SHIELD AND SCEPTER

SHIELD AND SCEPTER

K. M. WARFIELD

ALSO BY K. M. WARFIELD

Scales and Stingers (Heroes of Avoch Book 1)

Published in the United States by Creative James Media.

978-1-956183-60-3 (trade paperback)

First U.S. Edition 2023

For Sean

Never give up.
Never surrender.
Never feed Thor after midnight.

CHAPTER

ONE

Jinaari balanced a full tray across his arm, using the wall to help steady it, while placing his left palm against the wood paneling. The portal to their suite of rooms opened to his touch. Shifting the tray again, he carried it into the common area.

"You could've said something," Adam said, walking toward him. Taking a couple of items off the tray, he continued, "I would've gone down to the kitchen with you."

"I was awake," the paladin replied. He placed the tray on a central table, grabbing a roll as he sat down. "Didn't see any reason to get anyone else up."

Adam picked up an empty plate and filled it with bacon and some fruit. Settling into a chair, he said, "I'm not the one who almost lost his arm. Thia would have my hide if she knew you were carrying that without help."

Jinaari grinned. "Then we'll just not tell her."

The blonde man laughed. "How's your shoulder feel? You're out of the sling. Does that mean you finally let her heal you?"

"More like she told me it was happening seconds before she did it."

"About time. You restricted her to her room, barely let her move around."

"She broke her back, her ribs, and a few other bones, Adam. Any magic she was going to expend had to be to heal herself."

"Thia's the Daughter of Keroys, Jinaari. She's got a well to draw from that's deeper than anyone else's. I'm pretty sure she could've healed herself and you in the same breath." He took a bite, his face serious. "Or is something wrong with her that you're not telling me? I know how bad you were when we found you. Honestly, I'm surprised you didn't bleed out from what Alesso did to you. Her injuries weren't as obvious."

Jinaari shook his head. "She's fine physically. The arrest warrant and Tomil insisting on the ceremony have her on edge. Drakkus has abandoned the chapterhouse in Dragonspire. The paladins are making their way here to Almair, ready to do what Garret commands. Keroys isn't going to turn his back, either. That makes two Gods, plus a host of fighters and all of Tomil's resources, with a vested interest in keeping Thia free and safe. Whatever crimes my mother has imagined, Thia won't be hauled before a tribunal anytime soon. Besides," he sighed, "the generals won't let her start a war of any kind until spring. The frost is heavy in the mornings. No soldier, no matter how dedicated to a cause, will march in winter."

"What about Cirrain? Has the Baroness declared for either side? The city's halfway between Dragonspire and Almair. The Beckenburg family could find themselves under siege pretty quickly."

Jinaari sat up straighter. Adam was right; Cirrain would be where the first real battle would take place. Pan's mother, and Thia's aunt, was Baroness there. If harm came to them, or

Elizabeth sided with his mother, the fallout would be extensive. "I'll write a note to Drakkus. The paladins will need to go through the area on their way here. They could help with a siege if Baroness Elizabeth is willing to let them ride out the winter. And he'd keep me informed about the politics." Elizabeth was a skilled diplomat, who cared deeply for those who lived within her lands. She would sympathize with their cause, but not outright challenge the crown's rule until there was no other option. "Cirrain's too important to fall. I'd rather fight a battle there than here on the streets of Almair."

"Is something going on in Cirrain?" Pan's voice had an edge of panic to it.

Jinaari turned in his seat, looking at the young man as he walked toward them. "Not that we know of. But it's in a strategic location. If I sent a note with you, would your mother be open to reading it?"

The brown-haired man nodded; his eyes wide. "Do you really think Queen Agrana wants to arrest Thia?" He sank into a chair.

"I don't know," Jinaari admitted. "She has prejudices that are clouding her judgement. I think part of it is fear."

"Thia's not scary!"

"Not to us, no. But that's because we know her, know what she's really like. To most of the world, though, she's part Fallen. Some are having a hard time believing Keroys would Mark her as his Daughter, allow her to work the type of magic she does. My mother's one of those people."

"So, she thinks like Alesso did?" Pan's voice was barely above a whisper.

Jinaari recognized the shift in his posture. Alesso's betrayal of the party had cut into each of them deeply. *If he'd come after me, after any of them, we'd understand it. What he did to Thia, though . . . the death I gave him was too clean.* "Not really.

Alesso's hatred was personal. Queen Agrana's is more based in what she heard from her father as a child. It's learned."

"But you don't think that way, and she's your mother. If you unlearned it, can't she?"

"I had a God to thank for that, and my training with Drakkus. Garret had a purpose in mind for me—"

"Keeping Thia safe," Pan interrupted.

Jinaari nodded. "Yes. And killing Lolc Aon. While hating the Fallen wouldn't have been a problem when we were hunting the Goddess, it would've been with Thia. I wouldn't have been as aware of where she was, what she was doing."

"How can I help?"

"I'll write a couple of letters. I need you to give them to your mother and Drakkus. Do you remember him? He was one of Garret's Paladins that got us out of the camp."

Pan nodded. "He's your Commander, right?"

"Yes. He's bringing all the paladins from Dragonspire here, but I think he should keep Cirrain safe. If you're carrying the messages, both will know they're from me without question. Will you do this? It could give us the warning we need if the Queen does decide to try and come after Thia."

"I'll go pack," Pan rose. "Is Thia awake? I want to say goodbye before I leave."

"I'm awake. What's going on?" Thia's tired voice came from behind him.

Turning around, he watched her walk toward the seating area. Her steps were even, confident. He couldn't detect any hesitation in her stride. The pale lilac eyes were tired, but it was early yet.

"Jinaari's sending me on a mission!" Pan exclaimed.

Her head swiveled toward him; a questioning look on her face. "What kind of mission?" she asked. Grabbing a handful of berries, she sat in a chair. Her gaze darted between the three men.

He looked at her. "Drakkus is on the march, bringing my brothers here. I want Pan to intercept him at Cirrain. If they winter there, we'll have warning if the Queen moves against you."

"Should I go? It could make Baroness Elizabeth more receptive to the idea."

"You can't," Jinaari shook his head. "Pan has to leave today if he's going to get there first. You've got the ceremony with Tomil coming up." He watched her face darken. "You already agreed that it was necessary, Thia. You can't back out now unless Keroys needs you someplace else."

"I know. That doesn't mean I'm looking forward to it." She looked at Pan. "Be careful, okay? Send word that you've arrived safe?" She turned to Jinaari. "Do I have time to write a letter for my aunt?"

"Yes. I haven't written the ones he'll take from me yet."

Thia rose. "It won't take long," she said. Without another word, she went back to her room.

"Guess that means I should do the same." He stood up and looked at Pan. "Pack what you need. Soon as the letters are in your hands, you have to get on the road."

"Be sure to stop in the kitchen," Adam said. "Elian will give you some food for the trip, and probably some apples for your horse."

Jinaari went to his room and sat at the table. The letters didn't take long to write. While the ink dried, he started to melt the wax for the seal. This was their best chance at an early warning. His brother paladins would have adequate shelter for the winter. Thia and Pan's family would be kept safe. The only wild card would be his mother.

"Jinaari?" Pan said from the doorway.

He finished pressing his signet into the melted wax on the second letter. "I'm done," he said, handing both sealed letters out to him.

The young man slid into the room and shut the door. "Before I go, I need to ask you something."

"What?"

"What are your intentions with my cousin?"

Jinaari blinked. "The same they always have been. Keep her safe. That hasn't changed, and never will."

A slight flush colored Pan's face. "I'm not stupid. I know you don't always sleep in here at night," he stammered. "It's Thia's decision, but I just need to know you're not," he paused, "taking advantage of her or anything. She's been through a lot and I know she trusts you more than anyone else besides Keroys. She deserves to be happy, not keep getting hurt."

"Are you done?"

Pan nodded.

"Whatever's going on between me and Thia is just that. Between her and me. I have no intention of ever hurting her. I never have. Is that enough?'

"Yeah." He took the two letters and put them inside his jacket. "I already have Thia's. I'll let you guys know if things start getting strange." Without another word, he opened the door and left.

Jinaari stared at the closed door. *Thia'd get embarrassed if she knew the others picked up on us. Adam and Caelynn won't care. This is between her and me, no one else.*

Jinaari rose and left his room. Adam was still out in the common room, eating. "Elian will give him enough food," Adam said. "How long do you think it will take for him to get there?"

The taller man shrugged. "Who knows? This is Pan we're talking about. You or I could be there within a week, less if the roads were good. He seems easily distracted some days." He looked over at Thia's door. It was open, but he couldn't hear her moving around. "Where's Thia at?"

"She went to help Caelynn," Adam said. Jinaari started to walk toward the bard's door, stopping at the sound of his friend's voice. "Don't. She knows what she's doing, Jinaari. Hovering over her won't help her and you know it. If she can help, then she needs the space to do it."

Reaching over to the plate of food, he grabbed an orange before sitting down. "I know that. It's just," he paused. "I saw her on the ground, Adam, and thought she was dead. I never want to see her like that again." He dug his fingers into the rind, tearing it away from the fruit. *I've only known fear like that twice in my life. Both times, it was because she got hurt. I'm not going to let a third happen.*

"None of us do," he replied. "I thought you were both dead when we got there. She survived. We all did. She's taken care of the two of you," he pointed toward Jinaari. "Now she's going to help Caelynn. It's what she does. She still needs you to keep her safe, but not be overprotective. She questions herself enough as it is."

"I get that."

"Then let her do it. I can't even begin to fathom how deep her stores go. She's working magic on a level people haven't seen for a century. If anyone can help, it's Thia. I wasn't able to do much."

Jinaari looked at his friend. "You and Pan kept all three of us alive, brought us back here. That's plenty."

Adam shrugged. "I know that's what you needed us to do. It doesn't feel like enough, though. You two do all the heavy lifting while we barely make a dent."

"Stop that," he stared at the warlock. "I couldn't have gotten her away from Lolc Aon alone. Not in one piece. You kept that spider from getting her, too."

"After I led her into the nest in the first place," he grumbled.

"Hey, I told everyone to check the wall and she ended up

falling into a pit because of it. That doesn't matter. We're a team. You and Caelynn know what to do so well that I don't have to tell you. I trust it's going to happen, and it does. Thia's learned a lot since she first came to us. She trusts you and me. I don't worry about anyone else dying because I know she won't let it happen. She's too damn stubborn."

The blonde man nodded. "You're right."

"Of course I'm right," Jinaari said as he sat back. "I'm glad you finally admit it."

"You're also arrogant, insufferable, and demanding." Thia's voice made him twist in his chair.

Caelynn stood next to her. The blue tint of her skin had faded. It wasn't gone, but it wasn't as prevalent as when they'd first come back. The bard's face was tired, but happy. "Everything okay?" he asked.

"Thia was able to regulate my body's temperature better. I shouldn't have the problems with heat anymore." Caelynn lowered herself into a chair and curled her legs up under her.

"I wasn't able to get rid of the color."

Caelynn broke into a grin. "You toned it down, though. It complements my hair now. Think of all the patrons who'll listen to me play." With a laugh, she shook her head and let the pink locks dance across her shoulders. "It's one thing to come see an elf play. No one else will ever look like I do. I'm an original!"

Thia walked around and found a seat. "Is Pan gone now?"

Jinaari nodded as he popped another slice of his orange into his mouth.

"What's next?"

"The ceremony's a few days away," Jinaari watched Thia's body stiffen at his words. "Tomil's adjusting it as much as he can, shortening it and making changes so you'll feel safe. You agreed it was necessary, Thia."

"That doesn't mean I'm going to enjoy it."

CHAPTER

TWO

Thia took a deep breath, her hands nervously smoothing the skirt of the dress. It was the second time she'd worn it. The first was when she and Jinaari had been guests of honor at her aunt's table. The time she had openly embraced what she was.

"Keroys gave me his Mark for a reason," she whispered. "Trust him, even if I don't trust myself."

"I trust you," Jinaari said, but she didn't turn around. "So do Adam and Caelynn. All three of us will be walking with you today. Even if we don't see them, Garret and Keroys will be there too." His image appeared in the polished brass surface of the mirror as he walked up behind her. "With two Gods watching over you, I doubt you'll fall on your face. If you so much as stumble, one of us will catch you."

"How do you do it?"

"Do what?"

She turned and faced him. "Handle people watching you all the time? Staring at you? You've done all this pomp and ceremony before. There's got to be a trick."

He gave her a puzzled look. "I don't understand. You've

had people staring at you your entire life. This isn't any different."

"It is, though." Looking down at her hands, she watched the sparks dance from her fingertips. "Before, I knew why they stared. It was fear, hatred. I learned to hide, blend into shadows. Today, there's no hiding. There's no choice but to let them stare."

He sighed. "Try to focus on one thing. It can be the back of the person walking in front of you, a spot on the wall. Keep your ears open, your face calm, and breathe. You'll be watched, yes. Every move you make, inflection in your voice, is going to be scrutinized. Stick to the script. Tomil isn't going to spring anything unexpected on you. Today is more about letting Almair know who you are, and that he supports you."

"I know," she paused, "it's just . . ."

His hands grasped her shoulders and turned her to face him. "You've spent your entire life hiding, avoiding notice. And now you'll have every single person in the city watching you as soon as we leave the inn. The scrutiny won't stop once we get back. You'll be a public figure from now on, even if no one can see the Mark Keroys placed on you. For a while, you'll feel vulnerable. Naked in a way." Thia blushed at his words, but kept her gaze locked with his. "That doesn't mean you'll be alone. I'm not leaving your side."

The door swung open, and she turned toward the noise. Adam stood in the opening, one hand on the knob. "They're here," he said.

Thia took a deep breath, forcing the nervousness down. Glancing at her hands, she watched the sparks danced. *Today, people need to see this as much as they do the Mark.* "I'm ready," she replied as she glanced back at Jinaari.

A smile appeared on his face for a moment. Gesturing with his hand, he motioned for her to go first. "Good. Let's go."

She walked toward the door. Adam stepped aside, giving her room to go through to the common area. Caelynn waited for them near the exit. The pink haired woman smiled at her. "Come on." Her voice was cheerful. "Let's go show Almair who we are." The bard's outfit was skintight, accentuating every curve. The colors chosen enhanced the blue tint to her skin instead of hiding it.

Focus on something in front of me, ignore the rest, Thia thought. *Jinaari's right. I'm not alone.* Taking a deep breath, she forced her hands to stop fidgeting with her dress. "Let's go," she said. Her voice was infinitely calmer than she felt. The door loomed in front of her, but no one moved. Were they waiting for her to go first?

"I'll go first, then Thia," Jinaari said. She relaxed as he gave the marching orders. "Adam, you're behind her. Then Caelynn. When we start the walk toward the palace, I want Thia between me and Adam. Just in case someone gets stupid."

"Stupid?" she asked, looking at the paladin.

He shrugged. He wasn't wearing his armor, so she knew he didn't expect much trouble. But his sword sat in the scabbard at his waist. "You know what I mean, Thia. No matter what Tomil officially decrees, minds won't change overnight."

She nodded again. Too many would see her as a Fallen witch, no matter what the Duke said. That was one reason they opted to do this outdoors, with a long walk by all of them to the palace steps. Why she wore this dress. *The only way for people to truly start to accept me as the Daughter of Keroys is if they see the Mark, watch me wield magic beyond what others can do. The rumors are so mixed! Some say I'm real, others that I'm nothing but a pretender. It's hard for anyone to know the truth if I hide.*

"Thia?" Jinaari's voice cut through her thoughts.

"Huh?"

"How are things with you?" he asked.

She smiled, relaxing slightly. "They're good."

"Good," he said, a small grin flashing across his face. "The sooner we do this, the faster we can get back here." He turned and headed toward the doorway. Raising his hand, he activated the portal that led down toward the common room in The Green Frog.

Thia kept her gaze focused on his back as he led them down the stairs. "Tomil's meeting us at the steps," he reminded them. "A contingent of paladins from the chapterhouse here in Almair is going to escort us. They'll be in armor, but it's more for ceremonial purposes. If anything does happen, stick with one of us. My brothers will cover our escape, even if it has to be down a sewer drain."

"There you go, worrying about nothing again," Adam said. "Tomil's recognizing us as heroes. No one's going to attack us."

"Not if they want to live, no." Thia barely understood what Jinaari muttered under his breath. "Just taking precautions," he raised his voice where they could easily hear him. "We could kill a thousand Forsaken and rid the Fallen of a malicious Goddess a dozen times over, but there's always going to be someone who won't think that's enough. They'll see Thia's eyes and think she's beneath them. Something vile, evil, and hate her just because of that. Tomil's declaration will keep her safe. To a point. If someone's drunk enough, angry enough, he'll try something stupid. My job is to keep her safe. That hasn't changed." The confident arrogance he put into his words was the same that used to irritate Thia. Now, though, that reassured her. No matter what, she was safe as long as he was nearby.

Wilim stood behind the bar, absently wiping the surface with a clean cloth. "I'm keeping it closed until you're back," he said. "Not going to have many customers until then, and you won't want to walk through a room full of drunks to get upstairs. The priestess is going to need her downtime after today."

Adam coughed behind her, and she turned her head. "Thanks, Wilim." He glanced at Thia. "I thought it would be best to make sure you wouldn't get random petitioners coming here. Wilim is going to hire some of Jinaari's brothers when they're not busy to make sure no one gets out of line."

"That's what I'm here for," Jinaari shot back.

"You deserve the chance to relax too, old man."

Jinaari stopped at the large oak door that led out of the inn. Glancing over his shoulder, he gave her a concerned look. "You ready?"

She raised her chin. There was only one answer she could give him, and she knew it. Going back hadn't been an option since they'd fought Drogon underneath Tanisal. "Yes," she said, her voice steady.

Jinaari opened the door and the blast of crisp air made her hesitate. Winter was fast approaching. The cobblestone streets were covered with frost in the mornings now. The sun had warmed all but the shadows, making wisps of steam rise from the alley in front of the inn. Twenty of Garret's Paladins snapped to attention as they exited. One came forward, bowing at Jinaari. "Keep to your charge, brother. We will take care of the rest."

"Thank you, brother. May Garret guide your sword." He turned back around, nodding once to Thia. As she walked forward, Adam and Caelynn fell in step alongside her. Half of the paladins turned and began to march two abreast down the narrow alley.

"Who is he?" Thia asked Jinaari as he walked next to her. Her breath came out in a small cloud. A sigil danced in her mind. Biting her lip to keep her teeth from chattering, she expended the magic needed. A soft, yellow light engulfed the four of them, chasing off the chill.

"His name's Lukas. He's one of the best of the Order here in Almair," he said. "He runs the chapterhouse in all but title. The Commander, Ransom, has been in failing health for some time. Garret hasn't called him home, though, so he remains."

"Do you think I could help him?"

He shook his head. "No. Sometimes it's better to let a life end as it should without giving it a push. Any help you'd give would be temporary." He held up a hand briefly, stopping her before she could speak. "I know what you're capable of, Thia. It's not that you couldn't do it. It's that I don't think you should. His soul belongs to Garret, not Keroys. The path is different than the one you walk."

"Don't think that means I won't help you if you're hurt," she shot back.

"I know that," he replied. "But the commander's faith would prevent whatever you would do. As I understand it, he spends most of his time in prayer. If Garret wanted him to die, it would happen. There may be a task that only he can do that's unfulfilled. We don't leave this life behind us until those are complete."

"The way you're talking, you'll be around to protect me until I'm dead. Even if I don't want you to."

"Yes." His face grew serious. "Planning on trying to do that any time soon?"

She shook her head. "No."

"Good to know."

The alleyway ended, and the paladins leading them spread out into two rows. Thia caught sight of Adam moving up alongside her. He tilted his head. "Relax, Thia. There are no giant spiders in all of Almair."

She shuddered and looked down. "There's days I still feel one pulling on the hood of my coat."

"Keep your head up," Jinaari whispered. "If it's down, you come across as weak. You're not, and they need to know it."

She snapped her head up, finally noticing the crowd. People stood two and three deep along both sides of the road, watching them pass. Taking a deep breath, she focused on Lukas's helmet. The whispers grew as they passed. Anyone who was paying attention would see her Mark, know who she was. What she was. She wiggled her fingers slightly, knowing the sparks would be noticeable that way.

That was the purpose of going to the palace this way instead of by carriage. Thia knew that the populace had to see her to begin to accept she was what Tomil said. She raised her chin a little more. Today, she had to endure the scrutiny.

The march would take them straight to the palace. "You're doing fine," Jinaari whispered as they walked. The wide steps leading to the keep were within sight. Tomil stood at the top, waiting. His crisp white uniform was trimmed in a deep blue. The same color of the gleaming sapphire that rested in the center of his crown.

"Priestess!" A child's voice broke through the silence. Thia's head swiveled toward it. Jinaari instinctively moved in front of her, and she felt Adam's hand grasp her wrist. "Please, my grandmother needs your help!" The young girl's voice shook with desperation.

Thia pulled her hand free from Adam's grasp and placed the other one on Jinaari's shoulder. "Let me see," she whispered.

He turned, glancing at her, and nodded once before stepping aside. A girl, probably around eight or nine, stood in the road. Her tunic was clean, and her hair fell in two straight braids. A single tear wove a path down her cheek. "Where is she?" Thia asked.

The child turned, pointing toward the line of people. Sitting in a wheeled chair was an elderly woman. Her wispy gray hair moved slightly in the light breeze. A blanket lay across her lap. Weathered hands rested on it; the knuckles twisted in odd, swollen angles. Her peaceful face was decorated with deep lines, and her eyes were covered with a milky white film.

"Jinaari," she kept her voice low, "I need your brothers to take a knee. Everyone needs to see what I'm going to do, not their backs."

"What are you up to, Thia?"

"Trust me." She walked past him and looked at the girl. "What's your name?"

"Myra."

Holding out her hand, she smiled. "I'm happy to meet you, Myra. Would you please introduce me to your grandmother?"

Myra took her hand and led her toward the old woman. The people standing nearby stepped back as they approached. Thia stopped and knelt in front of her.

"Myra, child," the woman said. "I told you not to bother the priestess. She is meant to do more important things than tend to me."

"Nonsense," Thia replied. "I am to do Keroys's work, and he cares as much for you as he does any other." Blinking, she realized she could see what the woman's problems were. There was no way she could heal her. "You know that he will call you to join him soon, don't you?" she whispered.

"Yes. Even Myra cannot fight that."

"Tell me, grandmother. What gift can I give you to grant you peace?"

She sighed. "What I want cannot be healed. It has been tried, many times, priestess."

Thia smiled, taking one of the woman's hands into her own. "I am the Daughter of Keroys, grandmother. Let me give you something to show you his love for you."

"I . . ." her voice cracked. "I would like to see the sun rise and set again. The birds as they dive into the harbor to catch fish. See Myra's face again."

Raising one hand, Thia placed it on the woman's cheek. "Then let it be so." Drawing on some of the magic in her stores, she made sure the woman felt no pain as the film that blinded her slowly drained from her eyes.

"Grandmother?" Myra breathed, then shoved past Thia as she embraced the woman. Thia rose, watching.

"Myra, child," she choked out as tears ran from bright green eyes. "You look like your father."

Thia smiled, quietly walking back toward Jinaari and the others. He nodded at her once, "That was well done."

"I told you to trust me," she teased him as she went back to her position between him and Adam. The paladins rose, but the clanging of their armor didn't mask the excited murmur among the crowd. Word of what happened was already spreading through the populace. "A single act of kindness is going to do more for changing opinions of me than any royal decree will."

"I'm not disagreeing with you," he said. The guard began to walk again, and the four of them followed suit. "Some warning would've been appreciated is all."

"There wasn't time. It wasn't planned, unless it was on Tomil's part."

"Everything's fine, Jinaari," Adam interrupted. "Thia needed to do that, and will again. Not everyone coming after her will be a threat."

Their escort climbed the steps ahead of them, creating a wide corridor of armed fighters leading up to Tomil. Thia grasped the front of her skirt, lifting the heavy fabric up enough that she wouldn't trip. Adam and Jinaari both held onto one of her elbows to steady her even further. "I can walk, you know."

"Just accept our help, Thia," Adam said. "We're family, after all. Supporting each other is part of what we do."

The steps ended at a wide platform. Tomil raised his chin, looking at the crowd gathered below. "We welcome into our city those whose bravery and strength kept a Forsaken from turning this world into a barren wasteland. These same people braved the road to Byd Cudd, slaying the Goddess Lolc Aon and freeing the Fallen of her evil. And now it is known to us that one is the Daughter of Keroys, and bears his Mark. Truly is Almair blessed by their presence.

"Sadly, Queen Agrana does not see what we do. She only sees Thia as Fallen. There is a human side to her. She has a sense of compassion and honor that is hard to describe. We are fortunate that the Daughter of Keroys, and her companions, have sought sanctuary within our city during the winter months. She has agreed to meet with any who would petition her for healing or advice. We will also seek her counsel regarding the actions of Her Majesty. War is never something to be courted. I remain committed to protecting each person who lives within Almair, every soul that relies on my strength for their safety. This protection now includes the four individuals standing before me. Make no mistake. I will not tolerate any hatred directed toward them. Or any of the Fallen that come to us to seek a peaceful life. So say I, Tomil, Duke of Almair."

"Thank you, your Grace," Thia murmured, dropping into a deep curtsey.

"Enough formalities." Tomil looked at each of them in turn. "We need to talk, without the city watching us. You've all got titles now, by the way. I wanted to make sure you'd be able to come visit me if you needed to without a dozen courtiers trying to stop you."

"What are you talking about?" Caelynn asked.

"Come inside, out of the cold. I've got lunch ready for us.

We'll talk while we eat." Tomil offered his arm to Thia. "If the Daughter of Keroys would be so kind as to allow me the honor of being her escort?"

Thia blinked, then placed her arm on his. "I don't know how to read you yet, your Grace."

He smiled as they started to walk into the palace. "The more you and I talk, Thia, the better of an understanding we'll have."

CHAPTER

THREE

J inaari walked down the private hallway that led to Thia's office. *I know Father Philip wants to keep her safe. That he gave her a space with a secret way in and out was more than I expected.*

The pathway was narrow, and rarely used. One end led to the central courtyard of the cloister; the other went to the palace. *It makes sense,* he thought as he approached the door. *Tomil's smart enough to know Thia won't trust him if it's all official visits with pomp and ceremony. That sort of life isn't what she wants. And he wants to earn her trust.*

The door was closed. Stopping, he leaned against it and listened. If she was with someone, he didn't want to interrupt.

He picked up Thia's voice, but he couldn't make out what she was saying. A woman, one he didn't recognize, replied. The sound of another door opened and closed. Whoever it was had left. Slowly he twisted the knob and peered inside.

Thia sat at a desk, her back to him. "Are you going to stand there all day," she said, not raising her head, "or are you coming in?"

He entered the room, closing the door behind him. "I

wanted to make sure the Daughter of Keroys was alone." Walking across the room, he sat in a chair across from her.

She raised her blond head, a slight frown on her face. "And what can the Daughter of Keroys do for the Champion of Almair?" she asked, clearly irritated.

Sighing, he said, "I suppose I deserved that."

"You don't want me to use titles on you, don't use them on me. What happened to 'it's just Thia and Jinaari when we're alone'?" Leaning back in her chair, she looked at him. "What's happened?"

"I got a message from Pan. He's made it to Cirrain safely, though his mother was sad you didn't choose to go with him."

"You wouldn't let me," she reminded him. "Besides, all of this," she waved her arms around the room, "is enough of an adjustment. Papa's family is nice and all, but I'm not ready to trust them yet. Not all at once, anyway." She cocked one head to the side. "What did she say about your mother?"

Jinaari sighed. "The Baroness is a skilled politician. If she openly sides with Tomil, you, or me, her lands will be the first to be hit by any force my mother can muster. For now, she is staying neutral." He watched the disappointment pass over Thia's face. She was doing better, but still hadn't learned to mask what she was feeling. Then again, they'd agreed never to do that around each other. "Pan also got my note to Drakkus. The paladins will be given quarter for the winter in Cirrain. Garret's the one that told them to move out, so Her Majesty can't argue with it. It makes sense for everyone if they stay in the city. Your family, and the population, is well protected. And we'll get the warning we need."

The door behind him opened and he rose from his seat. An older woman stood in the arched entry. Something was familiar about her, but he couldn't place it. "Pardon, Daughter," she said, "but a message from His Grace has arrived." She held out an envelope. Glancing at Jinaari, she hesitated, "I wasn't aware you had a guest. I shouldn't have interrupted."

"It's fine, Abigail," Thia told her. "This is Jinaari Althir. You're likely to see him often. Jinaari," she locked her lilac eyes on him, "This is Abigail Potiri."

He tilted his head to one side, looking at Thia for a moment. He recognized the name. Alesso's mother? Why would Thia hire her and not tell him? He bowed at the woman. "Milady," he kept his voice even.

The woman walked across the room and placed the envelope on the desk before turning toward him. "I know who you are." Her voice was quiet. "I don't blame you for my son's death. He made his own choices." She turned back toward Thia and dropped a quick curtsey before leaving, closing the door behind her.

He sat back down and looked at Thia. "When and why would you hire Alesso's mother to help you?"

She turned the envelope over in her hands. "Just today, before you arrived. She came to me and asked for some way to repay me for her son's actions. She didn't know what was going on until Garret threw him out at the chapterhouse. Ashynn did. She was the one that gave him the message from the Barren that led him, led us, to the conduit. His mother didn't have a clue." He drew in a breath, ready to protest, but she held up a hand and he waited. "Jinaari, she didn't know. She's horrified that he traded me for her, for starters. It took me an hour to calm her down. She came here, ready to die, over the shame she felt. I wasn't going to let her do that. You, Father Philip, and Tomil have been after me to get someone to manage appointments, etc. She can do that and feel like she's repaying me for what her children did. And I know she's not contemplating jumping off a cliff." Her face softened. "I was going to tell you. You brought up Pan before I could."

"What's Tomil want?" he asked, changing the subject. It

made sense. Thia wouldn't have handled having Abigail's death on her conscience well, and she did need the help. Petitioners were slowly trickling in.

He watched her break the wax seal and open the note. Her face fell and a look of resignation tinged with fear settled on her features. "There's an official delegation on the way from Byd Cudd," her voice shook slightly, but he caught it. "Tomil wants me to be there when they arrive and he welcomes them to his court."

"Does he say why? Or when they'll be here?"

The door to the private hallway opened and they both looked toward the newcomer. "The messenger said they should arrive within the next three weeks. Less if the snow stays in the mountains," Tomil said, leaning against the doorframe. "As to why I chose you, that's more complicated."

Jinaari rose and moved around the desk to stand next to Thia. Leaning against it, he looked at the Duke. "What kind of delegation is this?"

Closing the door, he replied, "One meant to cement relations between Almair and Byd Cudd. According to the messenger, the city went through a bloody civil war when you took out Lolc Aon. The current ruling faction wants peace, the chance to rejoin the surface world."

"Why me?" Thia asked. "I have no knowledge of the culture. I've only been down to Byd Cudd once," she paused, swallowing hard, "and it wasn't a vacation."

"They asked about you, Thia. You being in Almair is one reason this faction is looking for a treaty. Reading between the lines of the message, I'd say they see you as a savior, liberator."

"I didn't kill Lolc Aon," she said, "he did!" She pointed at Jinaari. "Why would they see me as anything?"

Jinaari caught the edge of panic in her voice. "Not many were in the chamber besides us when I did that, Thia. But there were slaves there when you defied her, let out the blast of light. Rumors grow with each telling. There's your lineage, and who knows what lies Lolc Aon and Herasta were saying to get the city to hunt you down."

"It's not true, though," she muttered. "I don't want to be worshiped as anything, let alone a savior of the Fallen."

"Half of what's said about me isn't true, either. Or Tomil." Jinaari said.

The Duke coughed. "I understand your hesitation, Thia, and I'll do anything you need me to do to make you feel safe when we meet them. The alliance would be helpful if Queen Agrana decides to march our way." Tomil paused; his face grew somber. "I need you with me on this, Daughter. I'm not just asking as a friend, but as the Duke of Almair. My people need the Fallen allied with us. You've told me yourself that the best way to integrate them back into surface life is one mind at a time. A show of unity between the crown and the Daughter of Keroys, accepting this delegation, will be a major step forward. Please."

Thia swallowed, looking at her hands. Jinaari saw the slight tremor, even though she tried to hide it. The torture Lolc Aon put her through was something she still struggled with, no matter how much he'd coaxed out of her. "I'll be there," she said. Letting out a long sigh, she looked at him and Tomil. "I want you both to promise me I won't be left alone with any of them. Not once."

"You have my word," Tomil said.

Jinaari placed a hand on her shoulder. "Not a chance." He raised his head and turned his attention back to Tomil. "What have you heard about things at the capital?" Distracting her would help. Later tonight, he'd get her to talk through her fears. They weren't without merit.

Tomil's voice was stern. "Nothing good. The Queen's not moving out of Dragonspire. Winter's coming fast, and any army she could get won't set foot outside the city walls at this time of the year. She's miffed at you," he pointed at Jinaari, "obviously. And you," he pointed at Thia. "She still thinks you're faking the Mark. Waking up and finding out that Drakkus pulled all of Garret's Paladins out of the encampment didn't help her mood. By the time you two took down Drogon and she headed back to Dragonspire, she had gone absolutely mad. Finding out that the paladins deserted the chapterhouse was another insult to add to her list."

"How do you know all of this?" Thia asked him.

"Amara's managed to get letters to me, some of them detail how bad Her Majesty has become." His face grew somber. "I don't want a war, Jinaari. And I certainly don't want to wear another crown. It's bad enough with the one I have now. I told you I'll protect Thia. I believe in her, same as I believe in you and your other friends. I'm a politician, though. Not a warrior. I can cement alliances, rally the troops, but they're going to need someone who knows what it means to wield a sword to lead them."

"Talk to Drakkus," Jinaari said. "He's Commander for a reason. Listen to his advice. I've never met anyone better at tactics or troop deployment."

"I've already sent word to him," he replied after a pause.

"Out with it, Tomil. There's something you're not saying." Jinaari stared at him.

He looked away for a moment. "The last letter from Amara. It was short, rushed. She was concerned that Stijyn was giving Agrana ideas. Today, I got word that Amara's been sent to Helmshouse. Queen Agrana's ordered the warlocks to keep her under lock and key, as I've threatened to have her murdered so I can marry Thia instead."

"That's ridiculous!" Thia said, aghast.

Jinaari nodded. "My grandfather was an expert at this. Amara's being used as a rallying cry. The only way to get the truth out, and have it believed, is if you and Amara get married as planned. If it's put off, or anything happens to her, the blame will be put on Thia."

"It's not my fault!" she argued with him. "You both know that!"

"We do, yes," Jinaari looked at her. "The rest of Avoch won't. This wedding's been planned since before we went to Tanisal. It has to happen." He turned back to Tomil. "You want it to happen, right?"

"With all my heart. No offense, Thia," he said, "but Amara's had my love from the moment we met."

"None taken," she said.

"I've got an idea," Jinaari crossed his arms across his chest. "Tomil, keep the wedding hype going. It's still, what, two months away?"

"About that, yes. We planned it as a way to kick off the Tallachan celebrations."

"Good. We have enough time to get her and bring her back."

Thia looked at him. "What are you thinking, Jinaari?"

"Later," he whispered. "Are you done for today?"

"I think so." She opened a ledger on her desk. "Yes. If anyone comes, I'll have Abigail tell them to come back tomorrow."

"I'll escort you back to The Green Frog. I need to talk with Adam and Caelynn."

"That's all well and good," Tomil said, "but I've got a feeling you're not telling me something."

Jinaari leveled a stern gaze at the Duke. "I'm not. The less you know, the better. Do your normal routine. When I can give you information, I will. Until then, what you don't know you can't accidentally tell someone. And we need secrecy if we're to get Amara out of this."

A shadow of concern and sadness drifted over Tomil's

face. "If anyone can, it's you. Please hurry, Jinaari. If she loses her life over politics, I don't know what I'll do."

"Put your public face on, Tomil. Don't let anyone know you're worried. Make sure you're never seen alone with any woman, especially Thia. You have to act like everything's perfect and you're an excited bridegroom." Jinaari turned toward Thia. "Do whatever you have to, then we'll head back to the inn."

He watched her rise and head to the door. Turning back to Tomil, he kept his voice low, "She's staying here."

"Are you sure you won't need her? The road to Helmshouse isn't a stroll past the docks."

Jinaari nodded. "You need her help with the group from Byd Cudd. I won't go alone, and I think she'll be safer here than with me."

Tomil looked at him, puzzled. "Why's that?"

"My family's trying to turn the world against her. No one would dare attack her in Almair, but they would on the road. I don't want people to die because of a rumor. It wouldn't sit well on her conscience."

"What about yours?" the Duke asked.

Jinaari shrugged. "If it keeps her safe, so be it. That's what matters."

Tomil nodded. "She won't like it."

"Doesn't matter. I'll get Amara here in time, don't worry."

Nodding, he said, "I know you will." Without another word, he left.

Jinaari stayed put, waiting. He heard Thia come back into the room as Tomil left. "What's going on?" she asked.

He shook his head. "Not here. I don't want to go over the plan twice. And I'd rather get back to the inn before the sun sets."

She grabbed her coat off the hook and put it on. "I'm ready," she told him.

As she reached for the door, he put a hand on her arm. "I'm always going to make sure you're safe. Remember that." His voice was low.

"What aren't you telling me?" she asked.

"Let's go." His hand touched the small of her back and pushed her toward the exit.

FOUR

Jinaari ushered Thia through the door to The Green Frog, anxious to get away from the freezing rain that had started to fall. "Head up," he told her. "I'll be there in a few minutes."

She nodded, her face still showing the concern it'd worn since Tomil left her office. He watched her disappear up the stairs before scanning the room. Caelynn was on stage, playing for the crowd. Inclining his head toward the staircase, he waited for her to nod in response. He tried to find Adam, but the warlock wasn't at any of the tables.

"Where's Adam?" he asked Wilim as he approached the bar.

The man mopped up some water with a rag. "Upstairs, I believe. Said he wanted to do some studying tonight." He placed a mug full of ale in front of Jinaari.

"Thanks," he said, grabbing at the handle of the tankard. Turning, he surveyed the room again. Lukas and a few other paladins sat at a table near the stage. "Their next round is on me," he told Wilim as he placed some coins on the bar before heading to the group.

"Lukas," he said in greeting as he got closer.

"Jinaari Althir. We are honored, brother. Please, have a seat with us."

Pulling out a chair, he sat down. "Next round is on me. It's already paid for, so don't argue."

One of the paladins laughed. "Thank Garret there's no prohibition against drinking."

Jinaari joined in the laughter, then turned toward Lukas. "Got a favor to ask."

"Whatever you need," he said, "just let us know."

"I've got to leave the city. I may not be back until close to Tallachan. If you can, I'd feel better if you station a guard or two outside of Thia's office at the cloister. Possibly one in the room, if she allows it. I don't want her going anywhere without an armed escort."

Lukas's eyes narrowed. "She's the Daughter of Keroys, Jinaari. That woman's got more power in her pinky than all of us combined. What threat could we possibly protect her from?"

"The kind that involves a knife in her back, for starters," Jinaari replied. "Yes, she's powerful. She's also naïve and doesn't read threats like we do." He grew serious. "I'll rest better on my journey knowing my brothers are watching her back."

"Then let your rest be untroubled, brother," Lukas nodded. "At least, on this matter. When do you leave?"

"By tomorrow morning. Gives you time to sober up." Jinaari rose. "Enjoy the round," he said before turning around and walking up the stairs.

Activating the panel, he walked into the common room they shared. Adam, Caelynn, and Thia all looked toward him.

"What's going on?" the warlock asked.

Removing his cloak, he threw it across the back of one of the chairs. "How much did you tell them, Thia?" he asked as he unbuckled his sword belt and leaned the weapon against the wall.

"Only what you told me, which wasn't much." Irritation tinged her words.

"Adam, do you know of any passages into and out of Helmshouse? Ones I could use if I wanted to enter unseen, and bring someone back out?" Jinaari asked as he sat down.

He blinked. "Several, actually. You'll never find them yourself, though. The tubes are designed for warlocks to use. Unless you've got one of us with you, you'll wander aimlessly. Might even end up back on the surface and have an avalanche bury you. Again." He paused, sitting back in his chair. His hands were folded in front of him. "You're going after Amara, aren't you?"

Jinaari nodded. "I have to. The only way to squash the rumor about Thia and Tomil is to bring Amara back here in time for their wedding. We've got two months, but I don't want to be gone that long."

"I can transport us with my staff to Raven's Pass. It's going to take us two weeks of navigating the tubes to find her, and as long back out. But that pass is rarely used any more. Too treacherous, especially this time of the year."

"All right. We'll leave as soon as we're ready. Caelynn," he turned toward the elf, "I talked with Lukas downstairs. He's going to make sure there's an armed escort everywhere you and Thia go. Unless you're both here," he pointed to the floor, "she's not to be left alone. For any reason."

"I'm going with you," Thia said.

Shaking his head, he looked at her. "You can't. You promised Tomil you'd be there to receive the delegates from Byd Cudd. They'll be here before we can get back."

She stared at him, and he saw anger flash over her face. "I'll send a note to Tomil, explain that I can't—"

"No, you won't," he told her firmly. "He needs you more

than we do." Before he could say anything else, she rose and stormed into her room, slamming the door behind her.

"I think tomorrow morning, first light, is best," Adam said. His words were measured, and Jinaari looked at his friend. Something wasn't right. "I'll need daylight to find the entrance, and I don't relish sleeping outside in a blizzard."

"Fine."

Caelynn stood up. "I'm going back downstairs to play." Jinaari saw her look at Adam and whisper something. Walking past him, she shook her head before saying, "Be careful. She'll kill both of you if one of you lets the other get hurt." She activated the portal and left.

"She'll talk to Wilim, make sure there's food for us by the morning." Adam rose. "I think I'll head to bed."

"I'll check my armor, then do the same."

His friend coughed. "I think you need to smooth things over with Thia more than to see if there's a missed speck of rust on your gauntlets."

"What are you talking about?"

"I've been around you long enough to understand that once you have a task, you focus on it. The expectation has always been you would make the plan, I help execute it. She doesn't know that," he pointed to her door. "All she knows is that we get to go on a rescue mission and she's being sidelined."

"Tomil needs her to meet this peace delegation. They asked for her specifically. She agreed to do it."

"If it wasn't for that, would you take her along?"

Jinaari nodded. "Of course. Her and Caelynn both."

"I think that's what she needs to hear from you."

"You think too much, Adam."

The blonde man smiled. "You've told me that many times. Usually when I'm right." He walked toward his room. "It's your choice, my friend. However, I think it's wise to make sure things are good between the two of you before we leave. If they're not, she's going to have weeks to nurse her resentment. And come up with creative ways to tell you she's peeved when we get back." He turned the knob of the door. "I'll be ready at dawn." Entering his room, he closed the door behind him.

Jinaari stared at it for a moment, then walked toward Thia's room. Testing the knob, it turned silently under his hand. The latch made a barely audible click as it opened. Sliding into her room, he closed the door behind him.

She sat in a chair on the far side, staring at the illusionary sea on the wall. No matter how many times he'd seen it, it still impressed him. "Adam really outdid himself with that," he said, pulling the other chair closer to her.

"He told me he wanted to get the details right, down to the smell of the saltwater air, because of everything bad I'd gone through down in Byd Cudd. He wanted to give me something beautiful when I woke up." She sighed. "I've thanked him several times. It's helped calm me down more times than I can count."

"How are things with you?"

Her head snapped toward him; her lilac eyes were stone cold. "You're leaving me behind while you go play the hero." The words came out as a hiss. "How do you think I am?"

"I'd take you with me, you know. If Tomil didn't need you." He kept his voice low.

"I can send a note and get out of it," her voice was steely. "They requested my presence, but I can decline. I don't want to find out what politics are like down there now."

"But it wouldn't be right and you know it."

"You and Adam are going to need me more than he does. I'll be what? Sitting there, listening to people tell me about a culture I've never been part of and feigning interest so a treaty can get signed? One we both know can be broken by a perceived slight?" She shook her head, "No. Keroys didn't give me the power he did to sit next to Tomil and be an advisor. He gave it to me to go out in the world and do things no one else can." The words started coming out in a rush. "I've heard stories about Helmshouse, the creatures that guard it. You'll need what I can do. Adam can't heal nearly as well as I can. Nor can you. Let him stay behind and be the diplomat."

"There's nothing in those tunnels that my sword can't kill, Thia. Adam was right that he needs to go. There are wards that only warlocks can take care of, and I'll be able to pass as long as he's with me. Those stories are meant to keep people afraid, keep them from snooping, that's all."

Her jaw clenched. She wasn't convinced. "Then send him and Caelynn. Your sister knows Adam."

"Thia, what is this really about? You're grasping at straws. It has to be me, and Adam's the only one that can get me in and out safely."

She looked out toward the illusion. "I don't trust her, Jinaari. Not like I do you and Adam. I'm anxious about this meeting and you're deserting me. I'm not sure I can do this if you're not there."

"You can. And you will. Tomil will do all the talking, you probably won't have to say a word. And what's this about not trusting Caelynn?" He moved the chair in front of hers. "Alesso and the Barren ambushed all of us. None of us knew it was coming." Reaching out, he took her hands in his. "You still trust me, right?"

Nodding, she said, "You know I do."

"I wouldn't leave you here, no matter what promise was made, if I didn't think you'd be safe. I've already talked with Lukas. There's going to be some of Garret's Paladins with you everywhere you go. They won't come up here, but you'll know where they're at."

"With all that armor on? The entire city knows where your brothers are." A small smile crept onto her face.

Good, she's coming around. "We're trained for battle, Thia, not sneaking into places. That's Caelynn's specialty. And one reason she needs to be with you."

"What do you mean?"

"She's going to be in the room with you when you meet the delegates. She'll be able to read them better than anyone, figure out how much of what they say is truth and how much is a lie. And she doesn't want anything to happen to you. I'm certain she thinks of you as a sister, Thia. I know you're cautious. Adam and I both earned your trust. Give Caelynn the same chance you gave us."

She nodded, and he squeezed her hands reassuringly. "We won't be gone long. It's possible we'll be back before they show up."

"What if," she swallowed, "things go wrong, though?"

"Not going to happen. We'll go in, find Amara, and come back out. Soon as we're clear of the tubes, Adam will bring us back here."

"Damn your arrogance, Jinaari. Things can and have gone wrong before. Getting in may be easy, but I don't think the warlocks are just going to let you saunter back out with your sister! If your mother sent her there for protection, they're going to do just that. You'll be chased as soon as she's missed." She shook her head. "I don't like the odds."

"They were worse going down to Byd Cudd. We all survived that."

"I'm not so sure about that," she whispered, looking down.

"Hey," he said, raising her head so he could see her eyes. "You came out of it. It's what needed to happen to receive what Keroys gave you, made us both admit something. That's more than surviving." She smiled, visibly relaxing. "Come on," he said as he rose and held out his hand, "you need to eat something. Let's go downstairs, have some dinner, and listen to Caelynn play. I wouldn't be surprised if Lukas has a story or two that'll make you laugh."

She took his hand. "Lukas?"

"If he's going to be keeping you safe while I'm gone, you should get to know him. And he needs to learn some things about you." He held out a hand, silencing her protest. "I didn't say you had to trust him, Thia. I know how long that takes. He's had the same training as me and he needs to observe you. Learn how you move when you're nervous. That sort of thing."

"You want him to know my tells," she stated.

Jinaari shrugged. "Pretty much. Not all of them," he grinned at her. "Some are not for him to understand."

Smiling back at him, she said, "Is he as arrogant, insufferable, and demanding as you are?"

"Not even close." He led her from the room and down to the main part of the inn.

The room was full. Caelynn sat on the stage, her hands working the strings of her harp while she sang. Most of the guests were listening, with a few tables holding quiet conversations. Lukas and the others were where he'd left them. "Over there," he pointed the table out to Thia. "Let's go."

As they approached, all four paladins rose. "Greetings, Daughter," Lukas said, bowing stiffly.

"Mind if we join you?" Jinaari asked.

"Of course not. Please, sit," he gestured to a pair of empty chairs. "Do you need something to eat? Drink?"

"Both, please." Jinaari made sure Thia was settled before he sat down.

"Of course. Donovan will take care of it." One of the other men left while Lukas sat down. "It's an honor to dine with you, Daughter."

"Please," Thia's voice was soft, "I'd rather you didn't call me that. Not here, anyway."

Lukas blinked, nodding. "If you wish. What should I call you, then?"

"Thia is fine."

Jinaari cleared his throat. "Around here, we keep things less formal. Titles become cumbersome and can discourage us from getting to know each other better."

"I'll agree with that," he replied. "My understanding is that all the official stuff happens elsewhere?"

"The cloister found a chamber that's rarely used. One which makes it so people can come to me if they need healing, or help with a problem, and I can take care of them. It's not large, and I'm trying to get it to feel more inviting, but it works," Thia told him.

Lukas nodded. A plate appeared in front of Jinaari, and he started to cut into the roast beef. "She won't be there much, though," he said between bites. "Once the winter's over, we'll be on the move. Keroys didn't give her the gift she has to sit in one place. There's still plenty of monsters in Avoch."

"Like your mother? Your brother?"

Reaching for his tankard, Jinaari leaned back in his chair. "What have you heard?"

"That one has gone crazy, and the other is egging her on. I hate to say this about your family, Jinaari, but you're the sanest one of the bunch."

He shook his head. "No. Amara is. She's got a grasp of how to play politics that I never could duplicate. Or ever wanted to."

"I've heard she's in Helmshouse, under the protection of the Solar herself. A keep full of warlocks is bad enough. I don't know anyone arrogant enough to try and get her out of there. Not without help."

Jinaari smiled. "I imagine anyone who would attempt that would have to be certain they could pull it off."

Lukas laughed, "Yes, they would. So, Thia?" He shifted his

focus to her. "I hear you grew up in River Run. My parents moved there once I was an initiate, and I've visited it from time to time. It's a beautiful area."

"It was from what I remember, yes." She paused. "I haven't been back for so long. I'm not sure I'd recognize anything."

"Where did you live? Was it in town or on a farm?"

"My father," she coughed and reached for her mug. Jinaari watched her movements. She rarely spoke about her father, or the village. "My father and I lived just outside of town. We had a small house near a barn that he said was falling down when he moved there. I remember a large oak tree that sat between the two. He made a swing for me one summer and hung it from one of the branches."

Lukas's face grew sad. "I know the place. The house itself is gone. A fire gutted it before my family arrived. The barn's been raided for lumber more than once. The swing is still there, on the branch."

"I knew about the house." She drew a deep breath, "Do you know if there's any grave marker nearby for Bran Tannersson?"

"I know there's a grave up there, but never went looking at the stone. Why?"

"My father died covering my escape with Father Philip. The villagers set the house on fire after they killed him. It was the last time I saw him." Jinaari saw the sadness in her face briefly. "I couldn't go back there and make sure he was laid to rest, and I've always wondered."

"Donovan?"

The young man sat up straight in his chair. "Yes?"

"I want you to head to River Run at first light. Take your drawing kit. Find out if Thia's father has been properly interred. Make a rubbing of the marker and bring it back to Thia."

"And if it's not him?"

Lukas glared at him. "Then do whatever you can to find his remains, put them to rest, and have the marker carved and put in place."

"As you command." The paladin rose and left the inn.

"That wasn't necessary," Thia started to protest. Jinaari reached out and put his hand on her arm, silencing her.

"Donovan's new to the Order, Thia. Just made his vows a week past. He's been itching for a mission of some kind. Anything, really, to prove himself in his own mind. We're not all inherently arrogant like your friend here," he nodded at Jinaari. "Most of us needed a small quest to take on in order to prove to ourselves we were worthy of calling ourselves one of Garret's Paladins."

Jinaari felt the tension leave Thia and drew back his hand. He tuned out the conversation, letting his gaze settle over the patrons in the bar. Many were regulars who came enough that he was starting to recognize them. They knew enough to leave Thia alone. The rest were enthralled with Caelynn's song and ignored anyone beyond the bard.

"Hey, pretty lady!" A gruff voice brought Jinaari's attention back to the table. A large man, almost his height, staggered toward their table. "Come dance with me!" His arm stretched out toward Thia.

Jinaari stood, his brothers rising just as quickly. "Thia?" His voice was low, and he didn't take his eyes off of the drunk. "Do you feel like dancing?"

"No," she whispered.

"Didn't think so." He motioned for her to move behind him. "The lady isn't interested, my friend. I recommend you find another partner."

A loud belch came from the man. "She ain't never danced with me, and I don't take no for an answer. Not from any woman." He lurched forward, stumbling into one of the empty chairs.

Someone moved behind Jinaari, and he caught the slight glimpse of pink hair. "Get her upstairs, Caelynn."

"What about you?" the bard asked.

Jinaari smiled. "I'm going to teach this boy some manners."

The drunk squinted at him. "Did you just call me 'boy'? I ain't no whelp! I'll beat you into the lap of whatever God you follow!"

"Please tell me you'll let us educate him as well, my brother," Lukas said as he came up next to him.

"I have no problem if you want to join in, but after the ladies are upstairs." He moved around the table, keeping his gaze on his opponent. "This is your last chance, friend. You can leave, or you're going to have a problem."

The man roared, charging at the group while swinging wide with his right fist. Quickly, Jinaari blocked it before landing a punch against the drunkard's jaw. He staggered back, shaking his head. One large hand went to his jaw. "Nobody hits me that don't want to be flattened!" the man said.

Adrenaline surged through Jinaari's veins. He knew Adam wouldn't care if furniture got broken in a brawl, but that wasn't the point. Not this time. The man advanced, raising his fists. "Let's do this," he muttered.

Five punches later, the man was on the ground, unconscious. Blood ran from his nose. "Damn it, Jinaari," Lukas said. "You said we'd get to play."

Turning, he smiled at the other paladin. "Next time, move faster. Otherwise, you get to clean up." He nodded toward the stairs. "How fast did you have to talk to convince her to go up?"

"Not fast enough. She saw the one punch you let get through. Took two of us, plus the bard, to get her inside."

Two more began to drag the drunk outside. Hopefully, he'd sober up enough to go home before it got too cold.

"He won't freeze tonight, Jinaari," Lukas continued. "I told them to put him on a wagon and take him to the chapterhouse. He's going to do some manual labor and reflect on his behavior as soon as the sun rises."

Laughing, Jinaari looked at Lukas. "That's an excellent idea." He turned toward the staircase. "I'm heading out at dawn, so I should get some rest myself. Thia is likely going to resist you being around at first. Don't take it personally."

"We won't. We're beholden to Garret, not Keroys. She will get the respect and courtesy she deserves, but we will do what we must to keep her safe." He held out his hand, and Jinaari grasped it. "Do what you need to do, brother. May Garret keep you safe."

"May Garret keep you safe, as well." He walked toward the stairs.

"What do you think I'm in danger from?"

Jinaari paused on the small landing and looked over his shoulder. "I just need to get in and out of Helmshouse. You need to keep the Daughter of Keroys safe. Trust me, you've got the tougher mission."

FIVE

Jinaari put his boots on, keeping his gaze on the bed. *It's not sneaking out*, he thought. *She knows Adam and I were going to leave at dawn.* Thia hadn't been thrilled with him after the fight and tried to argue her case to go with them again. *It's not that I don't want you with me. But a promise was made, one you need to keep. The Fallen are an ally we'll need if my mother does come against Almair.*

She stirred and he rose from the chair. "Is it time?" she asked, her voice sleepy.

"Close. I've got to pack my gear, get my sword and armor on," he said.

Sitting up on one elbow, she stared at him with lilac eyes. "Four weeks. If you're not back in that time, I'm coming after you."

"I'll get word to you once we have Amara. Stop worrying. Everything will be fine."

"Then why do I feel like it won't be?"

He shrugged. "I'm not sure. Talk with Keroys later, tell him what's going on. Maybe he can give you the peace you need." Walking over, he sat on the edge of the bed and looked at her. "We're coming back, Thia. Caelynn and Lukas will keep you safe until then. So will Tomil. If you have to, tell Abigail that you're not going to see anyone. Stay here until the delegation arrives and come back as soon as Tomil receives them. No one said you had to speak with any of them or participate in anything beyond the first meeting. If Garret is with me, we'll be back before they arrive." He smiled at her. "You worry too much. Adam and I will be fine."

Her face grew serious. "You don't know that."

"I know what I'm capable of with my sword, Thia. And what Adam can do with his staff."

"It's not your abilities that I doubt, Jinaari. It's what someone else can do that you can't anticipate or counter." She rolled over, putting her back toward him.

Rising, he walked toward the door. Glancing back, he saw she hadn't moved. Whatever fear she had wasn't going away. He had to get to Amara, though. Clearing his mind, he left the room and headed to his.

As he finished putting on his armor, Adam appeared in his doorway. "All ready?"

"Close," he said, placing his hand in a gauntlet. "Sword is out there." Grabbing the pack, he slung it over a shoulder as he walked out of the room.

Once they got into the common area, he dropped the pack into a chair before reaching for his weapon. Nodding at Adam, he asked, "That cloak going to be warm enough?"

"It should be. I don't plan to keep us in the weather for long. The tubes are climate controlled. We'll be fine once we're inside."

"Unless you count the creatures that make their homes in them," Jinaari said as he buckled the belt around his waist. He adjusted the hilt of the sword, making sure it was in easy reach, before reaching for his bag again.

Adam shouldered his pack, then grasped his staff with

both hands. "Those don't worry me. They're meant to keep outsiders out. As long as you're with me, they won't even wake up." He looked at Jinaari. "Everything okay with Thia?"

"Why?"

Adam shrugged. "It'd be nice to know if we were coming back to a warzone, that's all."

"She's not happy about staying behind if that's what you mean." Jinaari stepped closer to the warlock. "Let's go. If we can make it back before the delegation arrives, it'll make all of us feel better." He placed one hand on his friend's shoulder.

The room shifted as Adam cast his spell to transport them to the mountain pass. When their surroundings solidified again, Jinaari shuddered against the blast of ice-cold air. Snow covered the boulders on each side of the narrow path. "Damn," Jinaari said, his breath coming out in a cloud of steam. "I forgot how cold it was."

"We won't be out here long," Adam said. Jinaari watched his friend examine the rock in front of them. "Stay on the road and keep an eye out. I don't want to dig you out of an avalanche again."

Jinaari snorted. "I wasn't the one that brought it down."

"No," the warlock said, his hands running over the rock face, "but you were more than half dead when we found you."

"I was alive, though." The memory of that trip floated to the front of his mind. It was the first time he'd faced death, but not the last. "It's an important detail you gloss over."

"Part of my job is to remind you that you're human," Adam shot back. "Aha! Here it is." He touched the tip of his staff against the stone, and a red light outlined the entrance.

"Good. I was starting to wonder if you forgot the way." Jinaari grinned at his friend. "Did you plan to stand there all day and get snowed on?"

"You have to go first," he said, making a gesture with his hand. "It's going to shut as soon as I cross the threshold."

Jinaari walked through the lines, entering the tube. A white light surrounded him, and he started to warm up immediately. The interior was smooth, arching around him, and the earthen floor blended seamlessly into the sides. He stepped forward a few feet, giving Adam room to join him, but kept facing further down the hallway.

"There," Adam said from behind him. "Got it sealed. We can get moving now." There was a hesitation in his voice.

"Not yet. We rest for a while, let you get your strength back, eat something. Then we move." He glanced back at his friend. A bead of sweat trickled down the side of his face. "Don't even think about arguing, Adam. Between the transport and opening the way, your stores are low."

"We're on a time crunch, Jinaari. If you want to be back in Almair before that delegation arrives, we can't afford to sit here."

"I can't afford to have things come at us from both sides if you're not ready to fight back. The goal is to be back in Almair before Tallachan. Tomil and Amara need to get married as planned, and that's right as the holiday begins. If we can get done and be at The Green Frog again before the delegation arrives, then it happens. But I'm not taking unnecessary risks with your life, or Amara's." Jinaari swung his head from side to side as he spoke. He didn't hear anything beyond the two of them, but that could change fast.

"Fine," Adam said, sliding down the wall and sitting on the ground. "But no more than an hour." Closing his eyes, he appeared to sleep.

Jinaari knew better. Leaning against the wall, he waited. Adam would come out of his trance as soon as he replenished his stores, or the hour was up. His job was to keep them alive until then.

Lukas mentioned the Solar was protecting Amara, he thought. *I'll have to ask Adam about her when he's done.* When he'd been in Helmshouse years ago, most of his time was spent in the infirmary recovering. The warlock's leader never came in to check on them. Outside of Adam and his fellow initiates, he never spoke with another soul in the city. "I should've looked at a map of the city before we left," he muttered.

"It's not a city," Adam's voice broke through his thoughts. Turning, he saw his friend stand. "Helmshouse is a series of towers, occupied by students or masters. The Solar stays in the highest one, at the center, and overlooks everything. The tubes are more than passages in and out of the area. Each warlock makes one that goes to their own tower. It's part of our training."

"Is that where this one leads?" He pointed down the corridor.

"Not directly," Adam replied, walking closer to him, "but we'll be at the offshoot that does before nightfall tonight if we keep a good pace. Mid-day tomorrow at the latest."

Jinaari looked at him, puzzled. "If it's only taking us a day or two to get there, why'd you say two weeks to get in and another two to get back out?"

"Because we have to find where Amara's at, figure out how to get to her without detection. You'll be safe enough at my tower, but I need you to stay in a specific room if we get any callers. It's shielded. No one will be able to detect you. Not even the Solar." They started to walk down the tunnel. "In all honesty, I'm glad you made Thia stay behind."

"Why?"

"Look at the walls. Remind you of anything?"

He nodded. "The conduit leading to Lolc Aon."

Adam ran one hand across the wall. "It's not the same. Those were calcified scorpion exoskeletons, and spider webbing. This isn't. And we make sure you can tell night from day in them. For Thia, though," he paused, "it might've brought up memories she'd rather forget."

Adam was right. Traveling this way, less than six months after their journey down to Byd Cudd, would wear at her. "She's stronger than she believes," he said, "but you're right. This would make her hesitate."

"She's getting better. I don't know if it's because she can tap into all that Keroys gave her, or that she's proven something to herself. I wouldn't worry about her quite as much if another Alesso sold her out."

"Not quite?"

Adam smiled. "Honestly? I'm more afraid of what she'd do to anyone that tried to come after her like he did. It's a good thing you took care of him."

"It was fast."

"What?"

Jinaari's hand twitched on the hilt of his sword. "Alesso may have been a total ass, but he was still my brother paladin at one point. His death deserved to reflect that." He paused. As much as he disliked the man, he deserved a clean death. At least he was able to give him that. "Lukas heard a rumor that Amara's under the protection of the Solar herself. What are we going to run into trying to get to her?"

Adam let out a low whistle. "She's royalty, so it makes sense for her to have rooms in the central tower, guarded by some of the Solar's staff. Her Eminence spends most of her time in study or directing the instructors. I've got some maps in my tower, but I'll have to pay Her Eminence a visit first. That will help me determine if there's been any changes in the main tubes."

"What do you expect me to do while you're off doing that?"

"Stay in my tower, out of sight. And don't touch anything."

Jinaari grunted. "Afraid I'll break something?"

"No," Adam said. "I'm afraid that some of the things I

have in there will break you." He paused. "My kind of magic is different than what you or Thia can do."

"I know that."

"Not completely you don't. I have stores, same as you and Thia. But a warlock's magic is meant to influence the outside world. We bend things around us and shape them to do our will. The magic Thia does, it affects you physically. Mine goes after your mind. Warlocks rarely go outside of Helmshouse because we would decimate the world if we did. Ages ago, one of us become the advisor to the Duke in Tanisal. He twisted the Duke's mind, and it led to the destruction of the city."

"Wait. I thought the city was torn down by Nannan, because of what happened with the Corrupted Paladins of Silas and the Daughter of Hauk."

"Yes, that's the end result. But it started because of a warlock who couldn't resist playing mind games."

"Ouch."

"Exactly. One of the first tests we go through since then is to determine our morality, our sense of right and wrong. Failure results in immediate nullification of your stores."

Jinaari let out a low whistle. "That's harsh."

Adam nodded. "But necessary. Even untrained, anyone born with the ability is a danger to the rest of society. It's rare. Most end up as mages and/or leave to do other things. To embrace a warlock's life means a solitary one of study. Few leave Helmshouse once they are fully trained."

"You did."

"I didn't want to, not at first. But Her Eminence saw something I did not. Much like we did in Thia. This is my life now, and I'm glad for it. To be honest, I'm not sure what it's going to be like to be back to my tower. I'm so used to doing your thinking for you, listening to Caelynn's harp, or watching over Thia that silence will be hard."

"You don't talk while there?"

"Do you remember when you were in the infirmary?"

Jinaari nodded.

"Outside of talking with me or your brothers, did anyone else speak to you?"

He thought back, trying to remember. "No, I don't think so. There was noise as things moved around, but none of the healers spoke. I thought they were efficient at their tasks and that was it." He looked back at Adam. "Are you telling me that warlocks talk to each other without speaking?"

Adam nodded. "In a fashion, yes. We learn how to send impressions to each other, images of what we're doing or feeling."

"Is that why you want me to stay hidden? So that no one can read my mind, find out what I'm doing there?"

"It's more complicated than that. I think it's a good idea for no one to know you're here until we have a plan to get Amara out. The Solar remains neutral in politics and has since the Tanisal debacle. For her to grant your mother's request regarding your sister, well . . ."

"What, Adam?"

He stopped and turned to face Jinaari. "It gives me pause. Something's not right in Helmshouse. Given the history, I'm concerned. If Her Eminence has decided to take sides, this could escalate quickly." Shrugging, the blonde man continued, "But it could be nothing. As you often tell me, I think too much. Let's get moving. We're not going to get there tonight unless we pick up the pace."

Jinaari nodded, his mind racing. He hadn't considered that the Solar would take sides. The neutrality of Helmshouse was legendary. *Is this what made you nervous, Thia? What was Keroys warning you about that neither of us heeded?* For the first time since he'd entered his training as a boy, he felt unsure about what lay ahead.

Thia pushed the covers off the bed and sat up, swinging her legs off the edge. For a moment, she contemplated turning on the illusion. *It won't help,* she thought. *Not this time.*

Rising, she threw on some pants and a tunic before shoving her feet into her short boots. Glancing at the door, she hesitated. *They left already. Even if they're still out there, I won't get him to change his mind. I'm stuck here while they go play at being heroes. Dwelling on it won't make a damn bit of difference.*

She walked out into the common room and saw the doors to Adam and Jinaari's rooms closed. Frustration rose but she willed it back down. *Go downstairs, get breakfast. Then figure out what to do next.* Her mind wandered as she headed through the portal and down toward the bar's common area.

As she approached the small landing near the bottom, her eyes caught a movement from one of the tables. Her back tensed up and she slowed down. A young man appeared at the bottom of the stairs; around his neck was the same silver sword and shield that Jinaari wore. "Good morning, Daughter," he said, greeting her.

Pausing, she replied, "My name's Thia. What's yours?"

"Brennan." He paused. "Can I help you with anything?"

"I was going to get some breakfast for myself and my friends," she pointed toward the kitchen. "Where's Lukas?"

"Back at the chapterhouse. He wanted to make sure Donovan got off safely this morning." The tall man ran a hand through his dark blonde hair. "I can help you take stuff upstairs if you want."

"It's fine," she said, walking toward the kitchen. She could hear the morning cook humming as she worked. "There's only two of us. I can handle the tray without difficulty." *Just stop following me! Please!*

He nodded, stepping back a few feet. "I'm going to be over there," he pointed to a chair sitting close enough to the fireplace to keep the occupant warm, "if you need me."

Thia nodded, then pushed the door to the kitchen open. "Morning, milady," the cook said cheerfully in greeting. "What will you and your friends be wanting for breakfast today?" she asked, wiping her hands on the front of her apron.

"There's just myself and Caelynn, Elian. Something small and warm would be enough."

"Some oatmeal? Maybe with aged sugar?" Elian began to rummage through large crocks of supplies. "Where did the men run off to this early? Will you and Caelynn be joining them later on? Wilim told me that he prepared some travel packs for them last night." Oats were dumped into a small iron pot, followed by a flurry of other things. The woman eased it onto a hook suspended over the fire. Thia settled herself on a stool and stayed out of the way. Elian ran the kitchen at The Green Frog. Even Adam knew not to interfere with what she did. "I can't imagine those two could go anywhere without you ladies. They need you to keep them out of harm's way." She placed a small wooden tray on the center table and looked at Thia. "Or is there trouble between the bunch of you?"

"No trouble, Elian," Thia reassured her. "There's something they needed to do, and I made a commitment to His Grace. There was a chance they wouldn't be back before the event, so I had to stay here. Caelynn stayed in case there's a problem."

"Is that why I've got paladins refusing to leave the common room?" Elian placed her hands on her hips, shaking her head. "Which one decided you need people hovering over you? Because I'll give them a piece of my mind when I see them!" She picked up a wooden spoon and stirred the contents of the pot. "It was Jinaari, wasn't it?" She sighed, and Thia smiled a little at the sound. "That man . . . he's an arrogant one. I've never met anyone so certain he's the best at anything and everything as he is."

"It's not without reason," Thia said. "He's never failed at a task, and I doubt anyone can best him in a sword fight."

"He's not the brightest lad, though." Walking back to the tray, she picked up a bowl and carried it back toward the fireplace. Ladling food into it, she continued, "Wilim's told me plenty of stories. I didn't believe them at first, and then I met both of them. Jinaari may know how to use that sword at his hip, but Adam's the smarter of the two." She put the full bowl back on the tray and grabbed the other one. "You can tell him I said so, too!"

Imagining the cook going toe to toe with Jinaari almost made her laugh. "I've heard him tell Adam he thinks too much."

"Well, he thinks enough to keep Jinaari alive. To me, that's the right amount. As long as that man doesn't get the both of them, or you ladies, killed then I can live with the arrogance." She placed a small plate with dried fruit on the tray, along with a full teapot and two cups. "There you are, miss," she said, stepping back. "Will you be needing lunch later on? Or are you heading to your office?"

Thia got off her stool and walked over to the counter. Reaching across, she grabbed the tray by the handles and lifted it up. "I'm not certain yet, Elian."

"If you go, be sure to dress warm. It's been raining all night, and the streets are slick. Take one of those paladins with you. They'll keep you from falling on your way." She turned her back on Thia and started to season a large roast.

Backing up, she used her heels to push the door open. As she turned, she saw Brennan begin to rise out of his seat. "Stay there," she told him. "The tray's not heavy. I can manage without your help." He stood, but didn't move her way. Within moments, she was back in the secret area, placing the tray on the central table in the main room.

"That smells yummy," Caelynn said as she emerged from her room. "What is it?"

"Oatmeal with aged sugar. Elian gave us some dried fruit and tea, too."

Caelynn wrapped her hands around one of the bowls as she settled into a chair. "It's still warm!"

"It's not that far from the kitchens," Thia said as she sat down with the other serving. "And I convinced the current guard that I was capable of carrying the tray myself. This one listens, which is a surprise." She couldn't keep the sarcastic bitterness out of her voice.

Giggling, her friend looked at her. "Jinaari does listen. He just chooses to ignore what we say if he thinks his plan is a better one. Which," she sighed, "it tends to be."

They ate in silence. Caelynn put her empty bowl back on the tray and looked at her. "Thia, I know you're miffed about not going with them. He had his reasons. Jinaari never does anything, and I mean *anything*, without thinking about all possible outcomes. They're going to try to be back before you have to meet the delegation. If they can't, I'll be there. So will Lukas or another paladin. Probably as many as Tomil will allow in the room without risking a diplomatic incident." She paused. "There's time before that happens, though. What do you want to do today?"

Thia sighed. "I'm not sure. Elian said the weather was bad. I may stay here all day."

"And do what? Mope?" Caelynn shook her head. "Jinaari may think you can hide, but I know better. You've spent the majority of your life doing that, I know. It's natural for you, comfortable. But Keroys didn't give you that Mark for no reason."

"I know that," Thia shot back.

"Then stop hiding! You've got a job to do. There are people who are going to come see the Daughter of Keroys for healing. Even if no one shows up today, you have to be there. The fastest way to kill that rumor is to be seen. If you hide, then you give it ammunition. Gotta fight the perception head on to change it."

"How?"

Caelynn shifted, leaning forward and staring at Thia. "Be visible, keep people around you. Make sure you're never seen talking with Tomil without someone close by. Doesn't matter if it's me or one of the paladins. Use your secretary, cloister guards, whoever you want. If someone is always at your elbow, who can report about what's been said, the rumor will die. Keep a good distance between yourself and the Duke if you're talking with him. Make sure your body language is friendly but distant. You can't laugh at jokes or anything."

Thia shook her head. "I don't understand what you're talking about."

Caelynn smiled. "Think about Alesso if you have to. Or

Pan, Adam. Just don't think about Jinaari when you're around Tomil and you'll be fine."

"What?"

"You both keep things quiet, which is fine. Adam and I don't care. But I can tell when you're thinking about him. Your face is calmer, your body more relaxed. You can't be that way around Tomil or it'll add fuel to the rumor that you want him." She paused. "Or are you actually interested in him?"

Thia felt her cheeks grow warm. "Tomil's nice and all, but I don't like him as anything beyond a friend. Certainly not *that* way!"

"That's good to know." Caelynn smiled at her and winked. "Whatever's between you and Jinaari isn't my business. It's not like Adam and I broadcast when we keep each other company. But you've got to act like nothing's wrong until he gets back. It won't take long for word to spread that the two of them aren't in the city. People will be curious, especially our enemies."

Desperate to get off that topic, Thia asked, "What enemies? Beyond Queen Agrana? I mean, she's still in Dragonspire. She's not moving on Almair or Cirrain, is she?"

"What I'm about to say may shock you, but you need to hear it. Jinaari's great, but he's got blind spots. He doesn't always understand that keeping someone safe doesn't mean hiding hard truths from them. You need to grow up. Start taking control of your life instead of looking to us to show you the way. Yes, there's enemies. Tons of them." She gestured toward the portal. "In here, we're safe. Adam designed the inn and these rooms so we'd have a respite. He made sure that no one can spy on us, watch our movements once we come up here. Or shoot arrows at us from the roof of another building. Jinaari and Adam have been doing what they do for years. You don't correct wrongs without pissing people off. For every Alesso, Drogon, or Queen

Agrana, there's scores you haven't met. Ones that see you as a threat to their way of life. Tomil's trying to heal the divide between the surface world and the Fallen. And, yeah, the people here in Almair accept you for the most part. But not all of them. I'm your friend, Thia. Even if you don't trust me like you do the others. I'm going to keep you safe the best way I know how. And that's to make you aware of your surroundings, give you the tools to stop an attack before it begins."

She's right. I'm supposed to be a bridge, help the surface world overcome its prejudices against the Fallen. Demonstrate that there's a better way. How am I doing any of that if I stay hidden away? Sighing, she looked at Caelynn. "You're right. The problem is that I don't have a clue on how to do any of that. I'm as afraid of the Fallen as everyone else! People look at me like I know everything about their culture, forgetting that I was raised on the surface. Outside of a few hours, almost all of which was spent heavily drugged, I've never been to Byd Cudd. How can I help Tomil when I'm ignorant?"

"That's the best place to start, actually. You said once you were taught how to read Olc at the cloister, yes?" Thia nodded in agreement and waited for Caelynn to continue. "Is there a chance the teacher is still there?"

"No. I was given a book, that was all."

"Then we send a message to His Grace. The Fallen have traded with Almair for generations. There's got to be someone in the city that's the main contact, someone that's familiar with the language, traditions. We invite them to come to your office. Then we start asking questions about the culture, etc. You need to learn as much as you can before the delegation arrives, Thia. Adam's always telling me that learning about someone before facing them gives him the advantage. I'm going to learn with you. I may not stand next to you during the ceremony, but I'll be in the room. There's no way they can keep me out." She winked and a sly smile crept on her face. "They'd have to find me first."

Thia filled a cup with tea and rose. "I'm going to get ready. There's one paladin downstairs now, and I wouldn't be surprised if there's another before we leave."

Caelynn giggled, tucking her legs back under her and leaning back in her seat. "That's fine. It gives us someone to send notes with. And, if we go shopping, they can carry our packages!"

Thia disappeared into her room. Maybe she could pull this off. Caelynn's plan made sense. She had to learn as much as she could, as quickly as possible, or she'd appear weak when the delegation arrived. *I've faced a Goddess and a Forsaken, and refused the demands of both. Time to show the world what I'm capable of. Who knows? I may even start believing it myself.*

Less than an hour later, she and Caelynn went downstairs. Brennan stood quickly, looking their way. "We're heading to the cloister," Thia told him as they walked closer. "Caelynn will be with me, but I understand you have orders to follow."

The young man rubbed the back of his neck. "It's nothing personal, you understand. It's just that Lukas and Jinaari would have me digging latrine trenches if I didn't."

Thia smiled. "I understand. I may need you to carry a few messages for me once we get there. Would that violate your orders?"

"Your office entry is guarded, isn't it?"

"Acolytes of Keroys normally stand guard, either as a reward or penance. Why?"

"It would be better to have one of them deliver the message. Not to disparage anyone's skill, but yours isn't a martial order. They're not going to hold off a threat as well as I can."

Brennan's confidence reminded her of Jinaari. *Stay safe,* she thought. "I'll let you and Caelynn make that decision." If she'd learned one thing from Jinaari, it was to let those who understood tactics take the lead in them.

Opening the door, a blast of cold, damp air assaulted them. Thia raised the hood on her jacket and shoved her hands into the leather gloves. Thankfully, it was a short walk. Taking a deep breath, she dove out into the driving rainstorm.

Few people were out in the weather. The ones that were kept their heads down and moved quickly to their destination, or at least some sort of overhang where they could get a brief respite from the downpour. The cloister's wall came into view and she picked up the pace. A guard swung open the door, and the three of them darted into the partially covered courtyard.

Thia led them through the maze of corridors that took them to her office, avoiding the back entry. Caelynn knew about it, yes. But she wasn't sure she wanted Brennan to know. Not yet, anyway.

Stop being paranoid. He's one of Garret's Paladins. Just because Alesso was as well doesn't mean they all think like he did. Jinaari doesn't. Neither do Drakkus or Lukas. Still, having a way that Caelynn and she could escape without Brennan knowing appealed to her.

Abigail sat at the small desk near the door, rising quickly as they approached. The two acolytes snapped to attention. "Daughter," Abigail started to say as Thia put her hand on the door knob.

"Brennan's with us, Abigail. It's fine." She began to open the door.

"Yes, but—"

"Give her time to get settled," Caelynn said as Thia walked into the room. Instantly, she knew something wasn't right.

A tall man, his dark hair pulled back in a braid, rose from one of the chairs. Brennan's hand grabbed hers, and she moved behind him as his other hand went to his sword.

"I tried to tell you," Abigail whispered. "You have a guest. He was waiting when I arrived this morning."

The man bowed, his orange eyes standing out against his dark brown skin. "Daughter. I apologize if I startled you."

"Who are you?" Thia asked, moving past Brennan.

"My name is Kasmin I'chal. I am part of the Thahion delegation. Our ambassador sent me ahead so that I could meet with you, answer any questions you might have before the rest arrive."

Thia hesitated, then replied. "I don't want to sound rude, but what delegation? I've never heard of your people. You appear to be related to the Fallen."

Kasmin smiled, but didn't move closer to them. "We were once the Fallen. When you and your companions liberated us from Lolc Aon, we decided to distance ourselves from all that she represented. We now call ourselves Thahion." He spread his hands out, palms up. "If it makes you more comfortable, Daughter, have your guardian search me. I am here only to answer any questions you may have of our people and what has happened since you gave us our freedom."

She turned to Caelynn, trying desperately to calm the nerves that threatened to overwhelm her. This was too convenient. Moving away, she began to unbutton her coat. *If Keroys didn't want me to help them become part of the surface world, he wouldn't have Marked me. If he's who he says he is, I can't show any hesitation.* Taking a deep breath, she said, "Caelynn, would you please ask one of the acolytes to get us some tea? And let Abigail know I'll be busy for a few hours?" Turning around, she looked at Brennan. "Search him, please."

As the paladin moved toward her visitor, she continued. "It's not meant to insult you, but you did offer." She began taking her gloves off. *I've grown accustomed to hiding the sparks unless I'm working magic. This time, though . . .* Letting go of the small amount of magic she used to hide them, she kept an eye on her visitor. His eyes widened slightly, but that was his only reaction as the yellow sparks began to dance from her fingertips.

Kasmin nodded, holding his arms out while Brennan checked him for weapons. "Under the circumstances, I would do the same. Your history with our people has not been a kind one."

The paladin finished and walked back to Thia's side. "He's unarmed, Daughter."

Nodding, she gestured to the seat behind Kasmin. "Please, make yourself comfortable." She sat down, making sure there was several feet between them. Caelynn did the same, sitting as close to Thia as possible. Brennan stood behind her. Out of the corner of her eye, she saw him rest his hand on the hilt of his sword.

"The tea will be here soon enough. Until then," she let out a long breath and looked her guest in the face, "why don't we begin?"

Kasmin grinned as he leaned back in his chair. "Absolutely. Where would you like me to start?"

Thia folded her hands and placed them in her lap. "You said things had changed since my companions and I were last in Byd Cudd." She avoided using his words. "If that's the case, why don't you start from that point?" *We were trying to free me, not an entire race. The implications of killing Lolc Aon never crossed my mind. Adam would've thought about it, talked about it with Jinaari. Certainly, Keroys and Garret knew what could happen!*

She straightened her back and listened to the story Kasmin began to tell.

SEVEN

"We've got to be close," Adam muttered, the sound barely registering in Jinaari's tired brain. They'd been walking for hours. Initially, he set a quick pace. The warlock's assurance that they could rest, safely, in his tower that night spurred him on. *The sooner we get there, find Amara, the faster we're back in Almair. Thia needs me back before the delegation arrives. That rumor won't stop growing until Tomil and Amara get married, either.* "Find it yet?" he grunted. Delays always made him uneasy.

"Why? Are you tired?" Adam shot back.

Jinaari leaned against one side of the tube. "Not at all. You did promise me we'd be in your tower tonight if we moved fast enough."

"No," he replied, running his hand across the wall's surface, "what I said was we'd get to the offshoot that leads to my tower before nightfall." He glanced around. "It's not quite that time."

"We're resting in a tube tonight?"

"Most likely. Aha!" With an audible click, part of the wall slid away. A blast of damp, warm air hit him, accompanied by a stale, musty smell. Wherever that tube led, it'd been sealed a long time.

"Come on," Adam waived at him from the open doorway. "I can't keep it open forever."

Jinaari walked through the entrance, taking his time so his eyes could adjust to the dimmer light. Once he was past his friend, Adam resealed the opening. "Where now?" he asked.

"We rest here. It's getting too dark for us to make it to my tower." Adam sat down, his back against the wall they'd just come through. The blonde man was tired. Even in the meager light, Jinaari could see sweat dotting his forehead.

"I can make us light."

Shaking his head, Adam said, "Not a good idea. We'd be spotted. All tubes are going dark. If this one suddenly began to glow . . ."

"People would know it's occupied. Got it." Jinaari leaned against a wall, turning his head down the hallway. He lowered his pack to the ground and removed his helm, setting it on top. Absently, he rummaged around in a pouch and pulled out some dried beef. "How much farther? Any offshoots we need to worry about?"

"No, this goes straight to my tower. Shouldn't be anyone, or anything, between here and there except some dust." There was a tired edge to his voice. "It's been a while since I walked it, but I don't remember it taking more than a few hours." Jinaari heard him shifting and he looked toward him. The warlock had removed his pack and was using it for a pillow. "My legs were a lot younger then, though," he said as he wrapped his cloak around his body.

Jinaari sighed and took another bite of the jerky. It didn't matter what Adam said, he'd stand watch for a few hours. The warlock needed the rest, but he could wait.

The road here had been easy. Too easy. He didn't hold out much hope that going out would be as fast. Some would depend on Amara; she'd keep a good pace, but not as fast as he and Adam could do. They'd have to let her dictate how quickly they moved. *Soon as she's missed, they're going to come after us. I'd rather fight Lolc Aon again over facing a thousand or more trained warlocks. Adam's not been right since we got in here. His energy's low. I'm going to have to ask him about that, after we get to his tower. I need to be sure he's got the stores to get us back to the inn.*

His head snapped to his left and he stared at a shadow. Had it moved? Shifted at all? His hand wrapped around the hilt of his sword. Adam promised they'd be safe in this tube, but he had his doubts. Feeders were able to move through walls. All it took was them to catch the scent of human flesh, of fear.

Thia's face flashed in his mind and he shoved it aside. Caelynn was with her, and Lukas would make sure one of his brothers was as well. If he didn't think she'd be safe, he'd have brought her with them.

Yet the same unease she voiced to him had settled into his mind. *She was right about one thing. Something's wrong with all of this.* The timing was too perfect between the delegation and finding out that Amara was at Helmshouse.

It was as if someone knew exactly how to separate the four of them.

A quick movement in the darkness put him on alert. "Adam?" he whispered.

"I know," he replied. "Keep it busy for me."

He heard his friend moving as he turned toward the shadowy darkness. Three separate foes. "There's more than one," he muttered.

"Your sword is still God touched, isn't it? That didn't go away after you killed Lolc Aon?"

Jinaari let a tight smile flash across his face. "No," he said, "it didn't." Pulling the weapon out of the scabbard, he welcomed the soft light that it gave off. The blue aura was enough to show him what was coming his way.

The Feeders appeared human at first glance, which let them get close enough to their prey. Most victims didn't realize the figure wasn't solid until it had attacked. As soon as there was an opening, the creature would become a trail of vapor and infect their host, consuming them from the inside out.

Jinaari grabbed his helm with one hand, settling it on his head and closing the visor. As long as he could keep them at sword's length, he could give Adam time to cover his face. "Feeders!" he called out as he pulled his shield off his back. "And another that I'm not sure about."

"Shit!"

"What's wrong?" Jinaari asked, though he kept his gaze on the creatures. They moved with a slow, methodical gait. There wasn't much time left before they'd get to them.

"I don't have a way to shield myself."

"Stay behind me," he instructed. "They're not getting past me anyway."

The first one in the line screamed and charged toward Jinaari. Swinging his sword, he sliced through the mist that formed the creature. Blue lightning coursed through the two halves as the magic of the weapon worked against it. A second charged, swinging with a clawed hand at him as the first dissolved in a shower of sparks.

Parrying the attack, he spun his arm quickly and cleaved the creature. Looking past the dissolving body, he locked eyes with the third. The figure moved differently. It was clad in polished black armor, with a shield that matched. It wasn't a Feeder; dead eyes ringed with red stared at him through the helm. "Adam?"

"Yeah, I see it," he replied. "Thoughts?"

"We don't have time." Holding out his sword, he pointed

it at the creature. "I only offer this once. Leave us in peace, or die."

"I sense the fear in you." The deep, gravelly voice sent a chill down Jinaari's spine. "You are not the shield my Queen deserves."

"Who do you serve?" Jinaari demanded. *I should know that voice!*

The creature pulled his sword out of his scabbard with a steely hiss. "To me, she is perfection incarnate. To you, she is Thia Bransdottir." Without another word, he charged forward.

Jinaari sidestepped the attack, his feet moving around his pack on the ground as his sword sliced across the back of his opponent's armor. The blow was strong enough to slice through the metal, but there was barely a scratch. An unearthly laugh came from inside the fighter's helm. His foe spun around; his sword aiming for Jinaari's shoulder. There was something familiar about the movement of the attack. *It can't be!*

He parried the blow, stepping back a few feet. *I need to move him toward me, away from Adam.* "Who are you?" he demanded.

"I am your fate." He pulled off his helm and Jinaari stared in disbelief. Deep scars ran from Alesso's blood red eyes to his chin. "You cannot kill me, Althir. Not now. I serve a purpose you will never comprehend!"

"I was too kind the last time we fought, Potiri. I won't be as generous this time." He stared at his former brother. "And you're not getting anywhere near Thia."

"I am her shield. When she comes into her kingdom, she will choose me. And you'll be dead." He stared at Jinaari; a cold hatred burning in his red eyes. "Her feet are on the path already. By the time you return, she won't want to turn away from it."

A bolt of green magic shot through Alesso's armor. The Foresworn paladin's mouth turned upwards in a sick grin. "Remember my words, Althir. You will understand soon enough." A black shadow coalesced around his form, and he vanished.

Jinaari stared at the spot Alesso had stood in, his jaw clenched. He was right. This was planned. Slamming his sword into its scabbard, he stared at Adam. "You up for a few hours of walking? The sooner we can get to your tower, and find Amara, the faster we'll get back to Almair."

"Alesso's dead." Adam's voice echoed his own disbelief.

"It looked like him. Voice was right. Someone's managed to bring him back. Whoever it was either paid a high price or has stores that rival Thia's."

"Another God's Son or Daughter?"

Jinaari sighed. "I hope not." Thia's power amazed him. *To have someone else wielding the same amount, walking the world, possibly working against her . . .* his mind shuddered with the thought.

"Do you believe what he said? About Thia?" Adam asked.

Jinaari set his shield down before he bent down and picked up his pack. He threaded his arms through the straps and settled it on his back. "Not entirely. Potiri always was an opportunistic prick. He'd lie to anyone if he thought it would give him some sort of advantage over them." Picking the shield back up, he tightened the straps.

Adam gathered his gear and looked at him. "Which part do you believe?"

"Someone's messing with us, with Thia. That's obvious. She's safe for now. That delegation's still weeks away from arriving. I won't worry about her unless we don't get back before then." He leaned against a wall and looked at Adam. "You lead. You know where you're going, right?" It was more a demand than a question. *Someone's playing a game with me, and Thia's the target. But is it early on, or have they been planning something for years that I'm just now seeing?* His fingers pressed into the wire wrapped hilt of his sword. He hated having a foe he couldn't see, couldn't anticipate.

The blonde man nodded his head slowly. "It goes straight to my tower." His words were measured. "Care to tell me what's got you so pissed?"

"Care to tell me why doing magic that you've done dozens of times a day is now such a trial that you have to rest after opening a door?"

"Point taken. Let's get to my tower. I'd rather explain there than here."

"Then walk," Jinaari growled.

Adam turned around and headed down the tube, and Jinaari followed. The anger would go away. He knew that. What bothered him more was the sense of dread that settled on his soul. For once, he found himself hoping Thia would hide from the world until he got back. *Listen to Caelynn, don't run from my brothers. I have to believe you're safe until I get back.*

"Is there any way you can get a message to Caelynn when we get to your tower?"

"Yes," Adam replied, glancing back at him briefly. "What do you have in mind?"

"Encourage her to keep Thia isolated, let them know we'll be back as soon as we can. If you can, tell her about what happened back there," he gestured behind them. "She needs to know there's a threat from an unknown source. Word it however you want. But I'll rest better if she knows to keep a closer eye on Thia."

"I'll do that as soon as we get settled. I've got the right tools in my arcanium. It won't take long to set up once we're inside and you're in the shielded room."

"Can't I listen in?"

"Not unless you swear to stay perfectly still and not utter a sound. The spell isn't an easy one, and I don't need you interrupting me with questions."

They walked in silence, which was fine with Jinaari. Every step brought him closer to Amara, yes. But he couldn't shake the feeling that the message Adam was going to send would arrive too late. *Garret, keep her safe. Talk with Keroys, whisper in the ears of my brothers. Something. The last time I felt this conflicted was when you pulled me away so I could learn how to protect her. This journey isn't your doing, though. And I need to find out who's behind it before it's too late.*

"We're here," Adam said.

Jinaari looked up. A slab of white marble stood at the end of the tube. Adam ran his hand over it, and it slid aside. "I go first this time so I can disable the wards," he said. "Stay here. It won't take long." Adam walked through the opening and it shut behind him.

Jinaari looked back down the way they came. The inky darkness was solid, impenetrable. Not even a mote of dust shimmered in the air. For anyone else, it would be a deterrent. *I know the way. There's always another way to open a door.*

"It's safe now," Adam's voice called out from behind him. Without a glance back, Jinaari walked into the warlock's tower.

The room was warm, bathed in a soft light. Comfortable chairs sat near a fireplace; the light from the flames dancing off tables full of devices, books, bottles, and things he couldn't identify. Bookshelves lined the walls, reaching toward the top of the tower. "Over here." Adam stood near one set of shelves, holding a door open. "It's the best place for you to rest up."

"I want to listen when you contact Caelynn," Jinaari said.

His friend nodded. "I can make it so you hear me. You won't hear her, though. I can't amplify her voice enough. If you're in here, you won't be tempted to ask anything." His face grew serious. "My house, Jinaari, means my rules. Out there is yours. I may ask questions, but I've never once failed to do what you felt was best. You're the fighter, the tactician. I'm a warlock. You know what that entails. Here in Helmshouse, what I say goes. I'll tell you anything you need to know. Let's get this done and past us. Afterward, we can eat and talk."

Jinaari walked into the room. It was sparsely furnished with a large bed, fireplace, and a pair of chairs. A low table sat between them. Turning around, he asked, "How long?"

"How long what?"

"Until you reach Caelynn. You said something about needing tools."

Adam nodded. "Less than an hour. The hardest part, what will take the most time, is getting a response. If she's downstairs playing, or asleep, it may take a while. She'll know I'm calling to her, but she won't respond until she feels it's safe to do so."

Jinaari shrugged off his pack, dropping it on the floor. "Wake me when you get her." Turning around, he heard the door close behind him.

A wave of weariness washed over him. The fire chased away the coolness in the room. For a moment, he wondered how it had been started. *I'm surrounded by magic and people who can control it, manipulate the surroundings around me. That a fire suddenly roared to life is the least strange thing that'll happen.*

Fifteen minutes later, his armor was off and placed neatly at the foot of the bed. Pushing the blanket aside, he sat down and pulled off his boots. He glanced at the door; the light from the other room was bright enough to outline the opening. Another hour of waiting was a possibility, if not more. He lay down on the bed, throwing the blanket over him, and closed his eyes.

EIGHT

"Jinaari?"

He sat up, instantly alert. "Yeah. I'm awake."

"Caelynn's responding." Adam's voice echoed in the room.

"Do you need me to stay still or anything?"

"No. But you might miss something if you move furniture around. There's nothing in that room that can hurt you."

He pushed aside the blankets and swung his legs off the bed. The floor was warmer than he anticipated. Rubbing at his eyes, he willed the last bits of sleep out of his head. *I can sleep later.* Right now, he needed to hear what Adam said to the bard. He'd find out what her response was afterward. Reaching for his boots, he began to pull them on.

"We ran into an old friend," Adam started. "Alesso's been resurrected somehow." There was a pause, then he continued. "We don't know. All he said is that he would be his Queen's shield, that Jinaari wasn't worthy." Another pause, followed by a chuckle. "No, he didn't take it well. We need you to keep an even closer watch on Thia. Keep her in the rooms as much as possible. Alesso said she was his Queen."

The pause was longer this time. "What was the name again? I want to write it down." Jinaari rose and walked to the door, pressing his ear against it. He could make out Adam scribbling something. "Got it. How often does she plan to meet with him?" Another pause. "No, I don't think it's a good idea. Jinaari won't, either. If you can't convince her, though, then make sure you're there the whole time. One of the paladins, too. I'll be in touch when we leave, earlier if it's warranted." His voice was terse. "You've got a point. I'll talk to him. I'll call tomorrow night, same time. We need to stay on top of this."

A series of chimes rang out, followed by silence. Curious, Jinaari slowly twisted the knob. He opened the door enough to glance out into the main room.

"It's clear," Adam called out. "There's food on the table. Grab yourself a plate and I'll fill you in."

Opening the door wider, he walked into the room. A small table sat against one wall. Three different covered trays rested on it, as well as a couple of plates and mugs. Picking up a plate, he lifted the lid on one of the trays. Steam rose from the slices of beef. "Looks good," he said.

"I hope so. I haven't cooked for a while." Adam sat in a chair near the fireplace.

"If this is your cooking, my friend, I'm making you in charge of dinner every time we're on the road." Grabbing a mug of ale, he carried his food over to a chair near Adam.

"Not likely. I have help here that we can't use out there."

Jinaari took a long drink, then placed his tankard on a small table next to his plate. "You've stalled long enough. What did Caelynn say? The stuff I couldn't hear."

Adam sighed. "None of it is anything I call good. Seems the delegation sent someone ahead, a man called," he fished a piece of paper out of his pocket and read from it, "Kasmin I'chal. He was waiting in Thia's office when they got there. He said he was there to answer any questions Thia might have about what's gone on in Byd Cudd since we liberated them from Lolc Aon."

Jinaari let out a low whistle. "What else?"

"They're not calling themselves Fallen anymore. This Kasmin said they now call themselves Thahion. Caelynn said he's doing everything right, and it makes her nervous."

"How so?"

"He suggested that the paladin search him for weapons, for starters. Kept his distance, never hesitated to answer a question any of them asked. He also never asked where she lived, or anything of a personal nature. Thia's already agreed to meet with him again."

He stared into the fire. "This doesn't feel right."

"What part?"

"All of it." He sighed. "I have a feeling this was a set-up, a way to separate you and me from the two of them." *Or just Thia*, he thought.

Adam let out a long whistle. "That's an interesting theory. How'd you come up with it?"

"The only thing that would make me leave Almair right now is Amara. The timing of the message reaching Tomil about her being here, and the delegation coming, is too convenient. Then there's finding Potiri in the tube, this I'chal person," he paused, "it's just too neat. That's all."

"What exactly did the message from Amara say?"

Jinaari shook his head. "I didn't read it. It came to Tomil, and he told me about it and the rumor."

"The one where Tomil wants to kill Amara so he can marry Thia?"

Jinaari nodded.

"So, we're not even certain she *is* here. Or that there's even such a rumor."

Adam's right. I should've asked questions, read the message myself. Damn it! "If she's not, then she'll show up in Almair before we get back." Anger rose in him, and he grasped the arm of his chair tightly. "We have to find out if she's here, and fast. Being sneaky won't work. We don't have the time." *Thia may not have it, either.*

"First thing tomorrow, I'll pay a visit to the Solar. Her Eminence will appreciate the honesty. If Amara's not here, then someone's trying to drag Helmshouse into the politics of Avoch. If she is, we can plead our case. At the very least, I can get us where you can talk to her."

"Why not now?"

Adam stared at him. "Because it's three in the morning, and I need to rest. My stores are almost depleted."

"About that," Jinaari began. "I've seen you cast spells for a full day without breaking a sweat. You've transported us out of some tight spots. Outside of coming back from Byd Cudd, you were barely breathing hard. What changed?"

"It's a security measure. The tubes are designed to limit any warlock's powers to that of a novice, someone who has only just arrived at Helmshouse. We did that to keep our murder rate down."

"Murder rate?"

"After the one warlock caused so much havoc in Tanisal, we had a disturbance. Some warlocks took exception to the new rules and decided to start 'convincing' others to overthrow the Solar. They used the tubes to ambush some who vocally supported Her Eminence. The battle was bloody, and destructive. Many towers vanished from existence that day. In the end, we won. The Solar's new decrees went into effect. And everyone's magic became equal in the tubes."

Jinaari looked at him. For the first time, he saw the man's age. "How many of your friends did you lose?"

Adam raised his head. "Too many," he whispered. A shadow of grief and loss passed over his face briefly. "The ale's gone warm," he said, staring at his mug. "We both need the rest. I probably won't be here when you get up. I'll be back as soon as I've seen Her Eminence."

"I'm coming with you."

He shook his head. "I'll tell her you came with me, and why. If she feels the need to speak to you directly, that's up to her. I've been gone for a long time. She'll want to know everything I've done out there." Adam rose, and Jinaari followed suit. "I'm likely to be chastised for not writing."

"Were you under orders to? I thought Helmshouse kept out of politics."

"Oh, we do. That doesn't mean that we're ignorant of what goes on in the world." He took a deep breath. "It's hard to explain."

"Try."

"When you dedicate yourself to this path, you make concessions for the magic. Normally, warlocks remove themselves from the world. The longevity of our life is dependent on the field of study we choose. If we leave Helmshouse, go out into the world, that erodes slowly. I don't age as fast as you do, but I will eventually do so if I remain out there. The reason we keep an eye on what happens is so we can step in if, and only if, it's warranted."

"What made you leave?"

"Honestly?"

Jinaari glared at him. "What do you think?"

Adam sighed. "It was Thia. I didn't know it at the time, neither did the Solar, but Her Eminence discovered that a God had Marked someone. That there was a Son or Daughter out there. I was sent to find out who they were, who Marked them, and evaluate their character." He ran a hand through his blonde hair. "Near as I can tell, the news came a few years after her father was murdered and she went to the cloister in Almair. Her Eminence contacted Garret, and he sent you and the other initiates to bring me out." He held up a hand, stopping Jinaari from saying anything. "Don't. I know what you're going to say. I didn't know who I was looking for, or that you were part of it. All I knew was that there was a Son or Daughter out in the world. That one of Garret's Paladins would keep me safe, lead me to the one that was Marked. The details became clearer as time went on."

"You should've told me this," his deep voice was deathly quiet. "Years ago, when I was first given my medallion and we started to take care of problems."

"By that thinking, you should've told Thia about her Mark when you rejoined us under Tanisal."

Jinaari stared at him. "I had my reasons. You know that."

"As did I." He paused. "I think it's well past time for us to rest up. We're snapping at each other instead of listening. Here," he held out a piece of paper.

"What's this?" he asked as he took it.

"That's the name of the person who's meeting with Thia, and what the Fallen are now calling themselves. When you wake up, come out here. I'll secure anything that could hurt you before I leave. There'll be food, and you can do some research."

Folding it carefully, he nodded. "One more thing."

"What?"

"You told Caelynn you'd talk to me about something. What was it?"

Adam shrugged. "She suggested that I contact her more frequently than planned in case things change there. We won't be able to get there immediately, but at least we'd know what was going on when we did."

"I like it. You're the one that's got to do it, so it's your choice. Just . . ."

"Just what?"

"I'm going to be out here when you do. I won't interrupt

you," he held his hand up to stop Adam's protest. "If I have instructions, I'll write them down for you to relay. I can't help either of them if I have to wait a day." Holding up the piece of paper, he continued, "I'll try and find something while you're gone. Right now, this Kasmin has the advantage. We have to change that." Turning, he walked back to his room, closing the door behind him.

He sat on the bed, his head resting in his hands for a moment. This wasn't right. None of it. Raising his head, he stared at the fire. A wave of exhaustion washed over him. *I'm not thinking clearly. Adam was right about one thing; we had stopped listening.* Remembering the note, he opened it up and read the names again. *I'll sleep for a few hours, clear my mind. Then start looking for information. There's got to be an Olc dictionary out there.* Raising his head, he placed the paper on a small table next to the bed. *I just need to find it, discover what Thahion means. See if the name shows up anywhere else in their history.*

Kicking his boots off, he laid down on the bed and threw the blanket over himself. Closing his eyes, he waited for sleep to come. One more unanswered question floated in his mind.

If Adam had been sent to find Thia, what were his orders when he found her?

CHAPTER

NINE

The clatter of dishes chased away the last bits of sleep Thia's mind clung to. Sitting up in her bed, she pushed a hand through her pale blonde curls. It had to be Caelynn, but what was she doing up this early?

Pushing back the blankets, she swung her legs off the bed; her feet sliding into fleece-lined slippers. Rising, she grabbed her shawl and threw it across her shoulders as she went out to the common area.

"Morning!" The pink-haired bard called out. A tray full of food sat on a central low table. Steam rose from the teapot. "Did I wake you?" Caelynn asked as she poured a cup of tea.

"Yeah, but it's okay. What are you doing up this early?" Thia asked as she walked toward the chairs. Accepting the cup her friend held out, she sat down in a chair. Curling her legs up underneath her, she took a sip.

"Actually," Caelynn said as she poured a cup for herself, "I haven't been to sleep yet. I meditated some, but I've been awake for several hours now." Taking a sip, she looked at Thia over the rim. "I heard from Adam last night. After I finished playing and came back up."

"Are they okay?" Thia asked. *Please let them be okay!* The sense of dread she'd felt since Jinaari said they were leaving had remained with her.

"They're fine. They're in Helmshouse, in Adam's tower."

Startled, she coughed as some of her tea went down the wrong way. "Already? But Adam said it would take weeks to get there!"

"I know. He didn't tell me how they got there so fast, only that they'd arrived."

Thia studied her friend. "What else did he say?"

Caelynn sighed and put her cup down. "You won't like it."

She straightened her legs, placing her feet on the floor. Had something happened to Jinaari? Her hand shook enough that the cup rattled against the saucer as she set it down. "Tell me." She whispered.

"They're both fine. There was only one incident, and neither were hurt. It's more who they faced." Caelynn hesitated. "It was Alesso."

Thia shook her head in disbelief. "No," she said, "that's impossible. He's dead. Jinaari killed him."

"Adam didn't go into details, but they were certain it was him. You're a priestess. Do you know how he could be brought back to life?"

She nodded, her mind reeling. "It's not done. It's messy, painful for all involved in the ritual. If you die, there's a reason. It's not like Dangreth or other soulless creatures. There's no mind, no consciousness, to any of the animated dead. For a human to be raised . . ." she paused. "The damage it does to your soul . . . The only people who would have the magic stores to even attempt it would have to be a Son or Daughter . . ." Her voice trailed off. "They think there's someone else in the world with a Mark, don't they?"

"I really don't know. He didn't say anything about that."

"What did he say?"

"That they'd had a visit from an old friend. He said Alesso taunted Jinaari, told him he wasn't worthy of being the shield for his Queen."

Thia leaned back in the chair, her arms gesturing. "Then why does it matter? Jinaari renounced his titles. He's not the Lord Defender of Avoch anymore, doesn't serve Queen Agrana. What's the point going after Jinaari? Revenge for killing him the first time? Jinaari will do it again." She shook her head, exasperated. *Think*, she chided herself. *If Alesso's back, there's a high probability there's another person Marked in the world. If so, they're not friendly or they wouldn't have done this.*

"It matters," Caelynn leveled a direct look at Thia, "because Alesso said you were his Queen."

She shook her head. "No. I never want to rule over anyone. I have enough trouble being the Daughter of Keroys! I barely know how to help anyone who comes to me unless they need to be healed! I . . . argh!" She lurched forward, burying her head in her hands. *This can't be happening!*

"There's more." Caelynn's voice was barely above a whisper.

Raising her head, she looked at her. "More?" her voice cracked. Her chest tightened. *Why do I feel like I'm being shoved down a path I don't want to walk?*

"Adam and Jinaari both want you to stay here," she pointed to the floor, "in the inn. Don't go into your office. Probably not even downstairs if you can avoid it. They don't trust Kasmin. Honestly, neither do I."

"It's unanimous." She leaned back, her hands running through her hair. *Of all the times for you to be away from me . . . I need you here. But you're not, which means I have to do things my way.* "I understand what they're saying, Caelynn. But you were right yesterday. I can't just hide away if Jinaari's not here.

I've got you and the paladins. There were one or two down there this morning, right?" Caelynn nodded. "If I don't meet him as promised, he'll know something's wrong. I'd rather meet with him, keep you and the others in the room with me when we talk, than him to come here looking for me." *Besides,* she thought, *I have to get used to this. It's my life now. If Alesso's come back somehow, he's going to go after Jinaari again at some point. Depending on what the person did to resurrect him, a fight between them may not end the same. He may not like it, but Jinaari's going to need my help this time.* Jinaari was the best swordsman she'd ever known, and she normally wouldn't have doubts on the outcome. But if someone took the steps to resurrect Alesso, it was entirely possible they changed him where he'd be able to beat Jinaari. "Is there anything else? If there is, tell me now. Then we can decide how to keep me doing what I need to do but mitigate any new threats."

"Only that Adam's going to be in touch again tonight. He hadn't planned on it, but Kasmin being here, the run-in with Alesso . . . he wants to keep up to date with what's going on."

Thia nodded. "Is this something I can listen in on? If there's a threat against me, I need to know details. How can I anticipate an attack if I'm blind to where it's coming from?"

Caelynn laughed. "That sounds more like Jinaari than you."

"Maybe I've learned a few things from him. I'm not completely helpless. I get why he wants me to hide away if he's not here, but I can't do that. Whatever Kasmin wants, he hasn't gotten it yet. Otherwise, he wouldn't have suggested another meeting today. Let's see if we can't get him to let something slip that we can tell Adam tonight."

"I don't mind if you're in the room, but I'm not sure if he'll be able to hear you. He's casting the spell on his end. I don't know what's involved to make it happen."

"I don't, either. Warlock magic is so different from mine."

She paused. "I'll bring something to write on and a pencil. If he can't hear me, and I have a question, I can write it down."

"I hope you can talk and hear him as well. If not, your idea will work." Caelynn bit her lip. "I'm not sure about you seeing Kasmin today, though. Let's put him off, send a message to Abigail that you're not feeling well this morning."

"Why?"

"If he's who he says he is, he'll deal with it. Talk with Tomil, go to the market, whatever. If he starts sending notes back, pushes for you to see him anyway, then we've got our first solid proof that he's not all he pretends to be."

"What if he comes here, checking up on me?"

"The paladins won't let him upstairs. Even if he got past them, he can't access our rooms. He'd have to not only know where the mechanism was but be keyed to it. Stay up here and you'll be safe. It'll give us proof he's got an agenda when it comes to you. That's something Adam and Jinaari will need to know tonight."

Thia shook her head. "No," she said. "I'm going in and keeping the meeting."

"Thia," Caelynn looked at her, "Adam and Jinaari---"

"Adam and Jinaari aren't here." She stood up. "I am the Daughter of Keroys, and that means something. If I can't be out there," she gestured toward the wall, "then I'm going to do what he needs me to do. Right now, that's learning from Kasmin. Yesterday was a start, but I need to understand how things are structured in their society now. If they're really here to help Tomil against Agrana, great. If not, these talks with him should help us figure out what he's really after."

Her friend looked at her, nodding slowly. "Okay. How do you want to do this?"

"I don't want to even try to be sneaky. I'm going to take notes, right in front of him. I'll ask him to repeat something so I can get it right. You can read body language, right?

"Yes, but you just said you didn't want to be sneaky."

"I won't be. I'm not any good at it," Thia grinned, "but that doesn't mean you can't. Keep your eyes open for anything he's not saying. We'll set something up with Lukas, have him send a paladin in after an hour or something, claim I'm needed at the chapterhouse. Something like that. I'm not going to spend all day locked up with Kasmin. If we tell Lukas to do something, but not tell me what or when, then I'll be surprised when it happens. My reaction will be normal. We go with them, stay there for an hour or so, then come back here and compare notes."

"This could work."

"I hope so." Turning around, she headed for her room. "One more thing," Thia said, looking over her shoulder. "I think we should discuss what we do and don't tell Adam when he contacts you. Jinaari's got enough to worry about with his sister and everything. They both need to think we have this handled."

Caelynn nodded. "I agree. If we keep it to facts, don't share speculation on our part, then it's not a lie. They can stay focused on what they're doing instead of worrying about us."

"Exactly. We've got an entire chapterhouse of paladins that live down the road," Thia laughed, "plus all the guards that Tomil would send. And I'm the Daughter of Keroys. Is there really anyone stupid enough to try and do anything?" Turning back around, she opened the door to her room, closing it behind her. Leaning against the smooth wood, she slammed her eyes closed, desperate to hold back the wave of panic that was rising in her. *Who out there has enough power to bring Alesso back from death? Another Son or Daughter? If so, which god Marked them? Why didn't Keroys warn me? And how can they know so much about me to know to bring Alesso, of all people, back?* Opening her eyes, she drew in a deep breath. *I can do this. I have to do this. Keroys, if you're listening, I could use some guidance. I know what you want me to do, but not how!*

"I cannot do that, Daughter. You know that."

Thia stared as the air shimmered in front of her. Keroys smiled at her, his timeless face as calm as ever. "Is there another Son or Daughter out there? Can you at least tell me that much?"

He tilted his head to one side. "I cannot. The puzzle is for you, and your friends, to solve. That which is earned—"

"Is cherished more than what is simply given," she finished the saying. It was one of the fundamental teachings of her faith.

"If you know the lesson, then you know your path. I am not displeased with you. You have done so much, come farther than I had hoped for in a short time. You've unlocked your power, but struggle with how, and when, to use it. This is good. It is one reason I chose you to bear my Mark. Your strength is necessary for the days ahead."

Thia shook her head. "But I'm not strong. Not like you need me to be." She wiped angrily at the single tear that fell down her cheek. "I see so many paths but don't know which is the right one. And I feel as if I'm being shoved down one that'll lead to death for someone I care about."

"The one you choose will be the right one. You may not see it immediately, but it is. Is this any harder than facing that which Lolc Aon showed you? It's fear that makes you hesitate, Daughter. Nothing more."

"Hey, Thia!" Caelynn's voice called through the closed door. "You almost ready? We have to leave soon if we're going to keep your appointment!"

"Just a minute!" she said. Looking back to where Keroys had stood, she wasn't surprised to see he'd disappeared. She closed her eyes and whispered, "I can do this. He has faith in me, as do others." Rummaging through a chest, she pulled out her thickest set of pants and tunic. Dressing quickly, she thought, *I am his Daughter. I held off Lolc Aon, I can hold off one person.* Before she could lose her nerve, she shoved her feet into her boots and headed to the door.

"I'm here," she said as she opened it. She pulled her hooded jacket off a peg on the wall. "One more thing before we go."

"What's that?" Caelynn asked as she pulled her gloves on.

"Can you show me how Adam contacted you? I'm curious how it works, stuff like that. In case you're downstairs playing and he uses it."

"That's a great idea. I can't initiate contact, but I'll show you what it is, how to tell he's reaching out when we get back." She placed her palm against the wall, activating the portal leading down to the common room.

Thia let out a deep breath, trying to gather the calm public face she'd worked so hard to create. Maybe, just maybe, she could do this.

Caelynn moved fast enough that Thia had to sprint to catch her. As soon as they could see the common room, she searched for the paladins she knew would be there. Lukas was sitting at a table, talking with Brennan. His head swiveled her way.

"Good morning."

"Hello," she said as she came down the last few steps. "I'm going to go into my office. I'm expecting someone this morning."

"Brennan told me about this I'chal person," Lukas crossed his arms, leaning against the table. The movement was so similar to one she'd seen Jinaari do multiple times that she smiled at it. "I'm not sure I agree with this."

"It doesn't matter if you agree," Thia said. *Same arrogance, too!* "I do want to throw him off, though. He's anticipating being with me for the entire day. That's not going to happen, even with Caelynn and Brennan in the room."

"What do you have in mind?"

"At your discretion, send someone to my office with a note. I don't want to know what it says, or when it's coming. Word it however you want, but make sure it sounds like there's an emergency and you need my help. That'll end the meeting, Kasmin can go wander the city or whatever. We'll find you at the chapterhouse, stay for a time, then come back here."

"You," he turned to Brennan, "do not let her leave your sight. Understood? I don't care what she says." He looked back at Thia. "We'll do it your way. This time. If it doesn't go well, I'll put you under house arrest."

"Lukas," Thia stared at the tall man, her voice even, "if I want to leave the city, I will. Especially if that's what Keroys requires of me. I know Jinaari asked you to watch over me, but don't ever think that means you can bully me."

"Daughter," Lukas stared back at her, "I would never think about trying to bully you. However, I *will* ensure your safety until Althir is back. If that means restricting your movements, I won't hesitate to do it. I don't trust this I'chal, and you will not be left alone with him."

"I don't trust him either," she replied, "and I don't plan to be alone with him. Brennan was a credit to his vows yesterday. Caelynn will be with me the entire time, as well. If someone else comes, though, all three will be told to leave. I agree to your terms in regards to Kasmin, but that's it." Not bothering to wait for his response, she walked toward the exit.

She kept up a good pace, not caring who followed. She knew who it would be. *It's one thing when we're out in the world*, she thought. *It makes sense when there's a watch schedule. We have to take care of each other. Lukas is acting like he thinks the inn will be under siege tonight!* The few people out on the street moved out of her way, which was fine. She wasn't paying much attention anyway. The irritation in her grew with every step. How is it that everyone was so sure of what she could do, yet felt she needed to be watched every minute of the day? If Alesso had been resurrected somehow, Jinaari would need her help. Even if he didn't want to admit it.

"Thia?"

Caelynn's voice broke through her thoughts. "What?" Her frustration made her voice snap.

"You walked past the cloister."

Thia stopped, finally seeing where they were at. She'd taken a turn somewhere, and barely could see the walls of the cloister. Caelynn stood in front of her, concern on her face. "Are you okay?"

"Yeah," she said. "I was just thinking. That's all."

"About what?"

Shrugging, she started to walk again. "Everything. Nothing. It doesn't really matter, anyway." Thia headed back the way she'd come, keeping the wall in sight.

"It's not 'nothing', Thia." Caelynn's voice was low as they walked. "What's wrong?"

"I have this power. Keroys gave it to me for a reason. Yet I sit here, making small talk with someone I don't know, while Jinaari and Adam are out doing things. And I've got a host of babysitters who don't think I can use the bathroom without them observing." Bitterness crept into her voice.

"You're worried about them, that's all. It's understandable. Listening in tonight, hearing Adam's voice, should help." Her voice was calm, reassuring. But it only made Thia's anxiety go higher.

The entry to the cloister came into view. "Let's get this over with," Thia muttered.

CHAPTER
TEN

Taking a few deep breaths, Jinaari let his mind catch up with the recent events. One thing Adam had been right about; he needed to sleep.

One hand rubbed at his face, digging the last remnants of sleep out of the corners of his eyes. He didn't sit up, choosing to remain comfortably warm for a few extra minutes. The only sound he heard was the crackle and pop of the fire. *Adam said he'd be gone before I woke up. Probably a good thing. I'm not sure I'm ready to hear his answer about what he was told to do when he found Thia.*

Pushing the blankets aside, he got out of bed. It didn't take long to find clean clothes in his pack and get changed. Looking at the pile of armor, he grabbed the padded undershirt. It was damp with sweat. Draping it across the back of one of the chairs, he positioned it closer to the fire. *I won't need it for a while, might as well let it dry out.* The chance of a pitched battle in Helmshouse was slim. Anyone that came after them would have to get through Adam's wards first. If they were that skilled, his armor wouldn't save him.

He walked to the door and opened it. The room beyond

was empty. "Adam?" he called out. No answer. Glancing over to the table where food had been the night before, he saw a single domed plate. He stepped closer and saw a sheet of parchment with his name on it. Picking it up, he read it quickly.

Jinaari,

I'm heading out to meet with the Solar. I can't say when I'll be back, as I don't know how long Her Eminence will keep me. The deadlier elements of the room are deactivated, so you should be able to search without problems. We can discuss what each of us learned when I get back.

Including what I was told to do when I found Thia.

Adam

Putting the note down, he raised the lid off the plate. Eggs, sausage, and biscuits smothered in gravy sat waiting. His stomach growled in anticipation. Picking it up, he walked to one of the chairs and sat down to eat.

Between bites, his mind went back to the note. *How many years have passed since we were sent to bring Adam out? How many times have I trusted him to have my back?* His jaw clenched. *Adam's a brother of my choosing, yet he kept this secret all this time. He's ready to explain all of it now, though. That's something.*

His mind wandered over to Thia and the newcomer Caelynn had mentioned. It was too convenient. *The one thing that would get me out of Almair comes up right when Thia's agreed to do something that will keep her there. And then this guy shows up?* Frustration burned in him. It was one thing to fight a foe in front of him. He knew how to react to that kind of battle. One that involved manipulation, deceit? There were reasons why he never liked being at court.

Desperate to feel like he was doing something, he rose and went back to his room. Grabbing the piece of paper off the bedside table, he walked back into the main room and started scanning the shelves of books. Any that listed the Fallen, Lolc Aon, Byd Cudd, or Olc in the title got pulled down and placed next to the chair. Fifteen minutes later, two piles reached from the floor to the arm rest. Rubbing his hands together against the chill of the room, he breathed into them. "Damn," he muttered, "I need to get my gloves and a blanket."

The logs in the fireplace roared to life and a wave of warmth emanated from the flames. "Okay," Jinaari said. "What about some paper and a pencil?"

The plate from breakfast disappeared, replaced by the items he asked for.

Settling down in the chair, he grabbed the first book and started to read.

Three chimes interrupted his thoughts. Looking up from the notes he was taking, he saw a shadow form in the far wall. It began to take shape. Jinaari put the pencil down and began to rise, looking around for something close to him he could use as a weapon if he needed to.

"It's me," Adam said as he solidified. "No need to throw the book."

Jinaari sat back down, his finger marking the place where he'd stopped reading. "It was an option." He watched his friend walk across the room and sit in the chair opposite of him. "How'd it go?"

Adam shook his head. "Her Eminence wasn't thrilled with what I told her. But she agreed to help us. If for no other reason than to get us out of Helmshouse as soon as possible."

"Amara's here, then?"

"Yes, though not for the reasons you were told. The Solar said she came on her own, asking for asylum. Something about being afraid for her life if she stayed in Dragonspire."

"Let's go." Jinaari began to rise, stopping as Adam held out his hand.

"Not yet. The Solar is speaking with her tonight, letting

her know we're here to take her to Almair. Tomorrow morning, we'll be given access to her rooms. We'll leave from there, providing Amara agrees to go."

"Why wouldn't she?" Jinaari asked.

Adam shrugged. "I don't know, but Her Eminence insisted that it is Amara's choice to make. You can't force her to go any more than your mother could've made her to stay in Dragonspire." He nodded toward the pile of books. "Learn anything helpful?"

Jinaari shook his head. "Not much. Thahion means 'Unchained,' or something close to that, in Olc."

"According to Caelynn, Kasmin said they felt liberated from Lolc Aon once she was dead. Maybe that's why they went with it? They're free of the chains that bound them to the Goddess?"

"It's possible. I couldn't find any family name that matched the one you wrote down, or any other meaning for the word. I know you've got a lot of books here. Either I missed something, or what we need isn't in your library."

"That's odd."

"Which part?"

"About the family name. The Fallen were obsessive about that. Tracing your lineage back to Lolc Aon herself, or one of her favored priestesses, was a badge of honor. All children took their mother's name, or the name of the house they belonged to, when they reached adulthood. If there's no listing for I'chal, it's likely fake. Or they renamed themselves, like the society did."

Jinaari nodded. "I'm inclined to believe the name's not legitimate."

"Based on what reason? I don't like how this guy showed up as soon as we left either, but we can't jump to conclusions."

He began to count on his fingers as he spoke. "One, the

name doesn't exist in the history. I can understand wanting to distance yourself from family, but changing your name completely? No one does that unless they want to hide who they were before. Two, the timing. He shows up the day we left. It's too convenient. Three, he's exactly the one who can tell Thia everything she thinks she needs to know about what's been going on in Byd Cudd. Thia wouldn't want to meet this delegation without knowing something of what to expect, which means she would've been looking for a way to learn. But there's no way to confirm his story. He could be nothing more than a spy, sent to infiltrate court before the delegation arrives. A person designed to try and gain Thia's trust."

Adam chuckled. "We both know that last one won't happen quickly. Certainly not before we get back."

"Doesn't matter," Jinaari said, shaking his head. "That he's there, trying, is the goal. Even if she doesn't trust him, he'll influence how she sees the delegation when it arrives. If he can get her to lose her fear, make her let her guard down even a little, it could be enough."

"Enough for what?"

"That's the part I don't know." He looked at Adam. "Did the Solar tell you anything else?"

"She chided me for not keeping her informed. I hadn't sent her an update since we lost Flink and Kathra left us."

"I want to know everything you were told before you and I met. All of it."

Adam nodded. "I knew you would. You heard most of it last night, and I'd rather not repeat myself."

"You can skip that stuff if you want."

"Like I said, I didn't know particulars. Neither did The Solar. Having a God or Goddess Mark someone, though, is a warning to us. It means there's about to be a shift in the world, one that we can't ignore.

"The existence of Helmshouse depends on the warlocks

being separate from the world. Our lives sustain it as much as it does us. Having a Daughter or Son roaming the world . . . Jinaari, they wield so much magic that every single tower would fall between them taking breaths if they came here and wanted to destroy us. My job was to find this person, assess them. Make sure they had the moral character that would at least maintain the balance in the world, if not swing it to something positive. If Thia was Marked by Lolc Aon instead of Keroys..." his voice trailed off, and Jinaari watched his friend shudder.

"What would you have done if she had been? I need to know, Adam. So does Thia when we get back to Almair." That last point was important. There was no way he would keep this from her. "If she finds out from someone besides you, it'll shatter that trust she has in you. And it will come out. You know that. So, tell me so I can back you up when you tell her."

"I was to assess his or her moral compass. If I was certain the Mark wasn't from a deity bent on domination and conquest, I was to help them. Guide them on whatever quest they needed to complete."

"And if they weren't?"

Jinaari locked his eyes on Adam's and saw the hesitation in them. "If that was the case," he took a deep breath, releasing it slowly, "I was to either neutralize the threat, or bring them here so the Solar could." He picked at something on his pants. "In order to do that, I had to intercept them before they unlocked their power. That's why she connected me with Garret's Paladins. The Solar knew that was the best way to find them in time. And, given the vows your Order is required to take, we knew you'd take steps as well. Even if you didn't know why I was there."

"You were going to kill her?" He shook his head in

disbelief. "All these years, fighting next to me, and you never trusted me enough to tell me this?"

"Why did you think I was always so methodical at checking bodies after we killed something? I'm not a Death Mage, Jinaari. I was looking for Marks, hoping we'd found the person by accident. I watched Kathra, wondering if it was her, but nothing she cast indicated she had magic stores that surpassed the rest of us. I started to enjoy life beyond my tower and put my mission out of my mind. When you showed up with Thia and she laid waste to the entire graveyard without thought, that's when I realized it could be her." He looked away, then back at Jinaari. "I didn't miss the signs of the spider nest. I took us in there to test her. If she was Marked by Lolc Aon and not Keroys, they never would've come after her. When they did, I knew she wasn't evil. That I wouldn't need to kill her. Or let the Solar do it. By the time I knew whose Mark she bore, she was family, same as you. I'd die before I let anyone hurt her. You know that."

He paused. "As to why I didn't tell you, that's easier to answer. I didn't tell you because I swore an oath to not say a word of this to anyone until I found the Daughter or Son and knew what my next move would be. It was as binding as the one you gave Garret. I've never questioned that about you, and believed you'd give me the same respect. We barely had time to breathe between the spider attack, the scorpion pit, and you disappearing. When you came back, it seemed redundant. I knew I would support her, no matter the danger."

Jinaari tried to push aside the anger, but some remained. "There was time, Adam. On the beach, when she was asleep. On the ship heading back to Almair before we went down to Byd Cudd." He kept his voice even but watched his friend's face closely.

"I know. But why tell you when I knew nothing would

change? I wasn't going to hurt her. I was going to protect her, help her unlock her power." He tilted his head slightly. "Is that really any different than the reasons why you didn't tell her she was Marked before the first fight with Drogon? Or that protecting her was about more than having two Gods tell you to do it?"

The last remnants of anger left him. He was right. Jinaari hadn't said things to Thia for similar reasons. *And I wondered why she was so upset when she found out.* "No more secrets. I can't afford to not trust you."

"Nor I to not trust you," Adam replied. "You're right, I do need to come clean with Thia. Not until we get back, though. I want to have that conversation face to face. She deserves the chance to yell at me in person."

Jinaari chuckled. "She probably will. Caelynn may join in as well. Unless she's known this whole time?"

The blonde man shook his head. "No. It's not something we've ever talked about."

"I want to keep the conversation tonight light, Adam," Jinaari scratched at his beard as he spoke. "Let's not worry them if we can help it. Tell them we know Amara's here and will see her tomorrow. If they know we're coming back early, that should calm Thia down. I'm concerned about Kasmin, though. Do you think you'll be able to get anything new about him from Caelynn?"

"Only one way to find out. Let's eat, then I'll activate the crystal. From then, we wait for her to answer."

"Why not start it now?"

"Because, my friend, I'd rather not have to answer in the middle of my dinner. Her Eminence questioned me at length. To the point that I haven't eaten for several hours. I'm starving." Adam rose from the chair, walking past him.

Turning in his seat, Jinaari watched him head to the table. Two steaming bowls had appeared on it. Adam placed a spoon in each one, then picked them both up. "It's one of my favorites. It's not nearly as good as Elian's, but it's close."

He took the bowl that Adam offered. He was right; it wasn't exactly Elian's stew, but damn close. "One more question," he said between mouthfuls.

"What?" The warlock put his bowl down.

"If you thought she'd been Marked by Lolc Aon, would you have told me? Or just killed her when we slept?"

Adam shook his head. "I really don't know. After I saw her potential, my next step was to figure out who Marked her. When I saw the spider nest, I knew that would answer the question. If that had gone differently . . .." he paused, taking a deep breath, and releasing it slowly, "I may have killed her in the process of eradicating the nest."

"I did wonder about that," Jinaari said. "I know your strength. It was early in the day; you hadn't done any magic. You could've made the entire building go up in flames without breaking a sweat."

"Only I knew Thia wasn't Lolc Aon's Daughter. She was also terrified. I chose to get her to safety instead of flexing my muscles."

Jinaari ignored the jab. "I'm done," he said, putting his bowl down. Picking up the paper and pencil, he looked at Adam. "Where do I need to go? I won't get in your way, but I have to be close enough to write things down if she can't hear me."

Adam rose, pointing to the other side of the room. "I'll be at that desk. Bring over your chair and stay at one corner. Whatever you do, don't touch anything I'm handling. Or get out of the chair, bang your fist on the table, or try and break things."

"I don't do that without reason," he said. Standing up, he dropped the pencil and paper onto the seat before he lifted his chair off the ground and carried it to where Adam pointed.

On the top of the plain wood desk was an ornately carved box. "What's in there?" he asked, putting the chair down.

"Half of what I need. You might as well grab some of your books, this may take a while."

Jinaari walked back over, picking up two books he hadn't looked at yet. "I doubt there's anything in these, but it's worth a check," he said as he sat back down.

Adam removed his cloak and placed it on a hook by the door. "What are they about?"

Checking the spines, he read aloud, "*Illusion and the Fallen* and *Lolc Aon's Fall.*"

"You're probably right. Not sure there's much in either that will help figure out who this person is." Adam sat in a chair in front of the box, lifting the lid. Resting on bed of dark blue satin was a green gem. A fracture ran along one edge, making it appear that it had been broken in two.

"Where's the other half?"

Adam smiled. "In Caelynn's room, back at The Green Frog."

Settling into his seat, Jinaari focused on the gem. "That's going to be helpful on the way back."

"It can't leave this room. The half that Caelynn has won't work unless I initiate the contact. And I can't do that unless I'm here, in my arcanium, to feed it." He sat down at the desk. Pulling a white cloth out of a drawer, he laid it out in front of the box. Smoothing out the fabric, he continued, "Creating something like this takes more than magic, Jinaari. It requires regular care or it goes dark. Given how long I've been away, the reactivation wasn't easy last night." Adam looked at him intently. "Until I tell you it's okay to speak, or I've closed the lid, you must remain silent. You can question me all you like when we're done. This is hard enough without you second guessing what I'm doing. Oh," he smiled slightly, "and I want you to promise we won't tell Thia or Caelynn about how this works."

"Afraid they'll try to replicate it?"

"Caelynn won't. She knows better than to try. Thia, however . . . I think you'll understand once you see what it takes." He rolled the sleeve of his tunic up past his elbow. Jinaari noticed a large red welt on the inside of his bicep. "Now, work on that vow of silence."

"I didn't take one."

"Until I tell you differently, or that box is shut, pretend you did." Leaning forward, he rested his forearm on the white cloth. With his other hand, he picked up the emerald and placed it against the welt. Adam winced as the gem attached itself to his skin, burrowing into him enough that a trickle of blood began to drip onto the white cloth. He closed his eyes and Jinaari watched his friend regain control of his breathing as pain danced across his face. "Caelynn, it's Adam. Answer when you can."

His eyes shot open, and Jinaari drew back from the intensity he saw in them. "Now, we wait." Adam whispered.

Jinaari leaned back in his chair. *I hope she answers soon, for his sake.* Picking up one of the books, he began to read.

"Adam?"

Caelynn's voice was soft, but loud enough that Jinaari's head snapped up from the book. He glanced at Adam's arm. The gem pulsed with each breath he took, but the bleeding had stopped. His friend's face was relaxed. "Hey. Jinaari's right here, listening in. I'm going to have him say hello. Let me know if you hear him." Adam nodded at him.

"Hey," he said.

Seconds passed, and then she responded. "Okay, let me know when he tries."

Shaking his head, Adam said, "He already did. I wasn't

sure it would work. He's got a way to hand me notes if there's questions or instructions for you."

"Okay. Did you guys find his sister?"

"Yes. We'll see her tomorrow. We should be on the road back to Almair soon. Were you able to convince Thia to stay put today?"

"No," she hesitated, and Jinaari heard her draw a breath. "She insisted on meeting Kasmin again but worked out a plan with Lukas. He interrupted the meeting after an hour or so, citing some sort of emergency at the chapterhouse. I was with her the whole time, though. So was one of the other paladins."

Jinaari scribbled a note and passed it over to Adam. The blonde man nodded, then asked, "Did you learn anything useful in the meeting?"

"He's an illusionist, Adam. Almost as good as you, to be honest. He formed a miniature version of Byd Cudd out of nothing. Explained how each of the current ruling council was an elected representative of different jobs within the city. There was a huge black spot on the map that Thia asked about. It's where we killed Lolc Aon. Once the infighting was over, they herded the loyalists into what was left of the chamber and burned it with nightfire. There's nothing left but a pit of ash. She, um, didn't take it well."

"What happened?"

"Thia was, well, Thia. As good as she's getting, I could still see the guilt on her face. She blames herself for the deaths that happened after we left. She didn't anticipate what would come next."

Shoving another note at Adam, Jinaari forced himself to stay seated. He knew what might happen and should've prepared her for it. "Where's Thia now? Is she okay?"

"She's asleep. I made her go shopping when we left the chapterhouse, but she said she had a headache and wanted to lie down so we came back. I was going to check on her before I went down to play tonight."

No more meetings! Jinaari scribbled the words and slid them across the table at Adam. "Jinaari doesn't want her meeting with him again, and I agree. We're way ahead of schedule here and will be back soon. Tell her when she wakes up. It might make her feel better."

"I'm not sure we can keep her from meeting him, but I'll try. She called Lukas a bully this morning, and he swore he'd put her under house arrest if he had to. She didn't like that but knowing you're coming back will help."

"I won't be able to contact you like this again," Adam said. "As soon as we get Amara tomorrow, we're leaving Helmshouse. I can't bring this with me."

Caelynn sighed. "I understand. I'll do what I can to keep her in the inn."

The gem stopped pulsating and fell off his arm. Using his other hand, Adam placed it back in the box and closed the lid. Methodically, he began to wrap the bloodstained cloth around the open wound. "Something's wrong."

"Why do you say that?" Jinaari asked.

"The only people I know who can cast illusions as detailed as what she described have been trained here, at least for a short time. In Byd Cudd, they were prized. Celebrated, even. I'm certain this Kasmin I'chal isn't who he says he is. Because the name would've been recorded, either in our records, or theirs." Jinaari rose as Adam did. "First thing tomorrow," he said, rolling his tunic sleeve back down over his arm, "we pack up. Even if Amara stays, we have to leave. Thia's dealing with someone who can make water look so solid she'd walk across it without knowing she's drowning. Do you really want her to do that without us?"

"I'll be ready." Jinaari walked to his room, closing the door behind him. Ice cold fingers ran down his spine. "Damn it, Amara. You'd better be ready to leave, too," he whispered.

***

Caelynn watched the gem grow dark, signaling the end of the connection with Adam. She closed the lid on the box, then sat down on her bed. Cradling her head in her hands, she thought, *Damn you, Thia. I've never lied to Adam like that before!* She took some deep breaths and gathered herself, then headed back down to the common room.

Lukas had pushed several tables together. Spread out across the surface was a detailed map of the city and surrounding areas. He and several other paladins stood over it. Glancing up, he caught sight of her. "Did they believe you?"

Nodding, she skipped down the last few steps and went over to the table. "I think so. Adam said they've confirmed Amara is there and were meeting with her tomorrow. He thinks they'll be heading back here shortly after that."

Lukas nodded his head. "Then we work fast." Glancing around at the other paladins, he said, "You each have your sectors. Take your brothers, initiates, even the newest pledges. I want every single man out there looking for her, understand?"

"Yes, sir," they replied in unison before marching out the inn door.

"We'll find her, Caelynn."

She stared at him. "We have to. Telling Jinaari that Thia's gone missing is not something I want to do."

ELEVEN

Thia walked into the kitchen, intent on finding Elian's tea stash. The headache was growing; a dull pounding that no attempt to heal herself worked against. Her hands moved constantly, full of nervous energy.

"What's wrong, dear?" Elian said from behind her.

Jumping at the voice, she spun around and muttered, "I don't know." Words came out of her before she could stop them. "I can't focus on anything. Everything's irritating me, even things that don't bother me normally. I know there's a reason why Lukas and the other paladins are out there, but," she paused, "it's like I can't even breathe without being watched."

"I've seen this before," the older woman replied. Her warm hands enveloped Thia's and led her over to a pair of tall stools. The table held a teapot and two mugs on a tray. Compassion filled her face. "You've been going nonstop for months, and it's completely different from the life you had before you met the folks upstairs. Something tells me no one's given you time to do more than catch your breath. Here, sit down. You've had a lot put on you all at once, and you're about to boil over. How can I help?"

Thia felt a tear begin to fall down her face as she slid onto the stool. Angrily, she went to wipe it away, but Elian wouldn't let go of her hand. "Tears aren't evil, milady. They have a purpose, or we wouldn't be able to cry," the older woman said gently.

She drew in a breath. "It's just . . . I don't feel like I can breathe. It's like everything around me is waiting for me to say or do something, but I don't know what that is. What if I do the wrong thing? What if I don't do something and someone dies?" She paused long enough to take a breath. "Because of what we did, what *I* did, down in Byd Cudd, hundreds died. It wasn't just during the fight, but after. Lolc Aon's supporters were rounded up and slaughtered because they still believed in the Goddess we killed."

"Here," Elian said, handing Thia a cup of tea. The warmth of the contents seeped through the clay mug, and she began to relax a little. "Go ahead, take a sip. You don't need to stand on some sort of ceremony with me."

Smiling, Thia took a sip. The tea had a strong honey taste, with a hint of lavender. "It's wonderful."

"You haven't always kept things this bottled up, have you? There's got to be times you've shared your fears with Caelynn?" Elian asked, raising her own mug to her lips.

"Not her, no" Thia said, shaking her head. "Most of the time, I'd talk with Jinaari. He was there to keep me safe. I trust him." *And now he's gone.* The thought drifted through her head, but she didn't say it out loud.

"You don't trust her? Or Adam? What about the younger lad?"

"Pan?"

"Yes, that's the name. I haven't seen him for a few weeks now."

"He went back to Cirrain. And I trust Adam. He saved me from becoming spider food."

"Caelynn was with you the whole time, wasn't she?"

Thia nodded. "She was. I can't say there's a reason why I don't trust her. It's just that," she sighed. "I don't know." Her voice trailed off.

Elian looked at her. "You were raised by your father, yes? Then taken into the church by a priest?"

"Yes. Father Philip. Why?"

"And the other girls at the cloister? How did they treat you?"

She took a deep breath. "We didn't exactly get along."

The older woman tilted her head. "So, men have treated you well. Protected you, made you feel safe. Whereas women haven't. You don't trust Caelynn not because of who she is, but what she is. A woman."

"You could be right," Thia admitted.

"What I think you need, miss, is a few hours without all of that." She gestured toward the common room. "No guards on duty, no meetings with diplomats, no monsters to kill. A few hours of silence someplace besides up in your room. Time where you can come to terms with your doubts, realize that we all have them, and figure out that Caelynn's not the same sort of woman you're used to. Yes, she can be silly and loves to shop. But I've talked with her enough to know she would die before she'd let anyone hurt you."

"How, though?" She inclined her head. "The only place the paladins won't follow me is upstairs. Caelynn lives there, as well."

"Oh, the how is yours to figure out. I'm only the cook." She smiled at Thia. "But there's a door right there that heads out to an alley that is rarely used. It's covered, too, for several blocks. Local residents wanted to have a garden area off the street, so they made it happen. If I had the magic you did, I'd think about the best way to make all of them," she nodded toward the common room, "think you were safely up there," she pointed to the ceiling, "while you were really going that way. After all, you're the Daughter of Keroys. Who's going to question you for taking a nap?" Standing up, she patted Thia on the knee. "Finish your tea, take your time, and think about what I've said. I've got dinner to prepare." Elian spun around, talking to the few staff members in the room. "Back to work! You let the stew boil over tonight, you'll be scrubbing pots for a month!"

Thia sat there, watching as everyone put their backs to her and worked seamlessly under Elian's watchful eye. *She's right. I need to go somewhere besides here and the cloister and just think.* A sigil formed in her mind and Thia smiled. Reworking the symbol slightly, her duplicate formed in front of her. "Go upstairs," she instructed the image. "If anyone asks if something's wrong, tell them you have a headache and need to lay down."

The illusionary figure nodded once in understanding, then went to the door. She'd added enough solidity to the image that it was able to push the door open like a living person would. Darting a look at the kitchen staff, she saw Elian draw their attention to something so their backs were turned. Thia practically ran for the exit.

As soon as she stepped out into the cold air, she felt some of the tension leave. *I'm not in the clear yet.* She took a few seconds to calm her breathing. Never once had she imagined walking through a single doorway could feel so freeing. Turning her head, she looked to her right; if the paladins were to see her, it'd be from that direction. A single leaf fell past the opening, landing lightly in a puddle. Reaching up, she placed the hood of her coat over her head. That would hide her features, making it less likely she'd be recognized. *If nothing else, I know how to move without getting noticed. Or at least I used to.*

Keeping her head lowered, she walked down the alley. She didn't know where she was going, but simply put one foot in front of the other. *Not too fast*, she thought. *I'm more noticeable if I rush.* The cobblestone path opened to a busy street. Glancing around, she spotted the masts of ships in the distance. The harbor. Perhaps Captain Stone was docked. Would he remember who she was, or just know who she'd become.

Do I even know who I was? Who I've become?

She turned toward the bay. Not the docks, but she remembered seeing plenty of small beaches that sat away from the bustle of the ships. Real sand and surf instead of the illusion in her room. That felt right. She kept her head down and quickened her pace, dodging around other people.

Fifteen minutes later, she saw her spot: a small ledge about halfway up the hillside. The earth around it curved outward, giving her shelter from the winter wind. She could sit there, watch the sea, and think. No noise, no guards, no one wanting something from her that she didn't understand. Her pace quickened and she started to climb the narrow, overgrown path leading to her destination.

Inside the sheltered opening sat a large slab of rock. It was uneven, natural to the space, though the top had been worn smooth. Whether from use or nature, she couldn't tell. Still, she was grateful for something to sit on. Jumping up onto the stone, she leaned against the dirt wall behind her and pulled her knees up to her chest. *There*, she thought, *no one should see me. No one to take me back before I'm ready.*

Taking a few deep breaths, Thia stared out at the horizon. The water stretched forever; the waves rippling in the wind. Small patches of white danced on the deep blue ocean, disappearing as quickly as they formed. She felt the first few tears run down her face. *Elian said that it's not an evil thing to cry. Maybe she's right. Maybe that's what I need to do.* Her breath came out as a gasp as a sob rose in her throat. *How much have I ignored, pushed aside? Keroys wants me to heal the relationship between humans and the Thahion. How can I do that, if I let the past rule my future?* Lowering her head to her knees, she let all of the pain, sorrow, and grief that had built up in her come out in a surge. Her entire body shook with each wave. Memories of her father's death, her fear as she fell into the pit, all of it. Slowly, painfully, her mind replayed everything that had happened since she first left the cloister. This time, though, she didn't try to push any of it aside.

I can't hide anymore. Jinaari and the rest keep telling me I'm stronger than I know. I have to face this, embrace it! She forced herself to feel everything she had locked away. Not just the pain and fear, but the hope and trust. As her lungs fought for air through the sobs, the good memories began to replace the horrific ones. The laughter, the jokes between Adam and Jinaari. Caelynn trying to coax her out of her shell, giving insights into what made the other two the way they were. The absolute sense of security she had when Jinaari had caught her to keep her from the scorpions. The look on his face when she told him what Lolc Aon forced her to see.

"Daughter?" a man's voice interrupted her thoughts. "Are you all right? Have you been hurt?"

Thia snapped her head up. Kasmin stood at the edge of the opening. His orange eyes stared at her intently in the fading light. "I, um, yeah," she stammered. Wiping away the last of the tears with her hand, she unfolded her legs and sat up straight. "I'm fine. Why?"

He leaned against the wall, but didn't come closer. "If I can help in some way, I would do so. You only need to let me know how I may be of service." He tilted his head to one side.

"I'm fine, as I said." She drew a deep breath, willing her

emotions to calm down and restore the mask she had dropped. *I am, too. I haven't felt this in control of myself for a long time.* "What are you doing here?

"I found this place by accident the day after I arrived. I come here to see that," he pointed out at the ocean. The last rays of the sun were dying off, and the early evening sky was dotted with stars. "I'd read about the ocean, but to see it . . ." he took a deep breath and smiled. "We had some huge lakes near Byd Cucd. Some so large that you couldn't see the other side. But nothing like that." He pointed at the waves. "The water underground was still. If it wasn't, you ran for your life. But to see the waves and not fear what may be creating them calms me, reminds me that there is more to the world than what I've learned from books."

"The ones you read didn't talk about the sea?" Thia kept her tone light, but her hands dug into the edge of the slab. Judging from the encroaching darkness, she'd been there longer than she thought. *I've been missed by now. They have no way of knowing where I went, either.* The man stood between her and the path back to Almair. *Keep him talking, find out what he wants. Or the opening to leave without creating a problem for Tomil.*

"Oh, they did. But to see it in person," he paused, glancing back toward the water, "it takes my breath away." Turning back to her, he pointed to the slab. "May I?"

She moved over to the far edge but nodded. Kasmin sat down, keeping as much distance between them as possible. Her instincts told her it was still too close. *I should've moved to where he's at now,* she thought. *I'd be closer to the path.* "If you have the chance, you should book passage on a ship, head to another part of the world. Being out beyond the shoreline, where you're surrounded by water, it's as if you've left one realm and entered another."

"You've been on a ship that's gone out that far?"

She shook her head. "Yes and no. The few times I've been on one, we didn't have need to go that far out. You could watch the coastline move. If you were on the other side, though, it was nothing but water. It made me wonder what was beyond the horizon."

"I've had that same thought," he laughed.

Thia kept her eyes on the darkening sky. *He wants something. But what?*

He coughed. "I have a confession to make." Thia snapped her head around and looked at him as he spoke. "I overheard our ambassador express his fears about how we'd be welcomed. What happened to you . . . they felt it would be justified if His Grace would order us all arrested within moments of entering the city. I volunteered to come ahead, do what I could to make you comfortable with their visit. Try and get you to understand we're not what Lolc Aon and your mother were. I, ah, I was more than a little excited that I would be able to meet you before all the formalities." She noticed his fingers flex nervously against the stone slab. "I'd heard about you. We all had. I wasn't sure how much was true. May I ask you a question?"

"You can ask. I can't guarantee an answer until I hear the question, though." *There. That should make him think twice.*

"What little we knew of you before the liberation was propaganda put out by Lolc Aon or Herasta. We were led to believe you were held prisoner by Prince Althir and his companions, forced to worship Keroys. Not much else about you was available. However, I've been able to glean that your devotion to Keroys is genuine."

"He Marked me, Kasmin. That wouldn't have happened if I wasn't meant to follow him." Thia countered. "You still haven't asked a question."

He bent down, picking up a small rock and bounced it in

his hand. "The others . . . were you their prisoner? Or did you go down into Byd Cudd with them willingly?"

"Keroys made it known I was to help them, so I went with them to Tanisal. That's when we learned Lolc Aon was searching for me. I went with them down to the city because I felt safer with them than staying here." *There's enough truth in that to sound right but doesn't give him anything else. You taught me that, Caelynn.* She took a deep breath. "What were you told about me?"

He shrugged. "That you had been kidnapped as a child, forced to worship Keroys. No one ever mentioned you were Marked by him, or even how beautiful you were."

Thia's eyes widened in shock. "That's not a word I've ever used to describe myself," she muttered.

"That's a shame, because you're one of the most beautiful women I've ever seen." He whispered. Clearing his throat, he shot a quick glance at her. "I was nervous, meeting you the first time. I had no idea what to expect. All I knew was that you defied Lolc Aon, something none of the rest of us ever dared do and had companions whose deeds were so fantastic that they bordered on legendary. Or the stuff of nightmares."

She felt her cheeks grow warm. "Yeah, they're rather skilled at various things."

Kasmin nodded. "Where are they now?"

"You've met Caelynn."

"Of course. She's amazing. I was thinking of going to The Green Frog sometime to hear her play. I was told that's the only inn that she frequents." He paused. "I was thinking of the others. Wasn't one a warlock? And one your cousin on your father's side?" Suddenly, he threw the rock. It sailed past the cliff's edge to land in the water below. "I had been told you were a tightknit group and have been surprised none but Caelynn have come with you when we've met at your office.

So many stories have been told. It's hard to know what's rumor and what's real."

Thia didn't look at him. "Pan is visiting our family. Jinaari and Adam—" she started.

"Adam! That's the warlock's name!" Kasmin interrupted. "I don't know why I have trouble remembering it. It's not like there's another warlock with that name." He laughed. "The prince . . . his name is hard to forget. Is he as intimidating as they say? I've heard he's seven feet tall, among other things."

"Like what?"

He picked up another pebble. "Rumor has it that one reason Queen Agrana disowned him is because he had feelings for you that she felt weren't appropriate."

"The Queen isn't partial to someone who is, what did you call it? Thahion?" She watched him nod once. "Her prejudices run deep. I can't say they're without reason. Lolc Aon drove her followers to do some heinous acts."

"So, there's truth to the rumor?"

"Jinaari and I have saved each others' lives, Kasmin. I trust him more than anyone else I've ever known, outside of Keroys. Her Majesty doesn't trust me and resents the confidence her son has in me." *Anything else is none of your business!*

"What about Adam? Who is he in your world?" He held up a hand as she drew breath. "I'm not trying to pry, honest. There's a possibility that I'll have the honor of meeting them is all. I'd rather know who I'm facing over making an incident out of ignorance."

"He's a brother of my choosing. I trust him almost as much as I do Jinaari. The two of them have kept me alive, and sane, at times that others would've given up on me. Let me die." She paused. *Caelynn's done that, too. So why don't I trust her yet?* "As I was saying," she kept going, "they aren't far. They're taking care of a small matter but are in contact often."

She glanced out at the star filled sky. "It's late. I should return home."

"Have you had dinner yet? There's a small café near the docks that I've been dining in. I'd be honored if you'd join me." Kasmin glanced at her, a half-smile on his face.

"I really should return home," Thia said, jumping off the stone. "Perhaps another time, when the others can join us."

He stood as she did. "I understand. I don't like it, but I can see your side." He held out his arm. "May I at least have the honor of escorting you back?"

I'm trapped, she thought. *I can't tell him no without insulting him, and that doesn't help Tomil.* "It's not far," she said. The path was narrow enough to warrant single file. She didn't have to take his arm. "You don't have to, you know."

"I didn't mean to imply you'd be accosted. You're the Daughter of Keroys. I doubt any in the city would dare touch you without your permission." She heard him say as he began to walk behind her. "Despite what you may have heard about life in Byd Cudd, we're taught the ways of the surface world. I mean, yes. Lolc Aon had us at each other's throats, always trying to maneuver our House into a favorable position. But such things were done behind closed doors. We weren't knifing each other in the streets."

"Not until after we killed her," Thia muttered under her breath.

"Daughter?" There was a catch in Kasmin's voice, and it made her turn around. His hands were raised, palms up, and a look of wonder was on his face. "What's this?" he asked as white flakes slowly drifted down onto them.

"It's snow," she shrugged. Turning, she started to walk again.

"Snow? Like what falls on the mountain peaks?"

"It happens down here, too, during the winter if the

conditions are correct. Even with the sea right there," she gestured out to the inky water.

"It's beautiful," he said.

"Yes, but it's also slippery. Watch your step once we get to the docks. The streets are likely to be slick." Raising her head, she sighed. A group of armed men were going door-to-door down the line of buildings that faced the harbor. Either Caelynn or Lukas noticed she was missing and sent them to find her, or something else was wrong. She picked up her pace, watching the men closely. There were still several streets between them. If she could get to the first one, make it far enough down, she'd be able to evade them all the way back to The Green Frog. *Then what? Sneak into my room, pretend to be asleep or bathing for hours and not hear Caelynn calling for me? What if she's talking with Adam and Jinaari when I walk into the room?*

Her feet hit a patch of ice, and she began to fall. Someone grabbed her, but the momentum was too much and she fell on top of her rescuer.

"Did I hurt you?" she glanced up at Kasmin's face.

"Not at all," he laughed. "Unless you count an elbow to my ribs."

"Daughter!" Brennan called out over the clamor of the armor-clad paladins heading her way. "Thank Garret I found you." He held out a gauntleted hand toward her.

Taking it, she rose. "Is something wrong?"

"Nolan, escort Envoy I'chal back to his residence," Brennan began directing the others with him, but didn't release his grip on Thia's arm. "After that, start finding the other groups and let them know that we found her. Finnur, get back to The Green Frog and inform Captain Frazier. We'll be there shortly." He looked at her. "I'm going to insist on a slower pace, Daughter. I don't want you to be hurt."

Kasmin bowed. "Until we meet again, Daughter. Our

conversation tonight was a pleasure for me, and I hope we can speak openly again sometime soon." Turning, he walked away.

Her stomach fell. Between the tone of Brennan's voice, and how carefully he held her arm, she wasn't going anywhere. Not without force on her part, anyway. "I don't need assistance," she said in protest.

"We saw you fall, Daughter."

"My name's Thia."

He looked at her; his young face stern under his helmet. "It is, but formality is the core of civility. And I'm striving to remain civil to you right now."

"I thought we knew each other better than that." The slight pressure on her arm moved her forward, and they began to walk the street toward the interior of the city.

"We did, until you disappeared. It will be weeks before the Captain regains the trust he's lost in me."

Thia sighed. "You didn't do anything wrong, Brennan."

"Doesn't matter. I was to watch you. One minute, you're heading up to take a nap. The next, no one can find you. The first reaction was that I had become distracted and someone managed to abduct you."

The road bent to the left. The alley leading to the inn wasn't far now. "I'll talk to him, explain why I left. This was my decision." *I didn't think about what might happen to him when I cast that spell. Lukas must understand this was my choice over punishing Brennan.*

The Green Frog came into view; the windows for the common room were well lit. Two armed guards snapped to attention as they approached. One nodded to them while the other opened the door. "Brennan's back," he called into the building.

He released her arm as soon as they crossed the threshold. Lukas stood at the head of several tables that had been shoved together. He muttered something to the men surrounding him as they approached. As they darted past her, she caught sight of Caelynn standing on the landing leading up to their suite. Her face was a stony mask.

"Daughter, you had us concerned," Lukas said as she approached. "If you needed some fresh air, you could've said so."

"I didn't want to make a parade out of it. This was my doing, no one else was part of this." She pulled the gloves off her hands as she spoke. "Brennan did nothing wrong, nor did anyone else you had on guard duty. I apologize for making you worry, but do not penalize them for this." She gripped the back of a chair with her hands. A map of the city was laid out, with small markers in different areas. Had they done all this to search for her?

Lukas shook his head. "When he warned me, I thought he was joking."

"Who warned you? About what?"

"Jinaari, before he left. Told me that keeping an eye on you was going to be harder than what he was going to do. Until tonight, I thought he was exaggerating."

"She's the Daughter of Keroys, Lukas. Where she goes, and when she chooses to, is not something she needs to explain to you. It's not Garret's Mark she bears," Caelynn said from the staircase. "Jinaari has reasons to keep her safe. I'm willing to bet him asking you to keep an eye on her didn't include restricting her movements to the point of suffocation."

Thia cringed inwardly at the tone of her friend's voice. So much anger and pain were hidden beneath her words.

"She's right. You don't owe me an explanation, though I'm glad to hear this wasn't a problem with any of my men. Go upstairs, rest if she lets you. I'll talk with you tomorrow. If we can be honest with each other," he gave her a direct look, "then perhaps I can keep my word to Jinaari without restricting you beyond what you're comfortable with."

Glancing toward the stairs, she caught sight of Caelynn as she disappeared. "I'd like that, Lukas. Things should be back to normal by then."

"For your sake," he said, "I hope so. I like you, Thia. So do my men. We'd be here even if Althir hadn't asked us to be. We all got scared when you disappeared, but that one," he glanced over his shoulder toward the staircase, "she was ready to burn Almair to the ground to find you."

TWELVE

Thia put her hand on the rail, a wave of exhaustion washing over her. Her boots, wet with melted snow, took more effort than normal to lift onto the next step. *Get upstairs*, she thought, *make sure there's a fresh log on the fire. A long soak in the tub will feel wonderful before bed. I'll ask Caelynn what Adam and Jinaari said in the morning.*

Stopping in front of the entrance, she glanced back to make sure no one had followed her. There were only paladins left in the common room, plus Wilim, but it was habit. The only time she wouldn't do that is if one of her friends was behind her. The wood beneath her palm, worn smooth with their touch, vibrated slightly. The portal opened and she stepped through.

Turning around, she set her gloves down on the small shelf attached to the wall.

"We need to talk." Caelynn's voice was strained.

Thia stopped working the buttons on her coat, stunned. "Okay," she said, her hands finishing up. Shrugging it off, she placed it on one of the pegs below the shelf. "About what?"

"What in the name of all the Gods did you do today?" The words came out as an angry hiss.

Turning around, she saw Caelynn standing behind a chair, her hands grasping the back tight enough that her veins rose beneath the blue skin. "I . . ." she stammered, "I needed time alone. I don't know why you're angry. Sure, it's later than I thought I'd be gone, but you just told Lukas—."

"Screw him! This is between you and me!" Caelynn screamed, pointing at her. "Nobody knew where you were, Thia! I had to lie to Adam and Jinaari, make them think you were sleeping! I have *never* done that before! Ever! Not to the two of them!" She took a breath and Thia drew back from the ferocity of her words. "If you needed time alone, why didn't you just say something? I would've made sure you got it, plus kept anyone else away. Instead, we were tearing apart the city because we were terrified that you'd been abducted! And you get found by Kasmin!" She lowered her head for a moment. "I know you've been trying to keep it together, Thia. I've seen the cracks. Adam and Jinaari haven't, but I have. You've gone through more in the last six months than most people will in their lifetime. Eventually, something was going to give. If you'd just said something to me, I would've helped you."

Thia walked over to a chair and sat down, the weight of Caelynn's words hitting her like blows. "I'm sorry," she said, "I didn't think about that."

Caelynn sat down opposite of her. "You should've. I've been worried sick for hours! The three of you are my family, the only one I have left. I know you don't trust me like you do them, but I see you as a sister. I swore to Jinaari I wouldn't lose you again, and he trusts me not to. Even after what happened in the conduit. When I discovered you were missing, I thought I'd lost you forever."

"Wait, what are you talking about? What happened in the conduit?"

The bard's eyes grew wide. "Didn't he tell you what happened when you were taken?"

Thia shook her head slowly. "No. When I woke up, I asked if we'd lost anyone in the fight. He asked what happened when I was Lolc Aon's prisoner. Neither of us brought up how I ended up a captive until later, in Cirrain. Even then he only said that Alesso was behind it. I don't know anything beyond going to sleep in the room and waking up in a box, naked."

"I, um," Caelynn bowed her head; her pink hair hiding her face. Thia could see her hands shaking. "I was on watch with Alesso when you were taken." The words came out as a whisper.

Her stomach churned. "Go on," she said. *There has to be more! She wouldn't have given me over! Pan would've killed her! Jinaari and Adam would've made sure she was handed over to someone for judgement!*

"It was about an hour into my watch. Adam had woken me up like normal. He and I would share the watch with Alesso. We knew not to let Pan babysit him." She sighed. "Jinaari took a few turns, when we first started to go down, but Adam and I thought he needed to sleep more. That's when we volunteered to do it. Alesso wasn't a talker, and neither of us were interested in being friendly. There were a few times where Jinaari pulled him aside, when you were in the tent, and had words with him. I don't know what he said those times. Probably warning him to lay off you or something."

"Caelynn, what happened? I have a right to know."

The pink head bobbed in agreement. With a sigh, she straightened up and looked at her. Thia sat back, shocked. Caelynn's face was full of guilt. "Everyone else was asleep. He got up; said he was going to take a piss. Next thing I knew, something sharp hit my neck. I swatted at it and found the dart. Whatever they used; it was fast. I couldn't move, talk, nothing. I just fell over and laid there, helpless, while the fog entered the room. It made me even more tired. The last thing I saw before I blacked out was two of them stripping you, tying you up." Tears began to trickle down her face. "When I woke up, there was nothing left but your gear." She looked at Thia. "It was my fault. I heard footsteps in the conduit, thought it was Alesso. I should've known better, done something."

"It's not your fault." Thia's heart broke at the guilt on Caelynn's face. *She cares, and I repay it by doubting her?*

"It is," she insisted. "If I had paid better attention . . . we were all worried about him, that he'd betray us at some point. I shouldn't have let my guard down. We were so close to Lolc Aon's sanctuary! I thought we were in the clear, past all her traps."

Thia moved her chair closer. Taking her hand, she said, "Caelynn? Look at me." Meeting her gaze, she continued. "No matter who was on watch, it was going to happen. If it'd been Adam or Jinaari, they would've used a stronger sedative. That's all. It was perfectly planned. Alesso never said a word about the conduits until we found the one he was told to use. That room where we rested, all of it. I don't think it's your fault. Neither does anyone else." She paused. "I'm sorry I scared you like I did. That wasn't my intent, though I'm not upset about fooling the host of paladins downstairs."

Caelynn giggled. "Oh, Lukas was livid. And he doesn't hide it nearly as well as Jinaari." She sighed. "Are you okay? Really?"

Thia sat back. "I am now. You're right; I wasn't handling things well. I kept them bottled up too long. It's been one thing after another hammering away at me, and I'm woefully inept at dealing with the effects. I talked with Elian, and she suggested I go somewhere and let it all out."

"Thia," Caelynn looked at her, puzzled. "Elian's been out of the inn all day. One of her kids was ill."

"I talked to her, in the kitchen." She leaned forward, burying her face in her hands. "I know I did. She's the one that gave me the idea to make a duplicate of myself." Raising her head, she stared at Caelynn. "I'm not mad," she whispered. "I know she was there, along with several others. She had the tea set out, like she expected me."

"We'll have to talk to Adam about that, but I can't help but think it was a set-up of some kind. We already know Kasmin can do illusions, and he found you."

"You think it was him? A way to get me alone?"

Caelynn shrugged. "At this point," she said, "I wouldn't be surprised. If it was him, he's even better trained than we thought." She looked at Thia. "You won't like this, but the only way to make sure it wasn't him is for you not to be alone again. Up here, that's one thing. He can't come here. But out there," she waved a hand toward the exit, "is different. I don't want to suffocate you like Lukas did, but we gotta keep you safe."

"I understand."

"Good. I want to go back to what you said about making a duplicate. You can do that?"

Thia nodded. "Yes. It was only the second time. The first was when we'd come back from Tanisal. This time, I gave it enough magic to look and feel real in case someone stopped 'me.' Including instructions on what to say if someone asked where it was going. Once it left the kitchen, I slipped out a side door.

"I ended up near the docks. There was a sheltered alcove in the side of a cliff, with a path that led up to it. I hid in there and, don't laugh, I cried. It's like all the pain and grief I've held onto since Papa died came out at once. Kasmin found me as I was regaining my breath." She paused, "I'm sorry you had to lie to Adam and Jinaari. I thought I'd be back before I was missed. I didn't realize how long I was up there. Did they tell you anything?"

Caelynn nodded. "They're meeting Amara tomorrow. From what Adam said, they're starting back once Jinaari talks her into coming with them."

"I'll make sure I'm here when he calls again. I promise. And I'll tell them that it's not your fault. This was my doing."

"Whatever he's using has to stay in Helmshouse, so he won't be able to do it again. But they'll be back sooner than they thought."

Thia relaxed slightly. "I'm glad to hear it. Kasmin asked me questions about them. I tried to make it sound like they were close by."

"That's odd."

"What do you mean?"

Caelynn moved forward in her seat. "Think about it, Thia. In the two meetings you've had with him, you asked all the questions. He's never once asked one of you. Then, he somehow finds you when you're alone, vulnerable, and they start coming. I don't like it."

Thia ran a hand through her pale blonde hair. "It didn't seem odd at the time, more like he was trying to make conversation."

"What all did he ask you?"

Thia shrugged. "Where Pan, Jinaari, and Adam were. He was surprised he hadn't met them yet, just you." Her mind began to replay the conversation. "He got excited to hear Adam's name, claimed he never could remember it. Knows you play here, wanted to come and listen to you. We talked about rumors he'd heard down in Byd Cudd about me. About all of us." She felt her cheeks grow hot. "Said the one thing he didn't expect when he met me was for me to be pretty."

"Smooth."

"What do you mean?"

Caelynn rose. "He's trying to find out who you're close to, where they are. That's something I would've thought he'd been told before he was sent as an Envoy. The Barren, if not all Byd Cudd, knew we were coming and who we were. Why does he act like he doesn't know?" She moved to a small cabinet where the group kept some food and mead. "There's something about his claim not to remember Adam's name that bothers me. Something Adam told me in passing once." Shaking her head, she sighed. "I can't put my finger on it now. If I wake you up in the middle of the night, you'll understand."

"He said he'd heard that one reason Agrana was screaming for my head was because Jinaari and I were closer than she wanted. But that doesn't make much sense, either. Tomil was told Amara was sent to Helmshouse because he wanted her dead so he could marry me. Argh!" she flopped back into the chair in frustration. "Why are there so many people talking about things they know nothing about!"

Caelynn handed her a goblet. "Here." Thia took a sip of the wine while her friend settled into her chair again. "They talk because they can. When they see someone, who has something they want, they don't like it. So, they make up stories to make the other person look bad. It's possible both rumors came from Agrana. Or neither. There could be a score more that haven't reached Almair yet. The goal is distraction, to discredit you. If you're the Daughter of Keroys, slayer of the Forsaken, that's one thing. A woman who sleeps around and wants political power? A crown? That's different." Tilting her head to one side, she looked at Thia. "I wonder why this surprises you. From what you've said about life at the cloister, you know how vicious rumors are. One small comment taken out of context can become an avalanche of lies within minutes."

"That's different, though."

"How?"

Thia shifted in her seat. "They weren't jealous of me. I wasn't pretty, like them. I didn't have parents who were rich, well connected. There wasn't any reason for it. And now I'm being targeted not for *who* I am but *what* I am. I can't control that!" She rubbed at her neck, working on a knot in the muscles.

"First off, you're beautiful. Smart. Damn good at magic. All things that those girls weren't. Thia, you spent so many years hearing the lies they'd spew that you grew to believe them. It was easier to think something was wrong with you instead of them. Thing is, that's what they wanted you to think. I bet any number of them had things going on in their lives that were hard for them. Then you came along, outdid them at all the lessons, rose up to be trusted by Father Philip. You can't let the shadow of the past dictate your life now." Caelynn moved closer and put a hand on hers. "You rejected the life that you would've had with your mother, accepted the one you have now. Part of that is understanding that we all love you for who you are, not because you're Marked. We don't fear you, Thia. To us, you're beautiful, kind, and have a sense of what's right. I know I've blurred the line in my life. Adam has, too." She giggled, then her face grew serious. "You're the only person that's Jinaari's equal in that arrogant sense of honor he has. I think that's one reason why he trusts you as much as he does. He knows that you'll do what's right, even if it's what hurts you the most."

She felt tears form in her eyes. "But," she hesitated, "what if I don't know what that is?"

Caelynn smiled. "We all have that fear. Even Jinaari, with all his bravado. I'll never admit this if you tell him, but I saw his face while you were unconscious after the fight with Lolc Aon. He was trained for battle, and it tore him up watching you fight one that he couldn't help with."

"And I repay him by running off, scaring you and his brother paladins to death, and having unsupervised conversations with someone who may be a spy. Way to go." Thia couldn't keep the self-loathing out of her voice.

"No, Thia. You did what you needed to do to find your strength again. That's all. We were watching you far too closely for all the wrong reasons. As to consorting with spies, I'm wondering if that's not a bad idea."

"What do you mean?"

Caelynn sat back, curling her legs up underneath her. Smiling over the rim of her goblet, she said, "He's obviously interested in something, Thia. Something he can only get from you. Let's invite him to come listen to me play, have dinner in the common room with you. We'll work it out so you know it's not an illusion. I may not have near the stores the rest of you do, but I can weave some magic into my music. We'll sit you both near enough to the stage that I can pick up if he's lying to you."

"But what if I say something wrong? I'm not sure I didn't earlier tonight. The way he reacted to Adam's name, for example."

"That's nothing. The thing most don't know is that no two warlocks have the same name. There never was, or ever will be, any other who uses that name. Adam told me it was part of the final ceremony granting them their full powers. They had to choose a new name; one no other warlock ever used. That way, if they screwed up in a big way, it was easy to know which one." Caelynn put her drink on the table and rose. "I'm heading to bed, and suggest you do the same. Tomorrow, we start playing games with someone who has no idea what's about to happen to him. By the time the men are back with Amara, we'll know exactly who this Kasmin I'chal is and what he really wants in Almair."

Thia stood up. "You really think we can pull that off?"

"He's respectful of your power, which is good. But he's shown that he has little knowledge of who or what I am. That'll be his downfall."

Thia turned and headed to her room. Pausing at the doorway, she looked back. "Caelynn?"

The pink haired woman stopped. "Yes?"

"Jinaari once told me there's different kinds of family. The ones we were born into, and the ones we chose. I didn't have a sister growing up. Would it bother you if I told people you and I were related?"

Caelynn smiled. "There's nothing I'd like more."

THIRTEEN

"Jinaari? You awake?" Adam's voice echoed through his room.

"Yeah, I'm up," he replied from the edge of the bed. Glancing over his shoulder, he saw the door open and his friend enter. "What's going on?" he asked as he pulled one of his boots on.

"We've got a visitor."

The tone of his voice made Jinaari pause. Glancing up, he saw the serious set to Adam's jaw. "I'm almost dressed. Or do I need to put my armor on?" he asked as he pulled on the other boot.

"Just put on a clean shirt. And don't take all morning." Adam turned and walked out of the room, closing the door behind him.

Jinaari pulled his pack closer. Flipping the top open, he thrust his hand into the opening and searched for a clean tunic. *Whoever is here, they have Adam spooked. Amara? No, that doesn't make sense. He'd have let her come into the room. A messenger from Almair?* Concern for Thia and Caelynn washed over him and he threw the tunic over his head as he rose.

Pausing at the door, he made out Adam's voice. It was low, and he couldn't understand what he was saying. Twisting the knob, he opened it and walked into the other room.

Adam turned, and Jinaari saw the visitor. The tall, regal woman with silver hair inclined her head at him. "Your Royal Highness."

"Your Eminence," Jinaari said, bowing stiffly. "I am honored, though that title is not mine any longer."

"I am aware of your refusal to your mother, Jinaari Althir. I also know the mantle may yet be yours to wear." She folded her hands in front of her. "After Adam told me of your adventures, and of who the Daughter of Keroys is, I spent time in meditation. I fear Thia Bransdottir is not the only one Marked that walks Avoch."

"There's another Son or Daughter?" Jinaari glanced at Adam. "We thought it a possibility. Alesso Potiri was brought back to a life of sorts. Only someone Marked by a God could do this."

"In the vision that led to Adam joining the outside world, I saw the symbols of both Keroys and Lolc Aon layered over each other. This is why I commanded him to not just find the Son or Daughter, but to neutralize them if the Mark was of Lolc Aon. What wasn't clear until last night is that three children were born. One bore the scales of Keroys. Lolc Aon had two in mind, nurtured them, but did not place her Mark on them until it was known that you and your companions were heading to Byd Cudd."

"I took care of the Goddess, though." Jinaari said. "Shouldn't that have neutralized her Son or Daughter?"

The Solar shook her head slowly. "If a God or Goddess dies while their representative still lives, their power goes into them. However, the person cannot access it. Not directly. If that Son or Daughter has a child, the God that was killed is reborn in the infant."

Jinaari's heard sank. "Let me get this straight. Lolc Aon can come back if the person she Marked has a child?"

The Solar continued. "Yes. All the Gods have some foresight. They can sense if their current lifespan is in peril, take steps to ensure their return. This is what Lolc Aon did. However, the woman was killed. That means the Son is left." She leveled a direct look at Jinaari.

His hands gripped the back of the chair, but he remained calm. "We need to get back to Almair," he said.

"Agreed. Gather your gear, see to your sister. She cannot remain here much longer. Your brother will come for her or send others to threaten the peace of Helmshouse. I would have the three of you leave before that happens. There are many here who need my protection. And Avoch would not survive if those individuals were left to roam freely." She bowed again and walked through the solid stone wall.

"Was she even here?"

Adam nodded. "Yes. Her Eminence is able to bend her form around objects. It makes it easier for her to be where she needs to be at a moment's notice. You're welcome to throw the chair if it makes you feel better. I never cared for that one much."

He shook his head. "It won't help," he muttered under his breath. Looking at his friend, he said, "You know the way to where Amara's at, right? We're not waiting on some sort of guide?"

"I know the way."

"Once she's ready, how far until you can transport us back to Almair?"

Adam shrugged. "There's several tubes leading from the guest towers. Most will go straight outside. An hour, maybe two, of travel and we'll be good. We've got a good chance of being back in The Green Frog by late afternoon."

Jinaari straightened and turned toward his room. "I'm getting my armor on. I'll be ready in less than half an hour. We leave then, get Amara, and get out."

"Agreed."

He started to walk when Adam's voice stopped him. "Caelynn's not going to let anything happen to her, not after Alesso tricked her. She'll keep Thia safe until we get there. Your brothers are watching, too."

"It's not who's watching that we know about that worries me. It's the ones that we don't know." Twisting the knob, he walked into the room and closed the door behind him.

Sitting heavily on the bed, he cradled his head in his hands for a moment. *Damn it*, he thought, *I should've listened to you, Thia. You knew something was wrong, felt it, and it's worse than either of us could ever imagine. Garret, talk with Keroys. She's going to need his guidance before I get back.*

Raising his head, he stood up and pulled the padded undertunic off the back of the chair. At least it was dry. Methodically, he started to put his armor on. With each buckle, his sense of calm purpose came back. *I know this life. This is who I am. I was given a task, one I vowed to see through. My shield to guard her, my sword to protect her, my life for hers if needed. It's time to get back to work.*

He buckled his helm to the outside of his pack, where he could reach it easily, and then wrapped his belt and scabbard around his waist. He held the blade out, checking it carefully for nicks in the edge. The ethereal blue light embedded in the steel kept it sharp, but his training never wavered. It had to be ready for him to wield, no matter how many Gods touched the blade. Satisfied, he slid it into the scabbard and slung his pack across his back, adjusting his shield so it was within easy reach. "Adam," he called out as he opened the door, "you ready?"

"Almost," the warlock's voice floated down from above him. "Go stand by the door. I have to take care of something and I don't want you getting hurt by accident."

He walked over to the portal and waited. The blonde man floated down through the center of the tower; a shower of sparks flying from his staff drifted like dust across everything around the room. As it settled, the contents either faded away or turned to ash. Landing gently, he tapped the floor three times with the butt of the thick rod. "We're good," he said, nodding at Jinaari.

Turning around, he pushed open the door. Beyond was a well-lit tube. He walked into it and waited. Adam followed, closing the portal and sealing it shut. "This way," he said, moving past Jinaari.

"How far?"

"The Solar made it so we'd have a direct connection to Amara's room. When we find a door, it'll be the right one."

They walked in silence, which suited him. They'd known each other long enough that small talk wasn't necessary. Anger roiled in him. This was all too perfect, and Thia had felt it. She'd warned him, and he ignored it.

"What's the likelihood Amara won't want to go with us?" Adam asked.

"She will. The Solar said we had to take her away before Stijyn came for her or sent people. Last I heard, she wanted to marry Tomil. I'm more interested in why she came here and not to Almair when she left." Was it really their mother's doing? Or did she come on her own somehow? He was going to have to ask her when they were heading out.

"We're here."

Adam's voice cut into his thoughts. Ahead of them was a

large wood door, bound with iron. A key sat in the lock. "That's odd," Adam commented.

"What's odd?"

"That there's a key in the lock. We don't do that to guests."

Grabbing the key, Jinaari twisted it in the lock and then opened the door. "Amara?" he called out. "It's Jinaari. I've got Adam with me." Crossing the threshold, he looked around the room.

Things were scattered as if someone had been searching for something. Rugs were wrinkled, with corners thrown back. Chair cushions were tossed around the room, and desk drawers left open. No fire burned in the hearth.

He heard something in another room. He glanced at Adam as he slid his sword out of the scabbard. The two men crept forward, listening for clues. If it was Amara, she would've answered him when he first came in.

Adam pressed his back against the wall nearest the doorknob, waiting for his signal. With a nod, Jinaari charged through the opening as soon as his friend twisted the handle.

The bedroom was even worse. Clothing and blankets strewn everywhere. "Forkke! Gnat came back! Don't hide!" a small, frantic voice screeched from behind an open wardrobe.

Moving slowly, Jinaari crept forward. When he was close enough, he quickly moved the armoire door, and the creature squealed.

"Gnat not hurt Pretty Lady! Don't hurt Gnat!" the cobalus screamed. His long ears drooped from the top of his head, which was covered with wisps of white hair. He held up his thin arms, "Gnat not armed! Gnat just looking for his friend!" He peered at Jinaari from large, green eyes, "You look like Pretty Lady. Who are you?"

Jinaari put his sword away. "I'm her brother. Where is she?"

Tilting his head, Gnat asked, "Which brother? Are you Nice Brother or Mean Brother?"

"I'm the nice one. Me and my friend," he gestured at Adam, "are here to take Amara someplace safe. Where our mean brother won't find her."

Gnat's face lit up and he pushed his way past Jinaari. "Forkke! Gnat find you! Why you hide from Gnat?" He grabbed something off the floor, cradling it like a baby.

Jinaari whispered, "We're getting nowhere fast." He took a step toward the cobalus, but Adam raised a hand to stop him.

"Let me. You're not going to be able to strong arm him into anything." Jinaari nodded and stepped back. "Gnat," Adam knelt, looking the creature in the eye. "My friend and I are in a hurry. Do you know what happened here? Where's Amara?"

"Pretty Lady had a visitor, said her brother was coming to take her away. Only Pretty Lady was worried it was Mean Brother and not Nice Brother," he squinted, pointing at Jinaari's sword. "Gnat knows you said you were Nice Brother, but that didn't look like nice pokey." He looked back at Adam. "Are you Magic Friend? Pretty Lady said that Nice Brother had a Magic Friend who could fix Forkke!"

"Um, yeah. I'm the Magic Friend. What's wrong with Forkke?"

Jinaari leaned against the wardrobe, his arms crossed. This was taking too long.

"Forkke got sick and I put him in here," he stroked the bag. "He look like sand now, not all clear and round."

"Where's Amara?" Jinaari asked again.

"Pretty Lady begged Gnat to take her out of here in Gnat's special tunnel. She was afraid it was Mean Brother who was coming. But Gnat move too fast and Pretty Lady hurt her ankle. Gnat found out that Forkke got lost, so Spoone is guarding Pretty Lady while Gnat searched for Forkke."

"Adam, we don't have time . . .".

The warlock nodded. "I know." His head swiveled back to Gnat. "Is she far?"

Gnat shook his head; strands of hair flew in all directions with the movement. "Not far. Gnat and Forkke can take you. But only if Magic Friend promise to fix Forkke. He's Gnat's bestestest friend ever, except for Spoone." The creature's ears drooped. "And Nyfe, but Gnat lost Nyfe a long time ago." A single tear fell from his eyes.

"I'll do my best, Gnat. But my friend and I are in a hurry. Can you take us to his sister now?"

A loud explosion echoed through the room, and everything shook violently. "What was that?" Jinaari asked.

His friend stood up, looking out a window. "I've not heard that sound in a century. There's a tower under attack," Adam said, his voice strained. "My tower."

"Shit," Jinaari said, running to the window. A single tower in the distance was engulfed in flames. Dark smoke poured from the windows.

"We don't have time to figure out who, Jinaari," Adam turned around. "Gnat, we have to go. Now. Show us your tunnel."

"Follow Gnat. He knows way to Pretty Lady. Don't worry. Spoone is with Pretty Lady."

A boulder the size of a house came flying toward the tower where they were, and Jinaari ducked instinctively. The room shook again, and cracks formed in the walls. Jinaari followed Gnat and Adam as they ran from the room. The cobalus went to a cupboard beneath a bookcase, deftly dodging the tomes falling off the shelves. "Tunnel in here," he said, diving into the darkness.

Adam glanced back at him. "Go," Jinaari commanded him. "I'll bring up the rear. That thing's the only lead we have for where she's at." He waited until his friend disappeared into the darkness, then drew his sword. *At least I'll see whatever's coming after us,* he thought. With the faint blue light illuminating the darkness, he crawled in after the pair.

The space was small. Grunting, he pushed himself forward. The sound of stone gouging into his greaves made him want to slow down, but the constant shaking around him propelled him forward. Adam was still in sight, but their guide was beyond the light of his sword. "Can you still see him?"

Adam glanced back, nodding. "Yes." His head swiveled forward again. "Gnat, how far is it before it opens up?"

"Not far. Nice Brother and Magic Friend stand up soon."

A low rumble began to grow, and Jinaari picked up his pace. The tunnel behind him began to collapse. "Adam!" he called out in alarm.

"I can see the end of the tunnel!" he yelled back. "Get your ass in gear!"

Ignoring the scraping of rock against his armor, he continued to crawl along the tunnel floor. A cloud of dust and debris rolled over him. Coughing, he lowered his head. The light from his sword dimmed in the dirt that rained down on him, but he kept moving. Something heavy bounced off his boot, making him wince with pain. The tunnel was collapsing around him. Mustering all his strength, he launched himself forward. Without warning, the floor beneath him gave way and he tumbled into a heap.

Someone pulled on his arm, and he looked up at Adam. "You got lucky," he said, pointing behind Jinaari.

The tunnel entrance was gone; a few rocks tumbled from where it had been to the cavern floor. An incandescent moss grew in small patches on the walls, giving them some light. Jinaari sheathed his sword, ignoring the scrapes on his chest plate. He could buff those out. His ankle throbbed insistently. "Give me a minute," he said, hobbling over to a large boulder.

"You okay?" Adam asked.

Jinaari nodded. "I will be." Working off his boot, he looked at the ankle. A sickly bruise was forming already, but no swelling. Testing it, he reasoned it wasn't broken. Drawing a simple sigil, he wrapped his hands around the joint and healed himself. Placing his foot back on the ground, he put some weight on it, testing it. "That'll work," he said, as he reached for his boot. "I hope there's another exit."

"This way," the cobalus said. "Pretty Lady down this tunnel. Gnat show Nice Brother and Magic Friend the way."

Jinaari sighed, watching the short creature scamper toward what appeared to be the only way out. "Adam?"

"Yeah?"

"This isn't one of your tubes, is it? This isn't warlock made."

"No, it's not. We're in the mountains themselves, beyond Helmshouse."

Jinaari looked up at him, "Can you transport us from in here?"

He shook his head. "I don't think so. See the moss?" Jinaari nodded, and Adam continued, "It's another security measure. We knew creatures lived here, and we didn't want them to get hurt by our presence. So, we modified the moss. Until we get outside, to the surface, I can't transport us."

Jinaari closed his eyes, bowing his head for a moment. Letting out a sigh, he glared at Adam. "We won't be back at The Green Frog tonight, then. That's what you're saying."

"Yeah."

"Any idea how long it'll be until we are?"

The blonde man shook his head slowly. "One problem at a time, my friend. Let's find Amara, make sure she's okay. Then I'll get my bearings and be able to find our way out."

Jinaari stood up. "Let's get moving," he said. "Until we get where he's taking us, I want you up by Gnat. You seem to be able to talk to him, keep him on track."

Adam smiled. "That's only because you're arrogant and demanding." He glanced toward the tunnel where their small guide waited, waving his arm for them to hurry. "Gnat's not bad. Just think of him as a young, inexperienced initiate."

"There's a problem with that," he growled as they started to walk toward the exit.

"Oh?"

"Young, inexperienced initiates don't make my teeth itch."

FOURTEEN

"Pretty Lady close now!"

Jinaari sighed. Gnat had been saying that for hours. It was only Adam's calm patience with their guide that kept him from asking if they were lost. At the same time, there'd been no offshoots from the tunnel. It only went forward.

"Hey, Jinaari!" Adam called out. "I think we're here."

"Wherever 'here' is," he muttered. Walking forward, he saw the pair had stopped in front of a pile of rocks. The tunnel continued to the left. Gnat scampered up the rubble, heading for a gap at the top.

"Pretty Lady! Gnat came back, like he promised! And he brought Nice Brother and Magic Friend!"

Jinaari put his hand against the wall. "There's got to be another way in." Stepping back, he watched Gnat disappear. "That gap's smaller than the tunnel we took to get out of her room. Amara wouldn't have climbed that, especially with an injured foot."

"Depends. Thia climbed up a rock wall with her wrist in a splint, and down the other side."

"Thia'd already healed herself," Jinaari said as he ran a hand across the surface in front of him. "The splint was there to keep it stable, that's all." It wasn't the only reason, and he knew it. She'd told him the real reason was to make Alesso think she wasn't as strong as she was. That, and she doubted how well she'd healed herself.

That was before they destroyed Drogon's device. Before she knew what she was and unlocked her magic.

"Over here," Adam said.

Jinaari turned. Part of the wall had moved inward, and Adam stood in the makeshift doorway. He looked down the tunnel both ways before going through.

The interior was awash with a soft glow as countless patches of the luminescent moss decorated the walls. Amara sat, her back against the far wall, with one leg bent. The ankle of the other was twisted in all the wrong ways. Her clothes were dirty. Small rips in the pants showed her scraped and bloodied knees.

"Jinaari!" she said, a pain filled smile filling her face. "I'd get up and hug you, but . . ." her voice trailed off.

"Don't even think about moving," he said as he walked over to her. Dropping his pack to the ground at her feet, he knelt beside her. Her brown hair was pulled back in a braid, but several strands had come loose and framed her pale, pain filled face. She reached out to him, and he wrapped his arms around her. "Are you okay?"

"I broke my ankle," she said, leaning back against the rock. "What are you doing here?"

"Let's get you healed first." He glanced at her feet, then back at her. "I can fix it, but it's going to hurt like hell."

She nodded. "Can't be any worse than how it's felt since I fell."

Jinaari scooted across the cavern floor to his pack. "Adam," he said as he reached into a side pocket, "I need your help."

"What can I do?"

He found what he needed; a small bundle of hard leather, wrapped with rawhide. Holding it out, he said, "Amara, I want you to put it between your teeth. Adam's going to hold you so you don't jerk. Sound carries down here, and we don't want to tell the entire mountain where we're at." Placing it in her hand, he turned his attention to the injured foot. He untied her boot and eased it off. Carefully, he rolled down her sock. The break was visible but hadn't broken the skin. Gently, he felt around the bone. It was a clean break, but it was going to take him physically moving it before he could cast any spell. Raising his head, he locked eyes with Adam. "Ready?"

Amara nodded, while Adam shifted her body so he could wrap his arms around hers. With a fluid motion, Jinaari snapped the bone into place.

Amara let out a muffled scream and Jinaari quickly wove the sigil for healing, letting his spell seep into her injured ankle. He looked back at her. "Better?"

Tears flowed down her face, and her breathing was rapid, but she nodded. She spit out the leather and it fell into her lap as Adam released her arms.

"I thought you were Nice Brother," Gnat said from behind him. "But you hurt Pretty Lady!"

"Gnat," Amara said, "he is my Nice Brother. What he did was necessary. I have to walk to get out of here, and I couldn't unless he did that." Her voice was strained, but stronger.

Jinaari glanced over his shoulder. The cobalus held a rock in one hand, ready to strike. "You did what you promised, Gnat," she continued. "We're going to stay here a night, maybe two, so that my leg heals all the way. After that, we'll need you to guide us again. Will you do that? For me?"

Gnat's arms fell, and the rock slid from his hand. "Why does Pretty Lady have to leave Gnat?"

"Gnat can come with us," she said. "I'll always find a way for Gnat to help me. I promised you that I'd make sure Forkke got better, remember? And Spoone kept guard, like you promised." She reached out and opened her fist. Resting on the palm was a large crystal shard.

Gleefully, he snatched up the crystal. "Spoone! You're my bestestest friend! Gnat proud of how you protect Pretty Lady!" He hugged the shard close to his chest, cooing softly. His head snapped up, his grin getting even larger. "Magic Friend fix Forkke!" Gnat ran toward Adam. Thrusting the leather pouch out, he said, "Fix Forkke now!"

Jinaari put Amara's sock back on, then grabbed his pack. "I'm going to put a splint around your ankle. Give it a few hours before you try and put any weight on it." he explained.

Adam rose, taking the rawhide bundle from her and walked toward Jinaari. "Here," he said, holding it out. "I'll distract Gnat, see if I can reform the sand into what he wants. I think you two have some catching up to do."

Nodding, he said, "Thanks." Once he found what he needed, he started to wrap her foot. "Why did you run? Didn't the Solar tell you we were coming for you?"

"All she said was that my brother was here to take me away. She didn't say which one." Amara said. "I had no idea if it was you or Stijyn."

He finished up and eased her sock over the splint before dragging his pack closer to her. He grabbed at some dried beef and handed it to her. "Here, eat this. It'll help."

"Thank you," she said. "I didn't think to pack any."

Handing her his waterskin, he looked at her. "Why go to Helmshouse? Why not Cirrain or Almair?"

She swallowed and rested the pouch in her lap. "Helmshouse was closer than Almair. I thought about Cirrain, but wasn't sure what Baroness Elizabeth would do if I did."

"Drakkus has the chapterhouse quartered there for the winter. He would've kept you safe, gotten you to Almair. Tomil's been worried about you."

"I didn't know. When the paladins pulled out, they didn't ask Mother's permission, or tell her where they were going. The Solar's neutral, politically speaking." She took a bite of beef, chewing it quickly before continuing. "Everything changed after you deserted us in the camp."

"I had a job to do. Being at court was not going to get it done. Mother said some things that weren't right, including some serious threats against Thia." He looked at her. "I renounced my titles, told her what she could do with them. And we left."

She looked up at him. "Did you do it?"

"Do what?"

"Mother was raving about you and the Daughter of Keroys after you left. Said that she wasn't going to let some mongrel get power in Avoch." She paused. "It drove her mad, Jinaari. Just the thought that you had taken a Fallen into your bed."

"She's as racist as Grandfather was."

Amara looked at him, her head tilted to one side. "It's true, then. Not that it's my business, but you know Mother. When we got back to Dragonspire, we had to stop her from taking a torch to your room. Stijyn's been making all the decisions, giving Mother some sort of potion that makes it so no one knows how delusional she's become. It's enough that most of the courtiers don't know what's going on, but it's accelerating. I'm not sure she'll ever be herself again." She sighed. "One night, I overheard Stijyn talking to someone. They were trying to think of ways to discredit the Daughter, drive a wedge between her and Tomil."

"Her name's Thia, Amara. Don't trip over titles with her.

And there's nothing beyond friendship between her and Tomil."

Smiling, she continued. "That's good to know. Their plan was to plant some rumors about them, then kill me and frame her for it. When I found out what they planned to do, I ran. I couldn't stay there."

"Stijyn wouldn't kill you, Amara. You had to have heard that wrong."

She shook her head. "He wouldn't, but his friend was ready to. He's obsessed with her. He thought the only way to get to her was by getting rid of you somehow." She tilted her head. "They know you won't leave her side. Did you leave her out there?" She gestured to the wall separating them from the tunnel. "I thought she was a healer." Her eyes grew wide. "She's not here, is she?"

Damn it! "When you heard this plan, where were you?"

"I was in Mother's outer chamber. She'd just retired for the evening. Stijyn and his friend were in one of the small antechambers. The door was cracked, and I heard my name, so I listened. As soon as I heard their plot, I ran." She sat up straighter and put her hand on his arm. "You think they planned all of this, don't you? Made sure I'd overhear them and run, and that you'd follow."

"It's possible. We had to leave Thia behind because a delegation from Byd Cudd is coming to Almair. Tomil wanted her to be there when he received them in court. We didn't think there'd be enough time between getting you and when they arrived, so she had to stay." Rage rose in him. They'd set a trap, and he fell for it. He looked at her. "Tell me about Stijyn's friend. Do you hear a name?" His voice was insistent.

"Stijyn called him, 'My Lord', and talked as if they were equals. Possibly deferring to him some. Which was odd because you know our brother."

"He only did that around Grandfather."

"Exactly. Whoever it is, Stijyn respects or fears him." She shifted. "He was Fallen. His hair was dark, darker than his skin, and he had it in a braid. I caught his face long enough to see his eyes were orange."

"When was this?"

She shrugged. "I've been in Helmshouse for two weeks, and it took time to get here. Maybe a month ago?"

Damn it! "Adam," he called out.

"I'm busy. What is it?"

"Forkke was round, not egg!" Gnat yelled.

"When you have time," Jinaari replied. Turning back to Amara, he said, "I want you to tell Adam everything you remember about this person when he's done with Gnat. Even the smallest detail."

She frowned. "What's wrong?"

He absently scratched at his beard. "Right after we left, someone showed up in Almair. Said he was sent by the delegation to help Thia learn what had gone on since we killed Lolc Aon. Thia's met with him at least twice that we know of, and none of us think he's being entirely truthful."

"You think he's Stijyn's friend?"

Jinaari nodded. "It fits too perfectly, especially if they were trying to pull me away from her side. I swore an oath, Amara, to keep her safe. To two different Gods. The only thing that could get me to leave her alone was Garret telling me I was needed elsewhere, or—"

"Or hearing I was in trouble but she couldn't come with you," she finished the thought. "It was a set up. They knew I'd overhear the plan and run." She shook her head. "But how did they know I'd go to Helmshouse?"

"You said it yourself. Cirrain's loyalties are fuzzy sometimes, and Almair was too far to get to quickly. This was your best, most likely, destination."

"Forkke! You're back!" Gnat's voice throbbed with tears.

Looking up, Jinaari saw Adam walking toward them. The cobalus was holding a clear orb like an infant, rocking it gently in his arms. "You fix his problem?"

Adam nodded as he sat near them. "I hope so. I added something to the sand. It won't shatter if he drops it."

"Good idea," Jinaari said.

"What's up?" The warlock looked at him.

"Remember when I said I thought this was all a set up? She's confirmed it." He bent one leg and rested his arm against his knee. "Stijyn's been running things behind the scenes back in Dragonspire. And he's got a new friend who's Fallen, and way too interested in Thia."

"One that's smart enough to make me hear exactly what I needed to in order to make me leave. Which would pull him away from her side," Amara's voice was quiet.

"It's not your fault," Jinaari said, tossing a pebble across the room.

"It's not yours, either," she countered.

Adam cleared his throat. "Did we get a name to confirm? There's lots of Fallen out there."

"I don't remember a name, barely saw what he looked like. I'm sorry."

"It's too perfect not to be, Adam." He threw another rock, this time he put some of his anger into it. The sound of it colliding with the wall echoed slightly. First, it was Potiri. Then they hear about Kasmin I'chal, but can't find the name anywhere. Add to it the Solar confirming that Lolc Aon had Marked someone as well. Damn it! He should've listened to Thia!

"We need to get back to Almair," Adam said.

Jinaari glared at him. "Yes, we do. We need to find our way out of here first. Or to a cavern where none of this damn moss grows. And our only guide is over there cradling an orb like it's a baby!"

"Let me and Amara work with him, Jinaari. We'll get out of here as soon as we can."

Jinaari didn't answer. The anger seethed in him. They'd set a trap, and he fell for it. Caelynn was with her, yes. That was something. The bard felt guilty about being on watch when Alesso betrayed them, she wouldn't let anything happen to Thia. *'Work through the anger, let it drive your purpose' was what Drakkus taught me. First things first. There's nothing I can do from here. Keep them alive, help Adam find an exit.* "Adam, work with Gnat. Scout the tunnel ahead but not so far you can't get back here. Once Amara's able to walk, we leave. I'd rather not spend a month down here looking for the way out."

"Gnat know way out!"

He looked at Gnat scampering over to them. "I'm sure you do," he said dryly. "How far is it?"

"Way out not far!"

Adam rose. "Why don't you show me which way it is?"

"Magic Friend come with Gnat!" Together, the two left through the hidden door.

"He has no concept of time, Jinaari," Amara said. "Not far for him could be the next bend, or weeks of walking. But he can get us out."

"I need us to get out tomorrow, Amara. Not in three weeks!"

"She's the Daughter of Keroys, Jinaari. Who would try anything against her? From what I hear, she's powerful enough to level all of Dragonspire if she wanted to."

"I made vows, promises. I can't keep them from in here."

She shifted, and he felt her gaze studying him. "You care about her." It wasn't a question.

"It's complicated."

"So, explain it to me. If you two are sleeping together, so what? It's not like I didn't seduce Tomil after our engagement was formalized! This is different, though. Isn't it?"

"Thia knows *me,* Amara. She didn't know about my family connections at first. There's a level of trust we have in each other. I don't have to worry that she's trying to gain favor with Mother, improve her standing at court. And I know her, probably better than she knows herself." He sighed. "I made a promise to her that anything between us would always be just that. Between us. I reasoned that it would keep her from being a target. No one could get to me through her if they didn't know we were involved. Or vice-versa."

"It's a great dream. But you know that's all it is: a dream. There's no way you'll be able to insulate yourselves from that. As long as you're protecting her, regardless of anything else between the two of you, there's the chance. You're each other's greatest weakness." Her voice dropped off.

Glancing over, he saw her head drooping. Wrapping an arm around her, he pulled her closer. "Get some sleep," he told her. "No one's going to hurt you now."

Wearily, she laid her head across his lap. "But what if they hurt you?"

"Shh. That's not going to happen." At least, not with a sword.

FIFTEEN

Something nudged his foot. Instinctively, his hand flew to the sword laying on the ground next to him.

"Hey," Adam whispered.

Jinaari nodded, but didn't move. Amara slept next to him and he didn't want to wake her up. *She needs it. We've been pushing hard.* "Anything happen?"

Adam shook his head. "It's been quiet, unless you count the snoring. I don't know who's worse; you or Gnat."

"You are," he said. He pushed aside the thin blanket and rolled onto his knees. "We've been walking for a week, Adam. There's got to be an exit someplace. Can't we clear the moss from an area and have you transport us? Wandering around like this isn't helping Thia."

"I know you're anxious to get back. So am I. Gnat says there's a way out, and he knows this cave system. Clearing the moss isn't the solution. All it takes is us missing one small trace and we could end up in your brother's bedroom. What good would that do any of us, especially Thia?" He paused. "We've been lucky. Outside of the four of us, there's been nothing roaming the tunnels. That's a good thing."

"If I have to fight something to get us out of here faster, I'll do it. It's better than wandering for another week." Maybe today they'd find it. "Wake up Gnat. Sitting here won't get us out."

Adam nodded and walked toward the small figure curled up on a flat rock. "Amara," he said, "it's time to get moving again."

His sister stirred. "You lied to me," she grumbled.

"How?"

"You always said sleeping on a cave floor wasn't cold. Even my lungs are shivering."

"Check my pack," he told her. "I'm sure there's a spare tunic in there."

She sat up; her hands undoing the leather strap that held her braid together. Most of her hair had escaped it during the night. "I am not wearing one of those stinky tunics of yours. Honestly, do you ever bother to wash them? They reek of sweat and armor!"

He snorted. "I've been busy rescuing some prima donna princess who couldn't bother to grab a cloak when she ran away."

Amara laughed, and he found himself joining her. "You take things too seriously, Jinaari," she teased him. Throwing back the blanket, she grabbed her shoes. "Has she even heard you laugh? Or is she just as serious as you are?"

"Who?"

"Thia," she said, jamming her foot into a boot.

"How's the ankle?"

She grinned. "You didn't answer my question."

"And I don't plan to." He shifted to his knees, grabbing the pack and pulling it closer to him before taking the blanket from her.

"Will I meet her? Or do you plan to hide her from me?"

"You already have," he said, rolling up the thin pad she'd

slept on. "Back in the tent, when you were camped at the base of the mountains."

"Nonsense. That was at court, and we didn't get to talk. I do remember her saying something that made Mother bristle." She stood up. "But to answer your question, my ankle feels fine. Same as it has every morning since you healed it."

He felt her watching him as he secured the bedroll. Looking up, he asked, "What?"

"I understand what you meant, you know. About wanting to keep things just between you and her. We grew up together. I couldn't trust anyone, either. Half of the girls who said they were my friend were hoping to get to you. The other half pined for Stijyn. They weren't my friends. All they wanted was what they thought the connection would give them. That's one of the things I love about Tomil. Sure, he's a Duke and our engagement was a political necessity. But, when it's just him and me, none of that matters. It's just us." She grinned, and a mischievous light appeared in her eyes. "I've waited my entire life for you to find someone that you wouldn't chase away just so I could share all your dirty secrets with them."

"I'll get you back to Almair and then you're his problem," he snapped. One look at her face and he regretted it. Why was he so angry? "Thia hates the pomp and ceremony as much as I do. Good luck with getting her to stay long enough to hear any story you might want to tell her." He stood up. "You weren't with me when I was an initiate, and those stories are never being shared." Standing up, he shoved the pack at her. "Be useful," he said.

Shouldering the pack, she adjusted the straps. "I don't know why you're making me carry this. It's not like we've seen anyone for you to fight."

He adjusted his coif, then picked up his helm and placed it on his head. "Not yet. Doesn't mean there won't be someone later." Lowering his voice, he continued, "If you want to get to know Thia, be patient. Don't force yourself on her. Invite her places but don't be upset if she declines. Don't stand on ceremony or any of that nonsense. Tell her how you feel, and never try to lie to her. She trusts even less than you or I do, with reason. You have to earn it with her, and it takes time." He walked over to where Adam stood with Gnat.

"Gnat ready to fight!" He grinned, brandishing the rusty short sword they'd found.

"I sharpened it, Gnat. Don't wave it around unless you're in a fight. You might hurt someone by accident," Jinaari reminded him.

Ears drooping, he carefully put it back in the makeshift scabbard tied to his waist. "Gnat forgot. Gnat sorry. Gnat not want to hurt friends."

Looking at the other two, he said, "Let's get moving." Gnat scurried ahead of them, and Jinaari glanced back at Adam. Once he knew the warlock was taking position behind Amara, he turned and headed after the cobalus.

Several hours later, Gnat abruptly sat in the middle of the path. "Gnat hungry."

Jinaari nodded. The area had several boulders they could rest against. "Let's take a break," he told everyone. As the others began to eat, he took a closer look at the tunnel ahead of them. "Hey, Adam?"

Raising his head, he said, "What?"

"Is it just me, or is the path starting to go uphill?"

Squinting, he said, "I think you're right."

"Is the pack getting too heavy, Amara?"

"No. Why?" she replied.

Jinaari pointed up the path. "We're going to be heading uphill. I want you to be careful, watch your footing."

"Uphill? Like we could be near the surface?" a sliver of hope was in her voice.

"Gnat promised Pretty Lady Gnat lead her out!" Gnat nodded his head vigorously.

"How much farther?" Jinaari asked.

"Not far. First we go up and then we go around and then we go outside."

Jinaari drew in a breath, ready to ask Gnat what he meant by 'go around' but changed his mind. The explanation would be vague and incomplete, no matter how he asked the question.

"Here," Adam's voice broke through his thoughts. "You gotta eat, too."

He took the bread and dried meat. "Thanks." Taking a bite, he asked, "What were you and Amara talking about earlier?"

"She's immensely curious about Thia, thought she could get some information out of me that she didn't get out of you. Don't worry, she didn't."

He shrugged. "Amara's led a lonely life. Court isn't exactly a place where lifelong friendships are forged. I don't think Tomil's will be as cutthroat as it is in Dragonspire, but she needs friends."

"Caelynn will take to her. I know that." Adam smiled. "She's rarely met someone she didn't like from the start. Thia, though . . ." his voice trailed off.

"Yeah." He took another bite and lowered his voice. "It's been too quiet. I doubt we'll get out of here without a fight. When the attack comes—"

"You're sure there's going to be one?" Adam interrupted.

Jinaari nodded. "I do. The way's been too clean. No webs, no nests, not even ants. Just the damn moss and rocks. Which means someone cleared it out before we arrived, or whatever lived here was big enough to keep smaller animals away." He glanced toward Gnat. "I've never heard of a cobalus around here, have you? They normally live to the south, past

Tavisholm. What are the odds one would be here, find a way into Helmshouse that circumvents every security precaution you have, and manage to dig a tunnel into the one tower where Amara's staying?"

"It does seem odd, but Gnat's harmless."

"I'm not worried about him. But I wonder who is behind him being here. It fits together too perfectly." Picking up a small rock, he bounced it in his hand. "All of this is wrong."

"That means we have to set it right," Adam said as he started to rise.

"One more thing." The warlock paused and Jinaari looked him in the eye. "I can't afford not to trust you on this."

Adam stared at him. "I thought we straightened that out back in my tower. I told you everything about why I joined up with you, what my mission was. All of it. You're my brother, Jinaari. I have never once questioned what you thought was best, especially during a fight."

Was it anger or frustration in his voice? Jinaari met the stare, refusing to back down. "If I'm right, I need to know you'll get Amara out of here. And keep your word to tell Thia about your mission."

"I'm getting us all out," he snapped. "What are you talking about? I'm not abandoning anyone."

"I want your word, Adam. If things go wrong, you get her back to Almair. No matter what."

"You don't trust me?"

He stared at him. "This is wrong. Too wrong. You know it as well as I do. I got set up by someone."

"We both did. I should've seen this, same as you." Adam's face shifted. "You don't actually think I had any part in this?" he whispered.

Jinaari sighed. "I don't." *Not intentionally*, he thought. The smallest seed of doubt sat on his soul, though. "You're the thinker, Adam. Where I know tactics, you know people. If this

I'chal person is Marked, he's played a very long game. One that's about to come out in the open." He paused. "Amara said something to me earlier that's had me thinking."

"What was it?"

"She said that Thia and I were each other's biggest weakness. I'll protect her under any circumstances, and she's done the same for me. After we took down Lolc Aon and Drogon, the world knows this. Anyone out there that wants to get one of us to do something would go after the other one. It's a common tactic. That's why I need your word that you'll get Amara out of here. They're not after her, Adam. They're after Thia, through me. Get Amara to Almair and the balance shifts back in Thia's favor, because you'll have Tomil's forces behind you."

"You have it. But," he paused, "not unless there's no way to get you out with us. I already have to explain things to Thia. I don't want to add why you're not with us to the list."

"She'll understand. Eventually. I could be overthinking this, but I doubt it. If I'm wrong, we all get out of here. If I'm right, I'll be kept alive until I'm not useful anymore." Glancing up the path, he said, "Let's get moving." The sooner they got back to Almair, the faster this sense of doom would leave him.

The slope gradually increased. Within an hour, their pace had slowed considerably. Rounding another bend, he held up his hand. The passage ahead ended with almost a vertical wall of rock and dirt. An opening at the top was wide enough for them to crawl through, but not by much. "Gnat?"

"This is way out," the cobalus nodded excitedly. "We go up and then around!"

"I'm going to scout ahead," Jinaari said. "You three stay here." *I need to know what he means.*

Choosing his path carefully, he climbed up the mound. Halfway up, he caught the whiff of decay and burning wood.

He paused, listening. The echo of moans, accompanied by the crackle of fire and shifting of bodies, reached his ears. Inching forward, he brought his head up to the opening and looked through.

Small fires lit up a cavern below him. Three dozen well-armed men moved around the room. In the center, two hundred Dangreth shuffled about. To the right, above the horde of undead, a passageway led around the encampment. The ledge was about four feet high. Once they got on it, they should be able to go around. As long as they stayed low and moved quietly. He followed the path, trying to anticipate problem areas. It dropped down, out of sight, on the opposite side of the cavern. A patch of afternoon sunlight shone at the top of a short incline. *Gnat was right. We go around and out.* Carefully, he inched back from the opening and down to the others.

"Well?" Adam asked him as his feet touched the path.

"There's a way out," he started, "but we're going to have to be careful." He looked at Amara. "There's a small army in the cavern itself, mostly Dangreth, but there's a ledge that runs above the camp. If we move slow, stay low, keep quiet, we should get to the exit. I saw some light, so it won't take long once we're past them to be where Adam can transport us."

"How many Dangreth?"

"Too many. We can't fight our way through them." Kneeling, he began to draw a map into the dirt. "There's about a six-foot drop between the opening and the ledge, but there's a wall that will give us some cover. We all go up, then through one at a time. Adam, you'll go down first. I'll lower Amara, then Gnat, to you. When you get down, stay low below the wall's edge, and start moving. Watch your footing. One wrong noise and we'll have more company than we want." He looked at Adam. "If they realize we're there, I want you to blast the ceiling if you can. Don't overdo it, though. I'm trusting you to get us out once we're on the surface."

He smiled. "Are you saying you won't buy me another staff?"

"Not unless it's necessary. Those things are expensive." Jinaari stood, looking at each of them. "Watch your feet, don't sneeze, and we'll be in Almair within an hour. Let's go." Shifting to one side, he waited as Adam started to climb. "Gnat, I want you to come up last. I'm trusting you to keep Amara from falling."

"Gnat not let Nice Brother down! Gnat protect Pretty Lady!"

"Amara, turn around." Deftly, he unhooked the shield from his back and pulled it free. He secured it to the pack she carried. "Keep this with you. It's going to be tight enough for me to get through the opening. Follow my steps and stay close." Reaching up, he started to climb again. He heard her grunt slightly as she pulled herself up, but that was the only sound she made.

By the time he reached the opening again, Adam had lowered himself through. Glancing down, he saw the warlock crouching below the wall's edge. Jinaari motioned his hand, signaling Amara to take off the pack and lower it first. The hole wasn't tall enough for her to keep it on, at least not to get through quietly. Seconds later, she eased her body onto the shelf and let her legs dangle over the edge. Holding her hands, he kept her steady as she wormed down the other side. Her hands squeezed his briefly, and he let go.

Gnat came up next to him as he saw her shoulder the pack again and crouch down, moving out of the way so he could lower the cobalus. Within a minute, everyone was down and started to sneak toward the right. Crawling forward, he worked his body across the fissure and onto the ledge.

As soon as his feet hit the path, he dropped low and put

his hand on the hilt of his sword. Drawing it was out of the question; the light would only give them away. Just a few more yards and they'd be out of here. He kept his breathing even as his ears strained for any change in the camp.

The others stopped, and he caught up to them. A set of stairs had been carved into the earth, leading down to the exit. They had to go past the yawning opening of the cavern, though. Adam looked at him, whispering, "The rock formation's wrong. I can't bring it down without sealing our passage off, too. Not until we get out."

Jinaari held up his hand and slid past them. Peeking around the corner, he saw how far and steep the path to the surface was. The odds of the four of them sneaking out unseen were low, but they had to try. He glanced back at the army. The soldiers weren't paying attention, so he gestured at the others to run. As soon as they were past him, he followed.

"Intruders!" A cry rang out as soon as he stepped out.

"Run!" Jinaari screamed at the others as he pulled his sword out. He saw Amara grab Gnat and sprint after Adam. The camp awoke behind him, and the Dangreth began to howl.

Scrambling up the path, he saw Adam and the rest standing in a patch of sunlight. "Jinaari! Watch out!" Amara screamed at him.

Searing pain flared through his leg and it buckled, driving him to the ground. Twisting, he saw the arrow sticking out from the back of his left knee. With his free hand, he broke the shaft. The Dangreth were closing fast; clawed arms reaching out to his ankles. Beyond the horde, he spied Alesso; the distinctive red glow came from the helm of the black armor. He looked back at Adam. "Go!" he commanded. As the creatures began to pull him toward them, he saw the others disappear. Rolling over, he slammed his visor down and swung at the closest foe. The blessed blade turned three into ash before his arm was held down.

Alesso marched up, and Jinaari locked eyes with him. The last thing he saw was the pommel of Potiri's sword heading for his head.

CHAPTER

SIXTEEN

"Is this seat taken?"

Looking up, Thia saw Kasmin standing across from her. "No," she said.

Pulling out the chair, he smiled at her. "I didn't get your invitation until this morning. My landlord put it underneath some papers and forgot about it. Given that your assistant said you weren't taking appointments, I feared you were avoiding me. I hope I didn't say something inappropriate when we were watching the ocean."

She shook her head. "I've been busy." *Busy waiting for you to come here.*

"I can understand," he said. "While my primary mission was to meet with you, there were some other matters I was entrusted with. When does your friend usually start playing?" His tone was light, conversational.

"It varies. She comes down when the urge strikes, plays what she feels like."

He shifted in his seat, signaling for a bar maid. "Have you eaten yet?" he asked as he faced her again.

"I'm not hungry. Most of the time, we eat in our rooms."

158

Let him get his order in, then go upstairs and let Caelynn know he's here. I won't have to make a lot of small talk that way.

The door to the inn opened and she turned her head at the sound, hoping it was Jinaari and Adam. The two paladins in the corner shifted their posture, then relaxed as a uniformed man crossed the threshold. The messenger walked right to her without hesitation. "Daughter," he said, bowing and holding out a sealed envelope.

"Thank you," she said, taking it. The man straightened and folded his gloved hands in front of him but didn't leave. "Is there something else?"

"His Grace respectfully requests a reply," he said.

Sighing, she broke the seal. Opening it in front of Kasmin wasn't ideal, but she couldn't think of a polite way to get rid of him. Or the messenger. Inside the envelope was a small, handwritten note:

The delegation's here. Formal reception at court is tomorrow morning. Please come. T.

Sliding the note back into the envelope, she handed it back to the servant. "Please let His Grace know I will do as he requests."

The man nodded once, tucking the letter into a breast pocket, and left without another word.

"Everything okay?" Kasmin asked.

"It's nothing to concern you," she said. If he didn't know yet the delegation had arrived, he would soon enough.

He sighed and looked at her. "I thought we were friends, you and I. Yet I sense that there's a chasm between us. Is it because I waited a week to answer your invitation?"

"We both have duties that must be put above others. I didn't anticipate you'd jump simply because I said something."

She drew back from the intensity in his eyes. "Good. I was worried."

"About what?"

"I saw who you really are, that night in the shelter. You show the world the strength, but I saw a glimpse of the woman you hide. I would like to know that Thia more." He dropped his voice to a whisper. "I believe that vulnerability isn't a weakness, that we all need others to lift us up. Your world isn't centered on your cloister anymore, but it's just as small and isolated. Don't you have room for one more person in that circle?" He reached out and touched her hand.

Pulling herself free, she stood up. "I'm going to go see what's keeping Caelynn." Her pulse raced from the coldness of his touch. A sense of dread came over her at the possessive look on his face.

She walked toward the staircase, struggling to keep from running. *Well, I know what he wants now*, she thought. *Me!*

As soon as the common room disappeared below her, she began to take the steps two at a time. Her breath was ragged with panic as she slammed her hand against the key panel. The portal activated, and she ran through. "Caelynn!"

"Thia? What's wrong?" she asked as she emerged from her room.

Thia slumped into a chair. "Kasmin's here."

"That's good, right? We planned for this, invited him," Caelynn said as she sat opposite of her.

"It doesn't matter now. I know what he wants."

"What?"

"Me," she whispered. "He wants to court me."

Caelynn let out a low whistle. "Bold of him, but it makes sense with the other questions. You didn't give him any indication that you're serious about anyone else, did you?"

Thia shook her head. "No. I told him that I trust Jinaari, and that any other relationship between us was just that – between us and not something that involved the rest of the world."

"He probably saw that as you're not serious about each other. Did he say why it took this long to come here?"

"He claims his landlord misplaced the note. I'm sorry," she muttered. "I didn't hear much of the excuse. I was trying not to tell him what Tomil's message said and didn't ask enough questions. Spying is not my talent."

Caelynn shifted. "You got a message from the Duke?"

Thia nodded. "The delegation's reached Almair. The formal reception will be at court tomorrow morning. I have to —" She threw up her arms to shield her eyes from the bright light that suddenly flooded the room. A loud crash echoed off the walls. Blinking, she lowered her hands. Adam and two others stood in the remnants of what had been the central table.

"Anyone hurt?' the warlock asked.

"Adam?" Thia asked as she rose. "Where's Jinaari?" Small bits of wood slid off her lap and onto the floor.

He didn't answer her. Looking at the two with him, he said, "This is Amara and Gnat. They both could use a bath and a warm bed." He looked away from her. "Caelynn, can you get some clothes that Amara can wear later? I'll get Gnat settled in Pan's old room if you're okay with her using your bath."

Dread rose in her, and her mind went blank. Reaching out, she grabbed his arm and made him turn and face her. "Tell me."

"I'll tell you both, Thia. All of it. But we have to take care of them first." He moved her hand and nodded to the small creature. "This way, Gnat."

Thia stared at Caelynn, ready to scream. *Help me!*

The bard inclined her head, holding out her hand to the newcomer. "This way, Amara. Take your time. Something tells me Thia and I will be talking with Adam for a while."

Amara turned, facing Thia. Tears filled her dark eyes. She

opened her mouth to say something but stopped without a word. Following Caelynn, she disappeared into the room.

Thia stared at Jinaari's shield as the women left. Why would she have it? *He can't be dead!* She stared blankly at the wrecked table in front of her. Dread began to settle into her soul, making her feel as if she was under water. *He can't be! Where are you? Why didn't you come back with them? Why give her your shield?*

"Thia, sit down. This'll take a while to explain." Adam's hands were on her arms, urging her into a chair.

Angrily, she threw her arms wide, dislodging his grip. "What did you do?"

"Thia, let's sit down and hear him out. Please." Caelynn said as she closed the door to her room.

She fell into a chair, staring at Adam. "Start talking."

Wearily, the warlock sank into another chair. Placing his staff on the ground, he leaned forward. "Jinaari's not dead. At least, he wasn't when we left. And he told me, before it happened, that he would be kept alive should he be captured."

"What happened, Adam? Where is he?" Her voice was clipped, cold, even to her own ears.

"I don't know. Not precisely."

"What does that mean? How can you not know where he's at?" The questions came tumbling from her, each one causing the panic in her soul to rise.

"We left Helmshouse a week ago. Gnat, that's the cobalus, had taken Amara out before we were able to see her. When we went after her, the tunnel collapsed. He led us to where she was hiding, then through the mountain until we found the way out." He sighed, resting his arms on his legs. He looked away from her. "To get out, we had to sneak past a small army. At least two hundred Dangreth, and three dozen or more armed mercenaries. Jinaari got shot with an arrow in the knee, went down. He'd ordered me to get

Amara out, tell you everything, even if it meant leaving him behind. His reasoning was that he was too important of a prisoner for them to kill." Raising his head, he looked at her. A single tear fell from his eye. "The last I saw of him, the Dangreth were swarming over his body, dragging him back into the cave."

Thia stood up, crossing her arms across her chest. "Take me there," she demanded. "Now."

"I can't."

"Can't or won't?" she almost screamed at him. Staring at him, she tried to rein in her anger.

"I don't have your reserves, Thia. My stores aren't nearly as deep. Getting us here practically drained me." He held up both hands, and she bit her tongue. "I can, and will, take you where we left him. But I have to recover."

"How long?" she demanded.

"How long what?"

She stared at him. "Do I have to spell it out to you? Are you that daft? How long do you need to recover your stores?!"

Caelynn stood up and sat next to her, putting her hands on Thia's shoulders. The gentle pressure made her sit back down. "It'll be okay. He'll be okay," Caelynn whispered. She raised her voice. "Adam, would you be able to take us tomorrow afternoon?"

He nodded. "I think so. Why?"

Thia stared at the bard. "He doesn't have that much time!"

"Thia, the delegation's here. Court is tomorrow. We take Amara with us, leave Adam here to rest. Hand her off to Tomil, meet the Thahion as promised, and come back as soon as we can without causing a scene. We pack before we head out to the palace. It won't take long to change outfits when we get back. Then we go. All loose ends are tied up. There won't be any distractions, diplomatic incidents, or time we have to be back by. Adam said that he's not dead." She turned to the warlock. "You know that for certain?"

"It's something Jinaari mentioned. He's a tool, a way to get Thia to do . . . something."

"What do you think they can make me do?" Thia asked.

Adam ran a hand through his hair. "The Solar confirmed there's another Marked out there. When Jinaari killed Lolc Aon, her powers went to her Son. He can't access them, though. He's only a vessel."

"She can't be reborn without both parents being Marked," Thia breathed. She leaned forward, burying her hands in her face as nausea rose within her. *Maybe?* She raised her head, looking at Adam. "Did the Solar tell you if Lolc Aon had a Daughter, too?"

"The Daughter was killed." Adam's voice made chills run down her spine.

Thia turned to Caelynn. "If he's Marked, it all makes sense."

"What does?" Adam asked.

"Kasmin's downstairs. He's made it known he has an interest in Thia." Caelynn's voice throbbed with anger.

Thia felt her entire body shake with fear. But not for herself. *They'll keep you alive, but not unharmed. And all to get me to do something you'd tell me never to agree to.* "What else?" she whispered.

"What do you mean?" Adam asked.

She raised her head and stared at him. "What else aren't you telling us? You said he made you promise to tell me everything. If we're going to get him out of this mess, I need to know what he meant."

Adam shifted in his chair. "I'm not sure how to tell you this, Thia."

The anger took over again. "Try words, Adam!" *What could possibly make the situation any worse? Make him hesitate?*

He leaned back. Folding his hands, he didn't look at her. "A decade or so ago, the Solar realized there was a Daughter or Son in Avoch. The signs were unclear; she couldn't tell if it was Keroys or Lolc Aon that Marked someone. My mission was to find and evaluate them. I knew a paladin of Garret would lead me to this person, but that was it. That's why I began to travel with Jinaari. Over time, I put it out of my mind. I think part of me hoped they were dead, by our hand or some other way. Then, you showed up with him outside of Tanisal. When you decimated the graveyard, I started to wonder. Given your parentage, I was concerned." He took a deep breath and looked at her. "When the opportunity came to lead you through Tanisal, without the others, I took it. I knew the spiders were in that building, Thia. I took you in there as a test. If you were Marked by Lolc Aon, the nest would've come after me first, protected you at all costs. When they didn't, I figured either you were the same as the rest of us or Marked by Keroys."

Thia stared at him in horror. "What were you going to do if I did bear her Mark and not Keroys's?"

"My mission was to find you, evaluate your character, and eliminate a threat before you came into your magic if I thought you were evil. Or take you to the Solar in Helmshouse so she could neutralize your magic."

"You were going to kill me?" Slowly, she shook her head. Dying by Jinaari's hand because she'd turned to Lolc Aon was one thing; Adam had hunted for her, intent on killing her before she even had the chance to make the choice herself. "Did Jinaari know?"

"No, not until we were in my tower at Helmshouse. No one knew outside of me and the Solar."

Her pulse began to race. "I just . . . I can't . . ." she stammered. Leaping to her feet, she ran to her room. Slamming her hand against the framework, she stopped.

Tilting her head, she mustered what was left of her composure. "Is that it?" she demanded.

"Yes," he replied. "That's all of it." His voice was soft, full of regret and sadness.

"Caelynn, please let the Envoy know I won't be back down tonight. Make up some excuse, lie, whatever." She put her hand on the knob and turned it. "But make sure he understands I don't want to be disturbed. Tell Lukas the same thing. Outside of when we go to the palace, I'm not talking to anyone." Without another word, she swung open the door and slid into her room, slamming it shut behind her.

Thia leaned back and balled her fists. Bellowing in rage and frustration, she pounded them against the door behind her. *I told you*, she screamed at Jinaari in her mind, *not to go. Not without me. And now they're going to make me watch you die if I don't agree to give birth to something vile!*

Opening her eyes, she focused on the wall on the opposite side. The illusionary waves crashed upon the beach; their fury matching her own. *He led me into a spider nest! On purpose!* Grabbing a log from the rack, she threw it at the wall. Ripples of magic fled from the impact point, distorting the image. The log landed with a heavy thud on the floor.

The adrenaline began to leave, replaced with worry and grief. Stumbling toward her bed, she picked up a pillow before moving to one of the chairs. Hugging it, she caught the smallest trace of his scent. She let the tears come, waiting for the numbness to replace the pain, and stared at the wall.

SEVENTEEN

Adam stood up and took a few steps toward Thia's door. "Don't even think about it," Caelynn said, stepping in front of him.

"Caelynn, I have to," he started to say.

"No, you don't," she told him. "She's not going to listen to you right now, for one. And she said not to bother her. Let her get the anger out. Go downstairs, talk to Kasmin. Make him think she and Jinaari are having a happy reunion. Figure out if he's actually Marked or just someone who thinks she's special. But you *will* leave her alone until she's ready to talk to you!" She stood in front of him, hands on her hips, and stared at him.

His shoulders slumped in defeat. "Fine. I'll go down, have some ale with him. What's he look like?"

"He'll be easy to spot. Few Thahion come here." She relaxed a little. "I'll go with you, point him out. While you two talk I'll let Lukas know we'll need a quiet, private way to get to the palace in the morning. No one else should know Amara's back until Tomil sees her." Glancing over her shoulder, she continued, "I'll grab some food for all of us, too. What's the cobalus like to eat? I've never met one of his kind before."

"Gnat eats almost anything," Amara said quietly. Adam turned around and saw her leaning against the door frame to Caelynn's room. Drying her hair with a towel, she said, "Do you want me to help?"

"It's okay," Adam replied. "Thia's not exactly overjoyed that we left Jinaari behind."

She tilted her head to one side and gave him a direct look. It was one he'd seen Jinaari make many times. "I heard most of it, Adam. I may not be around you much longer, but I'd appreciate it if you didn't lie to me."

He glanced back at Caelynn, looking for some help. Instead, she shook her head slightly. "Do I have time to put on a clean tunic? I've lived in this one for a week."

"Just enough."

Moving quickly, he darted into his room and closed the door. *It wasn't a lie*, he reasoned. *She never asked. None of them ever did. Why would they, though?* One thing he liked about Jinaari was his insistence on focusing on the actions of someone, letting that dictate who they were. Titles, birthright, magic stores meant nothing to him. To any of them.

Sitting on the edge of the bed, he sighed. Maybe that was the real problem. Thia saw him one way, trusted him, and he just shot the basis of that trust out from underneath her. It'd taken time to build that up, and he shattered it.

"Jinaari was right. None of us can afford not to trust the others," he muttered. Throwing the tunic over his head, he thought about Caelynn. *She's always been protective of Thia, but it's different now. I wonder what happened between them while we were gone?*

"You done yet?"

Looking up, he saw Caelynn standing in his doorway. "Almost," he told her, pulling his boot back on. He leaned over to pick up the other one. "Something happened while we were gone, didn't it?"

She snorted. "I'll tell you. Later. Right now, I'm as pissed as she is and feel like holding onto my secrets." Shaking her head, she stared at him. "What is it with you two? You and Jinaari both knew who she was but didn't trust her enough to say a damn word! For all the times I heard both of you tell her she could trust you, yet you don't tell her things like this." She glanced away, then back at him. "Jinaari I can understand. He had two Gods, including hers, tell him not to say anything. What was your excuse?"

He shrugged. "I hadn't told Jinaari. Or you, Kathra, Flink . . . no one outside of me and the Solar knew why I was sent from Helmshouse. Over the years, I relaxed. I trusted all of you, forgot about my mission. I love this life, being with you. I didn't even remember what I was looking for until she decimated the graveyard in Tanisal. She was so scared of everything, I convinced myself there was no way she was Marked by Lolc Aon. But I had to be certain." He rose, stomping his feet to get them the rest of the way into the boots. "I promise, I'll leave all the lying to people like this Kasmin fellow. Soon as I come back up, you'll get a full report. So will Thia, when she's ready to listen to it."

Caelynn moved aside. "I'll try to get her to eat, if she lets me in the room. She's hurting, Adam. Until she resolves that, she won't want to see your face. If I'm not up when you come back, just get some sleep. Tomorrow's going to be bad."

"What do you mean?" he asked as they headed toward the portal.

"She's got to put on a public face, be who others expect, before we can get started on the rescue. Court is stressful enough; not knowing how bad he's injured is going to make it worse for her."

He nodded, understanding what she meant. Thia wasn't

used to being the focus of attention. Not after years of actively shying away from it. "I can go with you tomorrow," he said as they started down the stairs.

"No. We'll have Amara with us. Once Tomil sees her, that'll take some of the focus off Thia. What she needs is you to be rested and ready to transport us. Make no mistake, Adam. We're going back there tomorrow and finding Jinaari's trail. I suggest you listen to her, do what she says, for a while. She's grown up since you two left." The harshness in her tone surprised him.

They reached the landing that overlooked the common room. "Where is he?" Adam whispered as he looked around.

"There," she replied, nodding toward a table near the stage.

Adam saw the man and clenched his jaw. *It can't be!* "We may have a bigger problem than we thought," he whispered.

"Why?"

"He reminds me of a warlock I thought was dead." He turned and looked at her. "I won't know until I talk to him. I'll meet you upstairs soon." Descending the last few steps, he forced a smile on his face. No reason to alert him to Jinaari's absence, or Thia's current state.

Out of the corner of his eye, he caught sight of Caelynn heading over to the two paladins. Kasmin continued to eat, his head down, as he approached. "Is this seat taken?" Adam asked.

Kasmin looked up. A hint of recognition flashed in his orange eyes, confirming Adam's suspicion. "I'm expecting a friend."

Smiling, he pulled out the chair and sat down. "Thia's otherwise occupied." Laughing, he signaled for a mug of ale. "Some reunions are best done privately, you understand." He waited for the barmaid to bring his drink, thanking her as she left. "It's been a while, Samil. I thought you to be dead. I think all Helmshouse does." He kept his voice low, and his attention on the warlock across from him.

"That was the intent. How's Her Eminence?" He wiped at the corner of his mouth with a napkin, folding the cloth neatly before laying it on the table.

"She's doing well. Though I'm sure she'll be interested in learning you didn't die during the insurrection." He paused. "Or was that by design? Misdirection goes hand in hand with illusion magic. And you were quite talented at that."

"I had an excellent teacher."

Adam sat back, studying the man opposite of him. He shifted slightly under the scrutiny, and Adam caught sight of the inside of his wrist. A red mark, segmented like a scorpion's tail, flashed briefly but he saw it. "Tell me, Samil. How is it that a partially trained warlock ends up bearing the Mark of Lolc Aon?"

"How does a half breed end up worshiping Keroys? You and I both know that the Gods do as they will. My Goddess always hedged her bets. Made sure any Son or Daughter would be strong enough to do what was necessary before blessing us with her Mark. Can you say the same thing about Thia?"

"She's stronger than you realize. And she's not alone." Adam took a drink, setting the mug back down on the table. "But you knew that, or you wouldn't be here. I know you, Samil. You prey on those you think are weak, who are vulnerable. We beat you at your own game."

The other man's smile never reached his orange eyes. "I doubt that. Potiri did what I created him to do. Once I have Althir, Thia will do everything I ask to keep him safe." Pushing his chair back, he rose. Adam mimicked the motion. "Don't be surprised if the world begins to wonder about Thia's mental state. Especially if she can't trust the people she used to." His form shifted, disappearing without a sound.

Shit!

Glancing over, he caught sight of Caelynn heading back upstairs with a tray of food. He ran over, taking it from her. "We have a situation," he whispered.

"What else is new?" she said. "Upstairs?"

He nodded. He wasn't about to tell her anything where they could be overheard. She walked ahead of him, opening the portal so he could get in with the food.

Entering the room, he saw the broken pieces of the central table. "Take this," he said, holding out the tray. As soon as his hands were free, he walked over and picked up his staff. Weaving the spell, he focused the magic through the crystal and reformed the wreckage. "There," he breathed.

Caelynn put the tray down. "Start talking," she said as she sat down.

Amara came in and picked up a bowl before finding her own chair. Adam looked at both women. "Do you think we should ask Thia to join us?"

"She's not ready," Caelynn replied. "You'll just have to go over everything twice. Or one of us will fill her in later. Honestly, Adam, I wouldn't expect her to be listening to you this quickly. She's hurting."

He nodded, sitting as he lay down the staff. "I understand. It can't last long, though. Caelynn." He looked at her. "You saw me speaking with Kasmin just now, yes? Remember meeting him with Thia while we were gone?"

She nodded. "Yes. Why?"

"Who else saw him?"

"Brennan was with us. Abigail, Thia's secretary. The two that were with Brennan when he found them after she ran off—"

"Wait, what?"

"Thia got fed up with the scrutiny. The pressure of everything got to her. She created a duplicate of herself about a week ago, the same day as your last communication with me. After she cast the spell, she ran out a side door from the kitchen. Kasmin found her before the paladins did."

He stared at her. "You didn't tell us that. You said she was asleep!" The words came out in a rush of anger and confusion.

"You have absolutely no place to question what I did, Adam." Caelynn glared at him. "Not after what you hid from her, the spider nest, all of it. She was found. I didn't lose her like I did in the conduit. And you weren't here to help me watch over her! The two of you decided to run off without thinking things through. Kasmin didn't do anything to her. He asked some questions that gave us pause, we developed a plan, and then he stayed away from her for a week." Her words were clipped, precise.

"I don't mean to interrupt," Amara said, "but is this how you normally talk to each other? Jinaari made it seem like you were all on the same page with everything. You're as divided as the council."

"No, Amara," Adam said. He let out a breath, feeling the anger within him dissipate. "This isn't normal for us. We listen, respect each other's point of view. Somehow, our emotions are being heightened." He paused. *No secrets*, he thought. Looking at Caelynn, he continued. "Kasmin is a pseudonym. His real name is Samil. Decades ago, he was a student at Helmshouse. One of my best. He excelled at misdirection and illusion." He paused. "I wouldn't be surprised if he's behind the amplification."

"How do we fix it?" Caelynn demanded.

"This is old magic, stuff that originated before the Gods were first raised up by Nannan. There were some who would imbue certain objects with magic. They made it so these artifacts could influence others. I thought they were all destroyed, and the lore of how to make them forgotten. If Samil found out how to make one, and managed to place it with one of us, that would explain our reactions." He leaned forward. "Did he give you or Thia anything?"

"No." Caelynn's pink hair swayed as she shook her head. "Thia refused the first gift he offered her, said it was best done at court by the delegation. And she didn't say he tried to do anything beyond catch her when she fell on the street."

"Spoone," Amara said quietly.

Adam looked at her. "What are you talking about?"

"It was something Gnat said before he left me in the room. He said, 'Special Man said Spoone is magic. Spoone keep Pretty Lady safe. No one but Gnat and Special Man know how to find Spoone'." I was in so much pain from the broken ankle that I didn't question who he was talking about. I was afraid Stijyn had come to take me back, even though . . ." her eyes grew wide.

"Even though what?" Adam asked.

"Even though the Solar said Jinaari's name." She buried her head in her hands. "I know she said it was him, but I was suddenly afraid it was a trick. I found Gnat in my room that night, offering me a way out. This is all my fault."

Adam leapt to his feet and ran over to Pan's room. Throwing open the door, he saw the cobalus sleeping on the floor near the fire. "Gnat!"

"Gnat warm. Go away."

"Where's Spoone?"

Gnat rolled over, opening a sleepy eye. "Spoone is Gnat's bestestest friend. Spoone not do anything wrong."

"I don't think he did, Gnat." Adam chose his words carefully. "But I fear he might be broken, like Forkke was, and I want to fix him."

"Magic Friend fix Spoone? But Spoone not broken." He sat up. "Special Man said Spoone was perfect, he only needed his bestest friend Gnat to work." Reaching out, he grabbed at the small pouch at his waist. "Gnat keep Spoone and Forkke safe! Otherwise, Special Man says Nyfe will never come back!"

"Gnat," he said as he moved closer and knelt in front of him. "Do you remember what Special Man looked like? Or where you met him?"

Gnat's ears drooped. "He had dark skin, and eyes that looked like fire. His wrist had funny mark on it. Special Man found Gnat, said Gnat had to come rescue Pretty Lady because Gnat is brave." Tears welled up in his eyes. "Did Gnat do something wrong?"

"I don't think so. But I think Special Man did. I'll know when I see Spoone. If he did, I can fix it. Then we won't be yelling at each other anymore."

"Gnat heard lots of yelling earlier. Second Pretty Lady was mad."

"Yes, she is. But I don't think it was all because of me. I think Spoone is sick and made her madder than she would've been."

Gnat dug into the pouch and pulled out the crystal. "Magic Friend fix Spoone? Gnat not like Pretty Lady mad."

Adam smiled. "Neither do I, Gnat." Taking the crystal from the cobalus, he channeled a thread of magic. Just enough to see what was hidden within the shard. "There it is," he muttered as he found the small speck of magic embedded within the crystal's matrix.

"No!" Gnat roared.

Adam clutched the shard to his chest as Gnat leapt at him. Clawed hands began to dig at his. "Gnat save you from Evil Man, Spoone!"

"I'm trying to help Spoone," Adam screamed back, desperately trying to shield himself from the attack. A feral scream ripped from his throat as Gnat's sharp nails raked across his arms. Adam leaned forward, trying to protect himself and keep the shard in his hands. Gnat leapt onto his back with a screech. Pain seared through his shoulder as the cobalus sunk his teeth into his flesh.

"Gnat! Stop that!" Amara's voice screamed.

"He Evil Man! Evil Man trying to hurt Spoone!"

Adam was on his knees, desperately trying to breathe through the pain. Part of him wanted to fight back, but he didn't. "This isn't your doing, Gnat," he panted. "The person who gave Spoone to you put something in it that makes us angry. Makes us want to fight each other. I'm trying to get rid of it."

"Gnat, please. Don't you trust me?" Adam heard the tears in Amara's voice.

It's amplifying everything, Adam thought. *Anger, pain, frustration. No wonder Jinaari needed my word in the tunnel!* Quickly, he pushed aside all the negative emotions he was feeling and focused on the crystal again. Shielding what he was doing with his body, he directed a minute amount of magic into the shard. Anger rose again, and he fought against it. He forced himself to remember when the trust was solid; the laughter that made them family. Sweat dripped from his forehead, but he didn't break his focus. *This group, these friends . . . we're family. We may fight at times, but it's out of love and trust. Nothing is stronger than that. Nothing.*

A high-pitched whine began to emanate from the shard as it grew hot in his hand. *Don't drop it, don't stop*, he thought. Something lifted the weight off his back. In his mind's eye, he could see the magic he was using chip away at the speck of negativity deep within Spoone. Cracks formed along the dark surface, and he knew he was close. Ignoring his labored breathing, he pushed even harder. With an audible 'pop' the embedded magic shattered and dissipated.

Adam rolled onto his back and held it out. "Here you go, Gnat. Spoone's fine now." Staring at the ceiling, he took several deep breaths in an attempt to slow it down. His heart was pounding.

"Adam?" Caelynn came into view.

"I'm just winded." Turning his head, he saw Gnat cradling Spoone near the fire. "Watch out for him," he laughed, "he's got some sharp fingernails."

Her arm wrapped around him and pulled him into a sitting position. "Let's get you to bed," she said. "Can you stand up and walk?"

"I think so." With her help, he rose from the floor. The room spun briefly, but he kept his footing. "Amara?"

"She went to talk to Thia. Come on. Lean on me. I won't let you fall."

They stumbled toward the door. "You would've earlier."

"That's before I knew I was being manipulated. What did you say this guy's name was?" They walked at a slow, even pace across the main room to his door.

"Samil."

"You should've taught him some manners." She laughed, and the sound warmed his heart. "Then again, I think Jinaari and Thia would love the chance to educate him."

Glancing at her, he smiled. "It's been a while since I heard you laugh."

Winking at him, she kept them moving. "Right now, all I want to hear is you snoring." Her face changed as they stopped. "I'm serious, Adam. Even if Amara can get through to Thia, she'll want to go after Jinaari as soon as we get back tomorrow. You need to be ready for that." She twisted the knob and led him into the room.

Sitting on the edge of the bed, he sighed. "I want him back, too. He's my brother. Things weren't right between us when he was taken. I know why now, but that doesn't make everything instantly better. With him or Thia. I don't regret my actions, but I can understand why it bothers them so much."

Her hands pushed him down onto the bed. "You already know how to fix this. It's the same way you got them to trust you in the first place." As she threw a blanket over his body, he felt sleep work into his weary body.

"How's that?" he asked.

"One step at a time," she replied.

Adam nodded, closed his eyes, and fell into a dreamless sleep.

EIGHTEEN

Thia heard the door to her room open. "Go away," she said without turning around. "I was serious, Caelynn. I don't want to talk to you or Adam."

"Then it's a good thing I'm not either of them," a woman replied.

Thia heard the door close again, and someone walked closer to her. "I'm not good company, Your Highness. I'd be advising you poorly right now." Out of the corner of her eye, she saw Amara drag the other chair near hers.

"That makes two of us," she said as she sat down.

They sat in silence. Thia kept her eyes focused on the wall. As she calmed down, so had the waves. The emptiness hadn't left, even after the anger had. Jinaari was . . . somewhere. Being held by someone who would make demands on her in trade for his life. Demands she knew she couldn't agree to.

"That's impressive."

A fresh wave of grief washed over Thia, and she closed her eyes. "Your brother said the same thing the first time he saw it." She opened them but kept her eyes on the wall. Pointing to the log, she said, "I tried to break it, but it didn't work."

"I saw how mad you were, Thia. A bit of creative redecorating isn't surprising."

Thia chuckled. "That's a novel description."

Amara sighed. "Accurate, though. I've had a few moments in my life when I've wanted to throw things. There were always consequences if I did, though, so I resisted. In all honesty," she shifted in her chair, "I'm rather envious you were able to do that. I'll have to talk with Tomil. Something tells me a room where I can throw things may come in handy."

"Jinaari would say I was foolish, overreacting."

"Ah, yes. My brother and his arrogance. He doesn't understand that women need to let out our aggressions the same as men. He's got his sword, can always go to the practice ring and beat up a novice." She coughed. "Not beat up. What was the term he used? Educate them."

"What can I do for you, Your Highness?" *Maybe she'll leave me alone if I find out what she wants.*

"Dropping the formalities would be a good start." Thia felt the other woman watching her. "I thought you might want to hear what happened out there." Amara pointed over her shoulder toward the door. "You intend to take me to Tomil tomorrow, so it's unlikely you'd blast me into a million pieces. Adam was out of the question, and Caelynn's taking care of him."

Thia sat up straighter and glanced behind her. "Is he all right?"

"Gnat had something that was enchanted. It's why the three of you got so angry with each other. I had noticed some tension between Adam and Jinaari on the walk out, but I reasoned it was because he felt set up. Anyway, Adam figured it out. I guess the man downstairs you'd met . . ."

"Kasmin?"

"Yeah, that's the one. Adam said he was really a warlock named Samil, that he excelled at misdirection and illusion. We figured out that Gnat's friend Spoone had been enchanted to amplify negative emotions."

"Spoone?"

Amara smiled. "Gnat's got some imaginary friends. Spoone is a crystal shard. Forkke is a ball. When I first met him, it was a pouch filled with sand. Something happened to it. I knew Adam was a warlock and could restore Forkke, so I promised Gnat to get help if he got me out of Helmshouse." She paused, picking at some lint on the dress she wore. "Anyway, Adam was able to neutralize the magic. Caelynn was going to make him rest for a while."

"That makes sense." Thia looked back at the illusion in front of them. "What else did he figure out?"

"I don't know. Caelynn said something about you sneaking off, which made Adam mad. They started arguing and I asked if this was how you all acted to each other. Jinaari told me so many stories about the three of them, working together, it didn't seem right. Though he has lied a few times." She sighed. "That's when he figured out someone was playing with our emotions, amplifying them."

"Jinaari doesn't lie," Thia countered. "He may not tell me everything, but he doesn't lie."

"You're lucky. He told me sleeping on a cave floor wasn't cold, yet I haven't felt warm for a week now."

Thia thought of a sigil and cast the spell. The logs in the fireplace roared to life. "That'll help," she said. "It was getting chilly in here and I didn't notice."

"Thank you," Amara said.

Looking back at the wall, she fell quiet. *I've asked her why she's here a couple times and she hasn't answered. Maybe if I stop asking, she'll leave.* Still, something bothered her. "Can I ask why you have his shield?"

"He gave it to me to carry, along with his pack. The opening was narrow and he was worried he couldn't fit through if he had it on his back. Caelynn said she'd put them someplace, make sure they went with you when you go search for him." She went silent. After a short time, Amara spoke, her voice barely above a whisper. "I'm scared for him."

"Why?"

"It's my fault." Thia turned to look at the other woman. She had tears streaming down her face. "I was bait for a trap and he fell for it. I should've gone to Cirrain. Now he's a prisoner, a pawn."

Rising slightly, Thia moved her chair closer and sat back down. "He's resilient. Stubborn. Out and out refused to let me heal him once, even though his arm was in a sling. What could they do to him that would really cause him pain? I've seen him fight, Amara. He's taken blows that would've dropped anyone else to the ground, but he kept fighting. He may scream, curse at them, but he won't break. There's nothing they can do for that to happen. Tomorrow, we'll take you to Tomil. Once you're safe, we'll go search for him."

"They can, though."

"Can what?"

"Break him."

She shook her head. "I doubt it. He's the strongest of us, and I don't just mean with his sword. There's nothing they could threaten him with that would make him back down from his faith."

"All it would take is a threat to hurt you. It's his biggest weakness. And not just because he swore an oath to protect you. I saw his face when I'd ask questions about you. He cares a great deal about you, probably more than he's willing to admit." She shifted, looking past Thia. "I should've known it was him and not Stijyn that came to Helmshouse, even with the crystal's influence. He promised me years ago that he'd come if I needed him. Not stick around at court, mind you. He absolutely hates that world. I'm the reason he's where he is, wherever that is. And they'll use you to get to him, and him to get to you."

"They'll try, but it won't work."

Amara looked back at her. "How can you be so sure?"

"Because I know him, and he knowns me. He'd never want me to betray Keroys, my sense of what's right, to save him. And I wouldn't want him to do that for me. The guilt would weigh heavily on both of us, destroy us in the long run."

"You won't surrender to save his life? This is my brother!" Amara's voice cracked, and it broke Thia's heart to hear her pain at the idea.

Thia lowered her head for a moment, then looked her in the eyes. "Do you believe he would want me to birth a new incarnation of Lolc Aon, set her evil back onto Avoch, to trade for his life?"

Silently, Amara shook her head.

"I think you've got it backwards. We're each other's greatest strength, not weakness." She drew a deep breath. "I've never told anyone this, not even Adam and Caelynn. Garret and Keroys pulled him from us for some training. Before he came back, Keroys asked him if he would kill me if he thought I'd turned toward Lolc Aon. It was something Lolc Aon showed me when I was her prisoner. After," her voice shook, but she kept going, "he killed her and rescued me, he told me about it. He also said how much it would've hurt him to do. I know what I would've become if she'd won. Dying by his blade would've been the end I wanted. I wouldn't be who I am, have all the abilities I do, if not for him. Every time I doubted myself, he told me I was wrong. Over and over and over again, until I started to believe it. That's what I'm going to draw on while we look for him. His steadfast belief that I am a good person, worthy of being the Daughter of Keroys. And it's that strength I'll need supporting me when I refuse any offer to spare him. He wouldn't want me to do that, sacrifice this world so he lived. It'll be the hardest thing I'll ever do in my life, but I know that's what has to happen. So does Jinaari."

She stared at her. "You'd let him die? Without blinking? Thia, he loves you!"

Thia darted a look at her, stunned. "He said that?"

"Not those words, no," Amara said. "But I've known him my whole life, can read him better than he knows. He may not say the words, but I saw it in his face. Don't you care for him at all?"

"I care. Which is exactly why I'd be the one to do it. He deserves nothing less." She shifted in her seat. "It took Lolc Aon forcing her way into my mind to realize I had feelings for him," she whispered. "Confessing that to him was even harder than admitting it to myself. But that's between us. No one else. No labels, no demands, no promises beyond those we made beforehand."

"He said the same thing to me. I tried to get Adam to tell me more, but he refused." She tilted her head to one side. "You're right. His sense of justice and honor wouldn't let him live knowing what you agreed to do for it to happen. Can you promise me you won't do it unless there's no other option?"

Reaching out, she took Amara's hand. "Last resort, if and only if there's no other option left open to us. This is my promise to you."

"Thank you."

Thia coughed, desperate to change the subject. "Are you excited to see Tomil tomorrow?"

Amara nodded. "Yes. It's been several months. Our engagement was formalized during midsummer. Jinaari was in town, but barely had time to congratulate me afterwards. Something about picking up someone and heading to Tanisal to meet Adam. Mother called me back to Dragonspire when

Grandfather passed away. Tomil came with me, and the second reading of the banns happened. When the Forsaken showed up, travel was completely banned. She almost called off the wedding, but I convinced her not to." She paused. "Have you seen him lately? Do you know if he still loves me?"

"Don't worry about that. He's been worried sick about you." Thia smiled as an idea began to form in her mind. "Do you want to have some fun tomorrow? Or just show up?"

"What do you have in mind?"

"Just some slight misdirection. Did Adam say if the rest of the delegation was working with . . . what was his name?"

"Samil?"

"That's it."

Amara scrunched her face in thought. "Not that I recall."

"Let me sleep on it," she said with a yawn. "There's been rumors about Tomil wanting you dead so he could marry me. The best way to squash them is a very public reunion between the two of you, orchestrated by me. If the three of us are seen together when you're reunited, and we're publicly excited about you two getting married, my disappearance won't be as noticeable."

"I could help with that. If anyone asks, I could say you wanted to stay but were called away by Keroys. Who's going to argue with that? You're his Daughter!"

"It's got possibilities." Rising, Thia looked at Amara. "Jinaari's room is next door. Get some sleep. I'll think this through some more, talk with Caelynn. If we're going to surprise everyone, she'll know the best way to hide you until the time is right."

Amara rose and Thia escorted her to the door. As she held it open, Amara turned around. "I know I won't see you much. You'll be off on adventures with Jinaari. But I'll always be glad to see you when you come visit. You will visit when you're in Almair, won't you?"

Thia smiled and leaned against the doorframe. "If I can, yes."

Amara nodded, turned around, and walked to Jinaari's room. Thia waited until the woman disappeared and the door closed behind her. Raising her head, she saw Caelynn standing near Adam's door.

"You need to eat, Thia," she said as she pointed to the table.

"I thought this was broken," she replied as she walked over. Picking up a bowl and spoon, she imagined the sigil to reheat the contents as she settled into a chair.

"Adam fixed it. Between that, the shard, and transporting them here, he's spent." Caelynn glanced toward the warlock's room. "I don't know about you, but I'm thrilled that he made the rooms soundproof. That man snores worse than a horse with a cold when he's exhausted."

Thia laughed. "I don't think I've ever noticed. I was usually so tired by the time we made camp that it didn't take long to go to sleep." Scooping up a spoonful of stew, she took a bite. Her stomach growled in anticipation. *I was hungrier than I thought.*

"Did you and Amara have a good chat?"

She nodded, swallowing quickly. "She let me know there was something Gnat had that was making us angry. I'm glad Adam figured it out. I was ready to murder him, and I'm not sure why."

Caelynn looked at her, her head cocked to one side. "You don't remember what he said about his mission?"

"Oh, I do. It stung, but it's not much different than why Jinaari didn't tell me about being Marked. Or that Keroys asked him to kill me." She scooped up another mouthful and swallowed. "There were good reasons why they didn't say anything to me. Ones I can't argue with."

"What?!" Caelynn exclaimed.

Thia put down her empty bowl. "Before he came back to us, when we were under Tanisal, Keroys told him who I was. What I was. And asked him to kill me if he thought I'd turned toward Lolc Aon. If he did, my soul would've gone to Keroys no matter how much influence she had over me." She sighed. "It would've killed him, but that would've been preferable to doing her bidding. I know what that life would've been like, Caelynn. It was still death, but one that would've been excruciating and drawn out. And I would've caused others to suffer first." Shaking her head, she threw the images out of her mind. *It didn't happen, don't dwell on it.* "If we can't free him, you know what I have to do."

Her friend nodded. "I do. He will, too."

Thia shifted. "Good. Let's talk about something else. I want to surprise Tomil tomorrow with Amara. Thoughts?"

"I talked with Lukas. He's going to make sure we've got a quiet, quick way to the cloister early in the morning. Once we're in your office, we can use the back tunnel to get into the palace. Do you want to sneak her in to see him before court?"

A smile came across Thia's face. "I have a better idea."

CHAPTER

NINETEEN

Trumpets blew a fanfare, signaling the arrival of Duke Tomil to the assembled crowd. Footsteps echoed down the marble lined hallway. Most of the attendees were within the throne room already. Thia stood with Caelynn in a small alcove to one side of the tall, carved double doors. Amara was behind them, hiding under Thia's blue silk cloak. "Keep your hood up," she whispered to Amara. "He's coming. I don't want him to see you until we're introduced."

The court herald, an older woman with silver hair, walked in front of two armed guards. Tomil came next, glancing their way briefly as he passed. His face was the calm, regal one she knew well. If he realized who was behind them, Thia couldn't see it. She inclined her head while Caelynn and Amara curtsied. By his decree, she was his equal and should never bend a knee.

"Do you think he saw me?" Amara asked quietly.

"No," Thia whispered. The rest of his court filed past: advisors, council members, and two personal attendants

188

comprised the end of the procession. Caelynn started to move, but Thia put out an arm and stopped her. "Not yet."

"When?" she asked as the doors began to close.

Thia pointed to a single uniformed man standing at the front. "When he says so." The formalities of court were something she didn't understand, but she'd learned the rules. Or, rather, the rules Tomil established to make her feel as much at ease as possible. Watching the man closely, she could see his finger tap out in measured beats. Only when it ceased moving did she walk forward.

"Daughter," he said as they approached. "What are the names of your friends so that I may announce them properly?"

"Ciarán, please announce me and that I have a guest. Caelynn will not process with us, and my guest will reveal their identity at the proper time. I give my word that no harm will come to His Grace by their hand."

He inclined his head. "As you wish, Daughter." Turning around, he pulled open the massive doors. "Your Grace, Thia Bransdottir, the Daughter of Keroys, is here to offer her guidance. She brings with her a guest."

Caelynn snuck away, and Thia barely caught sight of her as she hugged the wall and disappeared from sight.

"Let the Daughter of Keroys and her guest come forth. His Grace is forever grateful for her insight," the herald's voice echoed through the vaulted chamber.

Ciarán stepped aside. Thia walked up the wide, deep purple carpet that led to the dais at the far end. Amara, her head down and hands clutching the blue silk cloak closed, stayed in step with her. Every eye was on them, and Thia kept her chin raised. If any doubted it was her now, that would stop as soon as she passed. The cut out back of her heather gray dress allowed for her Mark to be seen.

Tomil watched their approach, and he couldn't keep the

curiosity off his face. "Daughter," he said as they came to the foot of the long platform. "We are thrilled to have you join us today. May we learn the name of your guest?"

Thia smiled. "Oh, you know her name already, Your Grace." She nodded to Amara and stepped aside, watching Tomil's face.

As Amara pushed the hood back, his face lit up. Looking at Thia, he mouthed, "Thank you," as he stood up. "My Lords and Ladies, we are overjoyed and without words to see our betrothed come before us. Natasha!" he called out to the herald behind the throne.

"Yes, Your Grace?"

"Read the marriage banns," he said as he walked down the five wide steps to stand in front of Amara.

"But, Your Grace, they've been read twice now. A third reading is not to happen until you're in front of the priest, to begin the Tallachan celebrations," Natasha began to object.

Tomil didn't take his eyes off Amara. Instead, he reached out and took her hands in his. "I'm done waiting. Thia?"

"Yes, Your Grace?"

"If she's ready, so am I. I will marry her here, today, before this assembly. The coronation can happen as planned. But I am done waiting."

Thia's heart rose as she saw the tears forming in Amara's eyes. "As am I."

Turning to the herald, Thia said, "You heard them. Read the banns, please." Stepping forward, she placed her hands on theirs as the terms of the union were read aloud.

Someone crept up beside her and handed Thia a wide ribbon of white silk. Once Natasha was done, she looked at each of them. "Keroys knows your hearts and has brought you to this moment. By his laws, this can only be undone in three ways. I charge you to be true to each other, trust each other, and commit no violence against each other. Your duty to

Almair, to Avoch, are not absolutes. Treat each other with respect, love, and kindness. As you show compassion to others, show it threefold to the one you bind yourself to."

As she spoke, she wound the ribbon around their hands. "Tomil, do you accept this bond of marriage? Will you keep to the charges I have set upon you?"

"I will."

"Amara, do you accept this bond of marriage? Will you keep to the charges I have set upon you?"

"I will," she said, her voice quivering with happiness.

Placing her hands on theirs, Thia finished the rite. "Then let it be so. May Keroys bless you both with more joyous days than ones filled with tears in the years you will spend with each other." She stepped back, giving them space as they kissed each other.

From behind the throne, the herald called out, "Three cheers for His Grace and our Duchess to be!"

The crowd erupted in noise and applause as Tomil led Amara to a chair on his left. As they walked, they jointly unwound the ribbon but each kept one end. Once they were seated, they laid it across the wrist of the other so that the hands still appeared bound.

Tomil, his face beaming, looked back at Thia. "We would be honored, Daughter, if you would join us in our court," he said, gesturing to a seat to his right.

"I do so gladly," she replied. As soon as she settled into the chair, she whispered, "How long do you plan on doing this today?"

"Not nearly as long as before, now that you've brought her home," he whispered back. Natasha announced a baron that Thia didn't recognize. Tomil kept talking as he walked forward, "Where's Jinaari?"

Thia straightened in her seat. "Ask Amara later, when

you're alone. I'm leaving as soon as this is over. I'm needed somewhere."

He nodded and shifted his focus to the man kneeling in front of the dais. Thia began to look around the room. The Thahion delegation was here, but why hadn't she seen any of them? She caught sight of Caelynn who shook her head once. She didn't know where they were, either.

A cheer rose, bringing her attention back to the scene in front of her. The man was backing away, heading back to his seat, and smiling. "He must've gotten something he wanted," she muttered.

"He thinks he did anyway," Tomil replied. "Try to relax, Thia. They're next. You should be out of here within the hour."

As he spoke, the doors at the end opened again. Ciarán stood in the center. "Your Grace. It is my honor to announce the delegation of Thahion." He stepped aside and Thia rested her hands on the arms of the chair.

Four men and three women, dressed in vibrant colors and each with a wide, green sash across their chests, began to walk forward. They all had dark hair, but the skin tone varied between them. From her seat, she couldn't recognize any of them. *Do I really want to? Recognizing them means it's someone who kidnapped me or helped with what Lolc Aon did to me.* Taking a deep breath, she pushed aside the memories. *I have to keep an open mind. They want to change their lives, rejoin the surface world. Keroys said I'm to help bridge the gap.*

As the group approached, they spread out into a single line. Two of them set a wooden box, bound with iron, at the foot of the platform. "We welcome the friendship offered by the Thahion. You are welcome within our court." There was a steely note within Tomil's voice. She saw him raise his head and look across the assembled crowd. "If any here, or your households, show disrespect to our guests, you will answer to us."

The leader inclined his head. "We are glad to be here, Your Grace. We were unaware the wedding was happening today and did not bring your gift." He smiled at Amara. "Your Grace has honored us in including us in your ceremony."

"It was unexpected, but welcome. May we ask your name?"

"Of course. I am Laith Deos. I was elected by the Council to lead our group." He glanced at Thia. Folding both arms across his chest, he bowed. "Daughter, we are truly honored that you are here. Many of our kinsmen were present when you liberated us. They did not understand, as we did, that blind devotion to a mad Goddess is not a life worthy of living."

Inhaling deeply, she chose her words carefully. "Keroys would have me help the Thahion rejoin the rest of Avoch. Prejudices run deep on both sides, Ambassador. The scars of centuries cannot heal overnight. I will do what I can, with His Grace's assistance, to aid all who request it."

"Your words are wiser than you know, Daughter." Laith gestured at the chest. "This was found deep within Lolc Aon's lair. It does not belong to our people. It never did. We would return it to you, if you will accept it."

Thia glanced at Tomil. He nodded, and she rose. Walking down the stairs, she took a closer look at the box. The wood was new, and the iron fittings shone. She could see the small circular marks from the smith's hammer.

"We had the box made," Laith said as she walked closer. "The contents have been desecrated enough. We wanted to honor it as it came back to the surface."

Kneeling in front of the small chest, she felt something coming from inside. An energy that reminded her of what it felt like to be in Keroys's presence. *It can't be*, she thought. *It's a myth, a legend!* Sliding the bolt, she freed the latch and pushed the lid up.

Inside, surrounded by pillows to keep it from moving, lay a rusted rod. Grime caked every inch of it, making it look thicker than the lore said it was. Reaching out, she placed her hand around the center of the shaft. The dirt crumbled at her touch, allowing the gleam of silver to shine through.

"What is it, Daughter?" Tomil said.

She glided her hands over the length of the scepter, watching in amazement as centuries of neglect fell from it. "This is the Scepter of Avoch," she breathed. "Created by the Gods to make the tribes of man cease their warfare. It's been lost for centuries."

"Lolc Aon learned that her kin were not chosen to carry it, and she stole it when she took the Fallen down to Byd Cudd," Laith said. "That race is no more. We are, as we should have always been, the Thahion. And we shall fight for she who wields this."

Thia stood; the scepter cradled between her palms. The top third of the scepter was thicker; wide bands of gold etched with the symbols of the seven Gods. Surmounting it was a band of crystal carved with dragons. At the base, a braided leather loop was threaded through a hole.

Before she could react, Tomil and Laith sank to their knees. The rest of the room followed suit. The Duke looked up at her, his face impassive. "Almair is yours to command, Queen Thia."

Panic took hold. "Here," she said, thrusting it toward Tomil. "You take it. I have no desire to rule over anyone. Please," she begged him.

He rose, shaking his head slowly. "It's yours, no matter if you want it or not. I saw what it looked like, Daughter. If you were not meant to wield it, it would still be covered in filth." Turning, he raised his voice to address the room. "Much has happened today, and we need to speak with Her Majesty and the Ambassador alone. To hear their wisdom and know how to proceed." He turned, holding his hand out to Amara, and looked back at Thia. "After you," he said, gesturing down the center aisle.

Her body felt numb as her mind screamed for a way to escape everything. Somehow, she started to walk. *Put one foot in front of the other, breathe, keep your eyes on the door. When we're alone, I'll give it to him. After that, Caelynn and I will go back to the Green Frog. We'll wake up Adam, go find Jinaari. Breathe!*

"Ciarán, please take the delegates to the reception room," Tomil instructed as soon as the doors were closed. Turning to Laith, he said, "Amara and I will join you there shortly. There's food and drink for you all. I need to speak privately with Thia for a moment."

Laith bowed. "Of course, Your Grace." He looked at Thia. "Your Majesty," he bowed again. Straightening up, they followed Ciarán down the hallway.

"Over here," Tomil insisted, pointing to a small door to one side. "No one will bother us. I promise."

Thia nodded. She felt Caelynn's hand on her back, reassuring her. The scepter rested in her quivering hands. *This can't be happening!*

The room was small; four chairs, a pair of side tables, and a fireplace. Everything was plain, unadorned, and not what she expected. "Caelynn, do you mind?" Tomil asked as he pointed to the stack of wood waiting within the hearth. "Thia, sit." He guided her to a chair and she fell into it.

"I don't want this," she whispered.

Tomil and Amara sat across from her. "I know," he said. "But that's not what the Gods have decided. You're Marked by Keroys, Thia. You know better than the rest of us that we can't challenge their will."

Caelynn eased into the chair next to her. "There are three symbols of rule, right? The crown, the shield, and the scepter. Thia's only got one of them."

"She has two. Jinaari's shield is one, and he's sworn to protect you." Amara reached out and rested a hand on Thia's knee. "I don't know that he knows it. I caught a conversation between our grandfather and mother, when he was about to take his vows as Lord Defender. She didn't want to give him the shield, said it should stay within the vault for security. Grandfather insisted. Both expected Jinaari to inherit the crown, so his fighting with the shield made sense. Who would dispute his claim when he had two of the three artifacts?"

Thia closed her eyes as the fear rose in her again. "We need to leave," she said as she opened them. "This is something to deal with later. I may have . . . this," her hand ran along the smooth shaft of the scepter, "but it's meaningless without the shield back with Jinaari." She rose and looked at Caelynn. "What's the best way back to the inn? I don't need people on the street staring at me. We have to move fast." *Stay focused on what I can control, not what might happen.*

"Lukas is waiting at your office. We can go the same way we came in." Caelynn said. "Tomil, if I write a note can you send a fast runner to the inn? If we can warn Adam, he'll be able to grab our gear, maybe meet us at the cloister exit."

"There's pen and paper in the drawer over there," he pointed to one of the tables. "What do you mean about getting the shield back to Jinaari?" Tomil looked at her. "Didn't he bring Amara back?"

"No," Thia replied. "He was overwhelmed. I don't know where he is, but we're going back where Adam left him to start the search. I stayed long enough to get Amara safely to you and meet the delegation. This," she raised the scepter, "was unexpected." She turned around and looked at Caelynn. "How am I going to keep it out of sight?"

"Here," Amara stood and removed her cloak. Laying it across her arms, she held it out. "It's yours, anyway. Wrap it up in that to get back to the inn. I'm sure you'll be able to figure out something better after that."

Thia carefully wound the cloth around the artifact. It wasn't ideal, and word of what happened today was likely spreading through the city. Gossip was like that. As long as it got them back home was all that mattered. "Thank you."

Suddenly, Amara threw her arms around her and whispered, "Please bring him back. For both of us."

"I will," she replied. She looked at Tomil. "Try and keep the peace while we're gone. We can discuss the crown—and who's going to wear it—when Jinaari can be part of the negotiations." She turned and headed for the door. She saw Caelynn hand a note to Tomil, then follow her.

"Thia, are you okay?" the bard asked as they dashed for the hidden panel leading to the tunnel.

"Not here," she replied. Thia trusted Tomil, but the palace itself was full of so many others she didn't know. The very air buzzed with a combination of excitement, uncertainty, and fear. The last thing she needed was to have any conversation they had, or a single sentence out of context, spread throughout the city. *Or beyond it, to Agrana's camp. We have to act like he's with us, and we went to deal with something Keroys or Garret needed us to do.* If they could get back to Adam without being stopped, even better.

The secret door closed silently behind them, and Thia let out a long sigh. One hurdle down. Cradling the wrapped bundle, she grabbed the front of her skirt with her other hand. "We stop in my office, grab our coats, and get back to the inn. I hope Lukas kept enough paladins near the gate to cover our exit." Without another word, she started to run.

Lukas leaned against the door, pushing away from it as they approached. "What's wrong?" he asked.

"I'll get the coats," Caelynn said, pushing past Thia and into the room.

"I was given something unexpected." She pulled part of the silk away from the scepter.

Lukas let out a low whistle. "Is that what I think it is?"

Thia nodded. "We need to get back to the inn," she said as she adjusted the fabric again. "Quietly and as fast as you can. The sooner we get there, the faster Adam can transport us to where he left Jinaari."

"Jinaari's not there?"

Caelynn came out, closing the door behind her. "Let me," she said, holding out the coat.

As she fussed, Thia kept her focus on Lukas. "He was taken prisoner as Adam got Amara out. We're going to find him." She shifted how she held the scepter, letting Caelynn pull the sleeve onto her arm.

"Do you need any help?"

"No," she said, shaking her head. "You or anyone you'd send would only get in our way. I'll have Adam and Caelynn to help with the smaller problems."

"Don't forget Gnat," Caelynn said as she pulled Thia's hair out from under the collar. "He led them out. Maybe he can help us track him."

"Why do I think I'm missing pieces to a large puzzle?" Lukas asked. Placing his hand on Thia's elbow, he began to lead her toward the exit.

"Because you are," she told him. "One I'm sure we'll fill you in on later."

"Tell Jinaari he owes me several pints. Though I'd prefer if you didn't say he was right to warn me about guarding you."

"I'm not the one who ended up with the enemy, Lukas."

They rounded a curve and the gate was within sight. A small group of priests stood near it. "Need me to tell them to go away?" he asked.

Before she could answer, they moved aside. Adam and Gnat stood in the entry. "I brought the packs," he told her.

"We change first," she said, pointing to a door. "In there."

Caelynn ran forward, scooping up their bags as Thia headed to the small storeroom. The shelves that lined it were full of baskets. As soon as the door was closed, Thia set the scepter down on a bag of grain. "Let's hurry," she said as she wriggled out of the jacket. Kneeling in front of her pack, she pulled out a heavy tunic, leather trousers, the chain shirt, and the padded undershirt.

"Think that will fit inside your bag?" Caelynn pointed to the wrapped bundle as she traded her nicer tunic for a heavier, warmer one.

"I hope so. It'll fit inside, but the question is if it will stay there." Their packs held everything but remained lightweight. Given the nature of the scepter, though, Thia wasn't sure it would stay there. Or even allow her to put it inside. Sitting down, she pulled the thick, wool socks on her feet.

"What do you mean?"

"After all that time hidden in Lolc Aon's lair, it may want light. Something those bags don't have." She shoved her feet into her boots and grabbed the coat. "Soon as I get this on, I'll find out."

"I saw Jinaari's pack and shield with Adam."

Thia said, "I hope them being here is because of your note. I wouldn't be surprised if word had spread already, though. People knew where we lived. It's possible there was an entire mob that descended on The Green Frog, looking to get in my good graces." *Don't dwell on it. Focus. Use the skills he taught you. What might happen later won't matter if we don't take care of what needs to happen now.*

She put her gloves on and then placed her open pack on the bag next to the scepter. Shoving in the dress, she took a deep breath as she picked up the relic. "Please work," she whispered as she eased the bundle inside. Pulling her hand free, she tightened the drawstring and secured the flap across the top.

"Well?"

"I can feel disappointment, but there's a sense of understanding. It's hard to describe." Thia shouldered the pack. "But I know it'll be there if I need it. Let's go."

"Wait . . . you can feel disappointment? Understanding? Is it alive?"

Shrugging, she said, "I don't know about alive in the sense that you and I are. But there's a connection there, with me. Let's go. We'll talk about it more once we're where Jinaari fell."

Caelynn opened the door. Adam, Gnat, and Lukas turned around and looked at them.

"You know where we need to go, Adam," Thia said.

"I do," he said. "Hang on tight."

Thia and Caelynn each grabbed onto one of his arms, while Gnat hugged his waist. She took one more look at Lukas's face before it disappeared in a swirl of color and light.

TWENTY

Pain seared through Jinaari's body, chasing away the black void he'd been in since Alesso had driven his pommel into his face. He kept his breathing slow, listening for anything that indicated he wasn't alone. He could hear the pop and crackle of burning logs, but nothing else disturbed the silence.

He tried opening his eyes, but one refused to budge. Raising a hand to his face, he gingerly probed the area. Wincing, he tried to find the edges of the swelling. *I don't have time for this!* He tapped into the bare minimum of his magic stores, just enough to make it so he could see. *I don't know what's here, or what else I might need it for. Until I find my sword, or something I can use, my magic's all I have. And there's not much of that.*

Opening his eyes, he sat up. The room looked familiar, but he couldn't quite place why. Pushing aside the blanket, he swung his legs off and sucked in his breath sharply. Pain raced through his left leg. Gritting his teeth, he looked down. A blood-stained bandage wound around his knee.

Whoever his captor was took the time to strip him of his

armor and dress his wound, but not heal him. Carefully, he undid the knot that secured the bandage and unwound it. A small trickle of blood seeped from the wound, but it was manageable. He leaned over and took a closer look. The arrow was gone, but the skin was torn and bruised. Tapping into his stores again, he drew the healing sigil. *At this rate, I won't have anything to use if I need it before tomorrow*, he thought bitterly. *I need to find my gear.* Raising his head, he took a closer look at his surroundings.

Dark wood furniture, carved with animal heads, filled the room. Several straight-backed chairs, a few small tables, and the makeshift bed he sat on were the only furnishings. The walls were lined with bookshelves, with a ladder to reach the upper shelves. The frosted glass windows bore the Althir crest. The lodge? Why would his captor bring him here, a family home? Still, he knew the building. This had been his favorite room the few times he'd come before he joined Garret's Paladins. He wound the bandage around his knee. *If that's where I'm at, I can find a way out. Eventually.* He stood, testing his left leg. It was sore but held. He limped over to the table. Dropping into the closest chair, he waited. If someone was watching, they'd know he was awake.

The doorknob clicked as the tumblers turned. Right on cue.

"It's good to see you're awake, Your Highness. I was concerned the wound was infected," a man said.

Jinaari kept his focus on the fire, not turning around. He didn't recognize the voice, and he wanted to know who he was talking to before speaking.

A tall, slender man sat in the chair opposite of him. Black hair pulled back in a braid, orange eyes, and dark skin. Whoever this person was, Jinaari knew he could take him out within seconds.

The newcomer smiled. "Not who you expected? Alesso's

busy, as is your brother. Besides, I thought it best to get to know my guest personally." He tilted his head, looking at Jinaari's face. "Alesso hit you harder than I thought. Do you need help healing that eye?"

"No. I can see just fine. It's better to let some things heal on their own."

"I see." The man raised one arm, resting two fingers alongside his face. The sleeve of his tunic fell down, exposing his wrist. A red scorpion's tail was seared onto the inside.

"You're Lolc Aon's Son." He didn't ask, simply stated the fact. "Or do you have a name?"

"Several, actually," he dropped his hand. "Thia knew me as Kasmin I'chal. I'm certain Caelynn's communicated that to you. My former teacher knew me as Samil. Perhaps I'll come up with a new one, just for you to use."

Jinaari leaned back in the chair. The name was familiar. Something he'd read in Adam's tower. "Samil died in the insurrection of Helmshouse."

"Oh, I was certainly presumed dead. My master taught me how to alter what others see. I was an apt pupil. Strong enough to even fool him." He smiled, but it didn't reach his eyes. "I'm surprised Adam told you about me."

"We trust each other," Jinaari shrugged. *At least, we used to!* "Why am I here?"

"Oh, several reasons. I couldn't let Alesso leave you in the cave, bleeding on the floor. I'm certain Thia's browbeaten Adam into taking her on a search for you, and that's where they'll start. The last place you were seen, nobly sacrificing yourself so that your sister could escape to safety. Your brother suggested your grandfather's hunting lodge, and I happily agreed. It's comfortable, secure, and not someplace your friends will think of. Your issues with your grandsire are well documented, and I'm certain you haven't shared stories of your youth. You seem to believe that anything that went on before you met each other doesn't matter. But it does. I left enough clues that the cobalus will lead her here, eventually. I have no doubt about that." He paused. "But it'll be long after she and I have come to an understanding."

"You plan to threaten my life to get her to do what you want?" Jinaari sighed. "You don't know her."

Samil's smile faded. "On the contrary, I know her quite well. I know she'd walk away from everything Keroys gave her, same as she did with Lolc Aon, if it meant you were safe. It took my Goddess tearing her apart mentally, digging into every crevice of her mind, to get her to even admit she wanted you. I was there, Althir, while Lolc Aon shredded her. I learned at her feet how to manipulate Thia, tear apart every defense she thinks she has. I know every seed of doubt that was planted. I know what terrifies her, the things she won't admit to herself or to you. Before you see her again, she'll have agreed to every one of my terms." The cold smile returned. "But never let it be said I'm not an attentive host. This is your family's home, after all. I'm merely a guest." Rising, he tossed a key onto the side table. "A gesture of my good will if you care to take it as such. I don't plan to hurt you, Prince. I'm not one to lock others up in cages."

It was too easy. "And if I choose to leave?" Jinaari said as he rose.

Samil stopped, his hand on the doorknob, but didn't turn around. "If you can find an exit, I won't stop you. As I said, I don't believe in cages. Not like your friend does."

"What about my sword?"

"I'm having your armor repaired. You scraped the hell out of the breastplate. As to the sword, I'm not done studying it." He opened the door and left.

The door didn't close, and Jinaari resisted the temptation to simply run through it. *Think first, assess! He may not have locked the door, but he intends to keep me here. Somehow.* He glanced down at the key resting on the table. Picking it up, he slid it into a pocket. The armory would be where they were repairing his armor. The sword, though...Jinaari smiled. Whatever Samil was trying to do wasn't going to work. It wasn't going to tolerate the touch of someone Marked by Lolc Aon. After that, a way out.

Testing his knee, he gradually placed more weight on it. While still tender, it held. *What I need to do is rest it. Or have Thia work on it. Neither is possible right now!* Being quiet didn't matter any longer.

If Samil was telling the truth, his armor was in the smithy. He knew where that was. The sword would be a bigger challenge. *Just follow the piles of ash and screams of pain. It's God-touched, by two of them. I doubt even Stijyn could hold it long.*

He walked over to the door. *What had Adam said about Samil? Something about being able to make others drown in water while thinking they were on dry land. If this was the hunting lodge, I know this house. If anything's out of place, then I know Samil's manipulating things.* He wedged his foot into the opening and nudged it. It swung open, giving him the space to leave.

The hallway beyond was deserted. The murmur of voices carried from the end of the hall, where stairs led down to the main entry. He kept his pace slow, testing his leg with each step. By the time he reached the turn, he was walking normally.

Leaning against the wall, he glanced around the corner and down the wide staircase. Two figures, wearing the gray and green of the household servant uniform, took the last steps from the gleaming wood stairs and turned into the archway on the left.

"May I help you, Your Highness?" A woman's voice, strong and steady, came from behind him.

Jinaari turned around. The face was older, but familiar to him. "Maude?"

She nodded. "I haven't seen you in many years, Your Highness. You've grown into a man; one whose actions shook the realm." She tilted her head. "You're injured. Come. I'll take you to the chapel. The priest doesn't have much skill, but he can take care of some bruises and swelling."

"No, please. I'm fine. I can see and that's all that matters. What I need is to get to the smithy. My armor's being repaired. I seem to have misplaced my sword, as well."

"You know where the smithy is. I don't think anyone will ever get that forge moved. As to your weapon," her voice dropped. "Check the cellar. Too many of *them* have gone down there and not returned."

"Them?"

Maude moved her head slightly, looking around them. "Prince Stijyn's friend cavorts with Dangreth, and other creatures of that ilk." Her back straightened, and she raised her chin. "Are you certain you don't need healing, Your Highness?"

Jinaari heard footsteps as someone else came up the stairs behind him. "No, Maude. I'll be fine. However, if it puts your mind at ease, I'll go once I'm done at the smithy." Turning around, he saw another man at the top of the stairs. Clad in a chain shirt, with a short sword hanging from his belt, the bearded man stared at Jinaari.

"Your armor's not done yet," the newcomer sneered, "so don't go looking for it or you'll get lost. I was told to tell you. I did." He spat at the ground in front of Jinaari's feet. "I got better things to do than cater to some pretty boy."

Jinaari walked up to the man; his dark eyes focused on the other's brown ones. As he got closer, he said, "What's your name?"

"Why?"

"Because I want to make sure I don't have the wrong man later on." He kept his tone conversational.

"It's Tyree."

Jinaari smiled coldly, enjoying the way Tyree's face went pale. "Good. If you're still alive when I see you again, I'll find you. You need a pointed lesson in manners." Moving at a steady pace, he began to descend the stairs. Behind him, he heard Tyree let out a breath. The likelihood of them meeting again was slim, but he didn't know that.

When he reached the bottom, he walked across the polished stone floor and toward the double doors that led out to the courtyard. *What did he mean? It's not been that long since I was here. I won't get lost. The gouges weren't deep; they should be quick to buff out. If he's too busy, I'll do it myself.* Pushing them open, Jinaari stood in the doorway.

The courtyard was deserted. The smithy stood on the other side; no smoke or warm glow came from underneath the awning. A cold wind blew, causing the light dusting of snow to swirl. A shiver ran down his arms. *The house is as cold as the weather,* he thought. *Grandfather never would've let Samil take it over. So why did Stijyn offer it up?* He remembered what Amara said about their mother, how things had changed since the night he stood up to her. *If Stijyn's in charge now, he's ruthless enough to side with Samil. And stupid enough not to realize he's being used.*

He glanced up at the battlements that surrounded the courtyard. The wind grew, and he felt the winter chill through his clothing. Amara wouldn't let him live this down if she found out, not after he teased her in the cave about forgetting her cloak. She had all his gear, and his shield, though. *By now, Thia's seen her safely to Tomil. They'll come for me next, bring my pack. My job is to get out and find my way to where I was.*

Trouble was, he wasn't sure where that was.

It doesn't matter if I'm stuck here. Samil's a trained

illusionist. He has my armor, and my sword . . . Is he planning on impersonating me?

The answer hit him like a spear to his chest. Thia. Samil would impersonate him to get to her. That's what he meant by she'd have agreed to all his terms before Jinaari saw her again.

The daylight was fading quickly. He strode toward a staircase leading up to the walkway. His memory of this place was old, and that of a child. To get back to where he was, he needed to know which way to go.

His feet hit the last step and he slowed his pace. Walking forward, he rested his hands on the closest stone merlon. The valley that stretched out before him was white with snow. A single road twisted through what he remembered as grassy fields. The road met another. Depending on the way you took, it went to Dragonspire or Cirrain.

I can't go that way. Too open. Samil may say he doesn't lock people up, but he wants me to stay here until he's gotten whatever he wants from Thia. He shifted his gaze to the right. The forest stretched for miles. The hunting was good, but they'd been in a cave system when he'd been captured. One that ran close enough to Helmshouse for Gnat to get to Amara's room.

He began to walk to his left, keeping his pace even and slow. A few guards manned the parapet and he didn't want to alarm them. He wasn't looking for a fight. Not yet.

The overcast sky hid most of the horizon, but he remembered someone telling him to look for a single spire in the distance on a clear day. If it changed color, it was Helmshouse showing itself.

Positioning himself between merlons, he leaned against the stone and took a closer look at the foot of the mountains. A sheltered area, where one slope had slid down, caught his attention. Narrowing his eyes, he watched as the sun came out from behind the clouds long enough to illuminate a crevice in the rock. He started to map out a route in his mind, imagining running the path. *I have my way out. Now I need my sword.*

Turning around, he made his way back down the stairs. Halfway down the steps, he slowed down. *Something's wrong,* he thought. The snow was gone from the ground, and it was warmer. Glancing up, he saw a roof held up by large beams, where nothing but open sky had been.

Alesso stepped out of the shadows. He wore no armor, though a blade hung from his waist. He stared at Jinaari.

This is too easy. He kept walking, watching Alesso as he descended. "You look good, for a dead man."

Alesso shrugged his shoulders. "You look horrible. It's a good look for you." He spat at the ground. He kept his arms crossed, staring at him. "You always were too pretty for your own good."

"Is that your problem with me? I look better than you do?" Jinaari shook his head as he descended the final steps. "Honor is rooted in character, not physical features. Or is that a lesson you avoided like so many others?" He stopped seven feet away from the other man. "Why don't you go find out if your master has a task for you? I'd hate to tell your mother, again, that you were dead. It almost led her to suicide the first time."

"Don't you dare talk about her," Alesso growled. "She endured more at the hands of the Fallen than you know."

Jinaari shook his head. "How far have you sunk, Potiri? It wasn't enough that you betrayed Thia. It wasn't enough that you had every single one of our brothers turn their backs on you. It wasn't enough that Garret himself Foreswore you and kicked you out. Now you're the lackey for a Fallen Illusionist who wants to bring Lolc Aon back into the world? I knew you didn't have any honor, but even rats wouldn't crawl this low." He nodded, gesturing at the sword that hung at Alesso's hip.

"You're not even able to bring yourself to fight me like a man. Instead, you cheat. Just like you always have."

Alesso's red-rimmed eyes stared at him. "I beat you once. I can do it again." His hands began to unbuckle his belt.

"Beat me? One lucky shot was all you got. Then you tripped like a clumsy fool, and I gave you a final lesson. You couldn't beat me on your best day, and those are long past."

A feral growl came from Alesso as he threw the sword aside. Jinaari shifted his stance, anticipating the charge, and deftly moved clear. He drove his elbow into Potiri's back as he flew past. Twisting around, he said, "Are you sure you want to do this? We both know I'm stronger than you are."

The other man stared back, hatred in his eyes, but didn't answer. Instead, he swung a fist at Jinaari's jaw.

At the last second, Jinaari moved his head back and avoided the blow. As he did, he punched Alesso hard into his side. "That's for betraying Garret," he growled.

Alesso's other hand shot up, connecting with his jaw. Jinaari stepped back, swinging at his opponent's face. "That's for betraying my friends." Alesso staggered, stunned, giving him the time to pull his fist back again. "And this is for selling out Thia." The punch landed square on Potiri's nose, sending him flying across the small room.

The man's body hit the wall, and he fell forward. Spitting blood and teeth onto the flagstones, he struggled to his knees. "Stay down," Jinaari told him. "Don't be stupid."

"Is that what you said to her?" Alesso panted.

"To who?" He kept his fists up, ready for the next attack.

"Ashynn. Is that what you told her while you beat her to death?"

Jinaari shook his head. "What the hell are you talking about? I never touched your sister. I haven't seen her since you took her out of the caves months ago!"

Alesso raised his head, staring at him with hatred.

"Bullshit. Three weeks ago, she died in my arms as I woke up from the death you gave me. I saw you leaving the room. You were wiping blood off your hands. Her blood." He spat at the ground. "She barely had the strength to warn me, but she did."

"Three weeks ago, I was in Almair. I can prove it, if necessary." He relaxed slightly. "What did she say to you?"

"That I had to be a shield between you and Thia."

"Did she say my name?"

He shook his head. "No."

"I'm sorry Ashynn's dead. Thia will be, as well. But this wasn't my doing. You might want to think about who really would benefit by me not being at her side." Turning, he saw a door that he swore wasn't there before. *If it was, I didn't see it.* He walked to it, twisted the knob, and entered.

The room he woke up in was in front of him, almost exactly as he left it. A tray of food sat on the small table in front of the fireplace. Turning around, Jinaari looked through the doorway. The room where he'd fought Alesso was gone, replaced by the hallway he'd walked an hour earlier. *Damn it!* Slamming the door shut, he leaned against it. *Samil's playing games. No wonder he gave me the key to my room. Unless I find the right door, they'll all lead back here.*

TWENTY-ONE

Staring at the family crest set into the window glass, Jinaari shook his hand. Nothing was broken from the fight, except Alesso's nose, but there would be bruises soon.

Damn it! Who would've done that to Ashynn, but made it look like me? His eyes grew wide when the answer hit him. *Stijyn's not that stupid!*

They had close to the same height, same hair and eyes. Jinaari was more muscular, though. *It wouldn't matter. If he's thrown in with Samil, then there's spells to make him look more like me. I've seen Adam cast illusions that did that. What did he promise you, Stijyn? A crown? It was yours ever since I renounced my position. What could you want that Samil would promise?*

It wouldn't have been Thia. *Samil needs her to bring back Lolc Aon. The crown was going to be yours. Are you that impatient that you'd drive Mother crazy, discredit me and my honor, instead of waiting?*

He closed his eyes, knowing the answer. The myriad of lessons, schools, and tutors that came in and out of the palace had nothing to do with a broad education and everything to do with his brother's impatience. If he couldn't do what he wanted within a month, it was a problem with the teacher. Never Stijyn.

Pushing away from the door, he didn't bother to lock it. *I'm not even sure this is the lodge now. I could still be under the mountain, a few feet from where Adam left with the others. But they won't see me unless Samil makes a mistake, or Adam can find a problem with the spell.*

He walked across the room and sat in one of the chairs. The meal in front of him smelled amazing. His stomach growled. How long had it been since he ate? With a sigh, he leaned forward and picked it up. *They want me alive*, he reasoned. *I'm the guarantee that Thia will do what Samil demands. Garret, I know she's strong enough to tell them no. My life is not worth the horror she'd go through if she agreed.*

He ate in silence, trying to put the thoughts out of his head. What had Adam told him about illusions, back when they first saw the rooms at The Green Frog? *Something about there always being a single thread of what was real woven into the fabric. That it had to be there, or the subject wouldn't believe what they saw.* Placing the empty plate down, he rose and began to scan the wall above the fireplace. *If I can find the thread, pull it out of place somehow . . .* Jinaari knew he didn't have the stores to do it with magic, but he had the strength. One well-placed strike with his fist should do it . . .

It was tedious, but he began a minute examination of every inch of the walls. An hour later, he finished back at the first section and stepped back, swearing.

"You'll need help, brother."

Jinaari turned at the sound of Alesso's voice. He stood in the room, closing the door behind him. Under his arm was something wrapped in what could be a cloak. *A sword?* "Not from you," he growled, turning his back on the other man.

He heard Alesso cross the room and place two items onto the tile floor. "My life will be spent by the dawn. Should I live to see that, it will be gone before the sun sets. This I know, as I have chosen my brother over my life. I need to unburden my soul before death. Will you hear my confession, and grant me absolution in Garret's stead?"

The ritual words hit Jinaari's soul like a hammer strike. It'd been drilled into them since they were initiates: if a brother paladin knew death was coming, and asked to confess their sins, you heard them. To do otherwise was to go against Garret's laws.

Turning around, he nodded once. There was only one answer he could give. "I shall do as you request. May Garret find your words complete and without guile and allow his grace to lighten your soul." He gestured toward the two chairs before moving to sit down.

Alesso sat, drawing a breath. "I never wanted to be a paladin. My father sent me to train, after hearing you had entered as an initiate, with orders to befriend you. Our family's fortunes were long spent. The lands sold off to settle debts, and the house itself would be closed down in another year or two because we no longer could afford staff to maintain it. It was my task to become your friend, however I could, so that we had someone sympathetic to our plight when they arrived at court. I was also to use the connection to you to find myself a wealthy bride, one whose dowry would be enough to care for us all. And, perhaps, position Ashynn to a more strategic union.

"The first day I saw you, I was stunned. You were nothing like I expected. I didn't think you'd be as guarded as you were, suspicious of others. So, I tried to best you in the sparring ring. Outride you on a horse. Something where you'd notice me, ask me for help to improve. But you didn't need to. Every task we were given, you excelled at.

"When word came of my family being taken, I begged the commander leave to join the search party. He denied me. Instead, he sent you."

"He tried, but my grandfather wouldn't allow it," Jinaari said softly. "I was told to stand guard outside the King's bedroom while the searchers went."

Alesso nodded. "I believe you, but I didn't know that then. It was one more perceived insult you gave me, one more instance where you beat me. Only, this time you would have the glory of rescuing my family while I was mucking stalls. By the time we took our vows, I didn't see you as a brother. A fellow Paladin of Garret. You were arrogant, spoiled, and had your life laid out before you. Whereas I only had a promise I made myself to rescue my family one day.

"The jealousy grew like a cancer, second only to my hatred of the Fallen. When Garret and Keroys both picked you for the mission to Tanisal, I left before you and the commander did. I reasoned that, if I could beat you to Almair, I'd convince you to take me with you. That's why I was at the docks. Seeing Thia . . . I saw her as a way to find my family. Instead of asking if I could come along, help out, I attacked her. I regret that. Please let her know it wasn't personal, not that time.

"The day after I got back to the chapterhouse, Drakkus came into my room and told me to grab my gear. When I got to the courtyard, Garret was there. He told me I was going to protect the rest, including Thia, because you needed extra training. He put the *geas* on me so I would be forced to keep her safe and promised to speak with Lolc Aon about my family's release. But only if Thia remained unharmed until you got back to the group. He never told me she bore Keroys's Mark. I took the assignment for two reasons; the first was it was the best chance in thirteen years I'd had to find them."

"The second?" Jinaari asked.

Alesso raised his head and locked eyes with him. Jinaari

was shocked by the amount of hatred and jealousy in them. "The second was because I thought I could prove to all of them, including Garret, that I was better than you." He took a deep breath and looked away. "Then, Thia brought me back from the brink of death. I found out about her father, and that she'd never even been to Byd Cudd in her life. I began to see her not as a Fallen witch, but someone who was scared every minute yet found the strength to keep moving forward. When we came out of the cave-in and encountered the Fallen, I was tempted to trade her for Ashynn. But I also knew that would jeopardize getting my mother and father free and break the *geas* Garret put on me. You weren't back, Thia hadn't dismissed me, and I wasn't dead. No matter how much I wanted to do that trade, I knew I couldn't."

"And then I came back."

He nodded. "And then you came back. Thia healed Ashynn without hesitation, even though I almost handed her over. I knew what you were doing down there and wanted to help. That's why I tried to get you to wait while I took Ashynn back to the surface. I had to prove to you, to Thia, that I was worthy.

"It took us longer than I wanted to get to the surface. Ashynn was practically blind during the day for the first week. We managed to find a ride with someone, made it back to Almair. At the chapterhouse, I wrote a report for Drakkus, prayed. Ashynn began to come out of her shell, tell me what happened. The only thing she'd say at first was that Father was dead, but Mother was alive. I found out about a group of nuns that follow Hauk, and we set out for the convent. It was there that she gave me the letter. She'd been owned by a Barren woman, and there were instructions about how to lead Thia to one conduit. They knew you were hunting Lolc Aon, wouldn't risk leaving her behind, and planned it perfectly. I was told they wouldn't harm the rest of you, just take Thia home, and I'd get our mother back. Ashynn begged me to try. My *geas* was gone, and Garret hadn't secured Mother's release. I reasoned that I'd promised to free them, no matter what, before I took my vows as a paladin. While I knew Thia wasn't fully Fallen, I didn't believe she was worth my mother's life. I know better, now." He sighed. "That's everything up until you driving your sword through my chest."

"How you came back, the accusations you laid at my feet, need to be said. You know this."

"Death wasn't bad. It was the dark nothingness that surrounded me that was the worst. Knowing that it was my own recklessness, impatience, that caused so much pain. Not just for me, either. It was in death that I gained clarity when it came to Thia, realized that her purpose in this world was necessary and greater beyond any hurt pride I had about you being chosen over me. Through that blackness, I heard Ashynn screaming my name, begging me to help her. I felt my soul being forced back into my body. My lungs screamed in pain when I took that first breath. I looked over, and there she was. She was covered in blood from being beaten and whipped. The only thing that I recognized was her face. I rolled off the bed, stumbling to her, and fell. My legs wouldn't support my weight. I was close enough to her that I could touch her, reassure her. I asked her who did that to her. All she said was, 'He can't do it. You have to shield Thia from him.' It was her last act. I heard a sound and looked up. Someone that looked like you was wiping blood off his hands. He sneered at us, throwing the rag at her body, and left. Someone else lifted me up, gave me food. Helped me bury Ashynn. It was Samil. He said Thia was destined to rule Avoch, be a bridge between the Fallen and humans. And that you were keeping her captive, holding her back from doing what was necessary for your own gain. That I could be the shield that she needed, if I had the courage to do what was necessary."

"What was that? Kill me?"

"No," he shook his head. "I knew I couldn't do that. For all the jealousy, I knew you were the better swordsman. My task was to get you out of Helmshouse and down a tunnel, chasing Amara. There was only one way to go. I was to wait for you, let the others escape, but take you alive. And then make sure you stayed here until Samil came back with Thia."

"What changed?" Jinaari shifted in his chair. "Something did or you wouldn't be here now. I cannot grant you absolution in any way unless I know everything."

"I found the man who beat Ashynn. It wasn't you. And," he took a deep breath, "he's convinced that Thia now has the Scepter of Avoch. He's trying to get the army to march on Cirrain."

"Who was it? And when will they start to march?"

Raising his head, he met Jinaari's gaze. "It's your brother, Stijyn. I overheard him talking with someone after our fight. He's in charge, even though everyone thinks it's your mother. He wants to burn Cirrain to the ground before the snow gets too deep." He reached down and picked up the larger bundle on the floor. "Samil has left to try and convince Thia to join him. He took your armor, but left this behind. No one's been able to pull it out so he could duplicate it without dying or being hurt, including your brother. Wrapping it in the cloak was the only thing I could think of, and you'll likely need that anyway." He held it out.

Jinaari took it, laying it across his lap. Moving aside the thick wool, he let out a deep breath. Wrapping his hand around the hilt, he drew the blade free enough to see the familiar glow. "What's that?" he asked, nodding at the other item.

Alesso picked it up, turning the oblong box over in his hands. "Samil built this place, based on descriptions Stijyn gave him. It was made to keep you secure while he worked on

Thia. If my death doesn't happen by returning your sword to you, this will guarantee it. Samil knows his way here, because he made it. Stijyn needs help or he'd get as lost as you." He opened the lid, showing Jinaari a pair of glasses, and placed the box on the table. "If you wear them, you'll see what is real and not the illusions. Once your brother knows these items are missing, and you're gone, I will tell him I did this. Please," his voice cracked, "get out of here and find Thia before Samil does. I would die knowing you are at her side. You are the shield she deserves, Jinaari Althir."

He removed the glasses, and looked back at Alesso. "Let death come as it will. Meet it with honor and dignity. May Garret find it in his wisdom to take your soul to his realm, my brother."

Peace and calm came across Alesso's face as Jinaari rose. "May Garret guide your sword, my brother," he replied but he didn't get up.

"You're waiting here, then?" Jinaari asked as he unwrapped his sword and began to secure the belt to his waist.

"It is best. It won't be more than a few hours before he discovers the theft, and I made sure I was seen coming here. You won't be seen leaving, though." He pointed at the glasses. "There's more ways in and out of here than the staff know."

He secured the cloak, throwing the hood over his head. It was large enough to hide most of his body, and the dark color would make it easier to blend into the shadows. He turned the glasses over in his hand, but nothing seemed out of place. Putting them on, he jumped as the room around him changed. The gleaming dark wood table became a pile of rubble and skulls resting on a stone floor. Glancing at Alesso, he saw him sitting on a boulder. The bookshelves and other furniture disappeared, leaving a small room with a ladder leading up.

"He put me in an oubliette?"

"It was Stijyn's idea. I will be found, eventually. You need to be gone before then. Thia, and the others, need you."

He walked to the ladder and reached up, putting his hands on the rungs. Looking back at Alesso, he said, "I won't forget this."

"Tell my mother my death this time was honorable, please."

Nodding, Jinaari grasped the first rung tightly and pulled himself high enough to get his feet beneath him. Alesso's confession rang in his ears. Samil he could see . . . Stijyn's involvement angered him. *All you had to do was wait a few more years! I didn't want the throne, I never did. And what did he mean by Thia had the Scepter of Avoch? It's been lost for centuries!*

If she did have it, though, that changed everything.

Picking up the pace, he glanced up. There was still close to a hundred feet to go, but the light was brighter. Outside, then? *Don't overthink this*, he told himself. *Get out, make sure no one sees me, find the cave where I was when Alesso grabbed me.* Samil was right about one thing; Thia would've browbeat Adam into bringing her back to where he'd fallen. If he could get there before Samil set the illusion . . .

Ignoring the ache in his arms, he kept going up the ladder. Reaching the top, he peered up over the edge enough to look for anyone guarding the oubliette. Seeing no one, he scrambled out and stood up.

The opening was sheltered by a large bush. The leaves had died off for the winter, revealing the long, sharp thorns that jutted out from the branches. Jinaari's hand went for his sword, but he stopped. *No sense announcing my presence, and that glow would be noticed.* He pulled the cloak around him tighter; wrapping his hands into the folds of cloth to protect them. There was a small opening to his right. It wasn't large enough to pass unscratched, but he'd get through.

The thorns snagged the cloak, but he pulled free without ripping the fabric. Five minutes later, he was beyond the brambles. Looking around, he saw a tower in the distance. A cloud passed by, and the tower shimmered into a warm green for a moment.

Helmshouse.

Remembering how far they'd walked after leaving, he turned to his left. *The opening has to be this way. I only have to find it. And then find my friends.*

TWENTY-TWO

The shifting colors stopped, and Thia's body swayed. "You okay?" Caelynn asked.

"Just a little dizzy. Is it always like that?" she asked.

"I've transported you before, Thia," Adam said, concern in his voice. "What's different this time?"

She smiled at him. "I'm awake."

He chuckled. "That would do it. Come on," he waved behind her, "that's where we left Jinaari."

Turning, she looked at the area. The circular opening was rough, natural. She walked forward, looking at the ground. "You said he was injured?" The dirt was scattered. There'd been a fight of some kind, but she couldn't distinguish any footprints. Or see any blood.

"He took an arrow to the knee, inside the entry." Adam walked past her, pointing at the ground farther inside. "Up here, if I remember correctly."

"Gnat knows where! Gnat saw Nice Brother fall down!" The cobalus grabbed Thia's hand, pulling her forward. "Come with Gnat, um . . ." he looked at her, sadness in his large eyes.

"What's wrong, Gnat?"

"Gnat knows too many Pretty Ladies now. Gnat not sure what else to call you."

Thia smiled. "My name is Thia. You can use that."

He stared up at her, his eyes even wider. "Thia is Gnat's friend? Only friends let Gnat call them by their name."

"Yes, Gnat. We're friends."

The small creature began to dance gleefully, his arms wrapped tight around himself. "Gnat has a friend!!!!!!!!!!!!!"

"Thia," Adam called out, "over here."

She walked toward him. He knelt down, pointing to something in the dirt. A small, irregular spot, darker than the rest, drew her attention. "Is that blood?"

He nodded. "But not much." Glancing to his left, she followed his gaze. Deep shadows hid a lot of what was beyond the narrow opening. "There were a good two hundred Dangreth in there, along with dozens of mercenaries. There's no trail, which tells me they knocked him out and carried him."

"He would've fought back, taken a few dozen with him," Caelynn said from behind Thia. "Adam's probably right about what they did to Jinaari, but why take the corpses? This place has been scoured so we can't track them."

"Gnat can track anything!" The cobalus began to scamper around the cavern.

"They needed to take Jinaari alive. If he's dead, they can't use him as a bargaining chip." Thia stepped forward. *I have to find him before they find me!* Pulling the gloves off her hands, she used the sparks to illuminate the area. The light was enough for her to see details in the cavern. "I didn't expect them to leave us an easy trail to follow, Caelynn." She paused, looking around, "Adam, which way did you come from?"

He walked up next to her. "Up there," he said, pointing to their left. "There's an opening in the rock, up near the ceiling.

We came through, one at a time, then stayed below the rock wall."

Her gaze followed the path as he talked. "And there weren't any tunnels or anything that came off of the one you were in?"

"No. We found Gnat in Amara's quarters. There was an attack on my tower while we were there, and the one we were in was hit with debris. Gnat led us out, but the tunnel collapsed behind us. There was no way back, so we had to come forward. This was the first exit we found."

Thia turned to face him. "Your tower was attacked? By who? You didn't mention that before."

Adam sighed. "I think I chose the wrong word. It was destroyed, and I knew it would be. I wasn't expecting it to happen when it did, or as violently." Sitting on a rock, he lay his staff across his lap. "I've been gone from Helmshouse for a long time. When we arrived, I went to talk with the Solar, tell her everything I hadn't in the letters. She gave me a choice. My mission to discover who was Marked, and by which God, was over. I could either stay, go back to teaching, or I could remain part of the world. I chose to stay with all of you. The more important books and research I was doing were sent to my room back at The Green Frog. The rest either went to the libraries, to aid other warlocks, or were destroyed. I won't be allowed back, unless the Solar herself summons me, so my tower was destroyed as well." He looked at her and Caelynn. "This is my family, and I cannot imagine being without any of you for more than a day or two. To simply close that part of my life, shut you out of it without so much as a goodbye, isn't who I am."

"Did Jinaari know?"

Adam shook his head. "No, we didn't talk about that. With Spoone making us angry, and the trust he had in me shaken, it didn't dawn on me to bring it up."

"Spoone is sorry," Gnat said softly. "Spoone didn't want to make anyone say bad things."

"We know that, Gnat," Thia reassured him. Turning her attention back to Adam, she asked, "Why didn't he trust you?"

"I hadn't told anyone why I was sent from Helmshouse to begin with, Thia. He didn't know until we arrived that I was sent to find you. Or that taking you into the spider nest wasn't an accident." He chuckled. "I pointed out that my reasoning wasn't much different than why he didn't tell you about your Mark. That didn't go over well, and it shook the trust we have. After we found Amara, that's when the influence started. It was tense between us by the time we got here."

She let out a long breath. "It doesn't matter right now. What does is finding Jinaari." She looked at Adam and Caelynn, her tone serious. "When this is done, though, and we're back at The Green Frog . . . I think it's time the four of us sat down and had a long talk. There are too many secrets coming to light. I don't know why. We're still family. We chose to see each other that way. But we need to know whatever secrets, big or small, the others have. Not because it matters to us, but because others will use those against us. As a way to divide us. Agreed?"

Adam and Caelynn nodded, and Thia turned her attention back to Gnat. "Gnat, you said you could track where they went?"

He nodded enthusiastically. "Gnat find Nice Brother! Friend Thia stay here until Gnat says move!"

Thia watched him as he began to dart around the floor, pausing every few moments to look closely at something in the dirt. "It's obvious now, or I think it is, that Kasmin wasn't part of the delegation. I think we can take anything he told us and throw it out the window."

"His name's Samil, Thia. He was my student some time ago, before I left Helmshouse," Adam said.

She looked back at him. "You taught him?"

The blonde man nodded. "He was extremely talented at illusion magic, misdirection. At the time, he wasn't Marked. But I haven't had so many Fallen students that I didn't recognize him. He was on the edge of committing to the warlock life, had selected his name, when the insurrection happened. The Solar suspected him, rightly so, and had me put him in a cell. She decided to contain the threat until she could determine the best way to neutralize him. That area was damaged during the fighting, and I thought for certain he was dead in the rubble. I saw his body, or thought I did." He sighed, "I should've dug him out from the rubble, checked for a pulse."

"It doesn't matter now, Adam," Thia said. "We can't change that any more than we can change Drogon killing my father." She let out a deep sigh. "If you trained him, though, you know what he's capable of. I've seen his illusions; they're incredibly detailed. How can we find out if it's real or him playing games with us?"

"In order for an illusion to work, there has to be a single element that's real. Like the fence rail in your room."

"What about it?"

"It's real. I moved that wall back a few feet, added it, and then built the illusion around it. There are actually two separate spells; the first is a fake wall to hide the rail. The second is the waves and everything else beyond the fence. That's why you can touch it."

"Okay, so how does that help us?"

"Usually, the real aspect is something small and common. Or it's something that can't be easily duplicated. But, if you find that aspect and change it somehow, the entire illusion will collapse."

Caelynn asked, "How do we find it, let alone change it?"

Adam replied, "Finding it is the hardest part. Illusions work on our emotions. They're usually something we love or fear. Our brains either don't want to find something's not real, or are so afraid of what we see that we won't touch a thing, never discover that it's all fake. If you're not sure, you have to fight back. Even if it's the one thing you've always wanted. Changing it is simple. You can damage it in some way. Sometimes simply moving it to a different location within the illusion is enough to cause the entire thing to fail." He leveled a direct look at Thia, "Samil's Marked by Lolc Aon, Thia. I don't know when it happened, but he is. You have to be prepared in case he was there when you were her prisoner. If he was, he's going to play the same sort of games she did."

Closing her pale lilac eyes, she took a deep breath, calming herself before opening them again. Looking at Adam, she said, "I'm not afraid of those memories. Or what is hiding in the dark corners of my mind. They may shake me, but I won't stop because of them."

His gaze shifted between her and Caelynn. "Why do I think something big happened while we were gone that you're not sharing with me?"

Caelynn giggled. "Thia grew up, Adam. Deal with it. Besides," Thia watched her friend shift her stance, "you've had your secrets, too."

"True enough. Thia," he looked back at her, "I think your idea of us all talking and letting things out is necessary. Until we can do that, though, I have a request."

"What is it?"

"Do we get to watch Jinaari figure out he doesn't need to babysit you anymore?"

She laughed, "Let's get him back first. After that, it depends on how long before he clues in."

"Gnat find trail!"

Thia turned toward the cobalus's voice. He was jumping and pointing to a wall. "It looks solid to me," she said.

Her friends stood next to her. "Same here," Caelynn said.

"Only one way to find out," Adam replied. "Just don't push on any loose bricks or rocks without talking to another first."

The memory crossed Thia's mind, followed by a wave of sadness. *You saved me that time, Jinaari. Now I have to save you. But can I find you before they find me? Caelynn's right, I have grown up. But that doesn't mean I'm not afraid. It only means I hide it better. And, right now, I'm terrified that I'll lose everything I care most about.*

Walking over to the others, she looked at the wall. Gnat was pointing at the rock. "Nice Brother went through there!"

"How can you tell?" she asked.

"That!"

Thia looked down to where he was pointing. On one part of the stone was what looked like a smear of blood. Reaching down, she touched it gently. Most of it was dry, but the center of one drop stuck to her finger. "It's recent," she said. "Maybe a day." Looking up at Adam, she asked, "Was he hurt that bad?"

"No," he said, confusion in his voice. "Not when we left, anyway. And he had his armor on. Even with an arrow, the armor would've kept him from bleeding enough to leave a mark that big."

"If it is his," she said, straightening, "it still doesn't make sense. The rock's solid." She put her hand against the rough stone. "Unless . . ." Putting her hands side by side, she gradually separated them, keeping them flat against the surface. When they were a few feet apart, she felt the rock give way and her hands went deeper.

Adam let out a low whistle. "I'm impressed," he said as she stepped aside.

Taking a better look, Thia could see it now. The rock that made the wall of each tunnel was identical to the surrounding terrain, making it almost impossible to see the indentations. "The question is, which one do we take?"

"What do you mean?" Caelynn asked. "There's only one."

Thia's head snapped toward the bard. "You only see one?"

"Yeah, to your left."

"Adam?"

"You're seeing two, aren't you?" the warlock asked.

Nodding, she focused on the path to her right. The bloodstain was in the center post, with streaks going to the right. Placing her hand against it, she drug her hand against the stone, mimicking the smear. *If Jinaari left this, he was taken down the tunnel that only I can see. Or it's a plant and that's the way Samil wants me to go.* "When I move into the opening, what happens? Do you still see me or do I disappear?" Thia turned sideways, her body straddling the threshold.

"I see half of you."

"Caelynn, come hold my hand." She waited for the bard to grab it. "Don't let go. I'm going to go in far enough to turn and see if I can still see the three of you." Thia shifted her body, turning to face the opening. Adam was next to Caelynn, his face a mask. "Do you see me?"

"Pull her out!" Adam said.

Thia felt a tug on her arm and came back out. "Well?"

"We couldn't see anything but your arm. It's like the rest of you vanished." Caelynn said.

"If this is an illusion, what part is real?" She looked at Adam. "This is your magic, not mine. Is it anything like the wall in my bedroom?"

He reached out and touched the rocks. "It's beyond anything I taught him, but the principle is the same."

"Would there be a pressure plate, like I have? One we could turn off so you can see it?"

"It's possible. Yours is there more for you to have control, Thia. I use a verbal command for mine." He glanced at her. "I would've done that for yours, except you weren't talking when I put it together."

I was too busy trying to stay sane, she thought. *I lost a week of my life after being Lolc Aon's prisoner for a day. How long will he hold out against Samil? And what is he going to make Jinaari see?*

"What are you thinking, Thia?" Adam said from beside her.

"It's too easy," she whispered. "There's two tunnels, but I'm the only one who sees one of them. The smear could be left by Jinaari as a clue or put there to make me think he did it." She took a step back, squaring her shoulders. "Gnat, do you see both passages?"

"No, Gnat only see one."

"Can you tell if that's the way they went?"

The cobalus stepped into the opening and looked at the ground carefully. "Bad People walk this way. But more Bad People were in big cave when we left."

Taking a deep breath, she straightened her shoulders. "Okay, here's what we're going to do. Adam, take the others down the tunnel you can see. I'm going down the other one. Walk until you find Jinaari, the path stops, or you need to rest. That's when you turn around and come back here," she pointed to the floor of the cavern. "I'll do the same. We meet up, compare notes, then go deeper if we have to. If mine ends and you're not back here, I'll come after you."

"Thia, I don't think that's a good idea. We should stick together. Jinaari would have my hide if anything happened to you," Adam looked at her.

She smiled, "But it won't, that's the thing. Samil needs me alive."

"He's the Son of Lolc Aon, Thia. He's not going to hold back like you will."

"He may be her Son, but she's dead. And he's a trained warlock, not a priest. What he does, his skills, are nothing next to mine. He'll try to make me doubt myself, yes. Chip away at my confidence, use Jinaari against me, but it won't matter. At the end of the day, I still have more stores than he does. Keroys is alive, and with me. Lolc Aon isn't. Her power rests in him, but it's not his to use."

"I just think . . ." he began.

Grasping his hand, she interrupted him. "Adam, has anyone ever told you that you think too much?" She gave it a gentle squeeze. "I'll be okay."

He returned the gesture, smiling. "Yes, you will." He pulled her closer, giving her a gentle hug. "Gods be with you, Thia."

Stepping back, she smiled. "We'll find him, Adam. And things will be as they should be again." She nodded at Caelynn, then turned to Gnat. "I'm trusting you to take care of them, Gnat. You'll do that, right?"

"Gnat keep Friend Thia's family safe!"

Taking one more look at Adam, she said, "We'll see each other soon. Hopefully, one of us will have found Jinaari as well." Turning, she adjusted her pack so it rested evenly on her shoulders and started to walk down the tunnel only she could see.

TWENTY-THREE

"You're not letting her go alone, are you?" Caelynn whispered in Adam's ear.

He watched as Thia disappeared into what was solid rock to him. "I can't stop her, Caelynn. You said it yourself; she's grown up. With the magic she can do, I doubt there's anything out there that can hurt her." *Physically, anyway. She won't relax until we get Jinaari back. If we even can.* He turned around and looked at the other two. "Might as well get comfortable. We'll be here a while."

Gnat scampered back from the entrance to the other tunnel. "But Friend Thia said Gnat go down this way and look for Nice Brother."

Adam smiled. "I know that's what she said, Gnat. But that's not what we're going to do. We're going to stay here and wait for her to come back. I'm not going that way," he pointed down the passage, "until we all can."

"But you just told Thia . . ." Caelynn said.

"No, Thia told us to do that. And I happen to disagree with her logic. I couldn't stop her from going that way on her own, but I'm not leaving here until she comes back." Adam went to the opposite side of the cave and dropped his pack on the ground. "I don't know how long it's going to take her. Especially if she finds Samil. But I'm not moving until then."

Gnat walked closer and put Jinaari's pack and shield next to Adam's. "Friend Thia not get mad at Gnat for not helping?"

"She won't get upset at you, Gnat."

Caelynn snorted. "Thia may yell at you, Adam. And I will tell her this was your idea."

The blonde man smiled at her. "I'll save you the trouble and do it myself." Leaning against the cave wall, he looked at Caelynn. "It's not because I don't trust Thia to take care of herself. I know she can. If anyone's going to beat an illusionist, it's Thia. What I don't know is what we'd face down that way," he gestured toward the other tunnel. "None of us can heal anything major, my stores aren't full with the transport, and I don't know how good Gnat is with that sword."

"Gnat kill Mean Men who hurt Friend Thia!" he said, slashing at the air with his sword.

"I know you will, Gnat. And Caelynn would help." Adam looked back at her. "But you're not nearly as good as Jinaari is. The three of us can't take on a pack of Dangreth or hired mercenaries. I saw them, Caelynn. What was here would overwhelm us within minutes. What good would that do Thia or Jinaari? It would give Samil more bargaining chips to use against her. No," he shook his head, "I'm not going to let that happen. She's got enough to worry about."

He waited, watching Caelynn's face. He knew her tells, could see her wrestle with what he'd said. "It's just," she sighed, "I don't want to lose her again, Adam. She's my sister now, the only one I have. If she doesn't come back, I'm not going to be able to sleep until we find her. And if Samil tricks her in some way . . ." her voice trailed off.

Adam reached for her hand and pulled her closer. "This

was her choice, Caelynn. Same as it was when she made that duplicate and left the inn. I know what it means for you to love her, embrace her as your family. She's going to be fine. Trust her."

She rested her head against his chest and he felt her body relax a little. "I can't keep losing my family, Adam," she whispered. "One day, there won't be any way to rescue them."

"I know," he said. "It wasn't your fault before, and it isn't now. We've both lost people we loved. That doesn't mean Thia and Jinaari won't survive. They're resourceful, stronger than our families were." He held her close, one hand smoothing her pink hair. "We've had centuries to rethink our choices. I know I've analyzed everything a thousand times. The Gods kept us alive for a reason, Caelynn. Helping Thia and Jinaari is why." He paused, and she raised her head. "We're going to have to tell them everything, you know. Thia was right; secrets come out eventually. It's better they hear them from us."

"I don't know how to explain it to her, though. How can I tell her I knew what the scepter was before she put her hand over it? I don't want her blaming me for it choosing her!"

He pulled back and stared at her in shock. "What scepter? Caelynn, tell me what happened."

She met his gaze, and his heart began to beat rapidly. "The Thahion brought up the Scepter of Avoch with them as a gift to Thia. It chose her, Adam. She touched it and centuries of grime just fell away."

"Where is it now?" he said, his voice barely above a whisper.

"In her pack. It's giving her impressions. She's supposed to wield it. Tomil, the delegation, the entire court dropped to their knees and proclaimed her queen when she lifted it out of the box." She paused. "It's beautiful, Adam. The same as it was when our parents made it."

Adam let go of her and leaned against a boulder. "It's really happening, then." He ran a hand through his blonde hair with a sigh. "We'll find the words. We have to. Not until we have Jinaari back, and things calm down. If she's got the Scepter, and Agrana's got the Crown, we need to find the Shield and have them back Thia."

"It's Jinaari." Caelynn pointed to the shield that rested next to the paladin's pack.

"That helps. But neither of them wants to rule. Damn it!" He shook his head. "None of this will matter for a while yet. We'll find the words at the right time. Remember what we promised each other, after the attack? Honor their memories by living our lives the best way we knew how? That's why I went to Helmshouse, why you went to Tanisal to train in the bardic school. We both knew we'd find each other again, sometime, when we were supposed to. Lexi promised us that we'd find others who we would see as family. When a Goddess talks, I tend to listen. Especially when the world around me is burning."

Caelynn looked at him, her eyes full of tears. "I know. But will they both understand? This is huge, Adam. Confessing to them." She paused. "I don't want to lose this family."

He shook his head. "I doubt we will. They may get mad, yes. But we're family and they know that. Thia and Jinaari both need to hear the truth about our past, though. Think of it this way; they know us. It's not much different than why he didn't tell her about his family connections, that he was the heir to the throne. He wanted her to know him. They both know us now. And it's not like we knew anything was certain until the Thahion brought the scepter up from Byd Cudd."

"You have no idea how hard it was for me not to scream when I saw it."

"I can imagine." He looked at the wall Thia had disappeared through. "With luck, Samil won't know she has it. Not for a while yet." He pushed away from the rock. "We may as well eat something. I hope she's back within an hour, but we don't know for certain."

"I'd love some food." A deep voice said from the opening.

Adam snapped his head toward the sound. "Jinaari?" he asked, pushing away from the rock.

He walked forward. "Expecting someone else?"

The warlock stared at him. His shirt was torn and stained with blood; a massive bruise covered almost half his face. The hilt of the sword looked familiar enough, but he wasn't certain. "You look like hell. Where's your armor?"

"Samil took it." Jinaari moved closer. "I really could use something to eat."

"Here." Adam tossed a pack of dried beef at him. "You know it was Samil?" *Something's not right*, he thought. *I need proof!*

Jinaari caught the food and sat down on a large rock. "He told me, after I woke up," he said between bites. "Alesso did this," he pointed to the bruise, "and it knocked me out. I woke up in what I thought was a family estate. Found out later it was an illusion. Samil talked to me, let slip what his plans were." He looked around, "Where's Thia? Isn't she with you?"

"She's looking for you. What happened to Alesso?"

"He confessed to me, asked for forgiveness, then gave me this," his hand went to the sword at his side, "and a way to see beyond the illusion. I wasn't in a hunting lodge; I was in a damn oubliette. Climbed out, came here figuring Thia would've insisted on you bringing her here."

"Prove it." Adam said, crossing his arms across his chest.

"What?"

"You heard me. I trained Samil. I know how good he is. If you're Jinaari, then prove it to me."

Jinaari grunted. "You're being stupid."

"No, I'm being cautious. Which is something the real Jinaari would appreciate."

"Is that why you won't tell me where Thia went? I'm her protector, Adam. I can't do my job if I don't know where she is."

"Convince us you're who you say you are," Caelynn said, "and we'll tell you."

Jinaari sighed. "Ask me something, then. It's not like I've got a Mark like Thia does that I can show you."

"What was the last thing you said to me?" Adam asked.

He pointed to the opening. "I was lying in the dirt, over there, and told you to go. You disappeared with Amara and Gnat."

"What order did we come through the opening?"

He sighed. "You went first. Amara had my pack and shield, but couldn't get through with those, so we lowered that down next." He nodded to his gear. "Can I at least get that now?"

"Not good enough. Keep going," Adam said.

"Fine." Jinaari shot him an annoyed look. "Once you had the pack and shield on the floor, I lowered Amara. Gnat went next. I waited until you three were ready and had my gear before I came through. Now, where's Thia?"

"We won't tell you until we know you're who you say you are." Caelynn's voice carried a note of challenge.

"What more do you want?" Jinaari asked, his voice tight.

Adam heard footsteps and turned toward the tunnel entrances. Someone was coming.

TWENTY-FOUR

The tunnel ran in an unending path forward, without a bend or break in sight. Thia shrugged her shoulders, adjusting the straps on her pack, and kept walking. *I told Adam to keep going until they needed a rest. One of us will find Jinaari. We have to!*

She stopped, put her back against one wall, and let her body rest. Her legs ached, and her nerves wound tight. *I can't give up. He didn't give up on me. Once I find a door, something, I'll turn back. Unless I find Jinaari behind it, that is.* Glancing back, she realized she'd walked far enough that she could barely make out the exit. *When we have time, I'm going to have to talk to Adam. There's got to be a way for me to figure out distance and time when we're underground!*

A surge of strength flowed through her body, followed by a driving need to be out of confinement. Confused, she pulled the pack off her back and opened the flap. The scepter was on top. "You want out, don't you?" she whispered.

Thia threaded her hand through the loop and closed it around the bottom of the shaft. Feelings flooded her; belonging, acceptance, and a rightness that she'd only felt around her friends. "Tomil was right," she whispered. She pulled the weapon out of her pack, taking the time to look at it closely. "I may not want what you give me, but the choice isn't mine to make."

The bands of gold and crystal were thick, and the weight felt good in her hands. "The lore never said how you were to be used. Then again, Lolc Aon stole you before anyone could discover what your purpose was." She looked closer at the bands. Almost all the symbols were clearly etched. The crystal band bore dragons for Nannan, the mother of the Gods. The other bands were reserved for the individual deities: a sunburst for Hauk, a closed fist for Silas, a bow for Lexi, sword and shield for Garret, scales in balance for Keroys, a branch with three leaves for Ash. The final band, the one that should hold Lolc Aon's scorpion tail, was faded. The symbols were barely visible.

If I give in to Samil, her rebirth is guaranteed. That symbol will return. If I don't, will Nannan create another God to replace her? Will it be someone kinder? Or will the Thahion choose one of the other Gods to follow? She attached the scepter to her belt, surprised at how light it felt, and put her pack back on. *I can't worry about what may happen. I know, now, that doing what Samil wants would destroy Avoch. I can't let that happen.*

Resolutely, she started back down the corridor.

Fifteen minutes later, she stopped. The sound of feet shuffling echoed from the path ahead of her. The light from her hands illuminated enough for her to see the sharp bend the tunnel took. Extinguishing the sparks, she took a deep breath. *No sense alerting them,* she thought. Flattening her body against one side, she peered around the corner.

The tunnel bent sharply one more time. Beyond that, the flickering glow of torchlight illuminated an arched doorway. The wooden door was open. Someone or something was beyond it; Thia could hear them pacing. Even steps, probably human. Something tickled her nose and she sneezed.

"Who's there?" Jinaari's deep voice carried through the opening.

Relief flooded through her. She turned the corner and walked through the doorway. The next room was lined with cells, three on each side. Jinaari stood, his hands grasping the bars, in the middle one on her left. "Thia?" he asked, "where's Adam?"

"Down another tunnel, looking for you." She ran toward his cell door.

"Keys are over there," he said.

Twisting her head, she saw where he was pointing. A large iron ring with six keys rested on a hook driven into the wall. Quickly, she grabbed them and went back. "What happened?" she asked as she began to try keys in the lock.

"Alesso knocked me out, left me in here. I got to keep my armor, but my sword's gone."

"I'm surprised he could touch it," she muttered.

"It's not here, that's all I know," his voice was quiet. "How far until we rejoin the others?"

"I'm not certain. I lose track of time easily when we're underground. We had a plan to walk so far, then go back to the area where we split up. No one besides me could see this tunnel, so I came alone."

"No one else could see it?" he asked.

"Yeah," she replied. "It was like the one door in Drogon's tower, where Caelynn got hurt." The key twisted and the tumblers moved. She pulled the door toward her, opening it enough for him to get out. "Come on," she said, turning toward the way she'd come from. "We need to get back to the others."

"Thia," he said, grabbing her hand, "wait a minute."

She turned, looking at him. "What's wrong?"

A smile crossed his face. "Nothing, not now anyway. I spent way too much time in there, thinking."

"About what?"

"You and me." He sank to one knee, his hands grasping hers tight. "I can't hide this, not anymore. Whatever I need to do, I will do it. Just say you'll bind yourself to me. You're a priestess. Say the words now, and I will honor them. I want the world to know about us."

She pulled her hands from his and took a step back, stunned. "You're not Jinaari," she whispered.

He stared at her. "What are you talking about? It's me! Thia," he grabbed for her again.

She took two more steps back, her hand going to the scepter at her waist. "No, you're not. Jinaari would never say that." She loosened the tie, her hand catching the shaft as it came free.

His face shifted into Samil's, a tight smile on his face that didn't reach his orange eyes. "It would've made things so much easier for you if you believed it."

"I don't fear you, Samil. Why don't we do this now? That way, no one else gets hurt."

"Oh, no, Thia. I tried to give you a better way, but you rejected it. I won't give you a second chance. Next time you see me, you'll wish you'd taken me up on my offer."

Her arm snapped forward, swinging the scepter at his head. It hit him hard, and she stumbled back from the impact. Samil's eyes rolled back into his head as his body fell to the ground.

Adrenaline surged through her. *Run!* Her feet found the strength and she bolted for the door. Slamming it shut, she threw the bolt into the hasp before continuing back the way she came. *It was Jinaari's armor. I know it was. That had to have been the real part of the illusion. But I can't be sure what else in that room was real.*

After a few minutes, she stopped to catch her breath. The tunnel was the same, but she knew she had to slow down. *He was unconscious. I don't think I killed him, but that doesn't mean I don't need to be careful.* Looking down, she rubbed her thumb against the shaft of the scepter. It felt right to use it instead of magic, but now he knew she had it. *Does it matter? That's just one more thing he'll add to the list of what he wants from me. But maybe he won't realize how deep my stores go, either.*

Pushing herself forward, she slowed her pace slightly. It wasn't a leisurely walk, but she wasn't running anymore. Keeping her eyes on the path ahead, she made sure to listen for anyone coming up from behind her. *One foot at a time*, she thought. *If they're not in the cave, I go after them.*

The opening came into view, and she let herself relax slightly. Resisting the urge to run forward, she kept her steps even. Voices reached her, and she paused.

"Not good enough. Keep going." Adam said.

A man answered, but his voice was too low for Thia to make out what he said. Or who said it.

"We won't tell you until we know you're who you say you are," Caelynn's voice carried a note of challenge.

"What more do you want?" Jinaari asked, his voice tight.

Thia let out a sigh of relief and ran forward. "It's him," she said as she emerged into the chamber. Adam and Caelynn turned around, and she saw Jinaari sitting on a rock. His clothes were dirty and torn, but the sword rested at his hip. One dark eye was surrounded by a sickly yellow and purple bruise, the swelling reaching past his hairline.

"How do you know?" Adam asked as she rushed past him.

"Because I just knocked Samil out down that way," she replied, pointing toward the tunnel. She brushed aside his hair, assessing the size of the bruise. "I know you don't have the stores I do, but you could've healed this," she scolded him.

Pressing her fingers against his skin, she let the spell weave into his skin.

"Hey," he winced, "that hurt. I thought you were a healer, trained to help people who are hurt."

"And I thought you were a paladin, trained on how to avoid getting hit." The swelling began to go away as the color faded back to his normal skin tone. "Better," she whispered, staring at his face.

"Better." The trust and relief in his voice sent shivers down her spine.

Adam coughed, and she stepped back. "You said you knocked Samil out?" he asked.

Thia nodded. "He was impersonating Jinaari, wearing his armor. I don't know why, but it felt right to use this," she gestured to the scepter that hung from her hip, "instead of magic. That fight's still to come."

"He's not dead, then?"

"I don't think I hit him that hard. And I didn't stick around to check for a pulse." She looked back at Jinaari. "I know it was your armor, but I didn't think to try and strip it off of him."

"I can get another suit. Is that what I think it is?" He pointed to her.

Thia worked the tie as she spoke. "Yeah. The Thahion found it in Lolc Aon's lair, brought it back to the surface. For some reason, it likes me."

Jinaari let out a low whistle. "That changes a lot of things."

Caelynn said, "They presented it during court, after Tomil and Amara got married. The entire nobility present saw Tomil bend a knee and call Thia, 'Her Majesty'."

Thia threw her a dirty look. "It's not something I want. Ever."

"We know that, Thia," Jinaari said, his voice quiet. "A lot

happened to all of us, things we have to catch up on. Here isn't the place, though. How are your stores, Adam?"

"Good, though I'm not sure about getting us back to Almair tonight."

Jinaari shook his head. "We need to go to Cirrain. Can you get us there?"

Adam looked at him, puzzled. "That's doable. I may sleep in tomorrow, but I can get us there. Where do you want me to put us?"

"The center courtyard of the manor should work. Pan's there already, and enough of Thia's family will recognize us that it shouldn't be a problem. We rest, catch up in the morning. Then talk with the Baroness and Drakkus, get word to Tomil."

"Why Cirrain?" Thia asked.

He rose. "Alesso said that my brother's working on a forced march of the army, with the purpose of burning Cirrain to the ground before the snow gets too deep. If it falls, Almair will follow suit before spring comes."

"We can't let that happen," Thia breathed.

"We won't," he replied. "Adam?"

"Whenever you're ready," the blonde man said.

Thia and the others moved closer to the warlock. Glancing over, she saw Gnat sitting dejectedly on the ground. "Gnat, come on."

The cobalus raised his head. "Friend Thia want Gnat to come with her?"

"He'll be stared at," Jinaari whispered. "Staying here might be better."

She glanced at him. "He comes if he wants to. He saved you, Adam, and Amara. We owe a debt to him for that." Looking back at Gnat, she smiled. "Of course I want you to come with us. We're friends, right?"

With a cackle, Gnat pulled the pack and shield onto his

shoulders, scampered closer and hugged Adam's leg. "Gnat ready!"

Thia grabbed onto Adam's red cloak and steadied herself. The room shifted around her as he worked the spell. When it stopped, they were in the courtyard. She released her grip and swayed, though not as much as earlier.

"You're getting used to it," Caelynn said.

"I'd rather not," she replied. "My muscles may ache when we're on horseback, but this way takes too much out of Adam." She turned her head to her left, examining the warlock's face. He leaned on his staff, noticeably effected by the casting.

"Thia! Cousin!" Pan's voice rang out and she looked toward it. The young man was running full speed at her. Baroness Elizabeth and another man followed quickly. Pan reached her first, throwing his arms around her. "You came! How did you know? We just told Mother this morning! You'll officiate, right? Promise me you'll do that!"

"Pan," Elizabeth chastised him. "Your cousin and her friends have just arrived. And something tells me their visit isn't solely for pleasure." She met Thia's gaze. "Come, bring your friends. You can all clean up, rest. When you're ready, I'll be at your disposal."

Pan grabbed Thia's hand, pulling her toward the other man. "This is Eli. He's my fiancée. Promise me you'll perform the rite, Cousin! I know you follow Keroys and not Ash, but that's okay. Ash won't care, and it'd mean so much to me!"

"Hello, Eli," she said, ignoring Pan's chatter. "It's good to meet you."

The young man blushed but didn't reply.

"Thia," Jinaari came up next to her. "Come on, we're going inside. Pan, we've been busy for a few days. Give us time to rest, then we'll catch up."

"Oh, yeah. I mean, I want you to be my best man, you

know." He kept talking as they began to enter the house. "You're my closest friend, so there's that. And we want Caelynn playing and singing during the feast! Do you think Adam can use his staff to shoot off fireworks? Eli loves those and it'd be a great way to end the whole thing, with fireworks going off when we kiss. What do you think? Oh, and who's that?"

Thia looked to where Pan was pointing. "That's Gnat. He's a friend of ours."

"I've never seen a cobalus before. That's what he is, right? A cobalus? Is he staying with one of you or does he get his own room?"

"He can stay with me," Adam said. Thia saw Gnat relax slightly. His eyes were wide with curiosity and fear as they walked through the halls to their rooms.

"Gnat just want warm place near fire. Gnat not need a bed."

"Gnat," Thia looked at him, "you deserve a comfortable place to sleep. Everyone does." She stopped at the door to her room and dropped her pack to the ground. Rummaging inside, she pulled out the key. As she stood up, she watched Adam lead everyone else down the hallway. Glancing the other way, she saw Jinaari disappear into another room.

She picked up her pack, unlocked the door, and went in. Nothing had changed in the few months since her last visit. Fresh logs waited in the fireplace, and the room was chilly. Without thinking, she used some magic to light the fire.

As the heat began to warm up the room, she put the bag on the bench. Sounds came from the bath chamber. Sighing, she began to unbutton her coat. A bath wasn't going to hurt, and food was a must. She sat down next to her pack and tugged off her boots. Something didn't feel right. *If this is an illusion, then* . . . She stood up and walked to the workbench. Tucked into one of the drawers, behind some old rags, was her necklace. The one given to her as a token of the title she inherited from her father.

Her fingers found it and a sense of relief flooded through her. *It's real. No one, including Jinaari, knew where I put this. We're in Cirrain, together. It's not something Samil created.*

Someone knocked at the door and she turned around. "Who is it?"

"It's Elizabeth. May I come in?"

Thia put the necklace away and closed the drawer. "Of course," she said.

The door opened and her aunt came in. "I wanted to make sure you were all right. Pan cornered you so quickly I wasn't able to ask how things were going."

She smiled. "He's like that all the time, isn't he? I thought it was him being nervous around new people when we first met, but it doesn't stop."

"He only does that around those he trusts, or cares about. When the situation calls for it, he can control his impulses. Eli has a way about him that calms Pan down quite a bit. He's still excitable, but not quite as loquacious," she said as she sat down. "Word reached us from Almair, about what was found. Is that it?" Elizabeth gestured to the scepter.

"Oh," Thia replied. "Yes, it is." Looking down, she began to untie it from her belt. "Would you like to see it?"

"That's not necessary. However, I did want to warn you. When we're together, in view of others, I will defer to you. Until this mess with Agrana is cleared up, who rules is in question. We all talked about it, as a family and as nobility. Cirrain and the Beckenburg family stand with you. Some people, including the majority of the population of Cirrain, believe you are the rightful Queen of Avoch now. Others are more cautious, skeptical."

"Because of who my mother was." Thia nodded. "I expect that. Elizabeth . . . this is not what I ever thought of for myself!

I didn't ask for it, didn't chase it! I didn't want to be the Daughter of Keroys, and I still have days that I doubt I should bear his Mark! I don't know how to rule an entire kingdom!" The words tumbled out of her mouth.

"That's probably why the scepter responded to you. Any fool can rule over others. It takes someone who truly wishes only what is best for the majority of the populace, who is willing to sacrifice everything they personally hold dear to keep those they don't know safe, to actually govern."

"I understand. I think," she said. "But this is only one of three symbols. Unless the other two are in the possession of someone who sees things as you do, there's always going to be dissention. Unrest. People who will be willing to smile to my face while plotting to stab me in the back."

"Thia, you've had that issue your entire life. What you're facing isn't any different than how you were treated at the cloister. It's on a larger scale now, that's all." She took a deep breath, "What you say about the other symbols is true. Agrana has the crown; she's not likely to give it up easily. And either you'll have to wear it or place it on the brow of someone who will be not just loyal to you but honest. I don't know about the shield, though."

"Jinaari has the shield. It was given to him years ago, but he doesn't know it's *that* shield."

"Then you have his support. With the scepter in your hand and the shield to protect you, Agrana will have a choice to make. Do what is best for Avoch, or watch her short reign end with needless bloodshed." Elizabeth rose, and Thia followed suit. "I've stayed too long. I'm sure your bath is ready now, and I asked that some food be left in there for you, as well. I don't know your friends as well as you do, niece, but the best path forward is always the honest one. Tell him what you know, give him the option to accept the role that his mother didn't." She smiled. "I doubt you need to worry about Jinaari abdicating his responsibility to protect you, but that choice must be his to make." Walking past Thia, she reached out and squeezed her hand gently before leaving the room.

Thia went to the door, locking it after the Baroness left. Resting her forehead against the wood, she sighed. Her aunt was right. Jinaari needed to be told about the shield, and soon.

He's probably taking a bath, eating. I'll do the same, give him time, then go talk to him. Walking away from the door, the nagging worry in her mind wouldn't leave her. *We're in Cirrain. I proved that. So why do I feel like things aren't as they should be?*

Thia shook her head, pushing aside the doubt. She went to her pack, pulled out clean clothes, and went into the bath chamber.

TWENTY-FIVE

"Jinaari?" Thia called through the closed door, "Can I come in?"

She waited for a response, but he didn't answer. Twisting the knob, it turned easily. *That's odd*, she thought. "Jinaari?" she said as she slid into the room.

"Just a minute," his voice came from the door on the other side of the large bed.

Thia shut the door, leaving the key in the lock. The room was furnished with dark, polished wood furniture. A fire burned in the hearth, chasing away the winter chill.

"What's going on?"

She turned her head toward him. He stood in the doorway, a towel in his hand. An arrowhead, threaded with a cord, rested against his bare chest. "You forgot rule number 2," she teased him. *Why isn't he wearing his medallion?*

He blinked at her, rubbing the towel against his wet hair. "Huh. I must be tired."

The unease she'd felt since they left Almair began to rise. "So, Jinaari. How are things with you?" she asked him as she leaned against the wall, her arms crossed.

"That's an odd question," he replied. "Do you know where my pack went? Adam wouldn't give it back until I proved I was me, but it didn't make it into my room."

It's not Jinaari. He wouldn't have answered like that, left the door unlocked. And he never removes his medallion. "I, um, think Gnat had it. Which means it's in Adam's room. I can get it for you." *What's different? What could be the real aspect that sets the illusion? If I keep him talking, maybe he'll tell me where Jinaari really is.*

"Later," he said. He took a few steps toward her. "What did you need?"

"I was worried, wanted to make sure you were okay."

"Why wouldn't I be?"

"Jinaari, you just spent time being a prisoner. You said Alesso was there. How's that even possible? You killed him."

"I'm fine, Thia. All of Garret's Paladins are trained to survive hostage situations. As to Alesso, I don't know how. I don't have the stores, let alone the knowledge, you and Adam do when it comes to magic."

"What's that?" She pointed to the necklace. *That's got to be it!*

He looked down, one hand raising the arrowhead slightly. "This? I got shot with it, figured I'd keep it after I dug it out of my knee. Reminds me I'm not as immortal as I think I am."

"Do you need more healing? I took care of your eye, but a leg wound could be dangerous."

He walked closer. "I'm fine. See? No limp. I took care of that on my own." His lips turned up slightly. "Though," he said, moving closer, "I suppose you could inspect it."

"Maybe I should start with the arrowhead. If there's residue of a poison on it . . ." her voice trailed off as he stopped in front of her.

"It's right there," he whispered. "But I think any sort of poison would've affected me by now. It's been a day or two since I got wounded." He raised a hand, pushing some of her hair aside.

Her heart was racing, but she kept calm. *Keep playing along,* she thought. *If I have to, I'll break the illusion. But I need to know Jinaari's okay first.* She placed the palm of her hand against his chest near the arrowhead, letting one finger move across the metal. "It looks clean, not even drops of blood."

"That's because I washed it off," he murmured in her ear.

She felt his lips touch her skin. They were cold, dead. Unable to control her revulsion, she closed her fist around the arrowhead and pulled down sharply, breaking the cord.

"Bitch," Samil growled at her. His hands grabbed her arms and he shoved her against the wall. His lips pressed against hers; his teeth biting into them.

Thia reacted quickly, driving one knee up into his groin. Doubling over in pain, he released her. Grasping the back of his head, she drove it down onto her other knee. The bones of his nose crunched at the impact and he staggered backward, falling down.

She erected a shield around her, staring at his bleeding body. "No one touches me without my permission! No one!" Her voice shook with rage.

Samil began to laugh, pressing one hand to stem the flow of blood from his broken nose. Sitting up, he stared at her. "Now there's what I expect from Herasta's daughter. Someone worthy of being Lolc Aon's mother. Tell me, Thia. Do you make Jinaari beg before you ride him?"

"Where is he?" She stared at him, unwilling to react to his taunt.

"Someplace safe. Don't worry. When Stijyn arrives with the army, he'll bring Jinaari with them. And then we'll see how strong you really are, Thia. Because I have no qualms making him or any of your other friends suffer to get what I need from you." He leered at her, and her skin crawled. "Perhaps we should have him stay in the room as our 'negotiations' are concluded. He may learn something from me about how to properly control you." Samil smiled and then disappeared.

Thia twisted a hand behind her, fumbling for the knob, and stared at where he'd been. Dark red drops of blood stained the floor. Adrenaline and panic fought for control over her thoughts, but she got the door open. She bolted from the room, not caring if the door closed behind her. "Adam!" she screamed, shoving the broken necklace into her pocket as she ran.

The blonde man peered out of a room. "Thia? What's wrong?"

She stopped. "It wasn't Jinaari. It was Samil."

"Get in here," he said, moving aside so she could enter the room.

Thia dove into the room and headed for the closest chair. Falling into it, she leaned forward and buried her head in her hands.

"What happened?" Caelynn asked.

"Hold on," Adam said. Thia heard chairs being drug across the wood floors, and the clink of glass followed by liquid being poured. "Here," he said.

Raising her head, she saw him holding out a glass with amber liquid. The aroma of spiced honey rose from it. Without thinking, she took the drink and swallowed the contents.

The mead slid down her throat, dulling the edges of her panic. "I don't know that one will be enough," she whispered.

"Don't worry about that," Caelynn said. "I've got plenty."

"I'll bring the decanter over." Adam walked away. "When you're ready, Thia, we'll listen."

She took a deep breath and sat up, looking at both of them. "My aunt came to see me, told me word had come from Almair about what happened with the scepter."

"It's safe, right?" Adam asked as he refilled her glass.

"You know?"

"Caelynn filled me in, after we separated. Where is it now?"

"I left it in my room, and locked the door. I'm not sure it'll let anyone else touch it, either. Anyway, I went to talk to Jinaari. From what Amara said, he doesn't know the shield he has is *that* shield. I was going to tell him, explain what happened at court, give him the option to walk away. If he didn't, then I would've brought the scepter over to show him. When I got there, he didn't answer. The door was unlocked, so I went in."

"Jinaari never leaves his door unlocked," Caelynn said, stunned.

Thia nodded. "I know, and he even chided me about doing that when we came here the first time. Referred to it as 'rule number two'."

"Out of curiosity, what was rule number one?" Adam asked.

"That I shouldn't argue with the staff." She took a drink and kept going. "But, yes, I noticed the door was odd. I asked him about the rule, but his answer didn't make sense. So, I asked him a different question. One he's asked me a few times. Again, the reply wasn't right. He was wearing this," she pulled out the arrowhead and showed them. "He said it was the one he was shot with, that he was keeping it to remind himself he wasn't immortal. I remembered what you said, Adam, about something needing to be real. I asked if I could see it better, but he didn't take it off. He just came closer. He, um," she felt her cheeks grow hot, "tried to kiss me. But it didn't feel right, didn't feel like Jinaari, and that's when I knew. I pulled this off, broke his nose, and he fell back. He shifted form, became Samil, and threatened me before he disappeared."

"What kind of threat?"

"Stijyn's bringing an army here, that wasn't a lie. They're bringing Jinaari with them. Samil said he was looking forward to finding out how strong I really am, that he had no issue making Jinaari or any of you suffer if it made me agree to do what he needs from me." She downed the rest of the drink and held the glass out for Adam to refill. She could feel the alcohol begin to work on her but knew it would take a lot more to get numb enough to take the revulsion away.

Adam let out a breath, "We figured that's what was going to happen. I would've preferred we got Jinaari back first, but that's not an option now. We'll have to talk to the Baroness, find Drakkus, get word to Tomil."

"What about Jinaari?" Caelynn asked. "We can't just leave him in their hands!"

Thia stared at the mead in her glass, swirling the liquid gently. "He'll be alive when they arrive, Caelynn. Samil thinks holding Jinaari hostage gives him an advantage over me. No one wants a war. I don't think even Stijyn or Agrana do. I can't do what he wants, though. No matter what."

"Did Samil actually tell you what he wants?" Adam asked. "I know we've got an idea, but we could be wrong."

"We're not," Thia sat back in the chair. "After I got him away from me, he said he finally saw Herasta in me, that I'd make a suitable mother for Lolc Aon."

"Shit," Caelynn breathed.

"It's not happening, Thia," Adam reached out and squeezed one of her hands reassuringly.

She turned to look at him, her voice steady despite the alcohol. "No, Adam. It's not. I will kill Jinaari myself to keep him from being a bargaining chip. Garret didn't train him to kill Lolc Aon so that she could return. Keroys didn't Mark me to make it so I could give birth to a new version of her. And the scepter certainly didn't choose me so that I can drag everyone on the surface down to Byd Cudd with chains around their waists. I will die, either by my hand or one of yours, before that happens."

"Thia," Caelynn began to speak, but stopped when Adam put a hand on her arm.

"If that's what you want," he stared at Thia, his voice solemn, "then that's what we'll do."

"It's what has to happen, Adam. It's what Jinaari was prepared to do, on our way to Byd Cudd. I have access to so much power, it's terrifying at times." She swallowed, then kept talking, "Keroys wanted to make sure his sister couldn't access it before I did. Can you imagine what I'd turn into if her will became mine, now that I can tap into it all?" Staring at him, she continued. "It's possible I'll have to kill Jinaari. He knows that, if I do, it's what needs to happen. He wouldn't want me to spare his life any more than I'd want him to spare mine. That means he won't be able to kill me to keep Samil from having me. I need your word, Adam. Your promise you'll do this if it comes to that."

"This is crazy!" Caelynn whispered. "Thia, you're drunk and not thinking straight! Adam and I love you; you're our family! We can't kill you! Please don't ask us to," she pleaded.

Thia stared at the empty glass. "I know what I'm asking, Caelynn. Remember what I said back in the cave? No more secrets between us? I can't go into a fight with Samil and not trust you have my back. I'm going to do everything I can to beat him, destroy the part of Lolc Aon he carries. He is, however, Marked. The same as I am. And," she took a deep breath, shifting her focus to Adam, "he's had training in warlock magic. By one of the best."

He stared back at her, nodding slowly. "If there is no other option, Thia, I will do what you ask."

"Even if we free Jinaari, Adam. Saving his life is meaningless if Samil wins. You know this."

"I do, and so will he," he whispered.

Caelynn jumped up and started pacing, her arms gesturing wildly. "Great! What's the point of saving Avoch if we lose the people we care about the most in the process?"

"What's the point of living in a world devastated by evil when we know we could've stopped it from happening?"

Thia watched her words hit Caelynn hard. The pink haired woman sat back down, tears in her eyes, and her shoulders slumped in surrender. "You're right," she whispered.

Relief washed over Thia. "Let's not tell anyone else, this stays between the three of us. If we come out of this alive-"

"When we come out of this," Adam corrected her.

She smiled at him. "When we come out of this, we can tell Jinaari about our decision. But not until then. Even if we free him, Samil can't have me. Agreed?" She looked at her two friends, who both nodded.

Relief, working with the alcohol, chased the last threads of anxiety and fear from her. Yawning, she stood up. Her body swayed, and the other two grabbed her arms to steady her. "Adam, why don't you bring Jinaari's pack and shield to my room? Something tells me it'll be safer there."

"Only if you let Caelynn help you get there," he said. She opened her mouth to protest, but he shook his head. "You're drunk, barely can walk, and were attacked. You need sleep, Thia. Tomorrow, we figure out who needs to know what, get people started on defenses for the city. And figure out the best way to get Jinaari back and keep you alive."

Thia nodded, and watched Adam leave the room first. Caelynn kept the pace slow. "I know your reasons, Thia," she said, her voice thick with unshed tears, "and I see your point.

But please don't make us do that. I can't lose you a third time."

"It's not my first choice, any more than killing Jinaari is. But the alternative--"

"I know, it can't happen." They stopped in front of Thia's door. "I need your key."

Fumbling in a pocket, she pulled it out and tried to put it into the keyhole. Laughing, she finally got it on the fourth try. Once the door was unlocked, she pulled it out. "Don't let me go to bed until I lock it."

"Nonsense," Caelynn replied. "Adam's bringing Jinaari's gear, remember? We'll make sure it's locked when we leave, but you need to sleep." Gently, she guided Thia to the bed.

Sitting on the edge, she worked the short boots off her feet while Caelynn moved the blankets aside. The door opened, and both women looked up as Adam walked in. "Where do you want this?" he asked, holding up a pack and the shield.

"On the bench," Thia replied, gesturing to the foot of the bed, "next to my stuff. Put the shield near the scepter."

He walked around and put the pack down first. "Is there a reason?"

"Dunno," she said, "just a feeling. They were made to be used for the same purpose and have been separated for centuries. They probably want to get reacquainted." Thia's voice dropped as exhaustion took hold. Sliding into bed, she threw the blankets over the top of her.

"You talk like they're alive in some way."

"Maybe," she muttered as her eyes closed.

The dull ache surrounding her skull woke Thia hours later. The room was cool, and she pulled the covers close around her chin, willing the headache to go away. The pain subsided, but she needed more warmth. Opening her eyes, she saw the fire had almost gone out. The logs were nothing but kindling now; barely enough fuel to keep the fire fed. Sighing, she sat up and pushed the blankets aside. Placing her feet on the floor, her toes curled slightly as the cold seeped up through her socks.

She ran across the room, reaching into the bin next to the fireplace to grab a new log, and tossed it carefully onto the glowing embers. Yellow and orange sparks flew up as the burned wood crumbled to ash under the weight of the new piece. She waited, rubbing her hands together to keep them warm, for the fire to take hold before adding a second log.

Staring at the flames as they grew, her mind worried about Jinaari. *Are you warm? Do you know where you are? Samil promised you'd be coming with your brother, but not that you'd be treated well.* She remembered the discussions on the way to Byd Cudd between her, Adam, and Jinaari. *You tried to prepare me, keep me from panicking if it happened. I know you're strong enough to survive, but not if I'm strong enough to do what I may have to do.*

The room began to warm up and she straightened. Looking back at the bed, she thought about trying to get more sleep. *No, I'm awake now. There's a puzzle here, and I need to solve it. Samil's not going to bring Jinaari out where I can see him until it benefits him, when he wants to force me to choose if he lives or dies. He doesn't think I'll let him die, either. So, how do I keep Jinaari alive but make Samil think I don't care if he is? And keep myself safe at the same time?*

Her gaze went to the shield resting against the bench. His shield, the one he'd used more than once to keep her safe. Walking across the room, her fingers ran along the top edge. She knew almost every scrape and dent on it, just like his sword. Just like him.

Thia's eyes flew open, and her lips curled into a small

smile. *It could work! I need to practice, talk to Adam, but it could work!*

She grabbed a chair, placed it in front of the shield, and got to work.

CHAPTER
TWENTY-SIX

Thia stood on the stone battlements that surrounded Cirrain, encompassing the city behind the thick stone walls. A steady stream of refugees flowed through the gates. Baroness Elizabeth had sent word out that an army was coming, one bent on destroying the area, and offered refuge within the walls to all who wanted to come.

Someone walked her way, and she turned her head. Adam came closer, his red cape billowing around him. "Watching isn't going to speed things up, Thia."

"I know, but it gives me something to do. Besides waiting, worrying, and being asked questions I don't know how to answer."

He leaned on the wall next to her. "You're doing fine. Your aunt's got an amazingly clear head for a politician. Drakkus has the paladins working on fortifying things, making sure Samil's forces can't come up through the sewers. Between those two, we should be able to withstand a siege until Tomil sends reinforcements."

"That doesn't mean I like waiting," she sighed.

He looked at her. "What's really bothering you, Thia? I

haven't seen you this tightly strung since we were heading down to Byd Cudd."

"I don't know what they're doing to him, and I hate that," she whispered. "Even if our plan works, will he be the same arrogant prick we know?"

Adam laughed. "I don't think you should worry about that. Jinaari's strong, and that arrogance runs through his blood. He may be more demanding for a few days as he works out the anger, but no one can ever shake his sense of honor. They can't beat it out of him."

Thia smiled. "You're probably right."

"How's the practice going?"

"Good. I've got the base down. That part was easy. I'll have to manipulate the image as things progress, though. How about you?" She looked at him. "Your part's more crucial than mine. You're sure you can do it?"

He nodded. "Caelynn's been letting me practice on her. It's got some side effects that I didn't anticipate, so I've talked with Drakkus. I didn't go into details, mind you. But we're going to need a paladin with decent stores on hand when we do this."

"How bad is it?"

"For her, not too bad. We don't know how he is, though. It could be a lot rougher on him."

"If you've got the stores tonight, and she's willing, I'd like to try putting it together. You and I have to have our timing perfect on this, or it'll go horribly wrong."

"I'm game, and I'm sure she will be. As long as things stay quiet, I'll be fine." He looked at her, a smile on his face. "How are your stores?"

"They're good," she said. A horn blast tore through the air and Thia looked toward the sound. On the horizon, thousands of men marched in formation. "They're here," she whispered.

The soldiers around them moved into defensive positions. Drakkus bellowed from her left, "Get everyone inside and close the gate! Now!"

Someone touched her arm and she looked over. Adam's face was serious. "We need to get you into the keep."

"I can't see what's going on if I hide!" *I can't see him; know how badly they've hurt him!*

"Your safety is paramount, Your Majesty," Drakkus said as he approached. Thia cringed at the title. "Neither I nor any of Garret's Paladins will risk that. Being here, you're exposed. A trained archer could end your life with a single arrow." He grasped her elbow and began to walk her toward a guardhouse in the corner. "Adam, please escort the Queen back to the keep. I'll report to you myself, later, when everything's secure. If there's anything to even report."

"Come on," Adam told her. "Don't argue. Drakkus is bigger than both of us and can carry you inside if he wanted to."

She nodded and picked up her pace. *Drakkus is right. Me being out there, visible, is a risk. It's not the right time.*

Adam led her through the throngs of people taking shelter in homes or shops. They went past the massive gate. Soldiers were hustling the last refugees inside, pulling the huge wooden doors closed behind them. A voice called out a command, followed by the sound of chains on winches as the thick oak and steel bar was lowered into place.

"Thia, we can't stay out here," Adam whispered.

She looked around, realizing people had surrounded her, staring. Many began to kneel. "There's a time and place for ceremony," she said, her voice loud enough to carry through the crowd, "but this is not one of those times. Listen to the guards and paladins, go where they direct you. May the Gods keep us all safe within these walls." She walked toward Adam, who was waiting.

"May the Gods bless you, Queen Thia!" someone from the crowd shouted as she left.

"Keep moving," Adam hissed. "You won't do them any good out here."

They reached the manor house without incident. Pan and Eli were in the courtyard, trying to calm some horses. "Cousin! Are they here? Did you see Jinaari?"

"Inside," Adam said.

"I have to go inside, Pan," she said. "But, yes, the army's here and no, I didn't see him. They wouldn't let me stay up there long enough." Adam ushered her into the keep, closing the door behind them.

Servants bustled about with a purpose, each set to do a prearranged task once the siege began. "Elizabeth's going to be in the great hall," Thia said to Adam.

"Let's go."

Together, they walked through the keep until they reached the room designated to co-ordinate the response. Dozens of people came and went as the guards snapped to attention at their approach. "Your Excellency," one called out. "Her Majesty has arrived."

"Thank you," Thia said as they walked past. Straightening her back, she established her public mask. The one Jinaari taught her to create. "How are preparations going?" she asked her aunt.

"Well enough, Your Majesty. A message came from Duke Tomil not even an hour ago. The Almair reinforcements will be here tonight if the weather holds. If not, tomorrow. We won't be alone for long."

Thia nodded. "Good. Is Duke Tomil actually riding with them? I thought he'd have stayed back, let the paladin commander take the lead."

"I'm not sitting on my ass while my people die."

Thia looked toward the sound of Tomil's voice. He strode

into the room, a blue cloak billowing out behind him. His chain mail rattled as it moved, echoing in the vast room. "Amara?"

"Is safely back in Almair, with a few select troops who can get her out if she needs to." He stopped near her, bowing. "Your Majesty. My army will be here by nightfall. I've left instruction for them to make camp east of the city and try to hide from view. I don't know if Agrana knows we're here yet, and I'd like to keep it that way."

"Agrana's not in charge," Thia muttered. Walking over to a large table, she looked at the map spread out across the wood surface. "What's the best way to leave the city when they want to parlay?"

"Do you believe they'll ask for a meeting?" Tomil asked.

"I'm counting on it. Samil's the one who's behind all of this, and he's dying to meet me face to face again."

Tomil looked at her, puzzled. "Who's Samil?"

"The Son of Lolc Aon. He's had training at Helmshouse, manipulated both Agrana and Stijyn, just to get to me." Thia placed both hands on the table, staring at the map. *Damn it, Jinaari! You're the tactician, not me. I don't understand what half the icons sitting on the map mean!*

"To what end? What does he need from you that he'd sacrifice so many lives? Lolc Aon's dead. Can he even access his magic anymore?"

If I say it fast enough, she thought. Drawing a deep breath, she said, "When Jinaari killed her, Lolc Aon's essence went into Samil. He can't access her power, and I have no idea how deep his own stores are. Lolc Aon wasn't known for sharing her power. He's a trained warlock, which is vastly different than my magic. But his goal is to convince me to help him bring Lolc Aon back."

"How? Thia, she's dead. Even if part of her is in this Samil person, I don't see why he thinks you'd help him bring her back. Or even how it's possible."

"If a child is born of two parents who are Marked, and one contains the essence of a god, then that god is reborn in the child." She looked up as she spoke, staring at him.

Her words hit him and his eyes grew wide. "Damn," he said.

"And he's got Jinaari, plans to use him as leverage to get me to agree to this," she said. Thia shook her head slowly. "I promised Amara I'll do everything I can to save him, and I will, but if it doesn't work . . .".

He ran a hand through his hair, letting out a long sigh. "What can I do to help?"

"Work with Drakkus, be ready for anything. I'm hoping the meeting will resolve everything and the armies won't actually have to fight. Adam's going to make sure that Samil doesn't get me alive if it goes bad. If he doesn't, I need you to do it. But my plan is to rescue Jinaari, goad Samil into a one-on-one fight. He needs me alive, and that gives me the advantage."

"You'll want to go out here," Drakkus said, pointing to a section of the map. "It's a small door, but one we can keep guarded and locked. I can send some initiates out to put up a tent, get things ready. Or did you want to wait and see if they do it first?"

"I'm not sure we need a tent. I'd like things to be open, visible to everyone. I'm not the one who hides in shadows, not this time." Thia let out a breath. *I have to practice once tonight, the full sequence.* "If there's something up tomorrow, that's their doing. I don't have to go inside. But I don't want to waste lives, either. Tomorrow, I settle this."

"You aren't going out there alone. Jinaari would have my hide," Drakkus stared at her.

Thia looked at him, a small smile on her face. "Adam and

Caelynn will be with me. You, Tomil, and some paladins, as well. I leave it to you to pick them, Drakkus. If I tell you to stay back, do it. Understood?"

"Where do you want me, Your Majesty?" Elizabeth said.

"You stay inside the city, safe. If things go bad, I want you to make sure those who can survive do so. I've been watching you over the last week or so. The populace listens to you. If I'm dead, or Samil manages to take me alive, you need to be able to lead those who are left." Thia smiled. "I know, no matter my personal situation, that Avoch as we know it will continue through your efforts."

She caught sight of Adam motioning to her. Caelynn stood next to him; her face serious. *Time to practice.* She looked at the others. "I'm going to my room, get some rest. Tomorrow's likely to test even my stores."

Drakkus came around the table. "I'll walk with you."

The two walked through the crowded room toward the doorway where Adam and Caelynn waited. "Adam said you had a plan to get Jinaari free, but not many details. Only that I should wait near your room and have someone at the ready to heal him. What about you?" The commander's voice was quiet.

"You need to worry about him, not me. Either I'll come out of this fine, or no amount of healing will make a difference."

"I can't promise Althir will stay clear of your fight. He takes his duties as your protector seriously."

Thia nodded. "I know. I have something in mind which will force everyone to stay out of it. When I go after Samil, I don't want anyone else hurt." *Jinaari's been his prisoner for over a week now. Who knows what Samil's had him see, what type of torture he's gone through? I have to concentrate on my fight before I help him with his.*

Adam and Caelynn started to walk with them. Drakkus

looked over his shoulder at them, "I take it you two are staying with her tonight?"

"As long as she lets us, and probably longer. Don't worry, Drakkus. We'll keep her safe, make sure she rests."

"What about Gnat?" Thia asked.

"Pan and Eli have been giving him riding lessons," Caelynn said with a giggle. "It keeps him occupied, and safe."

Thia nodded. The cobalus was excitable, but she was concerned he'd get hurt in a large melee. Teaching him a skill would help him later, plus it gave Pan something to do as well.

Adam whispered, "Pan kept asking about you, Thia. He's worried you'll do something tomorrow, but he doesn't know what."

"What I'm doing tomorrow is ending this, Adam," she said. "Even if it's not the way Pan wants it to end."

TWENTY-SEVEN

The sun burned away the morning mist, making the day bright but cold. Thia took a moment to close her eyes and slow her breathing. *I will get him back. After that . . . Keroys, be with me.* She opened her eyes at the sound of footsteps.

Drakkus walked toward her, his face serious. "They're coming."

"How many are there?"

"Three on foot, one on horseback. Plus, some guards," he said. "One of them is leading another by a chain."

She felt Adam's steadying hand on her back, lending her some of his strength. "You have your instructions, Commander. Please, don't get in my way."

"Only if it's necessary, Daughter," Lukas said from behind her.

Turning around, she saw him walking toward her. "I'm not the one who needs rescuing, Lukas."

He shook hands with Drakkus, then gave her a tight smile. "Not yet anyway."

"You're the commander now?" she asked, pointing to a badge on his tabard.

"Garret called Ransom home. He's at peace."

Thia nodded. She hadn't known the man, but Jinaari and Lukas had always spoken of him with respect.

"What's it like in the camp?" Drakkus asked him.

"Cold. There's not a fire big enough or blanket thick enough to hold it off. I'd like to have words with whoever convinced Agrana that marching in winter was a good idea." Lukas said.

Both men turned to face Thia, and she met their gaze. "Well, Your Majesty? What do we do now?"

"We go out, I free Jinaari. If any of Agrana's troops try to interfere, discourage them."

"Form ranks!" Drakkus shouted at the paladins near them.

Caelynn threw her arms around Thia, and she welcomed the embrace. "Don't make us do it," she whispered in Thia's ear, "please."

"It's not my first choice," Thia said.

"Your Majesty?" Adam stood at her elbow; one hand extended.

Drakkus was putting his helmet on, standing at the front of the guard. Lukas and his paladins would form the back of the procession. Tomil and Caelynn would walk behind her and Adam.

It was time.

Thia put her hand on top of Adam's arm, surprised at how calm she felt. *This is going to work. It has to work. All of it.*

The small door opened and they walked through.

Outside the city walls, the surrounding terrain was packed dirt. Bits of frost remained in shadowy recesses where the mid-morning sun hadn't reached yet. She saw the group Drakkus mentioned. They stopped about a hundred yards from them, at the edge of the cleared ground. Even at that distance, she picked out Jinaari. His hands were bound. An iron band surrounded his neck, with a chain leading from it. His shirt, ripped and stained, moved in the slight breeze. The sun broke through the clouds, catching on the metal of the medallion around his neck. *It's him. He's got to be freezing!* Quickly, she shoved the thought from her mind. *I can't dwell on him, not yet.* Her vision followed the chain. Samil held the other end.

"Thia?" Adam asked.

"I'm good."

"He's not."

"I know," she said. "I can't think about that right now, though. We have a plan; it's going to work." She sounded confident, but inside her stomach churned with nerves. *I learned this from you, Jinaari. Show the world you're in control, even if you want to run, so that those around you don't.*

"I'm just saying he's not going to look better when you see him later. You saw what it did to Caelynn."

"Drakkus will go back inside to take care of him, get him stable once we start talking. When I'm done, I'll do the rest. Even if it's tomorrow." She took a deep breath. "If things go differently, it won't matter."

"They won't. Don't tell Jinaari this, but you thought of things I didn't." He chuckled. "If he finds out, he may decide you can do all the thinking instead of me."

"You're still his brother. I doubt he'd send you away. If he tried, I'd talk him out of it."

"You're family, too, Thia. I don't want to bury either of you tonight. Be careful. I know your power, and I helped train Samil. It'll be a hard fight to win."

She kept her focus on the Son of Lolc Aon. "I never thought today would be easy, Adam. But I'm not the same person that fought Drogon, or even the one that Samil met. He needs me alive, which means he's not going to try and kill me. He'll try to manipulate, hurt me, yes. But not kill me."

"Just don't change much more, okay? I liked the old Thia, but the grown up one you are now is a lot of fun to be around. Plus, you did say we needed to tell each other our secrets. I've got a few skeletons in my closet that are dying to come out."

"Oh?"

"Consider that incentive to come out of this the right way. If you don't, you won't learn all of them."

Drakkus held up a hand, signaling the procession to stop. The six men in front of her moved aside, forming a line on each side of their commander, but with room for her to move forward.

She walked up and stood next to Drakkus. Samil and the rest were within fifteen feet of them. Agrana sat on the horse, with Stijyn holding the reins. Her focus went to Jinaari.

A massive bruise covered almost half of his face. His dark eyes stared at her with suspicion and distrust. His sword, in the scabbard, rested at his waist. The tunic he wore was torn, stained with dirt and dried blood. His entire body shivered uncontrollably from the cold.

"This won't end well for you, Samil," Thia said, turning her attention back to him. "Surrender now. I'll talk with Agrana, see if we can't come to terms without anyone else dying today."

His orange eyes stared at her as he walked closer, and she cringed internally. "No one dies today unless it's your doing, Thia. Each and every drop of blood shed will be on your hands. You can prevent it by simply agreeing to my terms." He jerked the chain in his hand and Jinaari stumbled forward, falling to his knees between them. "Shall we start with his? Will you be able to watch while he dies? Or will you look away, knowing you could've prevented it?"

She stepped forward; her gaze shifted to Jinaari. "What are you going to do if I refuse?"

Samil smiled coldly. "Oh, I'd take my time with this one.

He'd feel more pain than you can imagine, all while you watched. Maybe I'll flay him, one inch of skin at a time. Perhaps I'll slowly break every bone in his body. Or maybe I'll do what Lolc Aon did to you and force him to confront the demons he hides in his mind. I was there, Thia, when Lolc Aon toyed with you. I know exactly how she did it, and I'd do it to him. Over and over and over again, while you watched. I'd make sure you heard every single scream I forced from his soul."

Her eyes grew wide. "You," she stammered, "you were there?"

"Who do you think opened the door and shoved you into the blood? Who do you think found the desire you wouldn't admit to yourself while she manipulated your fear so you'd crack just enough for me to open that door?" He laughed. "Who do you think was really on that bed?"

She slammed her eyes shut, turning her head away, before drawing a calming breath. "It doesn't matter what happened then. What does is what happens now. If I agree, you will let him go? Do I have your word?" Purposefully, she let her voice crack.

"I can't let him go free. He's too dangerous to be running loose, without someone to hold his leash. But," Samil said, "I won't hurt a single hair on his head. Here." He let go of the chain, tossing it forward. Jinaari winced as it hit his back. "You can even hold his chain if you like. Consider him a present."

Thia was in front of him now, staring at him. Jinaari looked up at her, his jaw tight. "You're not real," he snarled.

"Do you see any fear? Any anger or hatred?" she whispered the words, hoping they'd have the effect she wanted them to.

His head shook slightly as the doubt left his eyes. "Don't. My life's not worth it."

"There are people who disagree with you," she said.

"I know, but they'll get over it. Give me an honorable death, Thia. I welcome it by your hand."

She stared at him, a tear falling from her eye as she recognized her own words to him. "It's going to kill me to do it."

"If you don't," he said, "then everything we did to keep you safe was for nothing. Make it swift, for both of our sakes."

Leaning down, she murmured, "Trust me," as she placed her lips against his forehead. The skin was chilled, but she could feel some warmth within him. The heat from his body evaporated. *Keroys, give me strength. Garret, take him home if I fail.* Reaching down, she pulled his sword from the scabbard and drove it into his heart before anyone could react.

The sword flared blue as Jinaari's body fell prone, blood pooling out beneath it. From behind her, she heard Lukas order the paladins to hold their position. She stared at Samil, her face a stony mask. Irritation and disbelief played across his face briefly. "So much for your bargaining chip. I will not be controlled. Not by you, not by a Goddess that's dead. The only one I answer to is Keroys. Shall we do this?" She imagined a shell around them, similar to the bubble she used to get them to Drogon's tower. "It's just you and me, Samil. Everyone can see us, hear us, but they won't get hurt."

He sneered at her. "You're wasting your stores, using the shield. Which is fine by me!" Red beams of magic shot from his hands, bent on snaring her.

Thia dodged them but didn't fire back. Instead, she started to circle the edge of the barrier. "You crave control, Samil. But not over yourself. You want to control everything and everyone else. That's why you joined the insurrectionists in Helmshouse. You thought they'd set you up as the Solar, give you control. But it's as much an illusion as the ones you cast on yourself." Without warning, she sent a large ball of gold fire at him.

Samil blasted it, but Thia made it break into smaller balls. As he fought against them coming closer to him, she kept talking. "What did Lolc Aon tell you, before she died? That you'd be her equal? That she'd share power with you? She was incapable of that. You know it, too. All it would take would be for her to find someone else that interested her, someone who would make you angry enough to do something stupid, and you'd be dead. A footnote in history. Even if I agreed, your name wouldn't even be mentioned in the lineage."

The last ball of energy dissipated, and she took a closer look at Samil's face. A single bead of sweat trickled down his forehead. "You're weaker than I am," she mocked him. "You're nothing but a man who can't access even a third of what I can. Because Keroys trusts me more than Lolc Aon ever did you. All she gave you was a path for herself to return, nothing more. You need me alive. I, on the other hand, would rather never deal with you again." She imagined tendrils of pure energy radiating from her body and reaching across the ground to Samil. As they began to creep out from behind her, she saw his eyes grow wider.

"For the first time in your life, you understand fear. And that's the difference between you and me, Samil. I knew how it felt at a young age. To constantly want to run and hide from the likes of you. I conquered my fears. You haven't faced yours."

The bands of energy began to ensnare his arms and legs, wrapping around him and snaking their way to his torso. He fought against them but couldn't break free.

I have him contained. But how do I kill him?

Give me Lolc Aon, Daughter of Keroys. I would speak with my child about her behavior. The woman's voice echoed in Thia's mind.

A mighty scream pierced the barrier as a shadow blacked

out the sun. Glancing up, she saw the white dragon circling above them.

"Nannan?" Thia said, her voice filled with awe as the mother of the Gods stared down at her.

My son chose well when he Marked you, Thia Bransdottir. It is long past time that I correct my daughter's behavior. Send her to me, then do what you will with her vessel.

Thia looked back at Samil. His orange eyes were filled with panic. "No, please," he said, shaking his head. "I'll do whatever you ask. Don't do this." Another voice spoke in unison with his.

"And now you understand. We cannot control ourselves if we don't confront our fears." Raising one arm and pointing to the dragon, she said, "It's time to confront yours." Deliberately, she manipulated one of the bands around Samil. The needle-sharp tendril pierced Lolc Aon's Mark, and both the spirit of the Goddess and her vessel screamed in pain. "Your mother calls you home," Thia said. "Go!" She barked the command, throwing almost all the magic she had left into it.

The spirit left Samil and flew toward the top of the sphere. When it was close, Thia opened it. The dragon, her massive wings flapping while she hovered, opened her mouth, and closed it around the spectral image. A single nod to Thia in parting, and then she flew off toward the south.

Dropping the shield, Thia saw Adam and Caelynn running toward her. Samil lay on the ground, prone, but breathing. "Have the paladins restrain Samil, take him away, then go inside," she told them. "I'm not done yet." Her fingers untied the knot that kept the scepter on her belt.

"We're not leaving you, Thia," Caelynn said.

She turned around. "Do it!" she snapped. "If it worked, you're needed in there. Not here."

"Come on, Caelynn," Adam said, taking the bard's arm. "Thia's got this."

She watched them turn and head back to the city wall. Lukas stood, his face a cold mask. "My brother has fallen, Your Majesty. We would honor him and not leave him on the cold ground."

"Not yet, Commander," she said, her tone softer. "Restrain the prisoner. I doubt he'll resist but be ready for it. His power's gone, but he's still dangerous. Form an honor guard around Jinaari's body so it's not desecrated, but moving him must wait."

She saw him shift, recognized the motion as one Jinaari used often when he didn't like something he'd been told. "When, then? That," he gestured to where the corpse lay, face up with the glowing sword protruding from his chest, "is not how we treat our fallen brothers!"

"Soon. Trust me." Thia walked past Jinaari's body. Stijyn stood, holding Agrana's horse. Both stared at her in horror.

"You know what this is, don't you?" She held out the scepter. "It came to me, Agrana, not you. The shield is in there," she pointed to the city walls. "I give you until the midnight to renounce the crown. For once, think about what's best for Avoch and not for you personally. If you do not, we will bring the war you wanted to you. This land will be a killing field. We both know this. And we both know who will win. You've lost one battle today. Don't be stupid and lose the war."

Turning on her heel, she started to walk away. "Did my son mean so little to you, then?" Agrana called out.

Thia stopped and looked back. "No. He meant quite a bit to me. But I also know he wouldn't have wanted me to spare his life if it meant thousands dying or being enslaved. That's what it means to govern, Agrana. To give up what you hold most dear because it's what is best for the world."

She kept her pace even as she walked back into the city. As she passed Lukas, she said, "Walk with me. Please."

As soon as the door closed behind her, Thia leaned against the city wall and allowed herself to drop her mask. Her entire body shook, and her legs threatened to buckle beneath her.

"Thia?" Lukas said, his voice barely a whisper.

"I'll be fine," she said. "I need to rest. If you could get me to my room as quickly as possible, without a fuss? Please?" Waves of nausea and dizziness washed over her. *What was I thinking? Keroys, I think I found the bottom of what you gave me and scraped it dry.*

She felt someone's hand on her elbow. "I'll keep you from falling. Can we now bring our brother's body inside?" Lukas said.

Raising her head, she looked at him with a small smile. "He's not dead, Lukas. He's in my room."

"Then what's out there?" he demanded, pointing toward the door.

"It's an illusion of sorts. It won't dissipate until after dark, when no one will see it go away. It's something Adam and I came up with. I'd let you bring it in, but I don't have the magic left in me to change it again, not if I'm going to heal Jinaari." She looked him in the eyes. "He needs healing, too. I can't do that from here. So, please escort me to my room."

"If that's true, then Jinaari is going to be buying me beer for the next decade. Come on," he began to move her forward. "I'd like to see my brother, alive and breathing."

"As would I, Lukas. As would I."

He led her through the streets, the other paladins making sure no one came too close. The stares and whispers gave Thia pause, but she tried to ignore them. *I'm not done, not yet. I have to know he's okay. Tonight, if Agrana surrenders, we can decide who will wear the crown. But I have to know he's ready to still be the shield I need him to be.*

Some of her strength returned by the time they reached the hallway leading to her room. Drakkus stood with Adam and Caelynn, their faces concerned. "What's wrong?" she asked as they approached.

"He doesn't believe this is real," Adam said. "He thinks it's an illusion. Resisted Drakkus healing him, though he was able to do some." He looked at her, concerned. "Thia, he's lashing out at anyone that goes in there. It's not safe until he calms down. Or passes out."

"Give me the key," she said.

"I don't think that's a good idea."

"Adam, we don't have time. I can reach him. I know I can. But I can't do it from out here. Now, give me my key." She held out her hand.

He hesitated, then placed it in her palm. "We're staying out here, just in case."

"I'll let you know when it's safe." She waited for everyone to get out of her way and walked to the door. Taking a moment, she steadied herself. *Whatever magic I still have will have to be enough to heal him. At least enough to keep him alive until morning, after I've recovered.*

She inserted the key in the lock and turned it, making sure the tumblers moved before removing it. Twisting the knob, she opened the door enough to go inside and closed it behind her.

TWENTY-EIGHT

J inaari's body screamed with pain as the world spun around him. *If this is death, then I accept it.* Old wounds split open, and the cold air burned into the warm tissue. "Shit," he breathed, trying to fight against the agony.

The spinning stopped, and his stomach heaved. His body hit the ground hard. Opening his eyes, he saw a wood floor. A fire burned in the hearth not far from him. Raising his head, he shook it in disbelief. Two packs, and his shield, rested on the bench at the foot of the bed. A heather gray dress hung from a hook. Next to it, a blue silk cloak. Thia's room, in Cirrain? "Damn you, Samil," he said. "I won't keep playing this game!"

A key rattled in the lock. Jinaari struggled to his knees, his bound wrists making it difficult. The door swung open and Drakkus looked at him. "It worked," he said, breaking into a grin. The man turned, gesturing to the doorway. "He's here." Three others, all wearing the medallion of Garret's Paladins, came in. "Untie him first, get that godsforsaken collar and chain off, then heal him. You," he stopped one of them, "what was your name again?"

"Donovan, milord Commander. Donovan Pearce. I'm stationed with the chapterhouse in Almair."

"Go to the kitchen, get some food. Doesn't matter what, but Althir needs it. And some ale."

The younger man nodded and left.

The other two pulled Jinaari to his feet. He didn't fight them, but he kept his gaze on Drakkus.

"You look like hell. Adam told me you might, but I didn't expect this." He stepped forward as Jinaari felt the iron collar pull away from his neck. "Once you're free, I'm going to heal you. Don't fight me. Her Majesty will have my hide if you look this bad when she returns."

Her Majesty? Why would Mother care? "I don't care how I look. Her Majesty," he said, contempt in his voice, "can go inspect a latrine trench before I welcome a visit from her."

Drakkus shook his head. "I don't think we're talking about the same person, Jinaari."

The man working on his hands pulled the last of the rope away. Ignoring the sting as the raw skin was exposed to the air, Jinaari's hand went to the hilt of his sword. "Get out,"

"I can't do that," Drakkus said, staring at him. Walking forward, he continued to speak. "A lot has happened since you were taken. Let me heal you and I'll explain."

"No."

"Hold him," Drakkus commanded.

The other two grabbed his arms and Jinaari tried to pull free. Pain seared through his body while he struggled, but they held him fast.

"Jinaari, you're in Cirrain. Thia's out there," the man gestured toward the window as he walked toward him, "fighting Samil. Adam said they'd get you here somehow and that you'd probably be hurt. I'm going to heal you because I won't let her find you like this. After that, we'll leave you alone. Pearce will bring in some food, leave again.

Once she's done, she'll come here and see you. This isn't a trick."

His arm reached out for Jinaari's shoulder. Fighting against the others, he couldn't move it far enough away. He braced himself, expecting more pain at the touch. Instead, a wave of warmth washed over him. Most of the agony left, but not all of it. His strength, though, returned.

Quickly, he pulled free of one of his captors and used the momentum to throw the other against a wall. The one claiming to be Drakkus stepped back as Jinaari drew his sword, leveling the point at his chest. "Get. Out. I know your tricks, Samil. I'm not falling for them again."

The other man held up both hands, showing he wasn't armed. "I'm not Samil. He's out there, fighting Thia. I'm Drakkus Heath, your Commander."

Jinaari shook his head. "Get out." *I need to be alone, get enough magic together so I can walk, find a way out of this illusion! She's close, I know it!*

Something screamed, and they all turned toward the window. It wasn't human, or in pain, but it was loud enough to rattle the glass pane. Looking back at the others, Jinaari was surprised at the stunned look on the leader's face.

Drakkus nodded. "Okay. When you're ready, I'll be outside." He gestured to the others, waited for them to leave, before backing up to the door. Without a word, he closed it.

Jinaari didn't lower his sword until he heard the tumblers move. Shoving it home, he collapsed into a chair.

It was her. I know it. No one else would've said that to me. If she's nearby, so are the others. But how do I find them? And what made that sound?

Leaning forward, he rubbed his face with his hands. How long had it been since he'd slept? Eaten? Samil had manipulated everything he saw, interacted with, for over a week. He'd lost track of everything, including time.

The medallion!

Rising from the chair, he began to dig through the drawers. Thia told him she had left it here, on purpose. If he could find it, then he'd know this was real. If he couldn't, then he knew it was another trick by Samil. Desperation filled his mind as he searched. Finally, he threw the contents of the last drawer on the floor and stormed back to the chair. *Damn it!*

The tumblers in the lock moved, and he stood again. Staring at the door, he waited for whatever form Samil chose to take this time.

Thia entered, the hood on her coat falling away from her pale blonde hair.

"Go away," he growled.

Turning around, she locked the door behind her and placed the key on the small table. "Not until I know you're okay." She began to pull off her gloves but didn't look away.

"Locking yourself in a room with me is a bad idea, Samil."

"I'm not Samil, and I'm following rule number two. You taught them to me, so don't be surprised when I use them."

"No," he said, shaking his head, "I don't believe you. The real Thia is out there. She was ready to do what she had to do. This is another illusion to get me out of the way, manipulate her. It won't work. She's stronger than you, Samil. So am I." Adrenaline surged through his body. *I'm ending this!* Charging forward, he slammed her into the wall, expecting the illusion to shatter.

She gasped as he forced the air from her lungs; her body shuddered under his. "It's me," she said. "I can prove it."

He grasped her chin roughly; his fingers pushing into her jaw. "You're lying, Samil. That's what you do."

"You hate walking around in wet socks," she said, staring into his eyes. The pale lilac color didn't falter. Pressing harder against her jaw, he saw pain, but they still didn't change.

Blinking, he shifted his stance. "What did you say?"

"You hate walking in wet socks. You told me that, on the beach, after we got off Stone's boat. When you told me to change mine while you put your armor on."

He loosened his grip but didn't let go.

She kept talking. "I thought you were treating me like a child, telling me what to do, and refused to change them unless you let me help you with your armor. You mocked me; said you were fine. We came to a compromise. I helped you, then I changed my socks. Later, when I finally admitted I needed a rest, you told me you were impressed because I'd kept up with you."

He stared at her as the memory hit him. There wasn't anyone else around them when that happened. There was no way Samil would even know about it. "We fought, again. Only that time you called me an arrogant prick."

She nodded. "Because you were." Raising a hand, she placed it over his. It was warm. Every other time Samil had posed as Thia, her touch had been cold. Small yellow sparks flew from the fingertips. "You still are."

Leaning forward, he placed his forehead against hers. "And you're a stubborn witch," he said. "I didn't mean to hurt you." He brushed one thumb against her jawline; bruises were already discoloring her skin.

"You didn't know who I was." Her eyes were full of trust.

"I do now." He kissed her gently.

One of her hands brushed against a wound on his arm, and he winced. She pushed him away, concern on her face. "Sit down. I'm healing you, so don't try to argue."

He staggered back and collapsed on the bench at the foot of her bed. Taking a better look at her face, he was surprised. "You look exhausted. What did you do out there? How'd I end up here?"

Pulling a chair over, she sat in front of him. "Samil's not Marked anymore," she said. He felt her spell settle over him, knitting his skin and muscles back to normal. "Nannan came, took Lolc Aon's spirit away. I threatened your mother and brother, then came to check on you."

"Wait," he grabbed her hand, "Nannan came? The mother of the Gods?" he asked in disbelief. That would explain the scream he'd heard.

Thia nodded. Her body swayed slightly in the chair. "She did, told me to send her daughter to her. I'd already tapped most of my stores but found enough to do what she asked."

He watched her closely as he felt his body recover. Whatever she did had pushed her past any limit he knew of. "You need to sleep."

"There's no time," she said, her head drooping.

"We can't save the world in a single day. You've dealt with Samil, yes?"

She nodded. "Lukas has him in custody."

He rose, pulling her from her chair, and led her over to the side of the bed. "Anything else can wait until you've slept, recovered." He pushed her down on the edge, concerned. Her face was drawn. "Where's Adam and Caelynn?" he asked as he lifted her legs onto the bed.

"Outside, in the hall." Her voice was barely a whisper, and her eyes were already closed. He watched her for a moment, making sure her breathing was steady. *What price did you pay for my freedom?*

Turning around, he grabbed the key and unlocked the door. As soon as he opened it, Adam and Caelynn stared at him. "Jinaari?"

"I'm good," he said to Adam. Drakkus and Lukas stood nearby. "I'll take that food now, enough for the four of us. I'm starving, and we're going to be talking for a while."

Lukas said, "I'll get some."

Drakkus glanced at him. "I already sent one of yours to the

kitchen. Think his name was Pearce. You should be able to catch him on the way back."

"Got it," Lukas said. Looking back at Jinaari, he smiled. "You owe me a few rounds." Without another word, he walked down the hallway.

"I'm staying here," Drakkus said. "How's her Majesty doing?"

Jinaari started, glancing back at the closed door. "Thia?"

"Yeah. She's had a busy morning. A lot of people are worried about her."

"She's asleep." *Her Majesty?*

"I think we have as many stories to tell you as you do us," Adam said. "Can we come in? I promise we won't wake her up."

"Yeah, that's a good idea. I don't want to leave her alone." He moved aside enough to let the warlock and bard inside. "The food?"

"I'll knock when it's here," Drakkus said, leaning against the wall opposite of the door.

Nodding, he closed the door and locked it, putting the key down on top of Thia's gloves. Adam walked around, picking up some of the belongings Jinaari had thrown around the room. "You let her lay down with her shoes on?" Caelynn asked.

"She was barely awake."

"Come on, you can help. Shoes and belt, maybe her jacket if we can get it off without waking her. Then we get her under the blankets. The room's not that cold, but her stores are low. We need to make sure she stays warm."

He walked over to the bed and began to loosen her belt while Caelynn pulled off her boots. The clasp came free, and he went to pull it out from under her when he saw the scepter hanging from it. "Caelynn? Is that what I think it is?" he asked, pointing to it.

"Like we said, a lot has happened," she said, her voice quiet. "Can you lift her up? Then I can pull the belt out from under her. She won't roll onto anything that'll wake her up then."

He worked his arms underneath Thia's shoulders and knees, raising her enough that Caelynn could pull the belt out. "I've got her," he said.

She tossed the belt onto the bench, then pulled the blankets back. Carefully, he laid her back down and brought the quilt closer to her chin. Her breathing was slow and even. Turning away, he walked around the bed and moved the packs onto the floor. Adam and Caelynn had pulled chairs close enough to talk without waking Thia up. "How did she get that?" he asked, pointing at the scepter. "And how'd you get me from out there and in here?"

"Which do you want us to answer first?" Caelynn asked. "I can fill you in on the first, but Adam's better with the second."

"Let's start there, then." Jinaari leaned back against the footboard of the bed.

The bard took a deep breath. "The delegation from Byd Cudd arrived the same night Adam brought Amara and Gnat back. We took her with us to court the next morning, surprised Tomil. He had Thia marry them right then. When the delegation came forward, they had a box with them. It wasn't for Tomil, though. It was a gift for Thia. The scepter was inside, covered with so much filth you could barely see what it was. When she put her hand over it, the grime just crumbled away like dust. As soon as she picked it up to show Tomil what it was, he fell to his knee and proclaimed her Queen. Everyone else at court did the same. It chose her, Jinaari." She paused, looking at him. "It's not something she wanted."

"I can't imagine it would be. She's okay with it, though?"

Caelynn shrugged. "Resolved is a better word, I think. She's grown up a lot since you left. She's not letting fear control her like she used to."

"She's thinking clearer, too. Seeing possibilities that I miss."

Jinaari looked at Adam. "Like what?"

The blonde man leaned forward. "Like how to rescue you. She has the ability to create duplicates of herself. From what I can tell, they're not the same as an illusion. She doesn't need the real element that I do; just the ability to clearly and accurately envision someone else."

"It's damn good, too," Caelynn said. "She made one back in Almair. It was solid enough that it could open doors, even talk back to people." Giggling, she continued. "It was good enough to fool the paladins you asked to guard her."

"Why would she need . . ." he shook his head. "I'll ask her, later. Keep going, Adam."

"Her idea was to create a duplicate of you, one she could place over the real you, once she knew it wasn't an illusion to begin with. Once she did that and gave me the signal, I transported you here. She killed the duplicate, negating Samil's bargaining chip."

"Since when can you transport someone who isn't touching you?"

Adam stared at him. "I've always been able to, but it's hard. Not on me, but the person I do it for. Because I don't have your consent. We tried it a few times with Caelynn, to make sure the timing was perfect. We couldn't screw it up or Thia'd end up actually killing you. Even with her actively agreeing, it gave her nosebleeds and hurt. But not trying wasn't an option." He looked at Jinaari. "I know Drakkus healed you some, and so did Thia, but you still look like you need a month or longer doing nothing."

"I'm good. I've felt worse." He looked at Caelynn. "Go

back to why she made one in Almair."

"Lukas took your instructions a bit too seriously, and it was making her feel claustrophobic. Add to that just how much her life has changed, how many times it's been turned upside down, in the last six months." She stopped and looked down at her hands. "I saw it coming, but I kept hoping she'd open up with me, let me help her through it. Instead, she made a duplicate and ran off. I lost her again, like I did down in the conduits."

"That wasn't your fault," Jinaari said.

"I know, but I still feel guilty. Soon as I realized she was missing, I talked with Lukas. He started organizing the search while I went to answer Adam's call. I didn't want to lie to you two about where she was, but it wasn't going to do any good to tell you she was missing. It was only going to worry you, and you couldn't get back here to help with the search. I was hopeful we'd find her before you came back."

"Where'd she go?"

"Like I said, she was having trouble coping with, well, everything. She told me that she'd found some alcove near the docks that was sheltered, hidden. She went there and cried." Caelynn held up a hand, stopping Jinaari's question. "Don't. It wasn't her being weak or anything of the sort. Thia's gone through a lot, we all know it, and she can't just grab a sword and hit someone in a practice ring to let it out. When she came back, after we talked, I could tell it'd helped. I wasn't thrilled that it was Kasmin," she coughed, "er, Samil, that found her first. But that was before we knew who he was. I talked with Tomil last night. He didn't even know someone by that name had come to Almair. Samil made sure his contact was limited to the two of us, Abigail, or Brennan. He didn't come by the inn until the day Adam returned."

Adam spoke up. "I told Thia what happened, and she got mad. Amara was getting cleaned up, and Gnat was sleeping, so

Caelynn had me go down to talk with Kasmin. He'd shown up to listen to her play. I went down, realized who he really was, and tried hard to imply you were back with the rest of us. We exchanged threats, and he transported himself out. When I went back upstairs, we figured out that Gnat's friend, Spoone, had a problem."

I don't need more problems! Jinaari said, "What kind of problem?"

"Someone had embedded a spell within the matrix of the crystal, causing those around it to feel emotions that were ramped up, heightened. Specifically, anger, fear, doubt, mistrust. That's why you and I were snapping at each other after we got to Amara. It's why Thia and Caelynn both got angry with me for leaving you behind, and not telling them about my mission. I can't prove it, but it's something Samil was capable of. I managed to break the enchantment, but Caelynn still wanted me to leave Thia alone. She'd already said I had to bring them back to where I'd last seen you, once court was over, so I went to bed. Woke up the next day to Wilim pounding at the entrance to our rooms with a note from Caelynn. It said to get Gnat and all the packs, including yours and your shield," he gestured to Jinaari's left, "and to come to Thia's cloister as soon as possible. We met them at the entrance, and I transported them as soon as they were ready."

Someone knocked at the door. Jinaari rose and walked over. Picking up the key, he turned it in the lock and opened the door.

Lukas stood there, with another paladin behind him. Both held a tray full of food and drink. "Can we come in? These are getting heavy."

Jinaari moved aside and let them both in. As the younger man passed by, Jinaari noticed a tube strapped to his back. "What's that?" he asked.

"It's for Her Majesty," he said. Putting the tray down, he

raised the strap over his head. "I don't know if you remember, but the commander," he pointed at Lukas, "sent me to River Run when we first met you at the Green Frog."

"I remember," Jinaari said. "You were going to make sure her father was properly buried."

Donovan nodded. "He was, but the marker was poorly done. I stayed, worked with a stone mason to get something more fitting carved and installed over his grave. Once that was done, I did the rubbing as required." He handed the tube out to Jinaari. "I would be honored if you would give this to Her Majesty when she wakes up."

He took it, nodding. "I'm sure she'll be happy to see it."

Donovan smiled and headed for the door. Lukas looked at the three of them, then at Thia's body on the bed. "Everything okay?" he asked.

"She's tired, that's all," Jinaari said.

"I'm not surprised. I've seen people work magic before, but to see what she can do . . . I was tired within a minute of watching and she never broke a sweat." He looked at Jinaari. "You all look beat. Drakkus is setting up a guard rotation outside all of your rooms. The Baroness and Duke Tomil plan on holding court of some kind when Thia's ready. Given the ultimatum she gave your mother earlier, it could be a long night. You might want to get some sleep yourself."

"Ultimatum?" Jinaari asked, puzzled. He glanced at Caelynn and Adam, both of whom shook their heads.

"The last thing she did out there, after ordering me to take Samil into custody, was tell your mother to either surrender the crown or she'd bring war to her tomorrow morning," Lukas said. He paused in the doorway. "I saw Agrana's face. I don't know what she'll do, but that Thia has the scepter scared her. Agrana has the crown. Thia said the shield was here, in Cirrain. The big question is who has it and who they'll side with." He left, closing the door behind him.

Jinaari twisted the key. *Lukas is right. We have to figure out where the shield is, who should wear it, and hope they're sympathetic to Thia's side.*

"Who do you side with, Jinaari?" Thia's voice was soft, but full of strength.

Turning around, he saw her looking at him. "I don't have the shield," he said as he put the key down.

She sat up, pushing the blankets aside. "It's right there," she said, pointing to the end of her bed.

"What?"

"Amara told us that she overheard your mother and grandfather arguing before you were fully vested as Lord Defender. He pushed for it to come from the vault based on you being heir to the crown. Better for you to have both symbols of power instead of just one since no one knew where the scepter was. So," she continued, "I'll ask again. Who do you side with?"

"You. I'm surprised you have to ask."

Her head turned toward the others. "Mind giving us a few minutes?" she asked.

"Not at all," Adam said. "We'll grab a tray and go to my room, make sure Gnat's been fed."

Jinaari moved out of the way, letting them pass, before locking the door. He heard Thia chuckle. "Samil didn't know about the rules," she said. "That was one clue I had that it wasn't you."

"He impersonated me?" Jinaari asked as he grabbed a plate of food. Turning around, he saw her walk to a chair. She eased herself into it, slowly. *She's still exhausted.*

She took the plate he offered, saying, "Twice. The first time was obvious. The second . . . he had us going for a short time." She took a bite, and he felt her watching him as he sat down with some food. "So, Jinaari. How are things with you?"

CHAPTER
TWENTY-NINE

Jinaari stared at her, his fork halfway to his mouth. "I suppose I deserve that," he said, smiling.

Thia closed her eyes for a moment as relief flooded through her. "It really is you," she said as she looked at him.

He put his plate down on the bench. "I thought we settled that."

"Samil messed with both of us, Jinaari. I know it was you, out there," she gestured to the window, "and I wanted to believe it was you when I came in here when I was done. But I couldn't be certain until I asked you that question, heard your response."

"What'd he do to you?"

Her heart broke when she saw the flash of anger on his face. "Nothing I couldn't, and didn't, handle. At one point, I asked him that question. His reaction was what told me it wasn't you." She raised her hand to her jaw. "I don't know what I expected your reaction to seeing me would be, but this wasn't it."

She saw him trace a healing sigil with one hand as the

other touched her. A warm, gentle sensation danced across her face as his magic took away the bruising. "I wasn't thinking right," he said, his voice low. "I had convinced myself it was another one of his tricks."

Reaching up, she placed one hand on his. "I know," she said. "I saw it in your face when I walked in. That's why I didn't try and stop you."

"You should've."

"I've seen you angry before, Jinaari. I've seen the fear on the face of your opponents in battle. I am not now, nor will I ever be, afraid of you." Her cheeks grew red as she reached out and tentatively caressed his cheek. "You're stronger than I was when Lolc Aon had me. But I was there less than a day. Samil had you for over a week. I came close to killing you, and part of myself, today. You asked me to do it. I don't want to wake up three months from now and discover things aren't right with you." She looked down at her hands, taking a deep breath. "Things are different since the scepter chose me, more so than when you told me I was Marked. I don't want what happens out there to affect the trust you and I have. You told me I needed to talk about what happened to keep the memories from tearing me up from the inside. I need to know that's not happening to you." She raised her head and looked at him again.

"You've changed," he said, his voice low.

"I had to. The arrogant prick that normally tells us what to do was doing other things." She smiled at him, then said, "Talk to me, Jinaari. We trust each other, right? What did you say to me once? Hide from the world but not from you? Don't hide from me. Please."

"Samil let me know early on who he was, what he was," Jinaari began to speak. "I remembered the name from a book I found in Adam's tower, but it listed him as dead. My trust in Adam was shaken already. Samil being alive didn't help that."

"Because of why Adam was sent from Helmshouse to begin with?"

"He told you?"

"Yes. After he explained why you weren't with them."

Jinaari nodded. "I didn't know until we got to his tower. Once he told me everything, I made him swear to tell you. I couldn't afford not to trust him, but it bothered me— it still does—that he never said anything.

"The first illusion I encountered was an old hunting lodge of my grandfather's. Alesso was there. We fought, and he accused me of killing his sister. Later, he came to my room and asked that I hear his confession. He brought my sword with him, and some glasses that would help me see past Samil's illusions, get out of there. It was an oubliette. I climbed out, left him behind."

"What happened to him?" Thia asked.

He shrugged. "I'm not certain. He was convinced he'd be killed by Stijyn in the morning, once it was discovered he'd given me my sword and a way out. If it was even Alesso."

"You think it was an illusion? Adam said he saw him, too."

"I really don't know any more. Samil's damn good. With my sword being what it is, it's possible it wasn't taken like my armor was. It may have been hidden from me, though. Alesso could've been another illusion, the entire fight and confession another trick of Samil's." He took a deep breath, letting it out slowly. "When I got out of the oubliette, I thought I was near the cave where I'd been captured. I knew you'd talk Adam into bringing you back there. I started to search for it, for the three of you."

"I was rather adamant, yes," she giggled. "We went the next day, after court and all of that happened. Never saw the real you, though."

"You didn't find me because I'd never escaped. I went to sleep, exhausted, only to wake up back in the lodge. He did this several times, with different locations. The Green Frog, your cloister, the abandoned inn we stayed at in Tanisal. Even my chapterhouse in Dragonspire and here in Cirrain. He tried impersonating you a few times, but I'd always figure it out. Same with Adam and Caelynn. By the time he pulled me out of my cage and brought me out to see you, I wasn't sure what was real."

Her heart broke as he lowered his head. "What changed that?"

He raised his head and she saw the trust in his eyes. "When you said the same thing I told you, after I'd coaxed what Lolc Aon did out of you. No one else would know those words."

Thia looked around the room. "You managed to tear this apart, though. Drakkus said you thought it was an illusion. If you believed it was me outside, why the change when you got here?"

"I thought I was going to die. I was ready for that. It was honorable, and necessary. Before it happened, though, I was here. I didn't know Adam could transport me that way, or you could create duplicates. I thought Samil had done something to prevent you from giving me the death I wanted. To torment you, force you to agree to his terms. It didn't occur to me that you were behind it. After I chased the paladins out, I remembered you telling me you'd left your medallion here. If I found it, I'd know it was your room. That everything Drakkus had said was true. Only I didn't find it."

She coughed. "Top drawer of the workbench, on the left, buried behind a pile of rags and scraps."

He glanced at the area, then looked back at her. "I believe you. I saw the rags but gave up on that drawer. It's a good spot."

"You know this is real, then? I can ask Lukas where they're holding Samil, take you to him if you want."

"Only if you want me to kill him."

She sighed. "I'm trying to avoid more death."

"Is that why you gave my mother an ultimatum?"

"Yes," she said. "There are two armies out there, full of innocent men and women. Some are here because they believe in the person leading them, others because they were told to march. I want them all to go home, be with their families instead of out there, freezing." She reached out, taking one of his hands in hers. "I don't want to be a queen. It took me how long to even be remotely comfortable with the Mark I have? Agrana brought this war to me, here. All I wanted was to get you back, alive, and now I've got people giving me titles and bowing to me. And I didn't have the one person I needed to remind me that I'm strong enough to endure it all."

"It's that stubbornness of yours," he said, smiling. Standing up, he walked to the table near the door. "By the way, this is yours." He walked back to her, holding out a small tube.

"What is it?" she asked, taking it as she rose.

"Open it."

She undid the end, pulling out a parchment. Unrolling it, she gasped with amazement. "It's the rubbing of Papa's gravestone."

Jinaari nodded. "Donovan dropped it off when he and Lukas brought in the food." He walked closer to her. Reaching out, he brushed one hand across her jaw. "I'm sorry for that."

Her hand covered his. "I know. But it's one of the reasons I have to know you're okay."

"I'm good, Thia. If anything changes, I'll tell you. So, what's next?"

Scrunching up her face, she said, "You need a bath. After that, some rest. More food. Later tonight, a court. Tomil and Elizabeth both want to publicly pledge fealty to me, make it known they back the woman who carries the Scepter of

Avoch. The shield is yours and has been for years. You have a claim that's equal to mine. If I'm going to do this, I need you at my side. The Scepter is nothing without the Shield to protect it."

"And the crown? Who wears that if she surrenders it?"

Thia smiled. "I have an idea."

He arched one eyebrow. "What sort of scheme are you up to?"

"I don't scheme!" she said in protest.

His arms wrapped around her waist. "What you did out there," he said, "was a scheme. You somehow thought of a way to take away Samil's bargaining chip, keep me alive, send Lolc Aon back to Nannan, neutralize and imprison a master illusionist and trained warlock, and give my mother an ultimatum that she knows she has to answer. That, my stubborn witch, is a scheme I'm not even sure Adam could pull off."

"I did have to show him what I meant by a duplicate, explain what I was thinking of doing, a few times for him to understand," she said, returning his embrace.

His dark eyes grew wide with surprise. "You came up with it without his input?" Laughing, he said, "Please tell me you managed to make him feel at least a little awestruck. He's always been proud of doing most of the thinking. Having someone outsmart him like that would've been priceless to see."

"I admit, it did feel nice to watch his face when he understood everything. I think he was resigned that we wouldn't get you back without a fight. That we could work together to trick Samil, someone he trained, appealed to him." She wrinkled her nose and gently pushed him away. "Go bathe. Use mine so you don't have to answer questions from Drakkus. Your pack's there," she pointed to the end of the bench, "and has some clean stuff in it. I hope. The Shield needs to be as presentable at court as the Scepter if we're to make anyone believe we're united to do what we must for Avoch."

He leered at her. "Care to scrub my back?"

Her cheeks grew warm. "I've got a mess in here to clean up," she said. Turning him around, she pushed him toward the bath chamber.

Glancing over his shoulder, he pointed to her flushed face. "Nice to know not everything about you has changed."

Diving for the bed, she grabbed a pillow, but he'd darted through the door and closed it before she could hit him.

Thia sat on the edge of the bed, hugging the pillow. *We did it. We got him back. Now to convince Agrana to abdicate without a fight.* Looking around, she sighed. Jinaari had dumped the entire content of some drawers onto the floor, as well as pulled out most, if not all, of the clothing in the chest. Putting the pillow back, she rose and began to put her belongings away.

As she placed the blue silk cloak back where it belonged on a hook next to her gray dress, she heard Jinaari's footsteps behind her. Turning around, her heart skipped a beat as he leaned down, touching his forehead to hers. "Better?" he whispered.

"Better," she said as she returned his kiss.

THIRTY

"But," Natasha began to protest, "this isn't how precedence says royalty should be announced."

Thia resisted the urge to smooth the front of her dress. "Precedence be damned, Natasha. The Shield," she gestured to Jinaari, standing on her left, "and I are in agreement on this. You can announce us in the manner we've chosen, or we will find someone who will."

Natasha lifted her chin. "As you wish," she said, turning around.

"Be nice," Jinaari said, chiding her.

Facing the large doors that led into the main hall, she said, "I was." Adjusting the scepter so it laid across her left arm, she took a deep breath.

"You and I are going to have to talk about court etiquette," he said. "We're expected to look nice and play well with others."

"It's probably a good thing neither of us want to do this much," she said as the doors began to open.

"All rise for the Shield and Scepter of Avoch!" Natasha said, her voice loud enough to echo throughout the chamber in front of them. "Thia Bransdottir, bearer of the Scepter and Daughter of Keroys. Jinaari Althir, bearer of the Shield and Protector of Almair."

Thia rested her hand on Jinaari's, and they walked together behind the herald. Several hundred people knelt beside a swarm of chairs and benches on each side of the aisle. "They could've made it narrower," she muttered. "There's people standing."

"If they wanted a place to sit, they should've come earlier. As to the aisle, it's got to be this wide. The space will be necessary later," Jinaari said.

Ahead of them, three wide steps ran the length of a long platform. Five chairs rested on the top. Three were centered, and equal in height. Two more, one on each side, were smaller. Grateful for his steady arm, they climbed to the top before turning around.

"You sure you don't want to do the talking?" Thia said under her breath. Butterflies swarmed in her stomach as they faced the room. Everyone still knelt, looking at them expectantly.

"What you came up with is perfect. They've all seen your Mark. Right now, you've got their attention. Use it." He unbuckled the shield, lowering it so the point rested on the ground in front of him.

Thia took a deep breath and raised her chin, "Natasha?"

"You have," the herald cleared her throat behind them, "leave to make yourself comfortable."

She waited as the crowd took their seats. "Who has business with the Shield and Scepter?"

Duke Tomil appeared at the end of the aisle. "Almair would seek your wisdom and friendship."

"Let the Duke of Almair come forth and swear fealty," Natasha said.

Thia bristled as he walked forward, "I don't like that word," she muttered.

"Relax," Jinaari said. "We went over why it's necessary."

Tomil stopped in front of the steps, taking a knee before them. "Let it be known that Almair does recognize Thia Bransdottir and Jinaari Althir as the rightful bearers of the Scepter and Shield of Avoch. That their claim to the throne is right, just, and legitimate. Almair, her troops, and her people are yours to command."

"Together, we acknowledge your words and thank you for them," Jinaari said.

"Please, join us," Thia said, gesturing to a seat to her left.

Tomil rose, bowing at his waist, and walked to the chair.

"That wasn't so hard, was it?" Jinaari whispered to her.

"Says the man who once told me he never wanted to spend more than five minutes at court."

"Baroness Elizabeth Beckenburg," Natasha said, bringing Thia's attention back to the center of the room.

Her aunt walked toward them; head held high. Curtsying once toward Tomil, she sunk even deeper in front of Thia and Jinaari. "Let those who question the loyalty of Cirrain and the Beckenburg family know, here and now, that we do formally recognize the authority of the Shield and Scepter. Our lands, people, and resources are at your disposal, should there be need."

"Grateful are we to have the kinship of Cirrain. May all within the barony prosper," Thia said.

"Baroness, please join us," Jinaari said. Imitating Thia's gesture, he pointed to the chair to his right.

"Gladly do I accept," Elizabeth replied as she rose.

"What now?" Thia asked, her voice low.

"We sit down," Jinaari said, "and wait." He picked up his shield and turned around.

Thia followed suit, and they each took a seat, leaving one

between them. Carefully, she laid the scepter across the arms of the empty chair.

"Bring forth the prisoner, so that the Shield and Scepter may pass judgement." Natasha's voice was steady, but Thia felt the weight behind them.

Samil was coming.

The double doors opened once again. Lukas was at the head of the procession; the torchlight reflecting in his plate armor. Behind him, twenty of Garret's Paladins surrounded Samil. The warlock's arms were tied to a beam, and his fingers were splinted to keep them immobile. A gag had been tied around his mouth. A bandage, stained with blood, wound around the wrist where Lolc Aon's Mark had been. His orange eyes, though, held her. In them she didn't see defeat or fear. Instead, she saw naked hatred and a driving need for vengeance.

"He can't hurt you, Thia," Jinaari said, his voice barely above a whisper. "Adam gave excellent instructions, made sure they were followed. Even if he has any residual magic, he can't do anything but try and scare you."

"I know," she whispered back.

Lukas stopped, dropped to one knee, and lowered his head briefly. Looking at the two of them, he spoke loudly enough to be heard by the entire room. "I am Lukas Frazier, Commander of Garret's Paladins from Almair. At the command of the Shield and Scepter, I bring forth the warlock known as Samil for judgement for his crimes. They are numerous, and well documented. Many here in this room have witnessed them firsthand. What say the Shield and Scepter?"

Together, Thia and Jinaari rose. As she opened her mouth to speak, a bright light appeared at the foot of the steps, near Lukas. The glow faded, revealing a woman.

"The Solar," Jinaari said in her ear. "She runs Helmshouse."

Thia nodded her understanding and turned her attention to the woman. "Your Eminence," she said, inclining her head. "We are honored by your presence. How may Avoch aid Helmshouse?"

Jinaari leaned closer. "Nicely done."

"This prisoner of yours was once a student in Helmshouse. He is warlock trained, and had begun his trials, when he deceived us. While he is currently unable to use magic, he is far from being neutralized. As he was once part of our society, I ask that you give him to me for proper discipline."

Thia looked at Samil. A bead of sweat began to trickle down his face and his head shook slightly. She saw his mouth moving. "Can we remove his gag and let him speak?"

Lukas nodded. "That wasn't a precaution put on him, but more us not wanting to subject you to his mad ravings." He nodded, and one of the paladins closest to Samil removed the cloth.

"Please, no," he begged. "Don't send me back with her."

Turning her attention back to the Solar, she said, "I understand that, at one time, you wished to neutralize me in some way. Do you intend to kill him?" Thia kept her voice steady.

The Solar shook her head. "Death is not always the best path for a soul. What will happen is he will be taught the weight of his actions, how the consequences affected not just his life but all of Avoch. Some lessons will, admittedly, be painful. How severe depends on how receptive he is to what is being taught."

"He's a warlock, Thia," Jinaari said, his voice low. "If she takes him, deals with him in accordance to their laws, you won't have any guilt as to the outcome."

She took a deep breath, releasing it slowly. He was right. The only thing they agreed on was death, but the thought of condemning him didn't feel right. "The Shield and I agree, Your Eminence. On one condition."

"And that is?" she asked.

"If he ever comes out of Helmshouse, his life is forfeit."

"Agreed."

"No!" Samil screamed and lunged forward. Four paladins grabbed him as Lukas spun around, drawing his sword, and leveling it at his chest. "Please. I beg you. Don't let her take me back there!" His face was full of fear unlike anything Thia'd ever seen before.

"It is done." Jinaari took her hand, leading her back to the thrones, as the Solar stepped forward. She reached out, caressing his cheek. Samil flinched at the touch.

Thia glanced at Adam, who sat in the front with Caelynn, Gnat, and Pan. His face was sober, but she could see his jaw clench slightly. Whatever was about to happen to his former pupil made him cringe internally.

The Solar began to glow again, allowing the light to engulf Samil. He screamed, the sound echoing through the chamber. Without warning, the light and sound ended and both were gone.

A goblet appeared at her hand and Thia gratefully took it. Taking a drink, she steadied her nerves. *Part of me wants to ask Adam what will happen to him,* she thought. *But I think it's best that I don't find out.*

Handing the cup back to Natasha, Thia rose. "Earlier today, I spoke with Queen Agrana. I gave her a choice; surrender the Crown of Avoch by midnight, or we would bring war to her at the dawn. The Shield and I will remain here until that time is past. If any of you wish to seek your bed in case your sword is needed tomorrow, we give you leave to do so. It is our hope that she will choose what is best for Avoch over bloodshed. We would have you awaken to joyous news of peace over the horns of war. Please, go to your loved ones, your families. Eat with them, talk with them, and sleep well." She turned around and sat back down.

A murmur broke out from the crowd. No more than a dozen rose and made their way out of the hall. The rest remained, talking among themselves. "Why aren't they leaving?" Thia asked Jinaari.

"They will, eventually. Right now, they're more invested in what will happen if my kin show up. Here," he held out a bowl with apple slices, "might as well eat something. We could be here for hours."

"You're doing fine," Tomil said.

She turned toward him. "How's Amara?"

The Duke smiled. "Hopefully, she's gotten over being mad at me for insisting she stay behind. I'm not sure about the palace, though." He twisted in his chair, looking at her. "She said something about you inspiring her to do some creative redecorating. What does that mean, exactly?"

Thia sputtered, laughing. Turning around, she drew breath to answer him when the doors at the far end swung open. "Agrana and Stijyn Althir request an audience with the Shield and Scepter of Avoch," the herald called out before stepping aside.

Glancing at Jinaari, she straightened in her seat. "Shall I allow them into your presence?" Natasha asked.

She glanced at Jinaari. His face was calm. "Please do," she said to the woman behind them.

"The Shield and Scepter of Avoch do bid them to come forth."

"Don't rise." Jinaari said. "She has to come to us, surrender it to us, or it means nothing. There's no meeting halfway on this, Thia."

Agrana walked gracefully down the carpeted aisle, her hands hidden within the folds of her sleeves. Stijyn walked a step behind her, to her left. Both focused on Thia.

About halfway down, Thia saw Agrana's face shift as she realized Jinaari sat near her. Her eyes grew wide in amazement, while Stijyn's face twisted into something ugly. "He really hates you, doesn't he?" Thia whispered to Jinaari.

"He grew up hearing he was the spare, not the heir. It didn't exactly make it easy to be close to him."

The pair stopped at the bottom of the dais. Agrana wore a single gold circlet, inset with eight gems in different colors. She dropped into a curtsey, snapping her fingers at Stijyn. He bowed, but Thia could see contempt on his face.

"You were given a choice. Are you here to give us your decision?"

Her gaze darted between Thia and Jinaari. "How is he . . . I saw you kill him," she said, stunned.

"You saw what I wanted you to see, Agrana," Thia kept her voice even. "What is your choice? War or peace?"

"This is my choice." Reaching up, Agrana took the circlet off her head. She walked forward and placed it on the seat between Thia and Jinaari. Stepping back, she said, "Too long has my family seen our position as nothing more than something due to us. We have lost what it means to govern. May the Shield and Scepter choose among themselves who is best suited for the task."

"No!" Stijyn screamed, diving for the crown. "It's mine!"

Jinaari stood, throwing his shield in front of the chair, and staring down his brother. "Her decision is made. It cannot be undone. Stand back."

Stijyn stared at Jinaari and retreated back down the steps.

Jinaari looked at his mother. "Where will you go?"

"I plan to join a small group of educated women who are dedicated to Garret. It's past time that I thought of others. I need to regain my humanity before I can face you again." She turned, looking at Stijyn. Glancing back at Thia, she said, "Do what you will with my youngest son. He has much to account for." Agrana curtsied again and walked down the aisle.

"Commander Drakkus," Jinaari said as he walked closer to his brother.

"How may I serve the Shield?"

"Your chapterhouse has a new initiate. I recommend you keep him under careful watch. I don't want him leaving the compound until he understands the true meaning of honor and duty."

Stijyn spat at Jinaari. Thia gasped but stayed in her seat. *This was something we talked about.*

"I won't go. You can't make me."

Jinaari stood in front of his brother. "You are being given a choice. Go with Drakkus, spend five years in training. It's by far the better option than what the Scepter would give you."

Stijyn's attention went to her. "The Fallen witch? What could she do to me?"

Thia put both hands on the arms of her chair and rose, keeping her voice measured and calm. "I would have my people go through your troops, as well as their families and the supporting staff, and do a thorough inspection. When I got that report back, you would be stripped bare and tied to stakes in the ground. Once that was done, you would stay, in the cold, for one minute—"

"One minute versus five years of mucking stalls and cleaning chamber pots! That's easy!"

Jinaari shook his head. "I would let her finish."

Thia stopped on the step above Stijyn and stared into his eyes. "One minute for every hole found in a shoe, sock, or glove. Three minutes for every single person, man, woman, or child, who doesn't have a coat warm enough for the weather. Five minutes for every person who doesn't have a tent, cot, and enough blankets to not freeze at night. And ten minutes for each individual who cannot say they had a hot, filling meal in the last day. And I will not let them release you until the last second expires."

Stijyn's eyes grew wide as his face went ashen. "I'd freeze to death," he whispered.

"This is what happens when you covet power instead of understanding the responsibility of governing," she said. "Make your choice."

He glanced at Jinaari. "The paladins."

Jinaari pointed to Drakkus. "Tell him. You know the words that must be said. You watched me say them."

Stijyn, his face still pale with fear, knelt in front of the commander. "I do humbly submit to the will of Garret and ask to be given the chance to prove myself worthy of being one of his paladins."

"May Garret guide your soul as your body is molded to his purpose." Drakkus snapped his fingers and two paladins came forward. "Take this initiate, find him proper clothing. And make sure he's kept under constant watch."

Thia watched as the two warriors escorted Stijyn away.

"We're not done yet," Jinaari said as he touched her arm.

Nodding, she walked with him back up to the thrones. Jinaari moved his shield, making sure the crown was in full view, as she waited for the crowd to quiet down.

"The three symbols of Avoch are now among us. The shield and scepter have always been meant to be more than symbols, however. They are meant to protect and defend all within this land, regardless of station or rank. It requires us to be out, with the people, where we can be of use. Garret and Keroys both have a purpose for us that cannot be served by staying in a single palace and holding court. Thus, we have decided that neither of us will wear the crown."

The assembled crowd began to talk as she spoke. Behind her, she heard Tomil whisper, "Don't you dare put this on me. Amara will never forgive you."

Raising her hand, she waited for silence to settle over the room. "A wise person once told me that anyone can rule. But that it took someone truly dedicated to what is best for the majority of the people in their care, regardless of personal cost, to truly govern. That is what is needed in the one who wears the crown. The ability to fairly govern all the people of Avoch, regardless of the amount of coin in their purse or the color of their eyes. Someone who will be honest and communicate well. Someone that we," she gestured to Jinaari, "can trust to take care of the day-to-day business of this world while we're out in it, dealing with the fires." She looked past Jinaari. "Elizabeth Beckenburg, please come here."

Her aunt stared at her, stunned, and rose. With deliberate movements, she walked to the front of the dais and knelt before them.

"This is the last time you will do this. Will you bear the burden of the Crown, and do what we cannot? For the good of all Avoch?"

She looked up at Thia. Her face was calm, serene. "For the good of all Avoch."

Thia turned and lifted the crown from the seat. Jinaari put his hands on the other side of the circlet. Together, they placed it on Elizabeth's head. "Then let it be so."

They reached down, each taking one of her hands, and raised her up. They walked back to the thrones. Thia picked up the scepter as Jinaari slid his arm through the shield. Turning around, they faced the packed room.

"For Avoch! For the Shield, Scepter, and Crown! A joyous noise!" Natasha called out.

A cheer erupted. Thia stood there, taking a deep breath. For the first time in months, things felt right.

THIRTY-ONE

Thia leaned against the wall and watched the crowded dance floor. In the center, Pan and Eli danced with each other. Smiling, she took in the face of her cousin. *He's happy, and that's what matters the most.*

The last month had been a blur. The armies had been disbanded, sent home. Agrana stayed in Cirrain long enough to help Elizabeth gain control of necessary parts of the government. The day she left, Thia caught a glimpse of her and Jinaari. Something had changed between them. *He'll tell me, eventually. When he's ready. The private war between them is over, though.*

The music ended, followed by applause from the dancers. Within seconds, the musicians started again.

"It's almost time," Jinaari said from behind her.

"I know," she said.

"No regrets doing it this way?"

She shook her head. "No. It's going to be easier on everyone." For the last few days, she'd felt a restlessness. So had Jinaari and the rest. As comfortable and warm as it was in the keep, they knew it was time to move on. "We did what we needed to do," she said. "It's time for us to go start earning our keep."

"I'm still not sure about Gnat."

Turning around, she smiled at him. "I wasn't sure about Pan, but you said he was coming to Byd Cudd with us. That turned out well. Why not give Gnat the same chance?"

"Pan doesn't make my teeth itch."

She laughed. "Gnat's terrified of you. One stern glance and he'd be quiet for hours." She turned serious. "Plus, we were told he was to come with us."

"Yes, but that doesn't mean I have to like it." He looked past her, and she followed his gaze. Adam's red cloak billowed slightly on the other side of the room as he left. Caelynn followed, nodding at the two of them as she ushered Gnat ahead of her.

It was time.

Thia stole one more look at her cousin and his husband as they danced together. Weaving her way through the crowded room, she walked to the door that led to the corridor with her room. Jinaari followed her, stopping at his room. Pulling her key out of a pocket, she unlocked the door and went inside.

Her pack was ready. All she had to do was change clothes, put the dress inside, and head down to the stables. *Don't think about it*, she thought. *This is home now, same as The Green Frog. I can come back. This isn't forever.* Her fingertips caressed the worn surface of the workbench. "I understand so much more about you now, Papa," she whispered. "I'm glad for that."

Drawing a deep breath, she kicked off her slippers and changed into her traveling clothes. *It's not regret I'm feeling, only love. Leaving here is different than the cloister was because I know I'll be welcomed when I come back. It's not the last time. And I've got family coming with me.*

Folding the dress, she ran a hand over the fabric. So much

had changed, both in her and the world, since Keroys gave it to her. "It doesn't scare me to wear this anymore," she said.

"That's good."

Her head snapped up at the sound of Jinaari's voice. He stood in the doorway, pointing at the key. "I forgot rule number two again," she said, laughing.

"I'll remind you on the road. Come on. The others are waiting for us by now."

Quickly she shoved her feet into her boots. Picking up her coat, she said, "Is the way clear?"

"Lukas said it would be."

"Was that before or after he found the beer keg?"

Jinaari shrugged. "He's a paladin, Thia. Even if it was after, and he felt miserable, he'd make sure it happened. He wouldn't be Commander if he didn't."

She grabbed her gloves and put them on, then threaded her arms through the straps of her pack. With key in hand, she said, "I'm ready."

Jinaari moved into the hallway, giving her room to shut and lock the door. She put one hand on the smooth wood in parting.

"It's not forever," he said. "And we're going with you."

Thia drew a deep breath. "I know," she said. Slipping the key into her coat pocket, she turned down the passageway and headed to the stables.

Adam and Caelynn were leading the horses out of their stalls. Gnat sat on top of Adam's; his short legs stopping long before the stirrups. "About time you got here," he said. The cold night air making his breath come out in white puffs. "Caelynn was about to go look for you."

Thia went to her horse and secured her pack. "It was my fault. It was harder to leave than I thought it would be."

"Is that why you didn't say goodbye?" Pan's voice cracked.

Turning around, she looked at him. Tears stained his face.

Eli and Elizabeth stood behind him. "Yes," she said. Walking over to him, she embraced her cousin. "I'll miss you. But we need to be out there, doing what is necessary. And your life is here, with Eli. I'll be back. I promise."

He hugged her tightly. "You better write me, too. I want to know everything you do. I'll miss you so much!"

Thia let go and looked at Eli. "Take care of him, please. We're cousins now, too."

"I will," he said.

Pan stepped back and Elizabeth looked at her. "The Crown understands why the Shield and Scepter must go, but I would have my niece stay longer."

"And I would if we could. Avoch is in our hands, though. All three of us. We can't ignore that."

Elizabeth nodded. "Take care of her," she said, looking at Jinaari.

Thia turned around. He was already on his horse. "Of course," he said. "It's my job, even if she doesn't always like it."

She hugged her aunt quickly, then turned and mounted her horse. "We'll keep in touch," she said as Elizabeth moved closer to Pan and Eli.

Jinaari led them out into the courtyard, stopping when they were out of earshot. "Where are we going, Gnat?"

The cobalus's ears perked up. "Nice Brother wants to go where Gnat says?"

He nodded. "You're not from here, so I thought we'd take you home. Wherever that is."

"Gnat know the way! Not far! Maybe Furry Man has brought Nyfe back!"

Thia looked at him, confused. "Who's Nyfe and Furry Man?"

"Nyfe is Gnat's bestestestest friend ever! Even better friend than Forkke and Spoone!" His face drooped. "Furry Man said he was going to look at Nyfe, find out why he made strange noise. But then Furry Man never brought Nyfe back and Special Man told Gnat to come rescue Pretty Lady or Furry Man would never bring Nyfe back. Gnat not know where Nyfe is now."

"Does this Furry Man have a name?" Jinaari asked. Thia heard the exasperation in his voice and smiled.

"Furry Man said his name was Helix."

Pulling at the reins, Jinaari turned his horse around. "Let's go find this Helix."

He urged his horse forward, and Thia fell in line behind him. The gates of the keep opened, and they rode out into the darkness.

The Final Adventure Awaits in:
"Sword & Soul: Heroes of Avoch Book 3"

SWORD AND SOUL
BOOK 3

Coming May 2024

ACKNOWLEDGMENTS

If you've followed me on social media, you know that I'm a big Dungeons & Dragons player. I've played the game since the late 1970's/early 1980's. It's been a constant source of inspiration for books, stories, and a way for me to explore the possibilities of life. Sometimes it takes playing a character who's strong for us to find that strength in ourselves.

Since 2015, I've been playing with one group of friends. We've kept characters around while players had to leave the table for months on end, and found a way to stay connected during the pandemic. These people are my chosen family. We call ourselves The Murder Hobos.

I cannot let this book end without acknowledging the members. I think it's important to let the world know who they were, and which character they brought to life at the table. While the characters have changed and evolved between the game and the plot of the books, I tried to capture the core personality of each one.

Ed Brabant – Jinaari Althir
Dale Collins – Helix Yarnchaser
Joshua Collins – Pan Beckenburg
Jillian Morgan – Caelynn
Matt Morgan – Adam
Rob Rowland – Gnat
K.M. Warfield – Thia Bransdottir

About the Author

Born in the late 1960's, K. M. has lived most of her life in the Pacific NW. While she's always been creative, she didn't turn towards writing until 2008. Writing under the name of KateMarie Collins, she released several titles. In 2019, the decision was made to forge a new path with her books. The Heroes of Avoch series, along with a new pen name, are the end result.

When she's not writing, she loves playing Dungeons & Dragons with friends, watching movies, and cuddling up with her cat. K. M. resides with her family in what she likes to refer to as "Seattle Suburbia".

You can find K. M. at the following sites:

Twitter: @KMWarfieldbooks
    Her website: http://kmwarfield.com
    Via email: kmwarfieldbooks@gmail.com

www.ingramcontent.com/pod-product-compliance
Lightning Source LLC
Chambersburg PA
CBHW050750190726
48285CB00005B/1599